HOMA POURASGARI was born in Tehran, Iran and moved to United States to learn English at the age of 12. She received a degree in Business from Loyola Marymount University, after which she left to live in Paris for a year and attended the University of Sorbonne, focusing on literature. Multilingual, she has been traveling since the age of 5. She currently resides in Los Angeles, California. Lemon Curd is her first novel.

Lemon Curd

A Novel by Homa Pourasgari

Linbrook Press

This is a work of fiction. Names, characters, places, and incidents either are product of the author's imagination or are used fictitiously, and any resemblance to actual persons, living or dead, business establishments, events, or locales is entirely coincidental.

Linbrook Press
Published by Linbrook Press
PO Box 2325
Beverly Hills, California 90213

First trade paperback edition printing July 2006
The library of congress has catalogued the Linbrook Press paperback edition as follows:
Homa Pourasgari
Lemon Curd, a novel
ISBN 978-0-9779780-0-7
Library of Congress Control Number: 2006925750

Printed in the United States of America

This book is dedicated to all those who aspire
to write their first novel. Be patient. Never
give up. Believe in yourself
and others will too.

Acknowledgments

I would like to thank my teacher Jeanne Brennan who taught me how to write, Heidi Dvorak who showed me how to tell the story, my supportive friend, Tim Moore, who introduced me to Heidi, my mother without whose encouragement I would be stuck at a job I wouldn't like, my father who pushed me by calling every week and asking what chapter I was on and how many more I had left before I finished, my brother, the computer wiz, who taught me everything I know about software, hardware and the internet, my family and friends who were anxious to read my manuscript before it turned into a book, the staff of RJ Communications for providing answers to my questions, Jonathan Gullery for his great cover design and everyone who contributed to changing my project into a novel I hope you will all enjoy.

ONE

Anna Lisa Gibson swore at the never-ending Los Angeles traffic on a gloomy Thursday January afternoon as she drove toward Little Brit, her favorite British market in Santa Monica. She needed a jar of lemon curd, an English delicacy she preferred to jam, which she ate every morning with organic wheat toast and mocha java coffee. Surprises didn't sit well with Anna Lisa. She had to have a plan and if her plan didn't go her way, especially her morning, she was sure the rest of her day was doomed. That's the reason she needed to have her lemon curd for tomorrow morning.

When she finally reached her destination, she parked her metallic mint-green Saab convertible in a two-hour parking zone. As she walked into the store, bells above the door chimed as they always did when a customer entered the premises. The small market with a dusty cement floor was patronized by the British as well as the Americans who enjoyed British products. The cash register sat on a table at the front of the store. Next to the register was a small shelf filled with various hard candies, chocolates and biscuits, and a stand carrying imported magazines, newspapers and tabloids. The store, divided into four narrow aisles, was packed with teas, jams, unusual spreads and scones, beer and specialty sauces. Unlike a supermarket, it had a homey and warm feeling to it – a charming hole in the wall. Walking down the second aisle, she noticed only one lemon curd left on the top shelf. She tried to grab it but it was out of her reach. She asked a tall young clerk with pale yellow lashes for help. He was helping another customer and politely told her with his English accent that he would help her in a minute. Anna Lisa waited impatiently as she kept her eyes on that last jar. She watched a male customer walk in, pick up a few items and head toward the desired curd. As he reached up, he heard a woman's voice – hers – addressing him.

"Excuse me, but that's my lemon curd."

Neil Scott Whittaker turned around and assessed the lady who interrupted him. She was around his age – he was 35. From the serious expression on her face, her conservative gray skirt suit, soft pink blouse and a black thin leather briefcase, he assumed she was an ambitious uptight career woman. Her hair, pulled back in a ponytail reached the nape of her neck and complimented her oval face and big almond eyes. She was 5' 5", not skinny but rather curvy. He glanced at her full lips and then at her voluptuous firm breasts. She was real and amazingly beautiful without fake body parts, he thought as he admired her for some time before replying with a British accent, "Sorry but I must have heard you wrong for I thought you said this lemon curd was yours."

She looked at him more carefully now that he was closer. He was meticulously dressed in a double-breasted black Armani suit, a white cotton shirt and a burgundy silk tie. His wavy dark brown hair was short, and his height towered hers by at least six inches, but she didn't find him extraordinary. She preferred Mediterranean-looking men with football-player physiques as opposed to this lean man whose skin was white with a few fine lines around his round eyes and whose nose was long and narrow. His expressive midnight-blue eyes did make him appear handsome, she thought, but then, she preferred black eyes like her boyfriend's. "No, you heard right," she responded. "That's my lemon curd."

He glanced at the label on the jar as though reading it for the first time. "I'm sorry, I don't see your name on it unless your name is Samuel as in Samuel's Old Fashioned Lemon Curd."

His sarcastic remark did not escape her. "I had my eye on that jar before you came in," she said. "But I couldn't reach it. I've been waiting for the cashier to get it and, if you were a gentleman, you would let me have my lemon curd."

"I am a gentleman, but I am not giving you this jar. Don't you have a saying in America – first-come first-served?"

"You are the rudest Englishman I've ever met. That lemon curd is mine and you know it."

He didn't answer. After all, he was English and she was American and if anyone were entitled to this lemon curd, it would be him. What did an American know about lemon curd anyway? He ignored her, walked toward the cashier who had been listening to their ridiculous conversation for some time, paid him, and left.

Anna Lisa stood there in disbelief.

The kind cashier shrugged, looked at Anna Lisa and said, "No worries, we will have more in day after tomorrow."

"But I don't want it for the day after tomorrow. I need it today," she vented.

"Sorry, Miss."

She wanted to complain more but realized it was useless. Her favorite lemon curd was gone and that Englishman had it.

TWO

Her workdays were structured – Anna Lisa woke up before dawn, got on her stationary bicycle situated in a corner of her bedroom and pedaled for 30 minutes as she watched the morning news on her television set. The workouts were mandatory. Not only did the exercise assist her in dealing better with stress from work but it also helped her from gaining weight. After her workout, she'd take a shower and go downstairs in her white terrycloth robe.

In her kitchen, she'd take out a jar of lemon curd and two slices of toast from her beige fridge. Picking up her black Yale mug from the cupboard, she'd pour herself a cup of coffee prepared by a timer she'd set the night before. She'd sit on a chair covered with a salmon color cushion that matched the granite counter tops and dine on a square pine table with painted light peach flowers. Her belongings were incredibly organized since she hated clutter. After putting her dishes in the washer and rinsing the coffeemaker she'd head for the upstairs bathroom to blow dry her wavy chestnut brown hair straight and then pull it back so that it wouldn't frizz. She'd quickly make her bed and throw on a lace bedspread that matched her curtains.

Except today Anna Lisa was late to work and hadn't had time to make her bed or to have breakfast. It was about 8:20 on a Friday and she was in a lousy mood when she got to the parking garage of

Howard Brown & Co. in Century City, which was halfway between downtown L.A. and the beach. She noticed an unfamiliar car, a black Lexus, parked in her space. Since the parking attendant usually came in at 9, she had no idea who had taken it. She wasn't sure what to do. Parking on the street was scarce because of the residents who usually parked there. If she parked in someone else's spot, she was afraid she'd get towed. People in the building were ruthless when someone took their places, they'd immediately call the towing company. She had experienced that firsthand when she first started working there.

Anna Lisa decided to look for outside parking but after driving around the block several times she became frustrated. Damn it, she hated being late. Not that her tardiness would get her into trouble, but her boss, Simon, had asked her to be there at 8 so he could introduce her to a new staff member. This was not the best way to make a good impression. She was always hard on herself as though she had to prove to the world that she was perfect. Focus, Anna Lisa, focus; you must find a parking space, she told herself. Luckily, she saw a gardener parked at the curb in his white beat up truck piled high with mowers, rakes and shovels. She pulled up next to him and offered him $20 to relinquish his spot.

The Latino, who had thick leathery skin from spending too much time in the sun and one eye that was smaller than the other, looked at her desperate face and smirked. "Fifty," he said.

She raised her eyebrows. "Fifty dollars for a lousy parking space!"

The gardener shrugged and made an expression with his face which showed insolent indifference. He replied with a heavy Mexican accent, "Take it or leave it, señorita."

"I'd rather get a ticket than let you rip me off," she replied angrily and started to drive on.

"Okay, Okay, I'll take the 20."

"Too late, price just went down to 10."

"Fifteen."

Anna Lisa looked at her watch and then reached inside her briefcase. She pulled out a 10 and three singles from her wallet. "Thirteen and that's my last offer."

The gardener grabbed the money before she could change her mind and pulled out.

Anna Lisa parked her car and ran four blocks before reaching her office which was located in a 19-story high-rise owned by Howard Brown. This well-known enterprise for which Anna Lisa worked was started by Phil Howard, an Englishman and Shannon Brown, an American who now both worked out of their London office. Together they formed one of the largest marketing and advertising firms in Los Angeles and London.

Reflective bluish-gray glass prevented outsiders from seeing inside. The top three floors were used by Anna Lisa's employer and the rest were rented out to creative arts companies, business management firms and entertainment lawyers. Offices bordered the square building and in the center were oak cubicles and desks of employees who were lower in rank and salary. Beige carpet covered the floors and colorful modern artwork decorated the walls.

On the 17th were the corporate lawyers who negotiated fees, drew up contracts between Howard Brown, clients and agents and who took care of legal issues. The graphic arts department and the copy writers, the printing department, the photographers and the camera crew, the studios, and commercial actors and models interview rooms were on the 18th. The last level was occupied by the partners, managers and employees who dealt with clients. They were the ones who not only had to be great account executives and supervisors but also excellent communicators and salespeople who brought in the big profits.

All the departments had assistants, and assistants to the assistants. Leila Sultani, an assistant account executive, was Anna Lisa's best friend. She was talkative, petit and had short black hair. Each floor had a bookkeeper and an accounts payable clerk. Anna Lisa's boyfriend, Paul, was a bookkeeper. He didn't enjoy his work but didn't have a choice; bookkeeping was all he knew. Once finished with his undergraduate degree in business, he planned to move on to the marketing department. He wanted a higher salary and a large office. Anna Lisa, Paul and Leila all worked on the 19th floor.

Anna Lisa punched in her code at the front entrance and the door opened. The security guards who usually asked visitors to sign in hadn't arrived yet. She rushed toward the elevator and pushed the button several times as though it would force one of the six elevators to come down faster. A few minutes later, one opened, she got in panting and red-faced as the elevator took her to her floor. It was 8:30. Calm down, Simon will understand, she told herself. When the elevator stopped, she got off, greeted their receptionist, Bob, and hurried toward Simon's office.

Anna Lisa knocked and then went inside. Simon's office, tastefully decorated, was located at the northwest corner and was two times the size of Anna Lisa's. A glass wall on the north overlooked houses perched up on the hills and there was an enormous laminated cherry-wood desk and a large cushy swivel burgundy leather chair behind it. Two more chairs were positioned at the opposite side of his desk. The west wall overlooked the city and there was a cream sofa, two comfortable chairs and an expensive mosaic coffee table. Directly across from the sofa were the filing cabinets and above the cabinets hung framed posters of famous advertisements that Simon had created. A built-in bookshelf used for carrying reference books, a wet bar and fridge carrying mostly bottled waters, sodas and snacks and an entertainment center for looking up ad videos or listening to CDs of artists the firm represented faced Simon's desk.

Anna Lisa noticed that besides her boss, there was a man in the room with his back turned toward her. She looked at Simon and said, "So very sorry I'm late, my alarm didn't go off." She felt too stupid to admit she forgot to set her alarm the night before. "When I got here I couldn't find parking. Someone took my space."

As she said this, the stranger in the room who had been admiring the spectacular view of the city, turned and said, "I apologize, but I'm afraid that someone was me."

Her eyes widened and her jaw dropped open, but no words escaped her mouth.

"Anna Lisa, I'd like to introduce you to Neil Whittaker. Neil's from our London office," said Simon, a short man with a magnetic personality. He had stubbly gray hair, bright green eyes that matched his shirt, and a waistline that had expanded throughout the years.

Burning inside, Anna Lisa kept her composure when she said, "Did you enjoy the lemon curd?"

"Indeed, I did," he smiled.

"I see you two have already met," Simon said.

"Yes we did. Mr. Whittaker and I had a brief encounter at the market yesterday," Anna Lisa said, trying to hold back her discomfort.

Simon, who had known Anna Lisa for 10 years, heard the dryness in her tone. He had a mild temper and a spontaneity that sometimes annoyed the people around him because he would make plans at the last minute without any warning and expect his employees to immediately adapt to them.

"Anna Lisa, you and Neil will be working on the Olson account for the next eight months."

Olson & Olson was a cosmetics company started by Jane Olson and her now deceased husband. Their products and packaging were dated and needed to be changed. Their market shares had gone down by 20 percent within the past year and the board of directors was looking to replace the CEO of the company, who happened to be Jane Olson's nephew, Adam. Anna Lisa had first met Jane at a client's birthday party a year ago. She had been impressed by Anna Lisa's work and knowledge but held off. She preferred to keep the same old packaging, concept and products she had originally used and didn't like to change. Two months ago she heard the board may be looking for a new CEO and had contacted Anna Lisa for advice.

Anna Lisa tried hard to cover up her anger at Simon for making her share her account with Neil. "Great." She looked at him, faking a smile. "I'm having Diana show him around our offices, and I depend on you helping him get situated."

"Which office will be Mr. Whittaker's?"

"Yours, of course," Simon replied, but as soon as he saw her disappointed face, he scratched his head and added, "What I meant was you and Neil will be sharing your office."

Anna Lisa nodded and once again gave a tight-lipped smile. Preferring to work in solitude, she became frustrated with the entire situation. She was used to scattering her work around and brainstorming by herself. Some of her best work was done that way, and now she had to share not only the Olson account but her office as well.

Simon's assistant, Diana, knocked on his door and walked in. Her short, wavy strawberry hair was pushed back behind her large ears and her high cheekbones had a hint of rose blush. At 32 years old, Diana was an opportunist with an unkind attitude toward her subordinates pushing them around as much as possible. Wishing to be an account executive someday, she was incredibly polite to the partners, however, or anyone who could help her move up the corporate ladder. "Kimberly said you were looking for me."

"Yes, I'd like you to show Neil our departments, introduce him to everyone and answer any questions he may have."

"Gladly," Diana nodded and led Neil out of Simon's office, packed into a size 2 cream skirt and her extra-small tight black top, she wiggled when she walked.

"If we're done here Simon, I'd like to get back to my office," Anna Lisa said. Simon's first name was George, but since he didn't like to be addressed as George or Mr. Simon, everyone called him Simon.

Simon studied her unhappy face for a moment. "I don't think I've ever seen you this quiet. Is something wrong?"

Anna Lisa stared at her teddy-bear-like boss. The stubble on his head may have been gray but he had very few wrinkles even though he had celebrated his 67th birthday two weeks ago. "As a matter of fact there is, except I don't know where to start."

"I was afraid of this. I knew you weren't going to like sharing your account."

"Then why are you making me do this?" she asked, raising her voice, "I was the one who got us the Jane Olson account. I've been working on it for two months now and here you are handing my hard work on a silver platter to this Englishman."

"And I'm grateful to you, but we need both of you working on it. The partners are pushing up the deadline."

"I'll work longer hours. I'll get Leila to help me."

"Leila's busy helping two other account executives and has her own clients to deal with."

"I'll get Paul to help me."

"Paul? You can't be serious."

"He's smart."

"He doesn't know the first thing about marketing."

"I can teach him."

"We want the products to appeal to consumers in England and Paul doesn't know the English market."

"He can help me research."

"Would you listen to yourself? You're planning to do a lot of extra work for which you have no time as is. Besides, Paul is not the best candidate for this job. He comes in late and spends half his time chasing skirts."

"Paul?"

"Yes Paul. He spends most of his day flirting with the secretaries. I don't even know why you're with that guy. He's not right for you."

Anna Lisa knew Paul was a flirt before she had started dating him, but she had come to accept it. He didn't mean anything by it. "Simon, whether or not you like it, I love Paul. You hurt my feelings when you talk about him in this manner."

"I'm sorry. I'm starting to sound just like my wife, Jillian; butting into everyone's business," he said, reaching in his pocket for a tissue and blowing his nose. He had been fighting a cold for the past two weeks. "Look, your private life is your affair. *I just don't think Paul is ready to make a transition into marketing.* Perhaps when he's finished with his undergrad degree, we can talk more about this."

"And this Neil, what's so special about him? I believe he wouldn't be so extraordinary if it weren't for his English accent." Simon laughed. "You have no idea how much he knows, do you? He is a graduate of Oxford University with an MBA from Harvard. His reputation is well known all over London. He's a great marketing director and, frankly, I would think you'd want to work with him. He's brilliant."

Neil Scott Whittaker was responsible for the success of large accounts such as Austin's Building Blocks, which went from the number eight toy to number two in England, Zimmer's Frozen Foods whose company doubled their profits with televised ads, and Sullivan department stores whose sales figure grew by 50 percent. Business magazines and radio and T.V. stations had interviewed him. He was the number one employee at the London office and soon to be considered a partner. The only drawback was that he didn't know if Howard Brown needed him to be a partner in the U.S or in London, where he preferred to stay.

Anna Lisa wrongly thought that Simon preferred Neil to her and considered him to be better to handle the Olson account. She felt threatened and was afraid Neil was going to steal her show. "I suppose, compared to him, you think me dull."

"You know that's not what I think of you. I've always respected you. I've bent over backward, broken rules and backed you up when no one else would. And I'm still behind you. You're my right hand. But I also need a left."

Anna Lisa did not respond, and Simon could tell that she was mad. "Anna Lisa, I'm not giving away your account to him. I'm just asking you to share. And as much as I wish this were my idea, you working with Neil is a decision made by the partners at the London office. When Jane Olson's products are at every major department store, our company will make a lot of money and we'll all be well-compensated for it. It's a win-win situation."

She didn't see it that way. For seven years Anna Lisa worked an obscene amount of hours so she could one day become a partner. Simon hinted a few times that she was up for a promotion but she felt she was in a man's world. She'd seen it throughout her career: If a man and a woman with equal talent were competing for a position, usually the man got the job. So there she was watching all her hard work slip right through her fingers and there wasn't a thing she could do. That's the reason she preferred working with Paul. Paul would've been less of a threat if Simon had let her work with him. He was new to marketing and she could teach him. He would assist her but not take credit for her work. And yet, she couldn't tell Simon all this. She didn't want to reveal her insecurities. "But I can't work with Neil. I just can't see us operating together."

"What happened between the two of you yesterday?

"This has nothing to do with yesterday. I work better alone, that's all. I don't mind having an assistant but...."

"He's only staying for a year, and then he's going back to England."

"A year? Am I to understand that I'll be stuck sharing my office for a whole year?"

"You'll be working with him for eight months, and after that we will need his help promoting Lady Caroline's perfume line in England and in the U.S, which has nothing to do with you." He put his arm around her shoulder like a father. "Anna Lisa, please do this as a favor to me. I'll even try to get him his own office once the Olson project is over."

Anna Lisa sighed. Regardless of her close relationship with Simon, business was business and if she refused to work with Neil, Simon might take away her account and give it to Neil who was willing to cooperate and do what was necessary for the good of the company. Besides, she liked Simon. He let her get away with things most bosses wouldn't. "Fine, but you owe me big. And for my sanity's sake, would you please get him his own parking space?"

"Consider it done. Anything else?"

"No, that's it for now."

"You know I've always given you whatever you want."

"And I'm going to hold you to that," she said as she heard a knock on the door. It was Neil.

"I'm sorry Simon, but I have an appointment to attend. I'll see you Monday." He turned toward Anna Lisa, "Good-bye Leeza, till Monday."

Annoyed that Neil had abbreviated her name not just to Lisa but to Leeza and relieved that he wasn't going to share her office until Monday, Anna Lisa parked her car in front of an old building in East L.A and made sure her LoJack was turned on. It was still Friday and she couldn't wait for the day to end. After her meeting with Simon and Neil earlier, her day had taken one wrong turn after another and she did not know why sometimes God made her life so complicated. But when she walked into Brother O'Malley's Youth Foundation, she realized how lucky she was to have so much when his kids had so little.

The youth foundation located inside the rundown two-story stucco building was a non-profit organization started by Brother O'Malley called The OSSC – The O'Malley School of Second Chance. Classrooms were located downstairs and offices upstairs. Anna Lisa unlocked a sturdy ironclad door with her three keys and climbed up a long set of stairs covered with a cheap but clean navy carpet. To the left of the staircase was Brian's office. Brian was a young Mexican guy who sat in the front office and was in charge of administrative duties, bookkeeping, fundraising and whatever else was needed.

Anna Lisa knocked on his open door.

Brian was on the phone and signaled her to have a seat on a torn, red-vinyl chair. Anna Lisa took a seat and looked around. There were discolored filing cabinets, shelves filled with binders that carried grant requests and important documents reviewed by auditors. Brian's desk was covered with paperwork. He hung up the phone and acknowledged his guest. "Hey, how's it going?"

"Great," Anna Lisa said not complaining about her day or the fact that she had to hitch a ride from a friend for an hour's ride to a tow yard in Westchester. She could not complain. She had no right to complain; if anyone had the right to, it had to be Patrick O'Malley's kids. Most of them were in foster care, or ex-gang members, ex-drug addicts or both and in a constant struggle to find the right path.

"I suppose you're looking for Patrick?"

"Is he around?"

"Yes. He's free; you can go right in," Brian smiled.

Anna Lisa left Brian's office, walked several steps and then turned right down a narrow hallway toward Brother O'Malley's office. His door was open and she noticed he was busy writing a letter. In this day and age, he still handwrote all his correspondence and gave them to Brian to type. Anna Lisa knocked on the door and said, "Brother O'Malley, you wanted to see me?"

"Please, don't call me that; it makes me feel so old. Just call me Patrick," he said without looking up. "Have a seat."

Brother O'Malley was in his late fifties, had a beard and a mustache and wore his meals on his clothes. A large man in height, weight and influence, his long brown mustache blended in with his wide beard and to most people's amazement, he had a full head of curly hair. He wore a dark round neck shirt tucked into his black pants, which were two sizes smaller than his waist, forcing his large belly to hang out. But apparently no one cared about his messy hair or his dirty clothes because when he walked into a room, people respected him for who he was. He had a forceful personality and was able to collect money from large corporations and philanthropists. People had a difficult time saying no to him. Maybe it was in the way he asked or maybe his aura intimidated those people around him but, whatever the reason, at the end of each year he was able to raise enough to keep the foundation going.

Anna Lisa took a seat on one of the worn mustard vinyl chairs. With her back straight and her hands in her lap, she looked like a child who was about to be scolded for something she had done wrong.

"How long have you been volunteering for us?" Patrick asked as he wrote the last sentence of his letter.

"Two years."

"And how many basketball sessions have you missed with the kids during that time?"

"I'm not sure; two or three."

He looked up and blurted, "Seven."

Was she about to be fired from her volunteer job? And how in the world did this incredibly busy man keep track of her attendance? "I'm sorry but today was not my fault. Someone had parked in my parking space this morning and I had to…"

"I don't want to hear excuses," he said leaning forward on his desk, his fingers interlaced and his face looking stern, "that's what I always tell my kids. You know my kids expect to see you come rain or shine. They need consistency in their lives and depend on you."

"Yes sir," Anna Lisa replied sheepishly.

"Don't think I'm not grateful; I am. I appreciate you taking the time and being their role model. Juanita came up to me the other day and said she wanted to work in advertising just like you. She really looks up to you."

"And I care for her as well. I like all the kids assigned to me. You have no idea how important they are in my life."

"I know it, and that's why I wanted to ask you in person if you could try to be here more often. They love you."

She let out a sigh of relief. "Really?"

"Yes. You have touched their lives in so many ways. Jerome wants to go to college and be a doctor. Carlos has started working part-time at a gas station. He wants to be a car mechanic someday and work for Mercedes-Benz."

Feeling more at ease, she relaxed in her chair and replied, "I'm glad."

"I don't know what you're telling these children, but it's working," he commented, "So, how about it? Are you willing to put in more time?"

"Brother O'Malley..."

"Patrick."

"Patrick," she replied, "I'd love to but right now I can't. I'm in the middle of an important project but when I'm finished, I may be able to work something out."

"Okay then, but even if you could help us with fundraising, we'd appreciate it."

"I'll see what I can do."

Brother O'Malley got up with the letter in his hand and decided to take it over to Brian to have it typed. Anna Lisa figured that was his way of dismissing her so she stood up as well. They walked toward the stairs and after exchanging farewells, Patrick went into Brian's office and Anna Lisa headed toward her car.

When she got home, Anna Lisa went upstairs to her bedroom to change into something more comfortable and to call her grandmother's accountant of 30 years who was also her accountant. She pulled out the top drawer of her dresser which was sanded down to give it an antique look. Above the dresser was a rose vase filled with dried wild flowers and a silver-framed photo of her parents both at the age of 18, just before their car accident. Anna Lisa resembled her mother, who had a light complexion and wide hips. Her dark olive green eyes and chestnut brown hair, however, resembled that of her father's. Next to the picture of her parents stood two more frames, one of her maternal aunts and grandmother, and the other of her boyfriend. Anna Lisa was raised by her maternal grandmother and aunts.

Her parents died when she was only three months old. Their awful car accident had been reported on all the local TV stations and newspapers about how a drunk driver had caused a 15 car pile-up on the Hollywood Freeway. Among the victims were Tom and Lisa Gibson.

Anna Lisa put on a pair of pink flannel trousers and a white long-sleeve T-shirt, glanced at her parents' photo and wondered how her life would have turned out had her parents been alive. Throughout her youth, she had yearned for a mother she never knew and a father who had been absent in her life. As a child, she pretended to make cookies with her mom and to play soccer with her dad. It wasn't fair that her parents were taken away from her at such a young age, she thought as she put away the brown skirt suit she had worn earlier that day.

Her work wardrobe was usually plain and simple – a pair of dark solid pants or a knee-length skirt, a tailored shirt and a long jacket to cover her hips and not-so-perfect thighs. She'd add a pair of single pearl earrings, a round mother-of-pearl watch with a wide, black band she had inherited from her mother, and a delicate pearl necklace her two aunts had given her on her 21st birthday. Her shoes were either penny-loafers or sensible pumps and her purse a briefcase. Make-up was usually minimal – a light tinted moisturizer, mascara, pale blush and lipstick.

After removing her make-up and tidying up her room, Anna Lisa dialed her accountant and asked him to make a donation on her behalf to Brother O'Malley's foundation. She then went downstairs, made herself a veggie egg-white omelet and ate it while watching an old TV show – *Father Knows Best*. That night she dreamt she was five when her mom came into her room and tucked her in bed and her dad read her a bedtime story.

THREE

Monday morning came by at a speed of light and Anna Lisa wasn't looking forward to seeing Neil at the office, except that she needed to talk to him. She wanted to set down some rules since she was forced to share her work area with him. Her office was one of the larger ones, and it could easily accommodate two. The walls were light mocha, the chairs and sofas were covered with elegant taupe fabrics and the rest of the furniture was made of oak. Her swivel chair sat behind a desk with its back toward the view of the city. Neil's desk was to her left, away from the wall. She had shown up on Saturday with the movers to make sure that the furniture was arranged to her liking because she decided to create a pleasant and comfortable working environment for the two of them.

A calendar, desk mat and filing trays were among some of the accessories she had ordered. They had arrived in boxes and were set on his desk on Friday. Anna Lisa noticed they had been opened and arranged neatly on his table, his empty bookshelves now carried reference books and there was a stack of papers on his desk. She assumed Neil had been there some time between Saturday evening and Sunday.

Anna Lisa was reviewing the topics of her discussion in her head when he walked in wearing an impeccable dark gray suit, said a brief hello and went to his desk. He was frowning and seemed to be in a disagreeable mood, so she didn't reply. Instead, she went through her mail and the messages in her tray. He began by making phone calls to London. Soon each became so preoccupied with their work that they forgot about each other.

After a few hours passed, Neil's facial muscles relaxed. He even joked around with Kimberly, the new secretary Paul recently hired. Anna Lisa noticed his improved mood and said, "Perhaps we should go over some rules and expectations, Mr. Whittaker, since we'll be sharing this office for eight months."

He looked up in surprise. He thought she seemed stiff in her cream shirt and her hair pulled back into a bun. She would look so much softer if only she let her hair loose and wore something more feminine.

"Yes, perhaps we should."

"Would you like to go first?"

"No Leeza, you first." He stared at her with amusement.

"For one, my name is not Lisa, nor is it Leeza as you would pronounce it. My name is Anna Lisa, Mr. Whittaker. Please remember it." She crossed her arms over her chest. Named after her grandmother, Anna, and her mother, Lisa, she preferred to be called Anna Lisa. She didn't want to be confused with her grandmother, and she thought Lisa was too common of a name.

"I will if you call me Neil." He put his hands behind his head and leaned back in his chair.

His arrogant tone and lofty stance annoyed her. "I'll do no such a thing."

"Then that's settled, Leeza. Is there anything else?" He continued staring.

"Oh, what's the use? You have an answer for everything," she said throwing her hands up in the air and responding with a frustrated voice. "But let me assure you, there is one point on which you will not get your way and that's the parking ticket, the towing fee and a bill sitting on your desk."

He looked over his desk and asked with astonishment, "What ticket? What towing fee? Did someone tow my car?"

I should have had your car towed and saved my own instead, Anna Lisa thought. She frowned and became angrier as she recalled last Friday.

"You didn't answer my question," Neil repeated, "Did someone tow my car?"

"No, someone towed my car when you took my parking space," Anna Lisa replied through her clenched teeth.

He picked up the ticket, the towing receipt and another bill that was attached to it and glanced over them. "What is this bill for $13?"

"It's what you owe me because I had to bribe a gardener to give up his parking space." She didn't really care about the money but she blamed him for the mishaps of the prior week.

"Let me get this straight. You bribed someone so you could have their parking space?"

"That's right."

"But the space was in an illegal zone and thus you got a ticket and your car was towed away."

"Yes, and now you must pay for all the trouble you caused me."

He tried hard to suppress his laughter at her stupidity and the thought of her looking for her car and not finding it. "How did you get home?"

"My friend Leila gave me a ride to pick up my car at a tow yard in Westchester, near the airport. It took me an hour in traffic to get there."

"Near the airport? They towed your car all the way down there?" he asked as his eyes widened.

"Yes Mr. Whittaker, they did." When she saw the smirk on his face, she added, "I realize you find all this amusing, but I'd appreciate it if you'd just pay me back for all the trouble you have caused and be done with it. I'd like to put this unpleasant matter behind us and move forward."

He glanced at the papers in his hands. "I'm not going to pay for any of it. You got yourself into this mess. Get yourself out."

She pushed back her chair, got up, moved toward his desk and put her hands against the edge of his desk in a menacing manner. "Now wait just a darn minute. I wouldn't have gotten a ticket had you not parked in my parking space."

Neil lost his cool and stood up as well. He wasn't about to let a woman push him around. "And were would you suggest I park?" he asked bringing up his tone to match her raised voice. "The guest parking was temporarily closed due to renovation," he replied pointing his finger toward the parking garage, "and there wasn't a single space on the street."

"Yes but that didn't give you the right to steal my spot," she yelled at him.

"I didn't steal anything," he snapped back.

She put her hand on her waist and with a voice filled with irritation burst out, "Mr. Whittaker, I have no intention of backing down. You must pay for the entire expense."

"No. Absolutely not."

And so the two of them went at it, arguing back and forth. Neither one heard the light knock on the door that was already half ajar. The intruder walked in and remained quiet for some time. When she saw no one had taken notice of her, she cleared her throat and said, "Did I come in at a bad time?"

Neil turned and saw his sister, Juliet. "No, you came in at a perfect time. Leeza and I were just finished. Let's go have lunch before I lose my appetite," and with that he abandoned the fight leaving Anna Lisa in fury.

"She's impossible," Neil said to Juliet at lunch. They were eating at an Indian restaurant and were almost finished with their meal. The House of India was close to work. Most of the clientele wore suits and worked in nearby businesses. The walls were decorated with pictures depicting scenic views of India and the Taj Mahal. Waitresses dressed in saris and waiters wore turbans. Meals were decent but not as spicy as Neil would've liked.

At first, Neil had refused to talk about Anna Lisa but now, an hour after their argument over a parking ticket, he was ready to let out the steam that was forming inside him. "She has had it in for me from day one and all because of a stupid lemon curd. I had no idea American women were such idiots. I mean most women with an exception of a few have no sense to begin with, but–"

"Let me see if I heard you right, brother," Juliet said as she brushed away her blunt-cut, straight blond hair from her face. "You stole her lemon curd and later parked in her spot causing her to lose $10, to get a ticket, to have her car towed and to be late for work. Then she finds out she has to share her client and her office with you."

"Yes."

Juliet swallowed a piece of curried chicken in her mouth, patted a napkin against her thin lips and wiped off the sauce. "I think I understand why she doesn't like you."

"You do?"

"You don't?" Juliet asked looking at her brother with her small light brown eyes. She looked, spoke and behaved just like a younger version of her mother.

Neil took a sip of his Coke. He had no idea why Anna Lisa disliked him and said the first thing that came to his mind. "Because I took her lemon curd?"

"No doubt, the fact that the two of you had a bad start didn't help the situation any, but I think the main problem is that she doesn't want to share her client or her office with you."

"But I wasn't the one who asked for this assignment."

"I understand, and I think I know how to help the two of you get along better." If there were two things Juliet was good at, it was her ability to comprehend people and to assist in resolving their problems. Honest and sincere people delighted her; pretentious and superficial ones annoyed her. But because she had an easygoing personality, she got along with most people.

"Go on."

"You should invite her to lunch."

"Invite her to lunch? Are you out of your senses? We can't stand talking to each other for more than two seconds, and you expect me to put up with her for a whole hour with nothing to distract us but our conversation?" Neil waved at the waiter to bring the bill.

Juliet could tell he was annoyed with her but this didn't stop her from saying, "Look, you must find a way to get along with her. You'll be working with her for, how long did you say?"

"Seven months and 29 days, and less with any luck, that is if I can finish the project sooner."

"Eight months then. Plus, you will be sharing her office. You simply cannot go on like this. You must find a way to make amends."

"I will buy her a box of chocolate," Neil said jokingly.

"Well, it wouldn't be a bad start," Juliet said.

Neil decided to change the subject. All this talk of Anna Lisa was starting to irritate him again. "What do you think of the food here?"

"It would have been nicer if it had more flavor and their menu is limited. The restaurants back home have a better and larger selection."

"I agree." Back in London, Indian restaurants were abundant and the food tasted more authentic and spicy. Finding a great Indian restaurant in Los Angeles was probably as difficult as finding a great Mexican restaurant in London, Neil thought.

A dark turbaned waiter came over with a bill.

"Do you know where the loos are?" Juliet asked the waiter.

The waiter looked at her puzzled.

"She means the ladies' room," Neil said as he opened a black bill holder and glanced over its contents.

"Oh yes, just go straight," the waiter pointed toward the back, "and turn right."

"Thank you," Juliet said and got up. Attired in a pair of cream wool pants and a matching cashmere sweater, she dressed well, was almost as tall as Neil and incredibly thin even if she did have a hefty appetite.

Neil sat there and soaked in the atmosphere around him as he waited for his sister. A group of four men in suits were enjoying their meal a few tables away. A girl with black hair, wearing a red sari, was taking down orders. Two elegantly-dressed women and an older gentleman were looking at their menus.

After a few minutes, Neil saw his sister approaching.

"Did you miss me?" Juliet asked as she sat down.

The waiter came by and picked up the bill.

"I wish you lived here. I sure could use a friendly face."

"What a splendid idea! I'll divorce Mark, leave my three children and set up shop here instead. What do think?" she asked jokingly as she edged forward and rested her arms on the table.

Neil smiled at her quirky response. "How are Mark and my nephews?"

"The kids are back in school and doing great. Mark is busy taking care of them." She quaffed her water. "Tomorrow, I'm going shopping for them."

"Don't you get tired of shopping all the time?" Neil asked.

"Not really. I suppose that's why I love being the buyer for mum and dad's shops."

Juliet lived in London and traveled four times a year because her job was to shop for four men's boutiques in London. She was in charge of buying and inventory control while her parents managed the businesses. Having experience playing personal shopper to her clientele, she also helped dress Neil. She chose his suits, shirts and accessories during her travels.

"So, have you picked out anything new for me?" He hoped she had. He needed new clothes but hadn't had the time or the patience to stop at a mall even if there was a large outdoor Mall near his work.

"Honestly Neil, don't you think it's time for you to pick out your own clothes?" she frowned.

"You know how much I dislike shopping."

The waiter showed up with Neil's credit card. Neil signed the bill.

"I have shipped you a selection of suits, sweaters and shoes from Italy, and I think I can find you shirts when I meet with Juan Sanchez after our lunch."

"Who's Juan Sanchez?" He raised one eyebrow in surprise. Neil knew most of the designers because that's all his fiancée Sarah ever talked about.

"He's new. In fact, he's the reason I'm here. He designs men's apparel and his factory in Mexico makes them. I'm meeting him downtown to have a look at the samples he's showing."

"I've never heard of him."

"You will very soon. I'm trying to get his clothes in our boutiques before all the stores get their hands on him." She took out a small box of mints from her large brown leather purse, put one in her mouth and offered one to her brother.

Neil took one. "He's that good?"

"Yes, otherwise I wouldn't be here."

"And here I thought you came to visit your beloved brother."

"I am happy to be with you as always, but unfortunately," Juliet sighed, "we should get going. I reserved a taxi which is probably waiting outside as we speak, and you need to get back to work."

They got up, walked outside, where the taxi, indeed, awaited.

"What time am I going to see you tonight?" Neil asked, holding the taxi door for her.

"I shall be back at your place about seven."

His sister was staying with him for a month and he looked forward to sharing his evenings with her. "I shall make us my famous veal Marsala." Neil enjoyed cooking every now and then, especially when he had someone over with whom he could share his meal.

"I cannot wait to try it."

"See you later," Neil waved at his sister as her taxi drove off.

FOUR

It was February already. A month had gone by and Neil and Anna Lisa were still trying to get used to working in the same space. Today, time had passed by peacefully without either party exchanging but a few words until late in the afternoon when Anna Lisa got up to go see Paul. Neil ordered her in a bossy tone of voice to fetch him a cup of coffee on her way back and she glared at him as she walked away. When she reached her boyfriend's office, she found Kimberly, the new entry-level assistant standing quite close to him behind his desk. Anna Lisa got upset.

Paul was cute and women responded to his flirtatious behavior. Sometimes he would compliment them on their looks or gently hold their hands. With his black eyes and dark hair tied in a ponytail, a muscular body and six-pack abs, which he worked hard to maintain, he drove the ladies wild.

"May I have a word with you in private?" Anna Lisa asked Paul.

Kimberly started to head out when Paul yelled from his seat, "Don't forget to get the letter done before you leave."

After Kimberly shut the door behind her, Paul looked over to Anna Lisa and asked, "Is something bothering you?"

"Why is she always in a miniskirt and a tight blouse? Doesn't she own any work clothes?" Anna Lisa asked as she stood on the opposite side of his desk.

"She doesn't have a lot of money," he said swiveling in his chair.

"And why is she constantly hanging around you?"

"You don't like her?"

"I don't know her. But I feel like she spends too much time with you."

Unlike Simon's and Anna Lisa's office, Paul's office was small and had a rectangular shape. The entrance to his work area split the room into two halves. Facing the entrance were large wide filing cabinets and a window which showed a partial view of the city. On his desk, there was a picture of him and Anna Lisa taken at a friend's house and behind his desk was a beige chair pushed against the right wall. An empty desk and chair were situated against the left.

"I am the bookkeeper, and she's an assistant. I need her help. What's this all about anyway?" He was in charge of billings, writing up expense reports, reviewing employee timesheets, accounts receivable and taking care of day-to-day business of the 19th floor. In order to prevent employee theft, all the checks were cut by the accounts payable clerk and things like internal audits, payroll and tax issues such as Payroll taxes, quarterly tax and year end income tax return were outsourced to a large CPA firm. They were the ones who had trained Paul on how to organize the information they needed.

"Nothing."

"You're jealous," he said with a smirk.

"I am not." She looked at him with admiration. She loved his four o'clock shadow, his husky voice and funky clothes. Today, he was in a pair of sporty loosely fitted black pants and a fitted white round neck shirt, showing off his muscles.

"Yes, you are." Paul enjoyed watching women fight over him. He also knew how much Anna Lisa loved him and that fact turned him on.

"You spend more time with her than you do with me. We used to hang out all the time and now every time I ask to see you, you're always busy."

He got up, walked around his desk and put his arms around her waist. "Let's go out to dinner tonight. I don't have my class until tomorrow, and I'll devote the entire evening to you."

"Fine." She started to move away from him.

"Come here," he said as he pulled her back into his arms, "You know you're the only one in my life. I've been working hard so I can save money for our vacation in Greece." He nuzzled her neck.

She could hardly control herself as he pressed his body against hers. "I told you I can pay for both of us," she managed to say.

"It's not the same. I want to treat you," Paul replied and unzipped her brown knee length skirt, slid his hand in her panties and groped her butt. "You know, you're getting fat."

"Shut up."

"How much have you gained anyway?"

"None of your business," she protested, pushing him away.

"C'mon don't be mad." He tightened his grip on her and brought her closer so she could feel his arousal.

Anna Lisa removed his hand and said, "Not here, someone could walk in any minute." She zipped her skirt back up.

"But that's what makes it exciting," he said, pushing her skirt up, gliding one hand in-between her thighs and caressing her.

She removed his hand once more, put it around her waist and kissed him. "I promise we'll continue this tonight. I should get back to work now."

When Anna Lisa left Paul's office, her mood had lifted. She even felt playful and poured salt into a cup of coffee and served it to Neil. That'll teach him to ask an assistant for coffee instead of bossing me around, she thought.

"Thank you," Neil said in surprise. He didn't really want coffee and had asked for it just to irritate her.

The door opened and Simon walked in. "How are you two getting along?"

"Perfectly well, as you see. Anna Lisa was kind enough to bring me coffee."

"Anna Lisa brought you coffee? Humph," he said and scratched his head trying to remember what he came in for. "Oh yes, I came here to invite you both to dinner at my house. Say, around 7."

"I can't. I have plans with Paul," Anna Lisa replied.

"Change them," Simon said.

Anna Lisa could tell Simon was in one of his spontaneous moods again but this time, she decided to decline. "We haven't had time alone in a long time. I'm sorry Simon but I can't."

"What about you Neil? Can you come?" Simon asked.

Neil, who had just taken a big sip of his coffee, choked and spit some of it out.

"You're okay?" Simon asked.

Neil swallowed the leftover drops of coffee in his mouth and said, "Yes, the coffee was a little hot." He looked at Anna Lisa.

Anna Lisa suppressed her laugh.

"Well how about it, Neil?"

"I'd love to Simon, except my sister Juliet is flying back home tonight and my fiancée Sarah is arriving on an 8 o'clock flight. I am afraid I will be spending most of my evening at the airport."

"Well then, I guess it's just me and my wife. Maybe another time," Simon said, "You both have a nice evening."

After Simon left the room, Neil turned to Anna Lisa and said, "That was delicious coffee. What did you put in it, anyway?"

"Salt," Anna Lisa cracked a smile.

"I thought as much."

"I'm sorry but you asked for it."

"I did, didn't I?"

"Truce then?" Anna Lisa said.

"Truce for now, but knowing us, I'm not sure how long our truce will last."

"Me neither, but since we're both in good spirits, let's just enjoy the present."

"Agreed."

FIVE

When Neil and Juliet arrived at LAX, there was a long line for checking in and an even longer line for boarding the plane. Juliet decided to wait until the rest of the passengers boarded and they went up the escalator. A mélange of smells from fried food to coffee and sweets filtered through the air. The two walked passed several food stands and as they approached a seating area, Neil asked his sister if she wanted something to eat or drink.

"I would love a cup of tea."

"I'll get the tea; see if you can find us seats," Neil said as he walked away. He looked sporty in the hunter green pants and cream-and-green cotton knit sweater his sister had shipped him from Italy.

Juliet descended a few steps and settled on a brown wooden chair across from a fast-food place in a crowded noisy area where people ate or kicked back. Four Lufthansa uniformed employees sitting one table over were sipping frozen coffee drinks. At another table, a lady and a teenage boy were eating Chinese food with their carry-on bags next to them. To her right, a man was working away on his laptop.

Neil returned with a tray carrying their hot beverages. He added milk and sugar to their teas and they both sat there for a while, drinking and relaxing until Juliet broke the silence.

"How are you and Anna Lisa getting along?"

"We have our moments, but I'm hoping we can work together to pull this project off before we kill each other."

"I told you to take her out to lunch, but you didn't listen to my advice," Juliet said as she put on her thick white turtleneck that was wrapped around her shoulders. The air conditioner at the airport was making her chilly.

"Sorry Sis, but I don't think Anna Lisa and I make the best lunch companions just yet," Neil answered tartly. He didn't like to be lectured.

Juliet edged forward and changed her tone. "All I'm saying is you ought to use your charm to soften her up."

"She doesn't like me," Neil said, pulling back with frustration. "She put salt in my coffee and served it to me."

Juliet laughed. "At least she's not boring and has a sense of humor."

He finished off the rest of his tea. "I'm glad you find it funny, but I spit it out on my boss when I tasted it."

His sister laughed even harder. "I wish I could've been there."

"Whose side are you on anyway?" He frowned.

She shook her head. "I don't like to take sides."

"Funny, you don't have any problems taking my side when it comes to Sarah."

"Please Neil, let's not go down that road. I would like us to part on good terms," Juliet replied as the last call to board the plane was announced. "I suppose I should board if I don't want to miss my flight."

They walked toward the escalator without exchanging words. Juliet didn't like to discuss Sarah because she didn't much care for her nor did the rest of the Whittakers. They found her arrogant and distant, yet they tolerated her. On Sundays, when Neil spent time with his family, Sarah rarely joined him. She usually came up with one excuse or another and since the Whittakers didn't mind her absence, they never pressed her to join them.

Neil always felt the friction between his family and Sarah. Yet this friction did not stop him from wanting to marry her and when he told them about his engagement to her, they were disappointed but congratulated him all the same.

"What time is Sarah's flight coming in anyway?" his sister finally asked.

"An hour after your flight departs." Neil got off the escalator and walked with Juliet toward an entrance that led the way to various gates. Several security guards stood in front of the entrance allowing only ticketed passengers with a valid passport.

Juliet glanced at her watch. "I must go," she said. "I will miss you. The whole family misses you."

"I shall be back soon for my wedding. Give mother and father my love." He hugged his sister.

Soon after Neil said goodbye to Juliet, Sarah Weston arrived at LAX as scheduled. Neil was happy to see her as he kissed her amorously and embraced her for a longtime. He had been homesick ever since he left England a month ago. Sarah, who didn't work, was to stay for two-and-a-half months and then return home for her parents' 25th anniversary. Her grandparents and parents, now retired, made their fortune in real estate and investments. They spent most of their time playing tennis or golf, traveling and throwing frivolous parties while criticizing politicians and swearing that if they were in office, they could do a better job.

Sarah finally pulled away from Neil and said, "You did miss me!"

"It shows that much?" he said and smiled.

"Yes, you hardly gave me a chance to catch my breath. I like this side of you. We should be apart more often," she teased, looking at him with her pale green eyes.

"I'm just glad you're here."

"Me too," Sarah said, putting her arm though his. She wore a sable coat, alligator shoes and purse. Her silky dark blonde hair fell softly over her shoulders.

"Shall we?" Neil said and noticed she had piled five suitcases on a cart. He looked around for a porter but couldn't find any. He started pushing the cart outside with Sarah walking alongside him.

When Neil and Sarah were leaving LAX, Anna Lisa was having dinner with Paul at her favorite Italian restaurant – Luigi's kitchen in Santa Monica right across from the beach – around 8:30. East of Ocean displayed rows of expensive and not-so-expensive restaurants and the west had a wide path for people to jog or take strolls while looking over the Santa Monica beach and pier.

Luigi's kitchen was Anna Lisa's favorite spot because it was where Paul had taken her on their first date. Paul was well aware of this fact. He brought her here when she was mad at him. He knew it reminded her of their first date and hoped she would soon forget her anger. Before Paul, Anna Lisa dated men who found her pleasant and interesting, but they did not think she was interested in them. She listened to them with attention but she had the ability to hide her feelings and attraction. Her intelligence, independence, salary and position, well above average, bothered many. Although she tried hard to downplay her intelligence and her rank as an account executive, after several dates, men felt threatened and moved on. In her 37 years, she only had three boyfriends.

She met her first boyfriend at Yale, where she went to college. After developing a relationship as classmates, they began dating. One day, however, she found him kissing her roommate Erin under an oak tree near the school's library. His excuse was that he wanted to date other girls and wasn't ready for a serious relationship. After her discovery of her first unfaithful boyfriend, Anna Lisa had been protective of her second. She went with him everywhere, telephoned him constantly to check up on him and didn't allow him to go to clubs with friends. Her second boyfriend broke up with her because he thought she was too controlling.

With Paul, her third boyfriend, she had been distant at first. He worked on the same floor as Anna Lisa at Howard Brown and she had observed his interaction with the other employees. She knew he was interested in her but found him to be a flirt and a womanizer. His age bothered her as well. He was eight years her junior. But Paul had been persuasive. The harder she resisted, the harder he tried to capture her affection. He was used to women responding to his charm and he found Anna Lisa a challenge. He decided to befriend her and work himself into her heart.

Born in America, Paul was French by blood. His parents moved to Los Angeles from France before he was born. A year after their move, Paul was born and two years later his sister. After Paul was four, his mom left his father and took her daughter with her. Paul was raised by his father who had taught Paul to disrespect women and to manipulate, flirt and charm his way into their hearts. Paul, like his father, had had numerous girlfriends. He had disclosed some of his relationships to Anna Lisa and why he had abandoned each one. One drank too much, the other was incompatible and another was jealous of anyone he spoke with and so on. He had an excuse for every break-up and each was always the girl's fault. He told Anna Lisa how important her friendship was to him and every time she had a problem at work, he supported her, cared for her and tried to help her. This meant a great deal to Anna Lisa and, after a year, she let her guard down and agreed to date him.

With Paul, she learned to be flexible and to give him space. They had been together for three years. She loved him and wanted to marry him. All her life, she had been looking for that fairytale love – the kind of love her parents had shared. And although she thought she had found it with Paul, Anna Lisa knew her boyfriend wasn't ready to get married.

"How do you like Kimberly, your new assistant?" Anna Lisa asked Paul at dinner. They were seated in a dark corner. A round candle in a clear glass holder glowed in the center of their square table covered by a cream tablecloth.

"She's all right," he answered nonchalantly, looking around the restaurant. There was a birthday party going on at a table far away from theirs. Two couples were sitting a few tables down from them and behind the couples was a family with kids, parents and grandparents.

"I overheard her telling Diana she knows you from school," Anna Lisa asked with piqued curiosity.

"She's in my math class." He took a bite of his chicken fettuccini.

Paul didn't go to college after high school. He learned his bookkeeping skills by working at various jobs but always preferred to work in marketing. Three years ago, he decided to return to school and get his business degree with an emphasis on marketing.

"And?" Anna Lisa asked, feeling there was more to the story than what he was telling her.

"And nothing." He swallowed.

She wanted to know more about Kimberly but did not press him and changed the subject. "How's your school?"

"I have my business calculus exam next week, and I'm not looking forward to it."

Anna Lisa ate a piece of her grilled salmon. "You only have a year left before you get your bachelor's."

"And I can't wait till I'm done." He dipped a piece of bread in olive oil and put it in his mouth. "So, tell me, what's going on with you?"

"Well, I've been thinking about selling my condo."

His eyes widened. "Why would you want to do that? I like your place."

"I thought it would be nice to make a change. I've been checking out these beautiful high-rises on the Internet. They offer everything from swimming pools to tennis courts to basketball courts and gyms. And they have gorgeous views of the city, security, subterranean parking and valet."

"Is there a particular area you were looking at?"

"I thought somewhere close to work. Perhaps Westwood or Century City. What do you think?"

"Sounds great to me. If you make a move make sure your place has a basketball court. Then I'm definitely moving in with you," he said.

His comment excited her. She thought he was hinting at wanting to live with her. "I'll keep that in mind," she said and then couldn't think of another subject to talk about.

They both sat in silence and ate until Paul noticed Anna Lisa dipping a piece of bread in olive oil. "Don't eat that, you'll get fat."

"Stop it, Paul. You know how I feel about my weight," she said, feeling too self-conscious to eat the dipped bread. She left it on the side of her plate and instead sipped on her glass of water.

"Why don't you eat less then?" He had a fast metabolism and didn't have a clue about how difficult it was for her to lose weight.

"Can we change the subject, please?" Anna Lisa asked irritably.

Realizing he was getting her mad, he obliged. "Are you getting along better with Neil?"

Here was another topic she preferred not to discuss. "Yes when we don't speak, we get along perfectly well!"

"You'll get used to him. You didn't like me at first and look how I grew on you." He took a swig of his beer.

"True, but your manners are different from his. You're friendly and easygoing and he's arrogant and hard to get along with," she said. "I can't imagine any girl who'd want to be with him."

"You know he's engaged," He covered his mouth and used a toothpick to pick out a piece of chicken that was stuck between in his teeth. "I heard his fiancée's stunning and comes from money."

She was envious that Paul had used the adjective stunning to describe Neil's fiancée. "Where did you hear that?"

"Diana, Simon's assistant, told me," he answered resting his back against his chair, "She's friends with one of the administrative assistants in the London office."

Anna Lisa wondered about Neil's fiancée and what could she possibly see in him. "I guess my grandmother's right. There is someone out there for everyone."

"How is your grandmother?"

"She's doing well. I'm visiting her this Sunday. You want to come by?"

"I would except I'm playing football with friends from school."

At 29, Paul blended in with the younger students at his school since he was immature for his age. His immaturity was at times irritating as well as endearing to Anna Lisa who was approaching 40 in three years. They often argued over subjects he didn't comprehend but at the same time she liked his playfulness and silliness. Some men lost this childish quality as they aged and instead became too serious and boring.

"You can come by later if you like," his girlfriend said with enthusiasm.

"We're going to the movies later," Paul replied, but when he saw the look of disappointment on Anna Lisa's face, he added, "I can cancel."

"No, go. I'll go shopping with Grandma and my aunts." She noticed the waiter coming over with their bill.

Paul opened his wallet, pulled out his ATM card, and gave it to the waiter. Anna Lisa noticed a familiar picture. "Let me see, is that a picture of your mom?" She grabbed his wallet, noticing a woman with her arm around a young girl.

"It's a snapshot I took of her on Santa Monica Pier." He reached to take his wallet back.

She moved it away from him and asked in astonishment, "When?"

"About two months ago." He shifted in his seat.

"Why didn't you tell me she was in town?" Anna Lisa frowned.

"You were at that … that conference in San Francisco," Paul stuttered. "She only stayed for two days before leaving for San Diego to … to visit a sick friend."

"I wish you had told me." She raised her eyes and looked at him with disappointment. "I really wanted to meet her."

"I thought I told you," he said without making direct eye contact with her, "Besides, you wouldn't have been able to see her because you weren't in town."

"No, you didn't tell me," she complained. "Had you told me, I would've rearranged my schedule so I could at least have had dinner with her."

"May I have my wallet back, please?" Paul fidgeted nervously.

She ignored his request. "She looks very young."

"She's much older than she looks," he confessed.

"Is this your sister who lives with her?" Anna Lisa pointed at the young girl as she studied her face. There were a few freckles on the bridge of her nose and her cheeks, and her short, black bob looked very French.

"Yes, may I have my wallet back?" Paul demanded with impatience.

His girlfriend was about to hand it back to him when the page accidentally flipped to the next and she saw a girl's photo. "Diana, Simon's secretary?" She acted surprised.

"Yes," he answered curtly, wishing she would stop interrogating him further.

She felt jealous and insecure. "Why's her picture in your wallet?"

"Because– she gave it to me," he responded reluctantly.

Confused, she didn't understand his answer. "And why would she do that?"

"We used to date," Paul finally spat it out. Are you happy now? He wanted to say.

"You never said anything about dating her." Anna Lisa frowned. She wondered what other secrets he had been keeping from her.

"You never asked," he answered slyly.

"Don't play with me Paul." She flipped through more pages and saw pictures of girls she didn't recognize. "Who are all these women?" His girlfriend shook her head in disbelief.

"Girls I used to date," he said, regretting that she had possession of his wallet.

"I see." Anna Lisa compressed her lips. She handed back his wallet.

"If you give me your picture," he commented teasingly, "I'll put it in my wallet."

Her face was getting red with anger. "No thanks, I don't want to be added to your list of trophies."

"What do you mean?" he asked raising his voice.

"Nothing," she replied curtly. She had no intention of getting into a big fight with people in the restaurant watching them. She had already noticed a few heads turned in their direction.

Paul let out a sigh of frustration. "I don't see why you're so upset."

She glared at him with eyes that could shoot daggers and could no longer keep her voice down. She was fuming and whenever she was fuming at Paul or didn't want people to understand their private conversation, she spoke in French. Anna Lisa knew most Americans didn't speak the language. She attended a French school as a child and was fluent. "Do you not see? I'm your girlfriend and yet you have pictures of these girls in your wallet. Do you think that's appropriate?" She yelled at him in French.

"They're just pictures. I'm not sleeping with them," he answered back in French without caring about how upset he was making her.

"Oh, and that's supposed to make me feel better? Please take me home." She grabbed her jacket, and started walking toward the door.

"Thanks for ruining my evening." He had been looking forward all day to being with her and having sex.

Anna Lisa didn't answer. She was too furious to speak.

Even then he didn't give-up, because nothing was more satisfying than making passionate love after a fight. "Does this mean I can't spend the night at your place?"

Anna Lisa didn't respond.

"You know, I hate this silent treatment. You always do this to me when you're angry."

Anna Lisa finally replied, "If I speak when I'm angry, I may say something I'll regret later. If you were wise, you would give me time to cool down."

Paul did as she requested and they sat in silence for the rest of the ride home. When he got to her house, she didn't wait for him to open her door. She let herself out, and walked away.

Unlike Paul and Anna Lisa, Sarah and Neil had sex on the gray and maroon comforter, after their ride from the airport. Now, they both sat in bed with their backs against the silver metallic headboard at Neil's condominium.

"The flight was absolutely exhausting," Sarah complained. She looked sexy in a long silky bone negligée and he relaxed in a dark maroon Ralph Lauren robe.

Neil's condo, located on the high-trafficked Wilshire Blvd., was among the many classy high rises and Howard Brown had rented it furnished for him on a month to month basis. His place was south of Westwood Village which had a mix of ritzy restaurants for the business crowd working in the area and the residents, inexpensive and fast food restaurants for the UCLA students, plenty of movie theaters and shops carrying clothes geared to college attendees.

Sarah was tired but couldn't sleep. She picked up a long thin ivory cigarette holder from the night stand next to her side of the bed, pulled out a cigarette and held it between her lips. She flicked her gold Cartier lighter.

"I thought you were trying to quit," Neil said as he passed her a look of disapproval.

"I am. I haven't had one in a month," she said as she inhaled a puff of smoke with a feeling of utter satisfaction on her face. Nothing was more delicious than a cigarette after sex, she thought.

"Then why start now?" He tried to take it away from her but she wouldn't let him.

"Come Now, let me enjoy it in peace," she protested with her legs extended in front of her. She wiggled her red manicured toes.

Neil watched her with lust and desire. He wanted to tear off her negligée and have sex with her again.

"Don't look at me like that," she said, taking another puff.
"Like what?" he asked staring at her artificial breasts, which
looked very real. She had them done by one of London's top
plastic surgeons.
"Like you want to have another go at it."
"And why shouldn't I? I haven't seen you for a whole month."
He stroked her in-between her thighs.
"At least let me finish this," she said eyeing her cigarette. "I
deserve it after being on such a long flight."
Neil removed his hand and turned on the wide screen
television to distract himself from what he really wanted. "It's a
good thing you fly first class. You have no idea how the people in
coach feel."
Neil was middle-class and Sarah, high society. They met four
years ago at a party in the posh Chelsea district of London when
she was 19 and he 31. Like many men, he was attracted to her
instantly. She was tall with long slim legs, lovely hair that
extended to the bottom of her shoulder blades and big beautiful
eyes that enticed him.
"Like you would know?" Sarah commented with her usual
snooty tone.
"I used to fly coach all the time. Now the company pays for
my business-class tickets." He flipped through the channels. His
bedroom, large and modern, was covered with plush gray carpet
and furnished with a king-size bed attached to two night stands on
each side. To the left of the bed was a walk-in closet and further
down, a glass work desk overlooking Wilshire Blvd. and the
gleaming city-lights. In front of him was a faux fireplace and
above it, against the wall, hung his TV.
"Well, I can't imagine flying coach. I would rather stay
home," Sarah said irritably and got up to use the toilet. The master
bathroom had double sinks, marble counters, a separate bath
tub/Jacuzzi and an all-glass shower.
"You are spoiled," Neil remarked with a reprimanding tone
when Sarah came out of the bathroom.

She walked toward the bed and put out her cigarette into a crystal ashtray. "Spoiled? Did you know Emilia Spencer's father has his own private jet? I told Daddy he should get one." She shook a tiny mint spray bottle and squirted it in her mouth.

"And what did he say?"

"He's in the process of acquiring one." Sarah climbed back on the bed and sat close to Neil.

"Oh," he replied in disappointment, wishing her father would stop indulging her.

When Neil first dated Sarah, he had been impressed by her background, elegance and manners. He asked her where she worked and she proudly told him she didn't because if she took on a job, she wouldn't be able to take two-month vacations with her family. She usually hung out with friends, went shopping, pampered herself with facials and massages, played tennis, attended fashion shows and, at her convenience, helped out with charitable functions. However, tonight he wasn't impressed by her lifestyle and he wondered if she would ever be able to live more moderately.

"Dear, are we going shopping tomorrow?" she asked, gazing into his eyes.

He lifted her chin up with one hand, forced her mouth open with his, and gave her a long kiss before answering her. "I'm working a half-day tomorrow," he said, gently biting her lip, "but we'll have the next three days to ourselves."

"You mean two and a half?" she pouted.

"I thought we talked about this before your visit here," he replied, pulling away from her. "Howard Brown is compensating me quite well to live here and work on the Olson account. I don't really have a lot of free time."

"I'll call Charlie and have him show me around, then." Charlie's parents were old friends of the Westons and Charlie hung out with Sarah whenever he visited London. He was four years older than she.

"Do as you like." He turned off the triangular crystal lamp next to his bed, lay on his side with his back toward her and closed his eyes. He was angry with her and no longer felt like having sex. Neil didn't like Charlie, who lived in Malibu and came from money. His parents were in the business of oil and Charlie was in the business of spending their money. He traveled often, bought horses and race cars, and when he grew tired of them he gave them to his father to sell. Charlie was not a good influence on Sarah. Neil wanted Sarah to be around people who contributed to society rather than depleting it all the time.

"Neil?" she called him with sadness in her voice.

"Hmm?" he responded reluctantly.

"Are you awake?"

"Yes."

"May I come by the office tomorrow so we can have lunch?"

He turned toward her. "That would be nice. I'll send a car for you." He looked at her and marveled at her youth and naïveté. The women he met everyday were too busy working and planning their futures. They were always competing with him and wanting to have the upper hand. All Sarah desired was to be married, have a family and be with him. He knew she loved him more than he did her. He was her world. She needed him and he liked the fact that she needed him. He pulled her hair away with one hand, rolled on top of her and kissed her forcefully. Some time later after they had made love, they both fell asleep.

SIX

Neil already had an hour's head start when she walked in their office. It was Anna Lisa's turn to be in an irate mood. Still angry from yesterday over Paul's pictures, she said hello and headed straight for her desk. Her face looked tired; she only got two hours of sleep the night before. Focus, she said to herself, the Olson account is too important. However, before she could delve into her work, someone knocked on the door. Anna Lisa didn't respond; she knew it was Paul and wasn't ready to talk to him. When Neil noticed she was determined to ignore the knock, he said, "Come in."

Paul walked in with his funky khaki pants and white-and-green pin-striped shirt Anna Lisa had bought him for his 29th Birthday, three months ago. He said good morning to Neil, but before he could reply, Paul turned to Anna Lisa and told her in French they needed to talk. He was so used to people around him not understanding French that he completely forgot Neil was British and there was a good chance he spoke the language.

Anna Lisa responded that this was not the right time and that she was too angry with him. It was better for him to let her cool down.

Amused with their conversation, Neil pretended to be reading the material on his desk.

Paul insisted that Anna Lisa speak to him so she told him she was tired of keeping up with all the women in his life and the two of them went at it until Paul finally left. When Paul closed the door behind him, Neil looked up and said, "Boyfriend problems, Leeza?"

Anna Lisa looked at him and answered, "I should've known; you speak French."

"Oui, je parle Français."

"I suppose you speak Spanish too," she said in disappointment.

"Como esta usted? German and Italian, too, if you would like me to demonstrate."

She wrinkled her brows. "Is there anything you can't do?"

"Yes," he responded arrogantly, "but not much."

"Why is it the English think they're always superior?" She glared at him.

"Because we are; we used to rule the world," he said.

"And now we do. Get used to it."

"Your world is new," he stated in a calm but condescending tone, "but we've been around for years. Our history and culture is much richer than yours."

"We have more business sense than you do."

"Is that so? Then perhaps you may enlighten me as to why I was sent here to help you."

"Now, wait just a darn minute," Anna Lisa raised her voice, "I don't need your help. Simon forced you on me and if I had my way, I'd–"

Neil raised his hand and cried, "Enough. I refuse to pick a fight with you because that is exactly what you want. You're mad and irrational and you're directing your anger at me when you should be yelling at Paul for cheating on you."

Her jaw dropped open as she went over to his desk and put her hands on it. "For your information, Paul isn't cheating on me. He loves me and we're just having some...," She suddenly stopped, turned in the direction of her desk and said in exasperation, "Why on earth am I explaining myself to you? I'm not going to discuss my relationship with you because it's none of your business, but if you have any questions regarding the Olson account, now is the time to ask."

"I have questions but at the moment I'm afraid of you. You're too emotional and may fling something at me."

"Have I ever done that before?" she asked in anger.

"Not yet."

"Then perhaps it is wise for you to assume that I won't," she replied changing her tone. "Listen, I don't know why, but you bring out the worst in me. I'm sorry if I yelled at you. The sooner we finish this project, the sooner you can go back to England and be with your family."

Neil stared at her for a long moment. She looked masculine and rigid with her hair tightly pulled back and her black jacket draped over a white shirt and a pair of black slacks. Even her loafers resembled that of a man's. Yet, there was something feminine about her when she was quiet. He had stolen several glances at her when she had been unaware and had noticed she was rather pretty and pleasant when her facial muscles were relaxed and serene. He couldn't figure out why she disliked him. He never had so much trouble getting on with a woman until he met Anna Lisa.

"Well?"

"Well, what?"

"Is there something on my face that displeases you?"

He passed her a confused look. "No, nothing of the kind."

"Then why are you staring?"

"It's just that … that … never mind." He had no idea how to communicate with her. If he said white, she would say black. Would they ever be able to speak two sentences in a row without fighting? He wasn't sure.

"Mr. Whittaker, if you don't have anything to ask, I would like to get back to work."

Neil cleared his throat. "I've read about the board of directors and the lady who started the company," he said, reaching in his pocket for a pen to take notes, "but I would rather hear about them from you. I understand you have a good relationship with them."

"Yes, I do. They have a lot of faith in me." She grabbed her coffee cup from her desk, walked over to sit on the sofa and watched him look from one pocket to the other searching for a pen. He wasn't as hopeless looking as she had originally thought. Had she not been forced to work with him and met him under different circumstances, she might have found him agreeable. He was cultured and well-educated when he spoke. His clothes were always tasteful, pressed to perfection and spotless. He wore conservative dark suits, pale color shirts and colorful ties. Today he had on a navy suit, a yellow tie and a white shirt, which made him look like a gentleman. If only he behaved as such toward her. She stopped staring at him when he caught her eyes.

"Is there something on my face that displeases you?" he mimicked the same question she had asked earlier.

She ignored his smart ass remark and replied, "Fifty years ago, Jane Bradley did manicures and pedicures for celebrities and got paid very well. Five years later, she met Clark Olson; they fell in love and got married." She got up to lend him her silver vintage pen since she was tired of watching him search his pockets.

"Thank you," he said taking her pen. "I don't know where all my pens went."

"You're welcome." She walked back to the sofa. "A pen is a rare commodity in this building. As soon as you leave it somewhere, another person grabs it."

"Then I shall guard yours with care. Please, go ahead with your story." He felt bad that he had interrupted her.

"Where was I?"

"You were talking about the two of them getting married."

"Oh, yes. So after Jane married Clark, a business man from a wealthy Boston family, she decided to market her nail products. Clark helped by putting her in contact with investors. Back then, the competition wasn't as fierce as today and her business took off. They expanded, added other product lines and went public. Today all of their lines are doing well except for Jane Olson's products."

"Is it because of the quality of her products?"

"On the contrary, the quality is excellent," Anna Lisa said noticing him get up with her pen and a note pad to join her on the sofa, "In fact, her products are superior to most on the market today, but it's her old-fashioned ideas on how and where to advertise and her old packaging that's holding her back."

"Is the official name of her line Jane Olson's Nail and Beauty Care?"

"Yes, it is."

"I understand Clark passed away 10 years ago."

"He did," Anna Lisa nodded her head in agreement, "however, Jane still owns shares in the company and her nephew Adam, who is 30, is the CEO of the board."

"But Adam is young. I'm surprised his ideas are old."

"He is new blood for the company but he abides by his aunt's wishes," Anna Lisa said, "and now the board of directors is looking to replace Adam with someone more suitable, get rid of the Olson nail products, and buy out Mrs. Olson's who owns 49 percent of the shares. She's very upset."

"Rightfully so," he agreed.

"And Adam doesn't want to lose his job. He doesn't need the money but he likes his work and his aunt did start the company. It would be a shame to lose it all. Besides, the nail product line has sentimental value to her. That's how she met her husband – he was getting a manicure."

"You've got to be joking."

"No, I'm quite serious. Of course, fewer men got manicures back then but many do today. I love a man with polished nails."

"But that's absurd. It's girly."

"Don't knock it until you've tried it."

"No."

"Simon has and he loves it."

"I can't believe it."

"He goes once a week. It's not at all like what you think. Manicurists clean, shape and buff your nails and use these great creams so you won't have calloused fingers and hands," Anna Lisa said. "You should give it a try sometime."

My hands are not calloused, Neil thought, and changed the subject. "Now, I understand why they're spending so much money to promote their product."

"After we're done launching their product with brand new packaging, billboards, magazines and television ads, they will get their money's worth and so will the shareholders."

"And so the line will be saved and Adam will get to keep his job?"

"Not only that, but our company will end up managing their account for a long time."

"You think?"

Anna Lisa moved closer to him on the sofa. She was getting excited discussing possibilities for the Olson line. "Right now we're marketing the line to baby-boomers. But later we can use the same product with a few minor changes and come up with a new line geared to the career woman by simply changing the packaging and the mode of marketing, and giving it a different name."

"You really like their products."

"I do. I have samples," Anna Lisa said, walking over to her desk to reach in the drawer when the buzzer on Neil's intercom went off and a Miss Sarah Weston was announced.

Neil moved toward the door to greet her. "Hi darling," he said, giving her a peck on the cheek and noticing her stare at Anna Lisa. "Sarah, this is Leeza, my work colleague. Leeza, this is Sarah my fiancée."

"It's Anna Lisa actually," Anna Lisa said to Sarah. "But against my wishes, your fiancé has given me a pet name. Anyhow, it's nice to meet you," Anna Lisa said extending her hand to shake Sarah's.

Sarah gave Anna Lisa a lukewarm handshake and said, "Likewise." She then turned to Neil with a pretentious air and commented, "Really darling, why wouldn't you call Anna Lisa by her proper name?"

"It's a long story that I will not get into at the moment. Let us go and have lunch, shall we?" he said, putting his hand behind her back to lead her out of the office before she and Anna Lisa could have a chance to get to know each other.

Sarah, however, didn't budge. "You told me she was old and disagreeable but I see that is not true," She said, noticing a framed picture of a man embracing Anna Lisa on her desk.

Neil was embarrassed by his fiancée's remark as he cleared his throat and said, "I'm famished. Can we go eat, please?"

Anna Lisa, who didn't care about what Neil had told Sarah replied, "He did, did he? I'm not surprised. Unfortunately we had a bad start and we're trying to get along better, at least until this project is over. Isn't that true, Mr. Whittaker?"

Sarah picked up a burgundy frame from Anna Lisa's desk and studied Paul's face. "Is this your man?" He was not her type but he was good-looking, she thought.

"Yes, that's my boyfriend Paul."

"I'd love for all of us to have lunch someday soon," Sarah said.

Before Anna Lisa could answer, Neil interrupted them and declared that if he didn't eat, he would vanish into thin air, so the pair left.

Anna Lisa went to her drawer and pulled out her boring turkey breast slices sandwiched between iceberg lettuce leaves along with a small red apple. She was on a low-carb diet. She thought about how great Sarah looked. Her figure flawless, her outfit and jewelry subtle but very expensive and her hair long and satiny unlike her own, which was frizzy unless she spent hours fussing over it. She always wanted to look like the Sarahs of the world – slim, tall and delicate like a ballerina. For the past seven years she had tried every diet to lose her 20 extra pounds succeeding a few times only to gain it all back each time. It was as though her body was comfortable with her extra weight. She looked again at her unappetizing sandwich when she heard a knock on her door.

"Come in," she said.

It was Leila, her Iranian friend. When Anna Lisa had recommended Leila to Simon four years ago, Simon had agreed to start her off as an administrative assistant. At that time, Leila had a year left before finishing her bachelor's degree in business with emphasis in marketing and advertising. When finished with her undergrad, she enrolled in an MBA program at USC for which Howard Brown had agreed to pay. She was then promoted to assistant account executive.

"Who was that?" Leila asked with awe.

"Neil's fiancée," Anna Lisa answered with a cold voice.

"Very nice. She looked expensive." Leila wished she had that kind of money to buy couture. She walked over to the sofa and sat.

"Yes she is expensive, snooty and has a weak hand shake," Anna Lisa said with raised eyebrows. "She reminds me of J-ello."

"She seemed more like a crème brulée to me," Leila responded teasingly. She glanced around the office, noticing a picture on Neil's desk.

"On the exterior perhaps, but when you dig in I'm sure you'll find J-ello," Anna Lisa said.

Leila got up and picked up the chocolate brown leather frame sitting on Neil's desk and looked at the photo of him and his fiancée. He was in a navy suit with his arm around her waist, and she was wearing a classic spaghetti-strap taupe dress. Her softly curled hair lay over her shoulders and she had a perfect smile. "I think she's really pretty. She looks like a model."

"She is pretty and young too," Anna Lisa responded as she leaned back in her chair. "I wonder what she sees in Neil."

"Please don't tell me you don't find Neil attractive," her friend said in amazement putting the picture back where it belonged. She went back to the sofa, sat down and stretched her legs.

"Attractive, no; intolerable and conceited, yes. But then I'm not surprised," Anna Lisa replied. "He is British, and the British always think they're above everyone else."

"That's a prejudiced remark." Leila sat up. "I wonder what you say of me behind my back."

"That you're the best friend one could possibly have." Anna Lisa regretted that she had made such a remark. "You know I'm not prejudiced. It's just that Neil rubs me the wrong way."

"Honey, he can rub me anytime and I would never complain," Leila said with a smile.

"I'm afraid you're too late. He's already engaged and, besides," her friend commented as she got up, picked up a marketing research book from her desk and walked toward a book shelf, "I would stop hanging around you if he were your husband." She put the book on the second shelf and went back to her desk to pick up a yellow folder.

"My husband?" Leila said with excitement. "Oh, how I wish to have a husband like him. He's rich, handsome and pleasant."

Anna Lisa walked over to a filing cabinet, opened the top drawer, filed the folder away and shut it. "He's rich to be sure, but handsome and pleasant? That's a matter of opinion." She went back to her desk. "Anyway, let's not waste time talking about him. I'm hungry and want to enjoy my lunch."

"Why don't you lunch with me at my folks' house?" Leila got up and walked over to her friend's desk, "My mom made rice with tomato sauce, beef and green bean dish – *loubia polo.*"

"You know that's my favorite dish but I can't." She looked at her turkey wrap. "I'm on a diet."

"Again?" Leila said knowing her friend only too well.

"Yes I'm trying to lose 20 pounds," she responded with confidence. But the thought of her favorite dish was making her mouth water.

"In this lifetime?" Leila asked jokingly and smiled.

"Very funny," she answered with annoyance.

"C'mon start your diet tomorrow." Leila went around Anna Lisa's desk and pulled her hand. "You know my parents would love to see you. They always ask about you."

Anna Lisa resisted and removed her hand. "No really, I should stick to my diet. Paul thinks I'm too fat," she admitted sadly.

"That man loves to put you down, doesn't he?" Leila shook her head in disapproval. "I don't know why you take it from him. You don't need to diet, you look fine." She stared at her sandwich. "You are a funny friend – always tempting me to break my diet."

"C'mon, let's go," Leila insisted.

Anna Lisa stuck her sandwich back in her drawer and the two took off to Leila's parents' house.

Leila and Anna Lisa met in high school. The former had onyx eyes, straight short black hair styled like a boy's haircut, was two inches taller than Anna Lisa and her figure was petite and delicate. Leila moved to Los Angeles when she was 15 but still had a slight accent. Her goal in life was to marry a rich man, be a stay-at-home mom, have two children – a boy and a girl, preferably in that order – and live in a house with a large yard and a swimming pool. However, her Armenian boyfriend, Viktor, was always broke but loved her very much. She lived with her parents' because she spent all her money on clothes, shoes and jewelry and couldn't afford to rent her own place. Loud and outspoken, she had a difficult time keeping a secret. Leila's lack of discretion and her stentorian voice annoyed and embarrassed the people around her including Anna Lisa at times. Yet Anna Lisa loved her friend dearly and got along with her well.

Leila and her family were Muslims but lived in a predominately Jewish neighborhood near Pico Blvd. where the houses were old and charming, had slanted roofs with shingles and were built close to each other. The Sultanis' home was small but comfortable. Their neighbors were friendly and knew each other. They brought each other homemade cakes and fresh fruits from their yards. Leila's mother, Susan, knew how to read fortunes from Turkish coffee. She often had her Muslim friends and her Jewish neighbors over for Persian sweets, tea, Turkish coffee and a round of fortune telling. It was nice to see Muslims and Jews get along so well. Only in L.A. Anna Lisa thought.

Susan dyed her shoulder-length hair with red henna. She was short and plump. Her husband, Cameron, had gray hair, was few inches taller than his daughter and kept himself fit by jogging in the afternoons. The pair used to own two gas stations and a row of duplexes, which they rented out. As they got older, they sold the gas stations and kept their rental properties. They weren't rich but were happy and lived comfortably. Anna Lisa tried to spend time with them at least once a month, preferably more. They had adopted her into their family and treated her like a daughter.

As soon as the girls arrived, Leila's parents greeted Anna Lisa. Susan said with her heavy Persian accent, "Welcome, welcome, very good see you. You never come see us."

"I'm sorry Susan. I wanted to so many times but my work keeps me so busy."

"Work, work," Cameron said. "Why don't you get married and have children?"

"Leave her alone," his wife answered. "She doesn't need marry. She makes enough money; she can take care of herself."

Leila changed the subject, and settled into the living room. "Mom did you see my new shoes I bought yesterday?"

"No please, no more shoes," her mother said as she slapped her own face with two hands and turned to Anna Lisa. "How many shoes this girls needs? You tell me." With this she grabbed Anna Lisa's hand and pulled her into Leila's room. She pointed to a closet packed with clothes, some of the tags still unremoved, purses that still smelled of new leather and more than 50 boxes of shoes.

"But I got them on sale," Leila protested.

"She never has money," Susan complained to Anna Lisa.

"Mom, we have to get back to work soon. Can we eat please?" Leila said.

Susan invited them into the kitchen where they all sat around a square table covered with a brown paisley tablecloth. She served a delicious meal of white rice with saffron and tomato sauce, chopped beef sautéed with turmeric and cut-up onions and grilled green beans all mixed together. *Tahdig* – a crispy rice dish, salad with lemon juice and olive oil dressing, yogurt mixed with chopped cucumbers, walnuts and raisins and a basket of warm *taftoon bread* – a type of Persian bread.

"Eat, eat, why aren't you eating? Today, you eat. Tomorrow you diet," said Cameron as he filled Anna Lisa's plate.

"Dad, stop," Leila protested, "She has no room left on her plate."

"You girls are always on diet. Men don't like skinny women."

"You like?" Susan asked Anna Lisa about her dish.

"It looks delicious. I have to get the recipe from you."

"It's easy; you cook the meat and throw out the foam and then–"

"Oh Mom, she's not going to remember. We're not all great in the kitchen like you. You have to write it down."

"Okay, I write down," said Susan.

"Susan, do you go to a mosque?" Anna Lisa asked. She put a large spoonful of rice in her mouth. Iranians ate their meals with a large spoon and fork.

"Rarely, why you ask?"

"I'd like to go with you sometime. I've never been to one."

"We don't practice our faith," Cameron commented.

"God's in our heart, we don't need mosque to find God," stated his wife. "But if you want I take you."

"I'd like that," Anna Lisa replied.

"You Christian?" Cameron asked.

"I'm Catholic, but I don't go to church either."

"All religion is the same," Cameron remarked, "and people fight for nothing."

"He's right you know," Susan said. "Take the Palestinians and the Israelis for example. They fight over who gets more land while all these children suffer in the middle. You tell me how many more people have to die for a stupid piece of land?"

"If you ask me," her husband interrupted, "they should combine all the land and live together, help each other. Learn from each other, you know. So what if I'm Muslim, he's Jewish or you're Catholic? We're all the same."

Anna Lisa just listened. What they said made a lot of sense if they lived in a perfect world, she thought. Unfortunately they didn't. For as long as civilizations have existed, war has existed. Humans have always fought over material wealth, greed and power.

"You don't think so, Anna Lisa?" Cameron asked.

"Tea, anyone?" Leila said to distract her parents. She didn't want to get into a long political debate.

"I'd like some," Anna Lisa replied.

"Why you ask?" Susan said, "Just bring it for everyone."

Leila served Persian tea with sugar cubes and *baghlava* – a Persian dessert made of almond paste, rose water and sugar. Cameron took his tea, excused himself and left to go smoke a cigarette in the living room. Susan made Turkish coffee for Anna Lisa and offered to read her fortune. She turned the small teal cup in her hand and studied its content.

Susan held up two fingers and said, "Two women…Very jealous of you. Be careful."

Anna Lisa nodded skeptically. Who was jealous of her? She had no idea.

"You go on trip. Let's see in, one, two, three…Yes, in three months…may be little sooner," she said, tilting her head and shrugging one shoulder.

"A trip?" Anna Lisa asked in surprise and smiled. She got excited thinking Paul was going to surprise her and take her to Greece the way he had promised.

"But not with your boyfriend," Susan said as though reading her mind. "No. You go with a man. A tall man, you don't know very well."

Leila looked at her friend teasingly, "Anna Lisa, you sly thing. You've been holding out on me. C'mon tell me who is this mystery man?"

"There is no mystery man. Believe me I'm as curious as you are," Anna Lisa replied.

Susan frowned as she turned the cup. "Something happens. Something maybe not so good."

"Mom, you're not supposed to tell her negative things," Leila complained.

"Be quiet," Susan said to her daughter. She turned to Anna Lisa. "I see changes. Many changes. I don't know. Maybe new house...or new job."

"May be a new man," Leila sniggered.

"Go. Go watch TV with your father. Stop bothering me," Susan told Leila.

"Testy, aren't we?" Leila commented.

Susan ignored her. "Now, where was I? Oh yes. Everything is going to change for you and soon."

"How soon?" Anna Lisa asked. She was hanging on every word Susan was telling her and was starting to get butterflies in her stomach.

"In six months or less, but it's all good. At first, not so good, but then you will be happy. You'll see."

Anna Lisa was baffled by Susan's predictions.

Leila nudged her friend and said, "I wouldn't put too much thought into this. Mom has been wrong before."

"Put your index finger in the middle of the cup and press," Susan told Anna Lisa.

Anna Lisa did as she was asked.

"Now move it so I can see finger print." Susan scrutinized the cup for a moment. "I see love and commitment."

"From my boyfriend?" Anna Lisa asked excitedly.

"I don't know," Susan replied, the edges of her mouth tilting downward. "May be from this man you go on trip with."

"Oh," Anna Lisa replied with disappointment and wondered who the man was.

Leila looked at her watch and got up. "It's getting late. We should get going." Their one hour lunch break had turned into an hour and a half.

"You come back soon," Susan said to Anna Lisa as she stood next to her husband at the entrance and waved goodbye.

When Leila and Anna Lisa returned to work, Anna Lisa found red and white tulips arranged beautifully in a square glass vase on her desk. She read the card and smiled. The note was from Paul apologizing for the previous night. Then the door opened and he walked in.

"You like them?" Paul asked, walking toward her and reaching for her hands.

"Yes I do, very much." She looked at him with appreciation. She loved him completely with all his flaws. She loved his masculine fresh-smelling skin, the way he looked at her with his sad dark eyes when she was mad at him and the manner in which he brushed his big hands gently up and down her spine.

Paul knew well the power and control he had over Anna Lisa but he also knew when he was about to lose her. "So, you're not mad anymore?" He put his forehead against hers and nibbled on her lips.

"You hurt me last night." She let go of his hands and moved away. "We need to talk."

"Are you breaking up with me?" he asked nervously.

"No. Will you close the door and sit down?" Anna Lisa asked as she went over to the sofa and took a seat.

Paul shut the door and joined her.

"Do you see why I was upset?"

"Because of the pictures. I told you in my note I burned them," he said with his hands stuck in his pockets.

"But I didn't ask you to burn them." Anna Lisa frowned.

He looked at her confused. "I thought you didn't want me to have them."

"No, I didn't want you to keep them in your wallet, I have pictures of old boyfriends; I just don't keep them in my purse. Your wallet is a place for pictures of your family, friends and your girlfriend, not your old flames."

"I know," he nodded in agreement, "I told Kimberly what happened and she agreed with you."

"You told Kimberly?" Anna Lisa asked with a mixture of surprise and disappointment.

"Was that wrong?" He took his hands out of his pocket and straightened himself.

"Yes, you've only just met her," she replied with a hint of disapproval.

"But I had to talk to someone."

"Don't you have any male friends?"

"Yes, but they're like me. I was trying to get a woman's opinion."

Paul had a lot to learn, Anna Lisa thought, and she wouldn't be able to teach him everything in one sitting. "Fair enough, but confide in someone else next time. Kimberly works here and may gossip. I like to keep what goes on between us outside this office."

He pulled her toward him and kissed her. "You know you're the only one in my life."

"I know." Feeling scared, excited, exasperated and fantastic all at the same time, she put her fingers through his long hair and kissed him back. She was on a roller coaster high and didn't want to descend. He pulled her closer and she felt every inch of his body – hard, tight and strong. He moved his hands over her breasts, caressing them gently and then more roughly. Afraid that someone would walk in, she pulled away.

"What did you do that for?" he complained.

"Because I should finish up my work. Why don't you come over tonight and we can watch a video?"

"You'll make me dinner?" he asked excitedly.

"I'll order Chinese takeout. Say about 8?"

"I'm there." He fixed his hair, gave her one last kiss and left her office with a grin on his face.

That afternoon, Anna Lisa worked on her clients' advertisements. Neil was gone for the rest of the day with Sarah. When Anna Lisa finished up, she walked across the street to get her nails done at Hoffman's Nail Salon. Once home, she took a hot bath, put on a pretty black negligee, ordered Chinese food to be delivered to her apartment, selected a mystery suspense video and waited for Paul to arrive.

SEVEN

Saturday morning Anna Lisa's alarm went off at 9. It was actually 8:50, but she put her clock ahead so she could get in an extra 10 minutes of snooze without being late. Paul was sleeping next to her. Ursula, her housekeeper, had already let herself in about an hour ago. She usually began cleaning the downstairs bathroom and then the kitchen before she started vacuuming the dining room. She didn't want the noise of the vacuum to wake Anna Lisa but she couldn't care less about waking Paul.

Ursula, a tall, large German, started working for Anna Lisa six years ago. Anna Lisa compensated her well and found her other well-paying clients. Ursula considered Anna Lisa as part of her family and protected her dearly.

"Paul, wake up," Anna Lisa said as she got ready. He didn't budge. "C'mon get up, you're going to be late for your football game." She nudged him.

"Five more minutes," he said.

She sighed, shook her head and then kissed him on the cheek. "I've got to run. Love you." She headed downstairs in her ruby sweats, white tank top and tennis shoes. She was carrying a fresh set of workout clothes to change into after her hike.

"Good morning Ursula," Anna Lisa said when she reached the bottom of the stairs.

"Good morning to you as well," Ursula responded and handed her a glass of orange juice and her water bottle. Anna Lisa was planning to hike with her friend Nicole as she did every Saturday.

"Thanks Ursula." Anna Lisa gulped down the juice, "Got to go. Give my love to your children and say hi to your husband. Oh and please pick up my laundry. I left your check with extra money in the kitchen's right-hand drawer."

"I will take care of it."

As the door closed behind Anna Lisa, Ursula turned on the vacuum. She knew how much Paul hated the noise and she smiled. A few minutes later Paul dragged his lazy body downstairs and grunted, "Can't you dust or something instead of turning on that noisy machine?"

"I just finished dusting. Now, it's time to vacuum," Ursula said.

Paul grabbed his keys and left without saying good-bye.

Ursula was happy he was gone. As soon as he left, she turned off the vacuum and started dusting. She didn't like Paul because he had always been rude to her. He never greeted her and each time she tried to be civil to him, he ignored her as though she were far beneath him. She never said a word about this to Anna Lisa, because she didn't want to cause trouble. Ursula continued dusting and when she got to Paul's picture, she muttered, "She deserves better than you, and you know it. And if it weren't for Anna Lisa, I would let you be covered in dust." After she dusted the picture, she turned it to face the wall.

The hiking trail in Paseo Miramar in Pacific Palisades was just a 15 minute ride down the coast from Anna Lisa's condo. Affluent residents and nonlocals hung out there on weekends for the cool weather, upscale cafes and great people-watching. Anna Lisa and her friend, Nicole, went for the hiking trails.

After parking her car, Anna Lisa went to stand by a large cedar where she and Nicole always met. They met about four years ago when Nicole, her husband and their one-year-old daughter first moved into the house across the street from Anna Lisa's grandmother. They got into a conversation one day and Anna Lisa found out that Nicole used to teach high school before she became a stay-at-home mom, and her husband was a business consultant at a large corporation. Nicole discovered that Anna Lisa was single, that she was always busy with work and that she liked to hike, so the two made plans to hike every Saturday and Anna Lisa's grandmother offered to baby-sit.

Nicole finally arrived at the grounds and Anna Lisa waved at her. "Hi sleepyhead," Anna Lisa said when Nicole got closer.

"Hi, have you been here long?" asked Nicole. She was tall, had thin and wavy shoulder-length dirty blond hair, light brown eyes and a long face. When she smiled, her lips moved up high like that of a horse's, showing off most of her gums and projecting teeth.

"No, not very long."

"You're ready to go?"

"Sure am," Anna Lisa replied and they began their hike.

The trail started flat and steepened as they advanced and left little room for conversation. After a half hour, they reached a peak and stopped to take a water break. Looking down, they saw smog and muddy air, which hovered over the city. Heading downward, they talked about their week – their families, current events, the arts and their observation on life in general. Soon the path became more difficult as it changed directions again uphill and they tried to save their breath and energy until they reached a beautiful break area where a thin body of water cascaded over a series of rocks and landed into a creek. Like a forest, their surroundings were lush and green.

Anna Lisa who never missed a chance to prod Nicole about her relationship with her devoted beau said, "So, when are you and Eddie getting married?"

"Never. We have separate bank accounts and file separate income tax returns. For the first time in my life, I'm the one in charge of my finances and I like that."

Two years ago, Nicole's husband who owed a lot of money to creditors left the country and abandoned his wife. Nicole was stuck with a huge debt. At first she fell into a deep depression, cried constantly and vowed never to get married again.

"You know, California is a common law state. When you live with someone everything gets divided whether or not you're married," Anna Lisa commented.

"I've already taken care of that as well. I had a lawyer draw up a contract which basically stated what I have is mine and what he has is his. We don't owe each other anything once we go our own separate ways."

Nicole still remembered the creditors who didn't care about her sorrows. They called and sent letters to her constantly. After a month of harassment from them, she couldn't take it any more. She was afraid to end up on the streets so she took charge. With the help of Anna Lisa and her grandmother she sold most of her assets including a Range Rover, antique furniture and pricy paintings to pay her husband's creditors. She took a loan on her house, bought secondhand furniture and a used Honda and went back to teaching high school and studying for her master's degree in education so she could become a counselor.

"You have thought of everything, haven't you?"

"Well, once you get burned, you learn. Besides, I have a daughter to protect."

The private school where Nicole taught provided free daycare for her daughter. After work, Anna Lisa's grandmother helped out so Nicole could study.

"I understand."

"What about you?" Nicole asked, nudging her friend with her elbow.

"What about me?"

"It's time for you and Paul to tie the knot."

Anna Lisa picked up a dead branch from the ground and started playing with it. She was getting uncomfortable with the topic pf their conversation. "I'd like to live with him before getting married."

"Why don't you do it then?"

"He's not ready and I don't want to push him," she replied, tossing the branch into the creek.

"How long have you two been together?"

"Three years."

"That's a bit too long for him not to be ready," Nicole said, raising an eyebrow.

Anna Lisa knew her friend was right but didn't want to admit it. "C'mon let's start moving."

The trail pulled them up once more, then it flattened and awhile later geared downwards until they reached their starting point. Anna Lisa changed into dry clothes in one of the park restroom stalls, exchanged farewells with Nicole and headed for her office.

"Two women...Very jealous of you. Be careful."

Anna Lisa usually went in the office on Saturday because it was quiet on weekends and she was able to get a lot of work done without interruption. But when she arrived, she noticed her door was partially ajar. She walked in and to her surprise found Kimberly sitting behind her desk with her legs up on the table, chatting on the phone.

As soon as Kimberly saw Anna Lisa, she removed her legs and said to the person on the other side of the receiver, "Got to go. I'll call you," and hung up. Then she turned toward her superior, "What brings you here? I thought you were at that hiking thing."

"How do you know I hike on Saturday?"

"Paul told me."

She walked toward her desk and slammed her backpack down. "What're you doing in my office? You're not allowed to be in here."

"I just ... I just..."

"You just what? Happen to stroll in by accident?"

"Yes, I mean no," Kimberly said when she couldn't think of an explanation. "Simon asked me to write up a report he had dictated and since I had to leave early on Friday, I thought I would do it today."

Her nasal, high-pitched voice was grinding on Anna Lisa's nerve. "You have your own desk. Why don't you use it?"

"Your office is so much nicer and roomier," she said but when she saw Anna Lisa glowering at her, she relinquished the seat.

"Don't let me catch you in here again, is that clear?"

Kimberly nodded, picked up her work and walked out.

Anna Lisa was angry for a long time. She didn't care if people used her office but she didn't like Kimberly nor did she trust her. Her intuition told her the girl was trouble and Anna Lisa was sorry that Paul had hired her, but there was nothing she could do. She collected herself and began work on the Olson account.

Four hours later, when she finished, she decided to stop by Natalie Lu and pick up a salad and a tiramisu for dinner. Natalie Lu, a cozy café located on the artsy chic and spotless Montana Avenue, was located on the Westside, about a 10-minute drive from where Anna Lisa lived. One could easily miss it if one didn't know anything about it. Mostly locals from the Brentwood area were familiar with its gourmet menu.

After driving around the block several times, she found a car leaving. She pulled into the parking spot and walked towards the café. The day had turned much colder and drearier since her hike that morning. The combination of dark clouds and thunder threatened rain. As she went in, she noticed Neil and Sarah in line and decided to turn around and leave but Sarah had already spotted her.

"Hello, Anna Lisa, I didn't expect to see you here," Sarah said. She was wearing a beautiful camel cashmere coat, brown leather gloves and Salvador Ferragamo pumps. Not a hair was out of place and her make-up was flawless.

"Hi." Anna Lisa replied reluctantly embarrassed that she looked like a rumpled mess with her hair in ponytail, hidden under a white baseball cap. Her brown and white sweat suit and scuffed tennis shoes were no match for Sarah's designer outfit.

"This place has excellent pastries, doesn't it?" Neil said as though he was not at all surprised to see Anna Lisa there. He was clothed as beautifully as his fiancée. He had on a charcoal wool coat over his black sweater and pants and was wearing a pair of dressy dark gray leather shoes.

"Yes it does. How do you know about it?"

"Simon recommended it. He said it was a favorite of yours and his."

The interior of Natalie Lu had a warm feeling to it – the walls were painted in earth tone colors, straw baskets held various loafs of bread and the patrons were friendly and conversed with each other. A display case held scrumptious pastries, tarts and cakes and a large selection of coffees and teas. Another case offered tantalizing soups, salads, pastas and eggplant dishes.

"May I help you?" The pimply teenage boy behind the counter asked Neil.

Neil looked at Sarah. "What would you like darling?"

"I'll have a cup of English breakfast tea."

"Would you like anything with that?" the teenager asked.

"No, thank you. That'll do," she said, with a wave of her hand.

"And you, sir?"

"I'll have a cappuccino and tiramisu," replied Neil.

Anna Lisa looked disappointed as the boy gave the last serving of tiramisu to Neil.

A young girl with short brown hair behind the counter asked Anna Lisa, "May I help you, ma'am?"

Anna Lisa who didn't like to be addressed as ma'am because it made her feel old replied, "I'll have a Greek salad to go."

"Would you like anything else?"

"No. Well. Uh, was that the last piece of tiramisu you had? Do you have more in the back?"

"I'm afraid that gentleman took the last piece," the girl glanced discreetly at Neil, "Perhaps I can interest you in a mocha cake?"

"No, thank you. I think I'll stick with my Greek salad."

Neil, who had been listening to Anna Lisa's conversation, turned to the boy and said, "Sorry, I changed my mind. I'd like the tiramisu to go, and I'll have a slice of that mocha cake for here." When the young man finished serving him, Neil paid and directed him to give the tiramisu to Anna Lisa.

"This is for you, compliments of that gentleman," the teen said.

"For me?" Anna Lisa asked with wide eyes.

"Yes," he replied.

Anna Lisa looked toward Neil. "Thank you but no, I couldn't."

"I insist. It's the least I could do after taking your lemon curd."

Anna Lisa didn't know what to say except to thank him again and add, "You really don't need to..."

"I know. Bon appétit." He walked away with Sarah to find a seat.

"Do you fancy her?" Sarah asked when they sat down behind a small round table for two.

"Not at all, I was merely being polite." He offered Sarah a piece of the mocha cake on a fork.

She shook her head no. "You are a good sport, darling," Sarah said, unsure of what to think of her fiancé's relationship with Anna Lisa.

Neil gave her a half smile.

"She's not very pretty, is she?" Sarah sneered and sipped her tea.

"I think she's quite attractive."

"She's so plain, hardly wears any make-up and her hair is always pulled back."

"You can't blame her. With the kind of hours she has to put in, she probably doesn't have time to fuss," he said, "Anyway, I think she has that natural look." He took a bite of cake.

"Natural look, you say? People who look natural are simply too lazy to take care of themselves. It takes hard work to look put together."

"Perhaps that's not important to her," he said and decided to change the subject. "How are our wedding plans coming along?"

"I'm almost done with everything. I've booked us a place at the Ritz." She sat back and looked around her. Compared to her and Neil, everyone else was dressed casually, and she didn't like it. She was used to her fashionable social circle – this kickback L.A. attitude bothered her.

"Isn't that expensive?"

"Not to worry," she patted her fiancé's hand. "Daddy's paying for the whole thing."

Neil passed her a look of annoyance. "You know I don't feel comfortable with that."

"You really shouldn't feel guilty, he can afford it."

The sky gave out a loud thunderous noise and broke into rain. A gray-haired couple rushed inside to avoid the sudden downpour. Sarah checked to make sure she had her umbrella by her side.

"I don't feel guilty. I just don't think it is right for your father to pay for everything. I hope this isn't how it's going to be after we're married."

"Darling, you knew about my lifestyle when we started going out. And you hardly make enough to support me."

His facial muscles were getting tenser by the minute and he wondered if Sarah had any idea how insulting her comment had been. "I make six digits a year plus bonuses. They give me stock options, a matching 401K and other benefits. I think most people would consider that a nice living," he replied, clearly irritated.

"Well, you're not going to stop me from having things I enjoy. I'm simply not going to give those up."

"You don't have to give up anything but you ought to spend money more wisely. You can't run to your father every time you need something."

"Now, you're upsetting me. I don't want to talk about this anymore," she pouted.

"Fine," he said, feeling dissatisfied that the discussion of their finances came to a halt.

When Anna Lisa returned home, she arranged candles around her bathroom, lit them and filled her bathtub with hot water and lavender bubble bath. With her phone ringer turned off and a CD of Beethoven's piano Sonata No. 8 in the background, she melted into her long-awaited bath. After getting out, she smoothed on a cucumber-scented lotion, put on her terrycloth pajamas, wrapped her hair in a towel and started watching her favorite DVD – *Casablanca* starring Humphrey Bogart. On a table, she put her Greek salad and tiramisu on cream china plates with a gold trim that her grandmother had given her long ago, and poured herself a glass of chardonnay in a crystal wine glass.

The exhaustion from the hike and work finally caught up with her and at some point after eating and before the movie ended, she fell asleep. When she woke up, the DVD had rewound itself to the beginning. She got up, washed her plates, made herself a cup of chamomile tea and called Paul but he did not answer his home phone or his cell. He was probably with his study group, she thought; will try him later. She flipped through her TV channels and found an episode of *I Love Lucy*. Her mind started to wander about the events of her day – Paul in her bed, Nicole, the hike, work, Kimberly, and her run-in with Neil. Neil had been so nice to her at the cafe when he gave up his dessert for her. He suddenly seemed a tad warmer and kinder than when they had first met. She didn't know what to make of him. Only time would tell. She tried calling Paul again.

"Hello?" Paul answered.

"Hi, honey. I miss you."

"Are you at home?"

"Yes."

"Can I call you back?" Paul asked.

"Yeah, sure."

Two hours passed by and he didn't call back. She called him again.

"Hello?" Paul answered.

"I thought you were going to call me back."

"I'm sooo sorry. I forgot."

"Can you talk?"

"Actually this really isn't a good time. I have my study group here, and we're really jamming for the Monday exam."

Anna Lisa heard a background noise. A girl was cackling loudly as though on purpose so that Anna Lisa could hear her. She heard Paul telling her to keep it down because he couldn't hear. Anna Lisa finally gave up and said, "I'm going to sleep now. Just wanted to see how you were."

"Okay then, I'll call you tomorrow. Sleep well." He hung up leaving Anna Lisa wondering about where this relationship was going. Lately Paul was always busy with something or other. He never told her he loved her. He didn't want to get married or move in with her. And the trip to Greece he kept promising her – she doubted if it would ever happen. She felt like he was slipping away a little more each day. At times he was warm and at times he made her feel completely inadequate and unwanted. Tonight she felt empty, unloved and alone. Maybe she was just tired and needed a good night's rest. Maybe tomorrow would be a better day.

On Sunday, Anna Lisa ran five miles around her yuppie Brentwood neighborhood. Her condo, situated on a quiet shady street, overlooked the street and rows of maple trees. After her run, she took a long bath and went to her grandmother's house as she usually did where she saw not only her grandmother, Anna, but also her aunts and five young cousins. Her uncles rarely came. They'd rather escape their children and opt for watching sports on television.

Anna, 75 and in good health, looked 15 years younger than her age. Full of life and energy, she dressed youthfully. Her cotton-colored hair, always braided in a long single braid reached the back of her waist and her eyes were pale blue. Her younger aunt, Mia, was nine years older than Anna Lisa and her older aunt, Kate, 10.

After Anna Lisa's parents died, for months her grandmother mourned their deaths, but she had to move on and help raise the baby they left behind. Growing up, Anna Lisa had always been grateful to her family. Although she had a large extended family, she felt closest to her grandmother and aunts. That's why Sundays were always special to her – that's when she got to see the most important people in her life.

Anna Lisa's grandmother was making breakfast in her kitchen when the doorbell rang. The children were in the back room where all the toys and games were situated.

"Could you get the door?" her mother asked Mia.

"Use your key," Mia yelled out loud to her niece.

"I'm not sure which is worse, Anna Lisa always forgetting her keys or you yelling across the room," Kate commented.

"Oh hush," Mia protested.

"They're at home Aunt Mia," Anna Lisa yelled back. She had keys to everybody's house except that she didn't like to carry them because she liked to travel light.

"Oh, never mind, I'll get the door," Kate said to her sister.

Anna Lisa stood outside in front of a beautifully carved pine door waiting for one of her aunts to let her in. Her grandmother's house was located on the south side of Beverly Hills where homes were less pretentious and more practical than the north side. The front yard was modest, carpeted by green grass and separated in two halves by a brick path and a set of steps that led to the front entrance. The steps were bordered by colorful azaleas and purple lanterns that lit up at night.

"Hi Aunt Kate," Anna Lisa said, kissing her on the cheek.

"Sorry, sweetie, your Aunt Mia is very lazy," complained Kate. Like Mia, Kate was three inches taller than Anna Lisa, had hazel brown almond-shaped eyes and brown hair with golden highlights, which came down to her shoulder blades.

Anna Lisa walked through a short hallway where umbrellas were dropped into a pink floral china vase and coats were hung on a matching coat hanger. She followed her aunt a few steps down and turned right into her grandmother's large kitchen.

"Hi Grandma, hi Aunt Mia." Anna Lisa went to the stove to see what her grandmother was making. Anna had several things going at the same time, pancakes, eggs with chopped tomatoes, French toast, bacon and sausage. In the oven below she had freshly baked muffins and on the table there was a variety of jams, butter, baguettes, orange and nectarine juices. If she was ever hungry, all she had to do was knock on her grandmother's door.

"Gee Grandma, you think you have enough food?"

"Should I make some more?" asked her grandmother, worried that there wouldn't be enough.

"I was joking. Who's going to eat all this?"

"Did you eat before coming here? You better be hungry." Her grandmother had a big appetite but never snacked between her meals. She kept her weight in check by walking, swimming and playing tennis.

"Don't worry, I'm hungry," Anna Lisa said and walked over to pour herself a cup of coffee. Soon after, Anna Lisa's five young cousins emerged from the rear of the house. There were four rooms in the back, three of which were now converted into a home-office, play room and a guest room.

"Will you play soccer with us?" Jessica, Aunt Mia's eight-year-old daughter asked Anna Lisa.

"Not now, we're getting ready to have breakfast," Aunt Mia interrupted. "Take a seat over there and you can play when we're done."

"You know Steven came over yesterday to have dinner with us," Kate said to Anna Lisa. Steven Langley was Kate's brother-in-law. Anna Lisa used to work for him at a mid-size marketing firm before she started working for Howard Brown. Steven left to work for a much larger firm – Hamilton International – and two months later, Anna Lisa left to work for their competitor, Howard Brown. After Steven got settled in his new career, he asked Anna Lisa to join his team, but she had already been hired by Simon and had declined.

Anna Lisa sat down next to Kate and set her coffee cup down. "How is Steven, these days? Is he still the marketing director at

Hamilton International?" Hamilton International Inc., like Howard Brown, was a well-known marketing firm except that it was a corporation that demanded frequent trips outside the state and sometimes the country. Howard Brown was a partnership which did not require much traveling.

"He's making deals and doing very well," said Kate, pouring nectarine juice into her glass. "He still asks about you and wants you on his team."

Mia brought over a plate of French toast and pancakes and her grandma a plate of eggs and bacon.

"Yes, I know," said Anna Lisa. "He called me about a month ago and asked me if I was interested in being an account supervisor to manage three of his account executives. I thanked him for thinking of me but told him I wasn't ready to leave Howard Brown just yet."

"And why would you decline such an offer?"

"Because I'm happy where I am. Simon is a great boss, and I'm used to my environment. Besides, Steven has a temper," said Anna Lisa, spreading jam on her bagel. "Not that I can't handle his temper, but I prefer Simon's mild manners."

"Well, he said if you ever change your mind, he sure could use your expertise."

"Tell him thank you. I'll keep him in mind if I decide to move."

"Have some eggs," said her grandma as she passed the white china plate from across the table to Anna Lisa.

"Thanks Grandma."

"Tell me, how's your work? Are you happy?" her grandmother asked.

"Mostly yes. I'm having a little trouble with this account executive from the London office. We've been having a hard time getting along."

"I'm sorry to hear that," said her grandmother. "Have you thought about taking him out to lunch?"

"No," Anna Lisa replied, thinking her grandmother had lost her marbles. Why would she have lunch with someone she didn't get along with?

"You should," her grandmother told her. "People behave differently once they're outside the office. They're more relaxed and flexible."

Her grandmother had a point there, she thought. After all, Neil had been nice to her yesterday when he had offered her his tiramisu. "I'll think about it."

"How's Paul?" Kate asked.

"Paul's doing well. He's been really busy studying for his Monday exam."

"So he says," her grandmother commented. "I don't trust that boy."

"Kate, how was Vegas?" Mia asked to change the subject. She knew how much her mother disliked Paul.

"Nice and relaxing the way I like it."

"Mom, can we go and play? We're not hungry anymore." asked Josh, Kate's eldest child who was 13.

"You may after each of you takes your plate away and puts them in the dishwasher," demanded Kate.

When breakfast was finished, the table cleared and the dishes put away, Anna Lisa took out the trash. She looked around and took in the fresh smell of earth caused by the sprinkler system that went on early every morning. At least her grandmother's sprinklers watered her lawn unlike her neighbors', which watered the sidewalk or some poor soul's car parked in front of it, Anna Lisa thought. She walked back, went inside, passed the hallway, descended the steps and landed in the living room where she was able to see the dining area and then a sliding glass door that opened to a large backyard bordered by orange, pomegranate and lemon trees, colorful rose bushes and carnations. The patio chairs and tables were pushed aside so that the kids could play their soccer game. Turning left toward a mantel over a fireplace, Anna Lisa looked at the family photos kept in silver frames.

"You have everyone's picture here except Paul's," Anna Lisa protested when she saw her grandmother walk in the living room with a coffee cup in her hand.

"When that bum marries you, I'll add his picture," she replied, walking over to sit on the couch covered with a beige velour fabric embellished with pink roses. She set her cup on the cherry wood coffee table.

"Grandma!"

"I'm sorry Anna Lisa but you've been together for too long. When're you two getting married?"

"You know that's not important to me. What's important is we love each other."

"Huh."

"You know Paul loves me, he just has a difficult time saying it," Anna Lisa responded as a matter of fact even though she wasn't sure of his feelings at all.

"My dear, soon you'll be too old to have children. You've got to hurry up."

Her Aunt Kate dropped in the conversation. "Mom's right, you know. You should think about your future."

"What if I don't want children?"

"Nonsense," her grandmother said, "It's not up to you. You owe me at least two great-grandchildren."

Aunt Mia stepped in to bail her out. "Anna Lisa, the kids are waiting for you in the yard."

"Oh yes, I did promise them a game of soccer, didn't I? Excuse me Grandma." With that, the marriage conversation came to an end.

After Anna Lisa walked away, she turned to her Aunt Mia. "Thank you for saving me."

"What's an aunt for if she can't rescue her niece?" she winked and put her arm through her niece's arm as they went outside and closed the sliding glass door behind them. "Anyway, I thought the way they were cornering you wasn't fair."

"I suppose they mean well. I mean, it's not like I don't want to get married. I do. But Paul isn't ready."

"No man ever is. You have to tell them what you want at the right time. For you that time hasn't come up, but it doesn't mean it never will."

"But how do I know when it's the right time?"

"Trust me, you'll know. And when it happens, you hope he responds. If he pulls away, then you may want to move on."

Josh kicked the soccer ball up high toward Anna Lisa by accident. Anna Lisa caught it using her hands and threw it back to him.

"Be careful," Mia yelled at the kids. "Steer clear of Grandma's windows and rose bushes.

"It's all so complicated," Anna Lisa said.

"That's because we make it complicated. I think when two people really love each other, they're not afraid to spend the rest of their lives together."

"So, are you saying Paul doesn't love me?"

"That's a question you need to answer yourself," said Mia raising both eyebrows as the children dragged Anna Lisa away for a game of soccer.

While Anna Lisa was having breakfast with her family, Neil was with Sarah at a high class restaurant in Venice beach. The hostess directed them to a table overlooking the water. Yesterday's rain seemed as though it had never happened. Patches of fluffy white clouds scattered on the vivid blue sky and the sun glistened over the calm surface of the ocean. A busboy came to fill their water glasses but Sarah put her hand over hers and said, "I don't like tap water. Bring me a bottle of Evian."

The busboy left and a waiter came over and took their order.

"Where are you taking me today?" Sarah asked Neil. She was an enchantress who was well aware of her beauty. Her buttery skin emitted a healthy glow, a white linen headband matching her sleeveless dress kept her radiant hair away from her face and her flawless posture combined with the way she carried herself made her seem regal.

To outsiders, Neil and Sarah came across as the perfect couple. He was drop-dead-gorgeous in his eggshell shirt and dark purple tie that complimented his eyes. His aubergine suit and fine inky leather belt and matching shoes showed he was tasteful and attentive to details. His soft-spoken words and polite manners made him seem like a man with high standards of proper behavior. "I thought we'd start with the J. Paul Getty museum in the morning and Universal Studios in the afternoon."

"What? No shopping? You know I need a dress for the opera next week."

"Not again. You have taken up all of my closet space. Why don't you wear what you have?"

"Because I want something new. Besides, you should move into a bigger place. Your condo's too small."

"Need I remind you that my condo is a temporary place," Neil answered dryly. "I have two large rooms, two regular closets, a walk-in closet and plenty of shelf space. I really don't understand what you're complaining about."

"Where is my Evian anyway? The service here is terrible," Sarah looked for the waiter. "Now, what were we talking about? Oh yes, we were discussing the size of your condo. Honestly darling, I hope you don't expect me to live in a tiny space when we're married."

Neil wanted to live with Sarah before their engagement, but then she surprised him by proposing to him, a month-and-a-half ago. He told her he wanted to wait. Furious, she broke up with him and took off to her parents' vacation home in Tuscany. Neil didn't worry – it wasn't their first break-up. He knew she'd come back. And when she did, he told her he would marry her and they set a wedding date for September which was only seven-and-a-half months away.

The waiter brought the Evian. "It took you long enough," she told him.

Neil was embarrassed and thanked the waiter. He turned to Sarah. "Please do tell where you plan to live when we get married?"

"A large and well-equipped house, of course."

"I suppose you're planning to work to pay for this large house?"

"Don't be silly darling. I'll be busy raising our two children." She sipped her water.

"Well, at least you're planning to stay home and raise them unlike your mother who..."

"What? Stay at home? And I suppose next you'll say I have to stay up all night to feed them."

"Yes, that's what most people do," Neil answered sarcastically.

"You mean people without means. I'll have nannies to take care of them just the way I was raised."

Neil let out a sigh of frustration.

Up until the time he left London, Neil had been comfortable with Sarah and that was one of the reasons he had agreed to share his life with her. The other reason was, he was at an age when most people would want to be married. Sarah had flaws but, for most part, she was all right. She was young and they had plenty of time to spare before starting a family. She'd have to make some lifestyle changes such as learning to wear an outfit more than once or cutting down on her spending, but in time she would learn. She was lively, beautiful and came from a respectable family. He hadn't dated anyone since he had met her and didn't want to make an effort to date new girls and play the same old games – asking questions about what a girl did for living or how many brothers and sisters were in her family or what she did for fun, etc., etc., etc. He was tired of all that and too comfortable where he was. Sarah was used to his temper and idiosyncrasies, and he was used to hers. Except today she was getting on his nerves, and he was trying hard to control his temper.

The waiter came by and served Sarah a small fruit salad and Neil German pancakes with caramelized bananas and walnuts, orange juice, and hash browns.

"You know I could've made you a fruit salad at home," Neil said, wondering why they were eating out if Sarah didn't eat much.

"Yes, but then you have to wash the fruit, chop it and then there's all the dirty dishes that have to be loaded into the dishwasher," Sarah said. "This way someone else does all the work and we get to relax."

Neil wondered at the irony of the word relax. Sarah's entire life had been nothing but relax. "Don't you sometimes like to stay at home, cook a nice meal and enjoy it as a family?"

She picked up her soft, manicured hand and checked it for chips. "Yes, as long as I'm not the one doing the cooking."

"I suppose when we're married, you're planning to hire a cook?" He cut into his pancake forcefully as though he was cutting a tough piece of meat.

"Of course. Surely you don't expect me to perform domestic duties."

Neil wrinkled his brows. "And how are we to pay for all these luxuries if you have no intention of working?"

"I want to say Daddy will help us, but I know how angry you'll get."

"I see," Neil said holding back his anger. He wanted to discuss this further but he decided to save this conversation for another time. He just wanted to enjoy his Sunday.

EIGHT

"The meeting's in five minutes," Diana announced and left. Neil and Anna Lisa grabbed their files and headed for the door. On their way, Simon joined them and the three walked toward the conference room. One of the partners, in her late forties, and an associate in his mid-thirties from the London office, an executive administrative assistant ready to record the content of the meeting and Kevin, the chemist prepared to present new beauty products were already there. Jane Olson and her nephew Adam arrived at precisely 11 a.m. Greetings were exchanged; Anna Lisa was introduced to the two London representatives and Neil to Jane and Adam for the first time. The meeting was to last no more than an hour, but Neil knew better and had already ordered lunch to be prepared by the firm's favorite caterer at noon.

The conference room with large windows was long and rectangular. It had a pomegranate cedar table in the center, 10 coordinating leather chairs on each side of the table and two end chairs. In front of each seat was a business plan, an outline of the meeting, a pad of paper, a pen with Howard Brown's logo and a water goblet. Simon sat at the head of the table, on his right was Anna Lisa, Adam, a woman partner from the London office and the executive administrative assistant. On his left was Neil, Jane, the chemist, and the associate from the London office.

Each presenter stood up, and went to the opposite end from where Simon was seated to present his or her assigned portion of the project. Anna Lisa, appearing professional in her black gabardine suit, showed several different packaging ideas for the products. Looking smart in a dark olive suit and tie, Neil discussed the media through which the marketing would take place. Kevin, a skinny, nice-looking man in a gray sweater, introduced a new line of nail polish colors followed by a line of cleansing products, cosmetics, rejuvenating moisturizer and age-prevention cream.

"I don't like them," Jane said to Anna Lisa with her arms crossed in front of her chest. She was bony and wore an off-white turban over her thinning hair.

Disagreeing with his aunt but afraid to speak up, Adam gazed at her, looked away and let out an intense sigh. He had a boyish face, long jet black hair that was slicked back with gel, a faultless nose and thick luscious lips. He looked as though he belonged on the cover of a magazine with his dark-brown wool pants and mustard-colored shirt and tie, which showed off a dainty gold tie pin that coordinated with his cuff links.

The partner and the associate from the London office frowned.

Simon looked upset, but remained quiet and let Anna Lisa handle it.

Anna Lisa broke the silence. "Jane, which part don't you like? The packaging, the products or the media we're planning to use?"

"I don't like any of it," she said, her facial muscles getting tighter by the minute. "And the colors, they're too bold for a woman of my age."

Jane preferred pale and neutral colors like the outfit she was wearing today – a pink plaid jacket and skirt made by her tailor to fit her small figure and pumps that coordinated with her turban and leather purse.

"But Jane," Anna Lisa said, "times have changed. Today's woman of advanced age is looking for a youthful glow. These colors say 'I feel young, but I'm not trying to look like a teenager'."

"I must agree with Anna Lisa, Aunt Jane," Adam finally interrupted, "The packaging, the products and the colors fit well with our target market."

"But I don't want our products to be like others. I want us to be unique."

"I promise that your product will be unique," Neil joined in. "Your products are better than what is out there. We have test-marketed all of them and they are what the mature woman wants."

Jane shook her head. "And why so many moisturizers, creams and cleansing products? In my days a good soap and water and a cream were all a woman needed."

Neil glanced at his watch discreetly. It was noon already, and he knew that after a full stomach, one was always more agreeable. "Perhaps, we should break for lunch and talk about this later."

"I am a little hungry," Jane said.

"Me too," Adam agreed. Neil buzzed the intercom and soon white uniformed servers rolled in a long buffet table of stuffed mushrooms, salad with walnuts and goat cheese, sautéed veal with a light lemon sauce and capers, baby green beans, and roasted potatoes, fruit tarts, sparkling peach juice, Italian coffee and English tea. Jane pushed her chair back and got up to grab a plate as the rest of the group followed.

"Everything looks so scrumptious," Jane told Neil, who was standing next to her at the buffet table.

"Yes, especially the fruit tart," Neil replied, picked up a plate and utensils wrapped in a cloth napkin and handed it to Jane.

"Thank you," she smiled.

Thirty minutes into their meal, Simon got up from his seat to refill his beverage glass with sparking peach juice. The servers started removing the dirty dishes. Neil was busy conversing with Jane and Anna Lisa with Adam. A knock was heard on the door. Simon asked the person to come in.

It was Kimberly. She walked in and looked toward Neil, afraid to interrupt him.

Neil noticed Kimberly staring at him. "Well, what is it?"

"Your fiancée's here to see you."

"Didn't you tell her I'm in a meeting?" he asked with an upset voice.

"I did, but she insisted on seeing you."

Neil excused himself. Outside the conference room, he saw Sarah in pistachio knit dress and taupe pointy alligator shoes and purse. A floral print silk scarf, used like a headband was tied in a knot underneath her dark blond hair with the rest of the material laying over her dress. He greeted her and said, "Did we have plans?"

"No, darling," she smiled and fixed his tie with her soft delicate hands. "I thought I would surprise you and take you out to lunch."

"I can't. I'm right in the middle of an important meeting."

"I'm sure they can spare you for an hour or two."

"No, they can't," he replied through grinding teeth.

When they had first met, Sarah's idleness hadn't bother him because he only saw her two nights a week and on weekends. They would dine out, visit her parents, attend the opera, or go to the theater or a soiree. She always had a plan for a luncheon, a ticket to a show or an invitation to an event, and he enjoyed them until today when she interrupted his meeting.

Sarah put her arms around his neck. "I've missed you."

"This really isn't a good time. We'll see each other tonight," he answered, grabbed her arms gently and pulled them down.

She became angry at his lack of affection. "When is it a good time, Neil? Hmmm? You never have time for me."

"I have to go." Neil kissed her lightly on the cheek. "I'll see you tonight."

"I will not be home," she stated defiantly.

He stared at her and wrinkled his forehead. "Where will you be?"

"What do you care?" she answered with a hurt voice, "You're never around."

Neil tried hard to control his anger. "This is not the right time to play charades. We shall talk about this tomorrow." He walked back to the conference room, leaving Sarah standing there in fury.

When Sarah finally left, Kimberly, who had been eavesdropping the entire time, smiled. Trouble in paradise, she thought to herself, well, well. She could do better than Paul. Neil was a much better catch and Sarah just didn't know how to manipulate her man. Too bad for Sarah. She shrugged and began plotting.

Neil returned to the conference room and closed the door behind him. He looked over and saw Anna Lisa still talking to Adam. If she could convince Adam to agree with their ideas, convincing Jane would not be such a difficult task. As he watched Adam listening to Anna Lisa intently, he was assured that the meeting was going to be a success. He walked over to Simon and his English colleagues, who were standing near the window to stretch their legs. They discussed the next step of their plan.

After Anna Lisa and Adam's conversation ended, Adam started talking to his aunt.

"I think we should accept their proposal," he told his aunt.

"But we would have to make lots of changes," her aunt replied.

"Isn't that why we're here?" Adam asked, looking her aunt in the eyes. "Our product line may have worked 50 years ago, but it's not working anymore. These people know marketing, or they wouldn't be in business for such a long time."

"What if they're wrong?" she asked, passing him a worried glance. "What if these additions would hurt us?"

Adam shook his head. "Not likely. I've seen our competition at stores. We need to update our line or we're not going to survive. You have to trust me on this."

"You do realize, when I die, I'm leaving you my 49% share of the company. The decision we make today will affect your future." Jane didn't have any children and Adam was like her son.

Adam, who loved her aunt dearly, said, "First of all, you're not going to die. I won't allow it, and second, this is your company. You started it from scratch and I'm going to do everything in my power to protect your interest."

"In that case my dear," her aunt said smiling, "let's go make a deal."

Minutes later, everyone was back in his or her chairs discussing the product line.

"I've decided to accept the colors," Jane said. "I would like to make some changes to the packaging which we'll talk about later. I don't want advertisings at bus stops, but I agree with all the other types of media. Go ahead and submit the financial data to my accountant," she told Neil. She turned toward Anna Lisa. "Now let's talk about the cosmetics line."

"We really have fewer products than the other cosmetics companies and yet they perform better than all of the other products combined."

"Go on." Jane seemed to be more interested now.

"Why don't I let Kevin, our favorite chemist for our high-end products give you more details?"

Kevin drank some water to lubricate his dry throat. "We have a facial cleanser that gets rid of makeup and blackheads, exfoliates skin and tightens the pores all at the same time." He then handed the cleanser to Jane so she could examine it. "I would like to point out that all the products are gentle enough to be used on the face and around the eyes. After the cleanser, we follow with a day moisturizer and then the SPF30 cream," he said and passed on those samples. "Furthermore, we have a night cream that reduces the appearance of wrinkles. Most companies use a lot more products to do the same thing that ours do in fewer steps."

"And I like that, because the more products you put on the face, the more sensitive the skin becomes and soon it breaks down."

"My point exactly," Anna Lisa agreed.

Neil looked at Simon and then at his English colleagues. They seemed pleased. He also noticed Adam admiring Anna Lisa. Adam was tall, attractive and had a muscular physique. He seemed to get along well with Anna Lisa and that was good for business. So, why did Neil feel uncomfortable about the way Adam was looking at

Anna Lisa? He wasn't sure, but he was glad the meeting was coming to an end and soon Adam would be leaving.

Jane was the first to get up from the table, to thank everyone for their hard work and get ready to leave. Simon shook her hand and told her it was always a pleasure to see her. The partner and the associate from the London office expressed to Anna Lisa that they hoped she would someday visit them in London. Neil, after saying farewell to Adam, shook Jane's hand and told her he was delighted to meet her.

Adam uttered to Anna Lisa, "So, I'll pick you up for dinner tonight at 8."

"Perfect."

Neil was standing nearby, overheard the conversation and frowned.

Jane smiled.

That evening, Adam looking stylish in his brown leather jacket, picked up Anna Lisa at her condo in his black Aston Martin. She had changed into a pretty dark purple dress.

"You look nice," he said.

"Thank you." She gave him a big smile and said, "You smell great. What is the name of the cologne you're wearing? I really like it."

"It doesn't have a name yet. I've been working with a chemist to come up with a men's cologne. What you smell is a sample."

"I wonder, have you ever considered doing a men's line?"

"As a matter of fact, I've been thinking about it. Maybe after we're done with my aunt's products, we can discuss it further."

"No better time than the present. Why don't we talk about it now?" said Anna Lisa. The thought of marketing a new product always excited her.

And so they carried on regarding a potential men's line including shaving products, soaps and cream and before they knew it they were in front of Chez Philip, a French restaurant in

Westwood Village. Adam parked his car in a lot across the street and the two headed in.

Chez Philip was dark, the booths and chairs were comfortable, and the staff friendly. The entrance to the restaurant was small. A man in a black suit greeted them and took them to their table. Anna Lisa and Adam were at a square table where they could see the bar, the clientele and the busy outside street through a window.

After their orders were taken and dinner was served, Adam, who was eating the same dish as Anna Lisa asked her how she liked her food.

"I like it very much. These are the best lamb chops I've ever had."

"I think lamb chops and soufflés are their specialty," commented Adam who had picked out this restaurant because he wanted a quiet place that served great French food.

A waiter came by, poured more Bordeaux in their half-empty glasses and set the bottle, wrapped in white linen, back on the table.

"You know, I've been thinking about you," Adam stared at Anna Lisa and studied her face. She had a rosy complexion and eyes that expressed kindness.

Anna Lisa gave him an unwilling smile and hoped he wasn't trying to make a pass at her. It wasn't that she didn't like Adam because she did or that she wasn't attracted to him because she was. She met him through Jane two months ago and the two had enjoyed several lunches together, but she had a boyfriend and loved him very much. "You have?" she responded reluctantly.

"Yes, I really enjoy your company," he said, taking a bite of his lamb chop.

"Thank you. I enjoy talking with you." She pulled on her right ear, feeling unsure as to where this conversation was going.

"So, how's Paul?" he asked with curiosity. Adam had noticed Paul at Kimberly's desk when he had arrived for the meeting earlier that day, and they didn't look like they were discussing work.

"He's doing fine, thanks for asking."

"You two are still together?"

"Oh yes," she replied nervously. "In fact, he was over last night," she lied.

He passed her a cryptic smile. "Well, that's great."

Anna Lisa took a sip of her Bordeaux. "And you? Is there someone special in your life?"

"No, no one," he said with disappointment.

"What about those online dating services? I've heard many couples meeting that way."

A gloomy look suddenly spread over his face. "I don't feel much like dating. I'm still trying to get over my last love."

When Anna Lisa heard that, she felt more comfortable. He didn't want to date her after all. "When did you two break up?"

"Eleven months ago."

She was saddened by the tone of his voice. If Paul ever broke up with her, she would be devastated. "Why did you call it quits?" she wrinkled her brows.

"I didn't."

"Ah. She broke up with you. Have you ever thought about calling her just to say hi? Maybe she misses you as well."

He didn't answer.

Anna Lisa decided to change the subject because he looked like he was about to cry at any minute. "You know, you never talk about your family."

"There's not much to tell. I have two brothers in Boston and they're both married with children."

"Are you close to them?"

"I was when we were younger but ever since they got married, they've been busy with their own lives."

"And your parents? Do they live around here?"

"No, they're also in Boston. I visit them once in a while but they drive me crazy. They're so conservative that I can only stand listening to them in small doses."

"Yeah, families can be difficult sometimes. I love mine, but I also need time away from them."

"Do you have any siblings?" he asked with curiosity.

"No, I'm the only child," she answered disappointedly. She thought Adam was lucky to have two older brothers and wished she had at least one. All her life she had been raised by women and hadn't had a male role model to look up to.

"And your parents, do they live out here?"

"My parents died when I was three months old. My grandmother and aunts raised me." Growing up, Anna Lisa had always envied children whose parents picked them up after school.

"I'm sorry to hear that," he replied sadly. He thought he was fortunate that his parents were still alive even if they did argue most of the time.

"I've been thinking a lot about them lately. I wish they were around to see me all grown up."

"I think they would've been very proud of you."

"Thank you."

They continued conversing for a long time, sharing family stories and childhood memories until Anna Lisa let out a yawn.

"Excuse me," she said, "I didn't sleep well last night."

"You do look tired," he remarked, noticing her sleepy eyes, "Perhaps we should call it a night."

He signaled the waiter to bring the bill and after paying him, he helped Anna Lisa with her coat. Outside, the valet brought over Adam's car and the two left the restaurant.

When they reached Anna Lisa's condo, Adam said, "I had a nice time. I would like to take you out again sometime soon."

"That would be nice. Thanks for dinner and the next time we go out, it'll be my treat," she replied.

The doorman came over and opened her door for her.

"Until next time then," he said as Anna Lisa waved goodbye.

NINE

The day after her dinner with Adam, Anna Lisa was in her office, going over the changes Jane had indicated with Neil.

"Did you like her?" Anna Lisa said of Jane. She and Neil were sitting on the sofa with their work spread on the coffee table.

"She's a tough lady and knows what she wants," Neil responded.

"She's a sweetheart once you get to know her."

"Did you have a nice dinner with Adam last night?"

"Very nice," Anna Lisa answered without giving away any details.

Neil was disappointed with such a short answer, so, he pressed the issue. "It seems that Adam likes you."

"Yes. I like him as well. He's pleasant to work with."

"I think he has more than work in mind."

"What do you mean?"

"I saw the way he looked at you."

"No, Neil you're wrong, He's not interested in me."

"You called me Neil!"

Anna Lisa cracked a smile, "I guess I did. Maybe you're not so bad after all."

"Thank you, I think." He wrinkled his forehead.

"Listen, would you like to go and get a manicure and pedicure?"

"What?"

"Oh c'mon, try it," Anna Lisa insisted, "Hoffman's Nail Salon is right across the street."

"No. absolutely not," Neil protested.

Anna Lisa grabbed him by the wrist and pulled him out of the office. "If Simon needs us, tell him to reach me on my cell phone," Anna Lisa said to Kimberly, pulling Neil along with her.

The Hoffman Salon, Bathed in a soft yellow, offered a row of 12 cushiony chairs that looked like thrones. The front entrance was all glass. Once seated, customers submerge their feet in mini tubs of warm bubbly water, put hands in soapy bowls and lean back while the seats massage their backs. Anna Lisa liked Hoffman's because it was incredibly clean and they used her favorite product – Jane Olson's Nail and Beauty Care.

"I am not getting a manicure," Neil objected as Anna Lisa talked to the owner.

"Is it his first time?" asked Karen Hoffman. Five feet tall and in her early fifties, Karen had amber eyes and frizzy dirty blond hair which she pulled up with a rhinestone hair clip.

"Yes, he's a virgin. Treat him well," Anna Lisa responded.

"Don't worry, I promise you won't feel a thing," Karen said to Neil with a deep voice that started at the back of her throat and came out through her nose.

"You may want to take him to the back room where you take your famous clientele. I'm afraid Neil's rather shy."

"No problem," Karen said and led poor Neil to the back room.

This particular location was convenient for Anna Lisa. It was on the first floor of a business building and a few doors down there was a café. Anna Lisa walked to the café and ordered a chilidog and a frozen blue raspberry drink for herself. She took her time and enjoyed her lunch as she read the newspaper that was lying on the table. When it was time to get back, she bought Neil a chilidog and a blue drink as well. She then walked to Hoffman's and waited for

Neil who was also getting a facial but didn't know it. Her cell phone rang; it was Simon.

"Where are you?"

"I'm at Hoffman's with Neil."

"You finally got him to try out the product, hey?"

"More like forced him to."

Simon laughed, "What are you doing tonight?"

"I have no plans."

"What about Neil?"

"I don't know, you'd have to ask him yourself. Let me see if you can talk to him. He should be almost done." Anna Lisa walked over to the back room and knocked.

"Yes?" Karen asked.

"Could you ask Neil if he could have dinner with Simon tonight, around 8?"

Karen posed the question to her relaxed, pampered client. "Yes, he says he can make it."

"He can make it," Anna Lisa told Simon and hung up. She picked up a magazine resting on top of an oval glass table in front of her and started reading until Neil finally emerged, looking content.

"I assume you enjoyed it, Mr. Whittaker," Anna Lisa said jokingly.

"Yes I did. I even fell asleep for a few minutes," Neil said.

Neil reached into his pocket to pay, but Karen told him that Anna Lisa had already taken care of it.

"You must let me pay you back," Neil told Anna Lisa.

"Don't worry about it. I'm putting it on the expense report, and I'll get reimbursed."

"In that case, thank you."

"You're welcome," Anna Lisa said as the two walked back toward the office.

On the way, Anna Lisa handed Neil a white lunch bag and a large to-go cup. "Oh here. I almost forgot; I got you a chilidog and a raspberry drink."

"A chili what?" he asked as he looked in the bag and then at the blue frozen drink."

"Don't tell me you've never had a chilidog."

He shook his head no.

"Try it, it's really good," she said as they rode up the elevator. When they got to the 19th floor, Paul was waiting.

"Paul!" Anna Lisa said in surprise.

"You know, I haven't seen you all day," he said.

"We've been busy working, and then we had a meeting. I just took Neil to introduce him to the product line we're representing."

Paul looked at Neil and said, "And how was Hoffman's?"

"I take it you've been there as well."

"Oh, yes. Anna Lisa loves that place and gets everyone hooked on it."

"I enjoyed it," Neil said, pausing. "Excuse me, I think I'll go eat my chilidog and drink my blue beverage," he said, trotting off to the lunch room to give them privacy.

"How did you do on your test?" Anna Lisa asked Paul.

"What test? Oh, you mean my math exam."

"Yes, the very one," Anna Lisa said, raising her brows.

"I think I did okay. Sorry I wasn't able to talk to you Saturday night. There were all these people over and…"

"Don't worry about it," Anna Lisa said nonchalantly, "Well, I better get back to work."

"You're not mad, are you?"

Trying hard to hide her anger and scared to show him her vulnerability, Anna Lisa didn't want Paul to know that she had been home waiting for his call all night. "No. I just have to finish up. I'm having dinner at the Simons tonight."

"How come I'm not invited?" he whined.

"It's not a dinner party," she responded coldly, "It's just me, Neil, Simon and his wife."

"Neil? Why does he get to go?" Paul asked sounding like a child.

"Because we're both working on the Olson account. We had a successful meeting yesterday and Simon feels like celebrating, I suppose."

"When are you coming home?"

"I'm not sure, why?"

"I was just asking. I miss you."

"You didn't seem to miss me Saturday night or Sunday, otherwise you would've kept your promise and called."

"You are mad at me."

"I am not. I'm just very busy as you can see," she said, pointing to the pile of work on her desk

"Then I'll leave."

Anna Lisa noticed the disappointed look on his face as he headed for the door. "Paul, wait," Anna Lisa said, "I guess I am mad. Why didn't you call me back?"

"I told you, there were a lot of people over. We were busy studying and it slipped my mind."

"Great," she said slapping her thighs. "Soon I'll slip your mind all together. Really Paul, I feel as though you have stopped caring about me. You used to be so attentive."

He moved closer and hugged her tight. "I'm sorry honey, my school is so hard this semester. My brain is fried and I forget things – things that I shouldn't be forgetting," Paul said, pulling away from Anna Lisa so he could see her face. He looked into her sad eyes. "I care a lot about you. Come by tonight and I'll show you how much."

She paused for a moment. "If I come by, it might be late. Once Simon starts talking, he doesn't stop."

"I'm going to bed at midnight. I'm tired from all the late-night studying. If you get back before then come over."

"Okay then," she said and kissed him, "I've missed you too."

After Paul left, Anna Lisa finished her work. She then went home, took a bath, got ready and headed to Simon's house.

The Simons lived on a hill away from civilization – or so it seemed. As Anna Lisa followed the directions she wondered who would live in such a neighborhood." A left, a right, a right, a left, a left, a left, a right, a left on dark windy narrow roads that seemed to be going nowhere. Of course, most people would envy the Simons' neighborhood, which had large, upscale well-kept properties guarded by private security and one of the best public schooling systems, but not Anna Lisa. She finally found the house and buzzed the speaker at the gate. The gate opened. She was surprised they opened the gate without asking for her identity, but then she noticed the cameras. She drove up a long brick path surrounded by palm trees, and at the end of it, Anna Lisa was surprised to see Neil's car already there. She was sure he would get lost. How in the world this Englishman had found his way was not clear, but he had.

Simon opened the door of an enormous modern-looking structure, which was designed more like a fortress than a home, and said, "Did you have trouble finding us?"

"No, it was quite easy. This is some house." She thought she would never want to own something so ugly. The tall building was constructed of charcoal gray cement and algae green-glass. It seemed too contemporary, cold and uncomfortable, and Anna Lisa hoped the inside would look better than the outside.

"Thank you. C'mon in, we're all waiting for you."

The high ceilings, pale-gray cement columns and floors, pointy glass lighting fixtures and modern art work – kooky abstract paintings and scrap-metal sculptures – somehow all seemed to flow. Jillian, Simon's wife, greeted Anna Lisa and Simon left to go to the kitchen. She was a thin lady dressed in a plain white shirt and black ankle-length skirt. Her straight saffron-red bob curled under. At 55, she had alabaster skin, a brown mole on the right side of her upper lip and smelled like rose.

"At last, I get to see you. You've been a very busy girl," said Jillian. "It must be at least a year since I last saw you at the launch of Adrianna's perfume."

Jillian, a former-lawyer with a type A personality, was now retired. With her four children in college and too much free time on her hands, Jillian spent her time redecorating the house and getting into everybody's business.

"Hello, Jillian. It has been a long time. Thank you for inviting me."

"You are always welcome here," she said and looked around for her husband, "Simon probably went outside to be with Neil. Let's join them."

The back entrance of the house opened up to the patio which featured a turtle-shaped pond. A waterfall cascaded downward from the hills and emptied into the pond. The dim patio lighting gave the grounds a romantic feel, and several outdoor heaters worked to keep the cool temperature at a comfortable level. A square cast-iron table and four matching chairs with black cushions stood next to a horseshoe-shaped bar.

"Hello Neil," said Anna Lisa, catching him by surprise.

As he turned around, his eyes brightened. She was wearing an open V-back dark green-dress complimenting her olive eyes. Not in a pony tail or bun, her wavy hair hung loosely at her shoulders. She was wearing light makeup and a soft red lipstick. "Hello, Leeza," he said.

"Leeza?" said Jillian. She then looked at Anna Lisa. "Anna Lisa, I didn't know your name was Leeza."

Anna Lisa sighed. "It is not. Neil seems to like the name and has decided to christen me Leeza."

"Ah! A nickname; I like it. What would you like to drink?"

"Neil seems to be having a martini. I'll have one, too."

Once again Jillian looked around for her husband and saw him coming out of the kitchen into the patio with a plate full of appetizers. He offered them to everyone.

"Could you be a dear and make Anna Lisa an apple martini?" Jillian said to her husband. She then put her arm through Anna Lisa's and said, "C'mon, let me give you a tour of the house."

The tour started from outside, moved indoors to the upstairs bedrooms, then down the stairs and ended with the kitchen. The house had been remodeled by Jillian when she moved in a year ago. Besides the large pond, the immense and maze-like backyard had a beautiful garden, Jacuzzi, dry and steam sauna, tennis court, fully equipped gym, guest house and green house. Anna Lisa thought if Jillian hadn't accompanied her, she'd need a map to find her way back. Inside, it had 10 rooms, including a library, family, dining and living room, a recreation room with a pool table, and an incredible gourmet kitchen with two of everything – stoves, ovens, dishwashers, and sub zero refrigerators, copper pots and pans and high-tech kitchen appliances.

"You see dear," Jillian said as she showed off her kitchen, "I gave the help the night off. There are only four of us and I saw no reason why I would need them."

Simon and Neil came into the kitchen. Simon handed Anna Lisa her drink. They all moved back to the patio and chatted for a while until Jillian was ready to serve dinner. Everyone offered to help. The outside table was already set with four black plate mats and cloth napkins, square silver plate setting with matching wine glasses, silverware and two candleholders holding tall white candles and inky china dinner and salad plates. Jillian gave them each a prepared dish to take to the patio, and then they sat down to share a cozy evening.

Simon opened up a bottle of rosé and poured.

"The roast beef is delicious," Neil said to Jillian, "It's so tender. You must give me the recipe."

"It's a secret," Jillian said winking. "After all, you don't expect me to give away everything I've learned at the Cordon Bleu for free."

"I shall be more than happy to buy your recipe," Neil said jokingly.

"Money is not what I had in mind. I have to think of something better."

Anna Lisa looked at Simon, smiled and said: "Now I see where you learn your bargaining abilities."

"Come now, Anna Lisa. What do you have to complain about? You always get what you ask for," Simon said.

They all laughed.

"Tell me Neil," Jillian asked with curiosity, "how do you like Los Angeles?"

"I like the weather and the people I have met, but beyond that, it is too early for me to pass judgment," he answered politely.

"Simon tells me you did your graduate work at Harvard," Jillian said.

"Yes, I lived in Boston for two years and enjoyed it quite a bit."

"Then, why didn't you stay in the states when you were finished?"

"I received a job offer from Howard Brown in London."

"Yes, of course," Jillian said, looking at Anna Lisa and then back at Neil. "Did you know Anna Lisa went to Yale?"

"No, I didn't," Neil said, glancing at Anna Lisa. "I suppose that would make us rivals."

"Yes it does, in every possible way you can imagine," she answered playfully. At the beginning of their relationship Anna Lisa was so scared he was going to steal her client that she never thought she would ever warm up to him, and now here she was having dinner with him and enjoying his company.

Neil smiled at her response and thought of their first encounter at the Little Brit and their argument over lemon curd. How far along the two had come in the past three months.

Jillian sat back and enjoyed the chemistry between Neil and Anna Lisa.

When they were finished with their entrees, they helped themselves to a salad of mixed greens dressed with balsamic vinaigrette, grape-seed oil and fresh ground pepper. Simon offered his guests more wine – and they both declined because they had to drive.

"I thought the meeting went very well today," Simon said.

"We had a rocky start at first," replied Anna Lisa, "but we managed to turn things around."

"Oh? Was Jane resistant to your ideas?" Jillian asked Anna Lisa. Jillian knew about Jane because Simon usually talked about his work. When she called Simon at the office, she also would get the scoop on the clients as well as the employees from the secretaries who worked there. The assistants liked to gossip, and she liked to listen.

"Not just to mine but to Neil's and Kevin's as well."

"Yes, we all were worried at first," Neil said, "We thought we'd have to change everything."

"I thought Adam was the final decision maker," Jillian said.

"Hardly," Simon responded, "As long as Jane has her wits about her, she's not going to let anyone run the show."

"True," said Anna Lisa, "but I do believe Adam has a lot of influence over his aunt, otherwise today's meeting would have not gone so well."

"How do you like Adam?" Jillian asked Anna Lisa.

"I like him quite a bit. In fact, we had dinner last night."

"Oh?" Jillian said raising an eyebrow.

"No, it's not what you think. We've gotten to be good friends."

"Tell me," said Jillian, "is Adam as handsome as the ladies at the office describe him?"

"Yes, he is very handsome."

Neil was getting irritated with their topic of conversation. He suddenly felt in competition with Adam, but why? He had no reason to compete with him. He decided to get up and take his plate to the kitchen when Simon stopped him.

"I'll take that," Simon said, as he took Neil's dish along with his own and headed for the kitchen.

Anna Lisa started to stand up and help but Jillian intervened.

"Please, have a seat," Jillian said, "Simon and I will take care of it."

Jillian and Simon went back and forth a few times as they cleared the table. Neil left to use the restroom. Anna Lisa leaned back in her chair and enjoyed the evening. The stars were scattered across the dark velvety sky and the full moon shined above her head. She wished Paul was with her.

"So, where is Paul?" Neil asked Anna Lisa when he came back.

"He wasn't invited. Where is Sarah?"

"She wasn't invited either."

Anna Lisa looked toward the kitchen and noticed the Simons looking at them and whispering to each other. She turned to Neil and said: "Do you think we're victims of two matchmakers?"

Neil looked puzzled. "You mean this evening was planned?"

"Look at them. They're talking about something. I wonder if it's us."

Neil looked over and noticed they were being stared at by the Simons, who turned away knowing they were about to be discovered. They started loading the dishwasher. Neil turned to Anna Lisa and said, "I think you're right. But why would they do it? They know we're both involved."

"They must not like our partners," Anna Lisa said.

Jillian called the two from the patio intercom to announce that coffee and dessert would be served in the family room.

Neil got up and said to Anna Lisa, "Shall we?"

They went into the family room which overlooked a garden brightened by soft pink lights. There was a contemporary silver coffee carafe, four coordinating cups and saucers, a creamer and sugar bowl set on top of a curved smoky gray glass and pewter coffee table. A large black leather sectional and gray chairs were embellished with white pillows and two tall glass cylinder vases holding white calla lilies decorated the room.

As soon as Neil and Anna Lisa sat on the sectional, Jillian, carrying a tray of Vanilla soufflé, came in the room with her husband right behind her. After serving dessert, the Simons took a seat on the chairs.

Jillian started the conversation. "So Anna Lisa, how is Paul?"

"He's been working hard and studying for school. He has a year left before he gets his bachelor's degree," Anna Lisa said taking a sip of her coffee.

"And when are the two of you getting married?" Jillian asked, putting a spoonful of her soufflé in her mouth.

Anna Lisa brushed her hair away from her face. "Oh, we haven't made any plans yet."

"Why not? Doesn't he want to marry you?" asked Jillian.

Simon noticed Anna Lisa's awkwardness and interrupted his wife. "Anna Lisa, why aren't you eating?"

"You've got to try the soufflé, it's fantastic," Neil said.

"Glad you like it," Jillian responded.

Anna Lisa tried it. "Delicious. You're an excellent cook, Jillian."

"Thank you," she answered.

"Yes, my wife would make a great chef," Simon said hoping to divert the conversation away from Anna Lisa's personal life. "I told her she should think about writing a cookbook."

"Thank you dear," Jillian said to her husband. She then turned to Neil and asked, "How is your fiancée, what's her name – Sheila?"

Neil smiled reluctantly. "You mean Sarah. She's doing fine," he said taking a sip of his coffee.

"I hear you are to be married soon."

"Yes, in September."

"Hmmm–it's a shame both you and Anna Lisa are involved. You would make such a great couple."

Anna Lisa turned red.

Simon said, "Jillian, may I have a word with you in the kitchen?"

When they walked away, Neil whispered to Anna Lisa, "She is persistent."

"That she is." She looked at her watch; it was 10 o'clock. "Let's finish our soufflés and leave. I'm going to surprise Paul and pop by his place, and I'm sure Sarah is probably waiting for you."

"An excellent idea," Neil said while he continued eating. When they were finished, they graciously thanked their hosts and exchanged farewells. The evening came to an end more quickly than expected by all parties.

After Anna Lisa and Neil left, Simon said to his wife "I told you this was a bad idea. We shouldn't meddle. I've never seen two people finish their soufflés with such speed." He went into the living-room and bent down to pick up the saucers and the coffee cups. "Pour souls, they will probably end up with indigestion when they get home."

His wife started helping her husband by removing the dishes. "We tried. That's all that matters."

"What were you thinking when you planned this dinner? That Neil was going to leave his fiancée for Anna Lisa or that Anna Lisa was going to abandon Paul and fall madly in love with Neil?"

His wife started for the kitchen. "I just think Anna Lisa could do a lot better than Paul. Perhaps my cousin Stanley...."

Simon, who was right behind her, interrupted. "Oh, no you don't. We're not going through this charade again. I have to work with these people you know."

Jillian placed the dishes in the dishwasher. She turned and moved away to give her husband room. "You're too worried. I'm sure Anna Lisa appreciated what you were trying to do."

Simon put the cups and saucers in the dishwasher. "What I was trying to do? Don't you pin this evening on me," Simon said imitating what his wife had said earlier – "They're perfect for each other. They just need a little push."

"Say what you will but I think the evening was a success. These things take time. A few more dinners like this and the whole thing will be in the bag."

"Forget it. I have no intention of playing matchmaker again," Simon said, walking out of the kitchen and getting a drink.

After leaving the Simons, Anna Lisa drove to Paul's place located in southeast LA where windows had bars and a fistfight on the street was not unusual. He had bought his home a year ago because the price was within his means and the mortgage was cheaper than paying rent. The patch of grass in front of his dreadfully small house was brown. The entrance door was protected by a rusted iron gate to keep intruders out, although Paul's house had nothing to offer except sofas and chairs beyond repair, an old entertainment center and cheap wall decorations.

When Anna Lisa arrived at Paul's house, she thought he was home because his car was parked outside. She rang the bell several times but Paul didn't answer. She went around the back and knocked on his bedroom window and still no answer. She tried calling him on his home phone and then his cell but his message machine answered.

"Paul, are you there? Paul, pick up, I'm at the door," Anna Lisa said. When he didn't pick up, she said, "Well, I'm leaving now. Call me when you get this message."

Around the same time Anna Lisa left Paul's place, Neil arrived at his apartment and noticed that Sarah was not there. He changed into his pajamas, turned on the TV in his bedroom and, after a while, fell asleep. At two in the morning, he woke up and realized Sarah wasn't back yet. He got worried and called Charlie's house. Charlie's father answered.

"Hello, this is Neil."

"Who?" A sleepy voice on the other side of the receiver answered.

"Neil, Sarah's fiancé."

"What time is it?"

"It is very late, and I'm terribly sorry to be calling at this hour but I'm worried about Sarah. Has your son seen her?"

"Sarah's with Charlie. There was a group of them here earlier. They were all going to some birthday party. I imagine they'll be back late."

"Will you please not mention I called?" Neil asked feeling relieved that she was safe.

"Okay," said Charlie's father and hung up.

Neil waited up until four in the morning for Sarah and when he heard her key turn in the door, he pretended to be asleep. He knew she was late on purpose because she was still mad at him for not having lunch with her yesterday. She was like a child who retaliated when she didn't get what she wanted. No, he would not give in to her. She made a lot of noise to wake him up but he did not budge. She finally gave up and turned in.

TEN

Neil was at the dentist when Paul came into his girlfriend's office. Sitting behind her desk looking neat and businesslike in her maroon pant suit, Anna Lisa was about to make a phone call to a client but when she saw him, she put the receiver down.

"Did you get my message?" she asked.

"What message?" he said, walking toward her desk wearing a pair of loosely fitted brown pants and a cream fitted round neck shirt.

He was rugged and sexy, she thought. "I stopped by your place last night and rang the bell but you didn't answer. I even called you from my cell phone and left a message."

"You did? I must've fallen asleep waiting for you. I was soooo...tired last night, and this morning I was running late and didn't have time to check my answering machine," he went around her desk, took her hands into his and with a disappointed look said, "I'm sorry honey."

"That's okay. It's just as well. I was tired myself."

"How did it go last night?"

"It went well. Dinner was great. Jillian did all the cooking herself. And the conversation was interesting."

He let go of her hands and sat on her desk. "Did you and Neil argue?"

"No, we didn't," she smiled swiveling in her chair from side to side. She was thinking about how hard Jillian had tried to match her up with Neil. What a ridiculous idea, she thought. "Actually he was the perfect gentleman."

"Was he?" her boyfriend asked in surprise.

"I meant," she cleared her throat and stopped swiveling, "he was nice to me and didn't give me a hard time."

"That's good," he nodded. "I was a little worried about you two."

"Well, I have to get back to work. I need to make a few phone calls."

"I'd better do the same myself." He got off her desk, leaned over and gave her a long, erotic kiss, causing her to flush and get him aroused. "Let's finish where we left off, say tomorrow night at 8, your place?

How about we meet today at noon, my place, she thought. But she knew she had a busy day ahead of her. "Why don't we meet after 10 tonight?"

"Nooo–, tonight I have my math class and I want to get to bed early so I have lots of energy for us tomorrow night."

With a voice filled with discontentment, she said, "I guess I'll have to wait then, don't I?"

He stared at her with lustful eyes as he caressed the contour of her lips with his finger. "I can't wait till tomorrow night," he said as he kissed her one last time and left.

Two hours later Simon came into Anna Lisa's office and asked if she had seen Paul.

"I spoke to him earlier. Maybe he took an early lunch."

"If you see him, tell him I'm looking for him."

"Will do," Anna Lisa responded and went back to reading the test results from a focus group on one of her clients who wanted to change the scent of his hair products from almond to rose and his packaging from pale brown to dark pink. Compared to Jane, he was a small client, but Anna Lisa decided to work on his products first because Neil was at the dentist and she planned to work on the Olson account when he returned. She and Neil intended to work late into the evening. A lot needed to be done, and Anna Lisa looked forward to it now that they were getting along. Together, they would make a great team, she thought. Another hour passed by and Neil finally showed up with a numb mouth.

Because of the sick look on his face, Anna Lisa thought he had something major done on his teeth. "Root canal?"

"No, a cavity."

"Is that all? You look like a ghost."

"Well, it was a painful filling," Neil protested with a crooked lip.

"I take it we are afraid of the dentist," Anna Lisa smiled.

"A little," He tried to smile back but couldn't.

"I think I'll go get a cup of coffee. Would you like some?"

"No thanks," Neil mumbled, "I'm going to rest on this sofa and close my eyes for a few minutes."

"What did you say?" Anna Lisa asked not understanding his slurred words, but when she saw him collapse on the sofa, she understood.

Anna Lisa left Neil and walked toward the break room where she ran into Paul. She asked him where he'd been because Simon had been looking all over for him.

"Yes, I know," Paul replied in an irritating tone, "We already spoke. He needed a balance sheet and a P&L statement."

"You're okay?"

"Actually I'm not. I left my damn keys in the car and locked myself out. Do you know a locksmith?"

"I'm a member of Rescue and Tow. I can call them for you if you like." Rescue and Tow offered services such as towing and unlocking car doors.

"Would you?"

"Just give me your license plate number and I'll take care of it," Anna Lisa said.

He wrote it down for her on a piece of paper and thanked her.

She poured a cup of coffee for herself and left.

Half an hour later, Neil was still napping when Rescue and Tow called Anna Lisa to let her know the driver was waiting for

her in the parking lot. Anna Lisa picked up her membership card
and went to meet him.

In the underground parking lot, a grumpy middle-aged man
got out of his truck and pointed at a faded gold Dodge and said,
"This your car?"

Anna Lisa lied. "Yes, my keys are in there and I locked myself
out."

"Genius," the man mumbled and started working on the lock.
He finally managed to get the door open.

"You know you really should think about a different line of
work if you don't like what you do," Anna Lisa suggested.

"Yeah, yeah, whatever," the man grunted and drove off.

"Something happens. Something maybe not so good."

Paul's car was dirty on the outside and messy on the inside.
There were sweatshirts, books and magazines on the seats,
hamburger and potato chip wrappers and used tissues and napkins
on the floor. Anna Lisa lowered her head to reach for the keys in
the ignition when she noticed a Rebecca's Naughty Lingerie bag
sitting on the passenger seat of her boyfriend's car. Overwhelmed
by her curiosity, she peeked in the bag. In a black box, wrapped in
matching tissue was a red lace negligee in size small, a gift receipt
and a birthday card. The fact that her size was not small and her
birthday was a few months ago, pushed her to dig further. The
receipt had today's date. So that's where he was during his lunch
break, she thought and opened the card. The card wasn't addressed
to anyone but read – "Last night was great. Happy birthday
sweetheart. Love, Paul." Anna Lisa felt the blood drain from her
body and sensed a sharp pain in her chest. With trembling hands,
she quickly put the present back in its box along with the card. Her
eyes started to sting. The present and the card were meant for
Kimberly even if it wasn't addressed to her. He must've been in
bed with her the night before when she had called on him. How
could he have been with her knowing she might have stopped by.
She then remembered something he had said to her at the office

when she had told him she didn't want to fool around at work because she was afraid someone would walk in. He had replied, "That's what makes it so exciting." He was having sex with Kimberly last night when she rang his doorbell and knocked on his bedroom window. She felt sick to her stomach and wanted to vomit. How stupid she had been. All the nights she slept alone and the weekends she spent by herself because he had to study, he had been with her. Her legs felt limp when she tried to leave his car. Tears rolled down her face and after sobbing for a good 10 minutes, she finally got ahold of herself. No one at the office could know what had just happened. Anna Lisa felt as if her body had died, but she somehow managed to get out of the car and stop by the bathroom to check her face on her way back to the office. She splashed water on her face to get rid of the sticky tears and the red in her eyes but all the water in the world couldn't wipe the piercing pain she felt in her heart. Anna Lisa waited a few more moments before walking back to her office.

"There you are," Neil said when he saw her. "I must have dozed off. I feel much better now. He then took a closer look at Anna Lisa and noticed her red eyes. "Say, are you alright?"

"As a matter of fact, I don't feel so well. You mind if we call it a day?"

"May I do anything for you?"

"No, I just need to go home and rest." She picked up her belongings and left. On her way she stopped by Kimberly's desk and said, "By the way, happy birthday."

Kimberly looked up in surprise. "Thank you."

Now it was confirmed. Anna Lisa swallowed her tears and walked toward Paul's office. Luckily, he was there with Simon going over some figures. Anna Lisa wasn't ready to talk to him. She simply said, "Here're your keys."

"Thanks," Paul said.

"Are you done for the day?" Simon asked.

"Yes, I have an appointment. I'll see you tomorrow."

Hours after Anna Lisa Left, at 6 in the evening, Neil buzzed Kimberly's intercom. He needed some papers typed and faxed to a client.

"Yes?" Kimberly answered.

"Would you come in here, please?"

Kimberly got excited. Here was her chance to entice the most desirable bachelor of the office. To emphasize her already large breast implants, she tugged on her fitted shirt and opened the first two buttons. She checked her florescent pink lipstick in a hand mirror and fixed her mass of platinum blond hair. After reaching Neil's office with a racing pulse, she said, "You wanted to see me?"

Looking for the tape recorder and a fax number in his drawer, Neil failed to notice Kimberly's efforts right away but as he lifted his eyes, he was surprised by her tight outfit when he stated uncomfortably, "I have dictated a letter in here. Would you make sure to type it up right away and fax it to this number?"

Kimberly went around his desk and leaned over so to give him a better view of her breasts. "Is this the fax number?"

"Yes."

She stared at him with her big blue eyes. "Will there be anything else?"

Neil swallowed. "No that will be all, thank you."

Kimberly took the information and started to walk away but before she was halfway across the room, she dropped the piece of paper on which Neil had written the fax number and bent over to pick it up. Her skirt slid up revealing the cheeks of her butt hanging out from her tiny underpants. After slowly picking up the note, she straightened herself, turned and smiled. "Sorry, I'm so clumsy sometimes," and then headed once again for the door.

Neil said, "Wait a minute, there's something I want to show you."

Thrilled that her trick had worked, Kimberly turned and walked back to Neil's desk. She batted her lashes at him. "Yes?"

Neil took out a black binder from a bookshelf behind him. "Did anyone ever show you the office manual?"

Kimberly went around his desk to be closer to him. "No. I've never seen it."

Neil opened the manual, looked through the table of contents and found the section he was looking for. He opened up to that page, put a large red paper clip to mark the chapter titled OFFICE DRESS CODE and said, "I want you to read this carefully tonight so you might abide by its rules."

"Oh. Okay." Kimberly blushed in embarrassment. She took the handbook and rushed out of his office.

When she left, Neil organized his desk and shook his head at her stupidity. He knew perfectly well she was coming on to him and it was obvious the girl had no common sense. Why in the world would he trade his classy fiancée for the likes of her, he thought as he got up, put his jacket on and left to go pick Sarah up from his condo. They had plans to walk over to Westwood Village to see a romantic comedy.

Before the advertisement started at the movie theater, Neil sat next to his fiancée, soaking in the atmosphere. The film had been out for a while and though the theater wasn't crowded, people rolled in consistently as they looked for seats. An uptight bald man with a bucket of popcorn plopped down behind Neil and waited impatiently for the movie to start.

"What are you thinking about?" Sarah asked her fiancé.

"Hmmm?"

"Really darling, your body is here but your mind is not."

"Sorry," he apologized. "I'm just a little concerned about Leeza."

Sarah put her delicate hand over Neil's. "She's not your problem. Why should you worry about her?"

"Because suddenly today she was not herself. She seemed utterly distracted and upset."

"I don't see why this would be any of your business," Sarah complained.

The lights dimmed yet they still could see around them. When the advertisements started, Neil found himself having to talk a little louder. "It is my business when her well-being affects her work and, in turn, my work," Neil lied. In reality he was truly concerned. He had stood there for a long time after she had left, thinking what had gone wrong with her in such a short time. Earlier she was so energetic and bubbly but later she was completely out of sorts. Something wasn't right.

"Please Neil, no more talk of Anna Lisa or work. Let's just enjoy our time together."

"Blue raspberry?" He pointed his drink toward her.

She stared at the frozen blue concoction in disgust. "No, thank you. How can you drink that horrid beverage?"

"I guess that means no to the chili dog," he commented, taking a bite.

"Really Neil, your eating habits and your manners are becoming too American."

The uptight bald man behind them let out a sigh of frustration because they were talking and he wanted to listen to the advertisements. Sarah and Neil ignored him.

"Funny, the Americans think I'm too British," he commented, sipping on his drink. "So, did you say you were leaving next Wednesday or Thursday?"

"Thursday. I want to get back in time for Mum and Dad's 25th anniversary. I think you should come with me."

"I wish I could, but I have to work." Thank God he had to work, he told himself, or else he would be stuck conversing with bunch of boring and stuffy people who talked about nothing of importance.

"You always use that as an excuse."

"It's not an excuse," he replied, frowning. "Money doesn't grow on trees, you know." Perhaps it does for your parents but not for me, he thought.

Sarah nudged him and remarked, "Look, isn't that that secretary with Anna Lisa's man?"

He looked over in surprise at Paul and Kimberly. "I believe you're right."

"Maybe that's why Anna Lisa was out of sorts. They must not be together anymore."

"She didn't mention anything about it last night. In fact, after our dinner at the Simons', she was going over to see him."

"Then maybe he's cheating on her."

"Or maybe he's just out with a friend and they happen to both like the movies."

"An unlikely story. You are so naïve, darling."

At this point the theater darkened, the previews started, and the uptight bald man behind them told them to be quiet.

The same day Anna Lisa discovered her boyfriend cheating on her, she rented a black Toyota with dark-tinted glass, went home, put on a black, long-sleeve T-shirt, jeans and a baseball cap and drove to his house at 9 in the evening. She couldn't drive her car because he would recognize it. Scared and uncertain, Anna Lisa parked a few doors down from his house and locked her doors. She wanted to catch him in the act of betrayal. Had she confronted him earlier at the office, he would have denied everything. Paul had a remarkable ability to change and twist his stories to his favor. Anna Lisa had seen him do this often at the office with other women before she had started dating him. Why on earth did she let herself fall in love with a man who lied and cheated his way through everything? Her head was fuzzy for a long time, and she dozed off. It was about midnight when a dog's bark woke her up. She looked up and still no sign of her boyfriend. She waited.

Half an hour later, his car pulled up in the driveway. Paul got out and went to the passenger side and opened the door for Kimberly, who exited wearing a tight, black mini-dress. She looked cheap and floozy, Anna Lisa thought. They both went in the house. After waiting for a long time for the lights to go out, Anna Lisa went around to the back of the house. She knew Paul always forgot to lock the back door, but she had never intruded on him in this way until tonight. Carrying her shoes in one hand and opening the door with the other, she snuck in and felt her way through the dark until her foot hit the leg of the kitchen table. Wanting to scream, Anna Lisa shut her eyes and waited for the pain to go away. Finding her way out of the kitchen and into the living room, she stumbled on a beer can and cursed herself for not being more careful. She rolled the can away with one foot and continued feeling her way around the sofa where she almost knocked over the floor lamp and caught it before it hit the ground. She stood still for a few seconds to stop her body from trembling. Her heart was pounding hard against her chest. She could hear it loud and clear. Maybe she should turn around and go back to her car while she still had a chance, she thought. No, be strong and confront him, she told herself. Slowly, she started moving forward until she reached his bedroom and turned on the lights. She saw Kimberly straddled over Paul's naked body. Paul tilted his head to see who had turned on the lights. Anna Lisa looked straight at him and then at her. She walked out.

"Anna Lisa, wait," Paul yelled and pushed Kimberly away from him. He tried to run after her but he had no clothes on. By the time he pulled his pants on, Anna Lisa was gone.

At 6 in the morning, with swollen eyes, Anna Lisa went into her office, grabbed her files and wrote three notes: one for Neil and one for Simon both explaining that she wasn't feeling well and was planning to work from her grandmother's home. The last was Paul's which read – "Please do not contact me. I have no interest in your sorry excuses. When and only when I'm ready, I will talk to you. Until then stay out of my way or so help me God, I'll make sure both you and Kimberly will get fired."

Wanting to concentrate on her work, Anna Lisa wasn't about to let her emotions get in the way and decided to deal with them later. Not desiring to be home alone and scared that Paul might try to get in touch with her, she packed a small suitcase, her files, and her lap top and moved to work out of her grandmother's house. She knew Paul would never show up at her grandmother's home because her grandma made him feel uneasy – she was able to read right through him.

Her grandmother's small home office had no windows but still offered pleasant views. A muralist had painted a blue sky and floating white clouds on the ceiling, pair of French windows opening into a vineyard on one wall and scenes of meadows on the other three. Mango wood furniture gave the room an outdoorsy feel. A work desk sat in the center of the room next to a four drawer filing cabinet and a small round table with two chairs.

Anna Lisa began organizing her files when she heard a knock on the door. "Come in," she said.

It was her grandma looking young and energetic in her dark blue jeans and red sweater. "Anna Lisa, are you comfortable? Can I bring you something?"

"Thanks Grandma, I'm fine. I hope you don't mind, but I left your phone number with Neil and Simon."

"Sweetie, this is your home," her grandmother said kindly. "You may do whatever you please. I'm only glad you're not by yourself in your apartment. And when I get hold of that Paul I'll…"

"Grandma, you promised not to talk about him. I need to stay focused." Anna Lisa knew if she let herself relive the awful betrayal, she would fall apart and, frankly, she didn't have the time to fall apart.

"Say no more. I'll leave you alone." She closed the door behind her as she walked out.

———

Simon came into his office and noticed Anna Lisa's note. He felt bad that she wasn't feeling well, but not wanting to bother her at her grandmother's house unless it was absolutely necessary, he decided not to call her. Simon was the favored partner by his employees. He got along with everybody and knew how to communicate and motivate. Incredibly flexible, he didn't care when his managers came in or left so long as they got their work done and left him a number where they could be reached.

Simon put on his glasses and lowered his head to read the marketing data sitting on his desk when he heard a knock on his door.

"Come in," he said, removing his reading glasses and looking up.

It was Paul.

"Good morning," Simon greeted him, "What can I do for you?"

Paul wrung his hands and uttered in an uncomfortable manner, "I'm here on Kimberly's behalf."

"Oh? Why didn't she come in herself?" he asked, "She's not afraid of me, is she?"

"Well, um, she's rather embarrassed," Paul said. "Neil told her that she had to follow the dress code in the office manual."

"Yes, well perhaps Neil is right." He knew very well how Kimberly usually dressed.

"The thing is she doesn't own work clothes."

"Then tell her to speak with Diana. Maybe Diana could give her some pointers to help her out."

"Thank you, I'll let her know."

"Is there anything else?" Simon asked when he noticed Paul lingering.

"Have you seen Anna Lisa? She's usually here by now."

"She's not coming in today. She has some kind of a contagious virus and doesn't want to pass it to anyone."

"Oh," Paul said taking comfort that Simon had no idea about what had happened the night before.

ELEVEN

Six days had gone by and Anna Lisa was working from her grandmother's home. Whenever people wanted to stop by and visit, she told them she was still contagious with a virus and it was better to stay away. Working diligently day and night with Neil through fax, e-mail and telephone, it was as if Anna Lisa wasn't really without him. She hoped to finish the project ahead of time so she could take a vacation as far away from Paul and Kimberly as possible. She even stayed clear of her friend Leila, who could not keep a secret.

Unfortunately, time breezed by and the day finally came when she had to go back to work and face reality. It had been two weeks since Anna Lisa had last seen Paul and she wasn't ready, but at least she wasn't walking into the office with swollen eyes. Everyone asked how she was and expressed how happy they were to see her again. Neil's face lit up when he saw her. She knew he had missed her. Funny how this man who had infuriated her at first was now her friend.

"Feeling better?" Neil asked when he saw her.

"Much, thank you," Anna Lisa answered as she walked to her desk and settled behind it. She and Neil were to meet with the graphic designers.

Kimberly came in with a white long-sleeve shirt buttoned all the way up to her neck and a wilted-green skirt that fell below her knees. When her eyes caught Anna Lisa's furious glare, she turned beet red and looked down. "Here are the papers you requested earlier."

Anna Lisa stared at her clothes in disbelief.

Neil took the letters and Kimberly left the office in a hurry.

"Did you see what I just saw?" Anna Lisa asked.

"What are you talking about?"

"Am I the only one who noticed or did you see her work clothes?"

"Oh that. She and I had a little chat about the office dress code."

Anna Lisa's eyes widened. "You must've had some chat. I have never seen her dressed so, so…"

"Normal?"

"Boring is a better description."

"I think Diana helped pick out her clothes."

She guessed Diana didn't like Kimberly either since she chose such a hideous outfit for her. "But how did you get her to change?"

"I think I intimidated her."

Anna Lisa smiled. "Hmmm. Whatever you did worked. Thanks."

"My pleasure."

Anna Lisa glanced at her watch – it was 9 o'clock. "We have to meet with the graphic designers in 15 minutes."

"Tell me again why we have to see them?"

"Because they're supposed to show us a selection of designs for our packaging from which we need to choose one for both the American and the English market."

"But I already have one for our market. I had them drawn out in London. Why can't we use what I have?"

"Because what you showed me will not work."

"You don't know the English market," Neil said.

"And you don't know the American market."

"Why are you always so stubborn? You never want to compromise."

Anna Lisa sighed. "Just come with me and have a look and then we can decide. You may like my ideas."

Paul peaked his head in. "Sorry to interrupt," he said. "Anna Lisa, do you have a minute?"

Her body stiffened and she tried hard to push back her memories of the night of betrayal. Don't fall apart on me now, she told herself. Be strong and deal with your feelings when the Olson project is over. "Not really. Neil and I are about to leave," she replied swallowing the lump forming in her throat. Had Neil not been in the office, she would've broken down and cried.

Neil noticed the friction between the two and the coolness in Anna Lisa's voice.

"When you get a chance, will you stop by my office? We need to talk," Paul said and went away.

Anna Lisa wasn't ready to talk. She wasn't sure whether she wanted to break up with him or she wanted to stay. She decided to keep away from him until she could decipher the mixed feelings joggling inside her.

Neil and Anna Lisa left their office, took the elevator down one floor, and walked through a pair of frosted glass doors, toward the graphic arts department. The large office had four designers who sat behind diagonally angled desks while they worked. Anna Lisa and Neil met with two of the artists who presented several versions of the packaging designs. Anna Lisa thought three of them had potential for Jane's product line, but Neil didn't like any of them. Since he didn't want to argue with his office-mate in front of the two men who had labored over the drawings, he suggested they needed to think about them. At that point, the account executives took the layouts back to their office and argued behind closed doors. They finally realized that they could not compromise until Anna Lisa had a better idea of the English market and Neil a better idea of the American one.

Their quest for a compromise started one Saturday morning when they were to meet at Anna Lisa's house, and together venture out to stores to study current product packaging. Except that it was the wrong Saturday, or at least that's what Anna Lisa thought when Neil showed up at her doorstep. Still in bed, she heard a knock and dozed off. Ursula answered the door.

"Hello, my name is Neil. I'm here to see Leeza."

Ursula realized who Neil was right away. She had heard Anna Lisa complain about how much she disliked the nickname he had given her. Ursula looked him up and down as though she were buying a piece of merchandise. He was wearing a light peach cotton shirt, a pair of burnt brown, brushed-cotton slacks, freshly polished whiskey color shoes and a matching belt. He appeared cordial and dignified, she thought. Unsure if she should invite him in, she decided to interrogate him.

"Is she expecting you?"

He looked at the towering, intimidating woman standing in front of him with a bouffant, a royal blue garb that looked more like a uniform than a dress and a belt around her thick waist. She couldn't possibly be related to Anna Lisa, he thought. She didn't look anything like his coworker. "Yes, I work with her at Howard Brown, and you are?"

"Ursula, her housekeeper."

"Delighted to make your acquaintance," he said, extending his hand to shake hers.

"Likewise," Ursula said, taking his hand.

"Did she not mention I was to stop by?"

"No, she didn't."

"I suppose I can stay out here while you let her know she has a visitor."

"No, that's not necessary. Please come in," Ursula said, directing him to a seat in the living room. She told him Anna Lisa was still asleep, then climbed up the stairs to let Anna Lisa know about her unexpected guest.

Ursula gently touched Anna Lisa to wake her up but her employer swat her hand thinking Ursula was a fly.

"Ouch," Ursula yelped, "that hurt."

At the sound of her cry, Anna Lisa jumped up with her unruly hair sticking out from everywhere. "What? What? What happened?

"You have a visitor."

Anna Lisa rubbed her eyes and looked at Ursula dumbfounded. "Hmmm?" she replied with a groggy voice.

"Neil is here to see you."

"Who?" she asked not trusting her own ears.

"Neil, you know...your coworker. I told him to have a seat in the living room."

"What? He's here in my living room? Why did you let him in?" Anna Lisa whispered.

"Because he's gorgeous and said you work together."

"Yes but he wasn't supposed to be here until next Saturday. I haven't even showered yet."

"You shower, and I'll keep him occupied."

Anna Lisa couldn't believe it. Ursula never entertained Paul. In fact, she always did everything in her power to chase him out but now she was more than willing to entertain Neil while Anna Lisa showered. "Alright then, but I have to call Nicole first. She's expecting me at the hike."

"I'll take care of it. You go fix yourself up."

"Don't get your hopes up, Ursula," Anna Lisa said with narrowed eyes, "He has a fiancée and, besides, I have no interest in him."

Ursula shook her head in disappointment and started for the stairs. When she got to the living room, she gave Neil the morning paper and poured him a cup of coffee, informing him that Anna Lisa would be down shortly. She called Nicole and updated her on what had happened. And while Anna Lisa was getting ready, Ursula decided to make breakfast for everyone. She scrambled eggs, grilled bacon strips, pan fried sliced potatoes in olive oil and put cheese, orange juice, milk, toast, butter, jam and lemon curd on the table.

Anna Lisa finally emerged with her hair in a ponytail, wearing a pair of faded jeans, a white T-shirt and tennis shoes. But when she saw Neil – dressed elegantly – she felt uncomfortable about her attire.

"I'm so sorry, but I thought we were meeting next Saturday."

Neil got up. "I could've sworn you meant today. If you like, I can come back next week."

"Whatever you decide, you're not leaving till you've had my breakfast," Ursula said to Neil and directed him to the kitchen table.

Anna Lisa looked over at Ursula and then at Neil. "I think that's a hint for you to stay."

"Are you certain you have the time to do this?" he commented with a concerned look on his face.

"Yes. Ursula canceled my hike with my friend Nicole. After breakfast, we'll check out some of the department stores and smaller shops. We just have to finish by three o'clock, because I have to be somewhere."

He nodded his head in agreement and the three of them sat down to breakfast like one big happy family.

Neil couldn't believe how informal Anna Lisa was with her housekeeper. He took his time and enjoyed his perfect breakfast. Maybe he could steal Ursula and take her home with him, he thought.

Anna Lisa spread lemon curd on her toast and joked, "Would you like some lemon curd, Mr. Whittaker?" She remembered their first encounter and how angry she had been when he had taken her lemon curd and now there they were sharing a meal at her apartment.

Ursula glanced over at Anna Lisa and wondered why she was addressing Neil by his last name.

Noticing the mischievous look in Anna Lisa's eyes, Neil smiled and said, "Yes I would, Leeza." He recalled how much she had hated being called Leeza on their first day at work and now it didn't bother her at all.

When breakfast came to an end, Ursula urged Neil to come back again. Anna Lisa grabbed her purse and went outside while Neil followed.

"I like your housekeeper, she's nice." Neil opened the passenger door of his Lexus for Anna Lisa.

Anna Lisa got in. "She's much more than a housekeeper. She has always looked out for me and I her."

"I can see that," Neil said, "Where are we going, anyway?"

"Let's start with the Selma Jones boutique in Beverly Hills. They sell beauty products with different brand names."

After stopping at Selma Jones for half-hour, the two of them hit a series of department stores and upscale shops. They even stopped by Tress at an indoor mall to have a look at their products and packaging. They knew Tress would never carry Jane Olson's products since they carried their own, but Anna Lisa and Neil wanted to check out as many brands as possible before making their decision.

"I can't believe it's two o'clock already. I have to leave at three to coach a basketball team," Anna Lisa said to Neil.

"You know how to coach a basketball team?!" Neil asked in surprise.

"Not the way you're thinking." Anna Lisa started walking toward the escalator located near a department store. "I volunteer for a nonprofit organization. Today the kids have a game against another school and the real coach is out sick. I guess I'm it."

"What kind of nonprofit organization?" Neil asked as he walked with Anna Lisa.

"The kind that takes in troubled kids no one else wants. These are kids who've been kicked out of high school for drug problems, lack of performance, being members of a gang, or other reasons. The organization takes these teenagers and gives them a second chance when no one else will," she explained and got on the escalator.

"That's a noble cause," Neil said. "Mind if I tag along?"

Anna Lisa stared at him for a moment in silence.

"If you don't want me to come, I understand," Neil said.

"No, it's not that – it's just your clothes."

"What is wrong with my clothes? My sister gave them to me."
He got off the escalator and stepped forward so that the people
behind him could get off.

"You look expensive," Anna Lisa noted and followed him.

"Sorry?"

"Look, we're going to an area where the price of your watch
could feed a family of four for months."

"Oh," Neil said in disappointment.

"I have an idea," Anna Lisa said, "We can go buy you clothes
so you can fit in."

"Where did you have in mind?"

"Let's see," Anna Lisa said and walked toward the mall
directory. "We can start at The Stop."

"The Stop?" Neil replied, "Why that's a teenage store."

Anna Lisa chuckled. "You have a lot to learn about the L.A.
life. You see, in L.A., we dress different from the rest of the
country."

Neil wasn't sure what she meant but agreed to follow her into
a casual, inexpensive store that carried men's and women's
clothing and accessories. Anna Lisa picked out a pair of navy jeans
on sale for $25 dollars and a plain charcoal gray T-shirt for $10, a
baseball cap for $7 and a pair of men's white cotton socks for $3.
She stared at Neil's dressy shoes and decided to guide him to an
athletic footwear store. She chose a cheap pair of tennis shoes. All
in all, Neil spent far less on everything than the cost of his Italian
shoes.

When they were finished, they walked toward the parking lot,
got in Neil's car, and drove toward East L.A.

"Now you look very American," Anna Lisa said.

"I do?" Neil asked gaily.

"Yes as long as you don't speak, people will think you're from
L.A.," she smiled.

When they reached the outdoor basketball court of OSSC –
The O'Malley School of Second Chance, Anna Lisa instructed
Neil to sit in the bleachers with the two dozen other spectators and
went to greet her team. Ten minutes later, the game started. Neil

was impressed by Anna Lisa's coaching as she ran from one side of the court to the other, guiding her team, calling time outs to regroup and rethink their strategy and change players when necessary. By the game's end, after two hours, her team lost by one point. Even so, she kept up the team's spirit and told them they would do better next time.

"You're her boyfriend?" a 16-year-old boy from the team asked Neil. He had a nasty cut on his left cheek and a black kerchief wrapped around his head.

"No, I am her work colleague," Neil responded.

"You talk funny."

Anna Lisa came to his rescue. "Neil's from England. He lives in London."

The teenager got very excited and asked all sorts of questions about the city's various theaters. When Neil found out the he aspired to be an actor, he told him if he worked hard enough, someday he would be able to see the London theaters in person.

"If I work and save enough money, can I visit you in London?"

"If you make it to London, I shall help find you a student pension and show you around."

"What's a student pension?"

"It is an inexpensive boarding house where young visitors stay."

"Can we go see a Shakespearean play?"

"Certainly." Neil reached in his pocket, took out a business card and gave it to him. "Call me when you get there, and I shall help you out."

The teenager's face brightened as he took the card. He then took off to tell his friends.

Anna Lisa frowned. "Please don't make a promise you can't keep; these kids are very vulnerable," she whispered to Neil when the boy left.

"What makes you think I'm not being sincere?"

"Show him around London? C'mon Neil, give me a break. He doesn't belong in your world."

"You don't know anything about my world," Neil said sounding upset.

"I see how you dress and I've met your fiancée."

Neil's facial muscles tensed up. "You're so quick to judge everyone before you know anything about them," he said angrily.

Anna Lisa realized how mad she had made him and was sorry to have said what she had, but it was too late to take it back.

He glowered and shouted at her. "Why did you ask me to change into these clothes if you didn't think I belonged here?" He strode hurriedly toward his car.

Anna Lisa hasted after him and barely able to catch up, she got into the car but kept quiet. The ride home was incredibly uncomfortable. Neither spoke and when Anna Lisa couldn't handle the silence anymore she said, "You were right back there about me judging people too quickly. I'm sorry. I shouldn't have said what I said."

Neil turned to look at her and noticed her eyes were red. "I'm sorry too. I overreacted."

"Truce then?" She extended her hand to shake his.

"Truce." He shook her hand.

Besides looking at designs for packaging, Neil and Anna Lisa studied billboards, brochures, magazines and television ads.

"Please Leeza," Neil said to her one evening when they were in the conference room of Howard Brown analyzing TV ads, "it is time for us to stop. My eyes are exhausted and my stomach is rumbling."

But his coworker ignored his plea because when she was busy, she didn't have time to think about Paul. "Just one more ad before we–"

"No more. I am tired and starving. We should go eat."

His office-mate was surprised because she thought he went home every night to have dinner with Sarah. "What about Sarah? I thought you were having dinner with her."

"She went back home for her parents' anniversary and, to tell you the, truth a little distance will do us good."

"I'm having dinner at my grandmother's tonight. Why don't you come along?"

"No, I would not want to impose," Neil replied. "I shall order a takeaway on my way home."

"Impose? My grandmother makes enough food to feed an entire army. She'd love to have you, especially if you have a big appetite."

"In that case, I am famished enough to eat a whole army."

"My friend Nicole and her five-year-old daughter, Sam, will be there and I must warn you that Leila and her parents are coming as well," said Anna Lisa, "They're Iranian and incredibly kind, but they like to get into everyone's business."

"They can't be any different than Jillian."

"You're right; I almost forgot."

They both chuckled.

Once they left the office, Anna Lisa drove her car and Neil followed in his. When they reached their destination, Anna Lisa rang the bell.

Leila answered the door and was surprised to see Neil. "Hey, your grandmother's in the kitchen," she told Anna Lisa and then she looked at Neil, "I see Anna Lisa has been working you hard. Your eyes are pink."

"Yes," Neil gave her a tired smile, "she's ruthless."

"Come in, we're about to have dinner." Leila took him to the dining room table and introduced him to her parents, Nicole and her daughter Sam.

Anna Lisa went into the kitchen to help her grandmother and came out with a large casserole containing lasagna. Her grandmother followed her with a big crystal salad bowl. Anna Lisa greeted everyone and introduced Neil to her grandmother.

A lace tablecloth dressed the maple table. White China dishes, silver flatware, blue cloth napkins with napkin rings, and crystal wine glasses were set in front of each seat except Sam who had a Cinderella plate, pink silverware and a matching cup with a lid.

Food covered the table – minestrone, steamed asparagus and artichoke hearts, garlic bread, dinner rolls, chicken cacciatore, lasagna, eggplant parmesan and salad.

After everyone sat down, dishes were passed around. Anna Lisa's grandmother was at the head of the table. Nicole and her daughter Sam and Susan Sultani sat to her right, Leila, Neil and Anna Lisa sat to her left. Cameron Sultani was seated at the opposite end of the table from where Anna Lisa's grandmother was seated.

The Sultanis were quiet. It was Anna Lisa's grandmother who began with an interrogation.

"You're married?" she asked Neil.

Here we go again, Anna Lisa thought, Grandma's trying to set me up with someone she approves of. "Neil, would you like to try the eggplant parmesan?" Anna Lisa said trying to change the course of the conversation.

"Yes, I would, thank you," he smiled, knowing very well that his office-mate was trying to change the subject.

She cut a piece with a spatula and served him.

"You never answered my question," her grandmother said to Neil. "Are you married?"

Neil studied the vibrant lady sitting at the end of the table. She didn't look anything like his office-mate. Her small eyes were pale blue, her lips thin and her hair now white was probably light blond during her youth. Anna Lisa must look like her grandfather or father, he thought. "I am engaged. My fiancée is in London, and we are getting married in September."

"That's too bad. I was hoping you were single," Anna commented, glancing at her granddaughter.

"Would anyone like some garlic bread?" Anna Lisa offered. Her grandma was making her feel uncomfortable.

"I'd like some," Leila blurted.

She passed the bread basket to her.

"How's work?" Anna looked at Nicole.

"Busy," she replied, "This year I have more kids to deal with than last year."

Anna Lisa turned to Neil. "Nicole is a counselor at a private school."

"My mother was a teacher before she married my father," Neil commented.

"And did she like it?" Nicole asked.

"I believe she did. The world needs more teachers and counselors."

Nicole raised her wine glass, "I'll drink to that." She took a sip.

"How's the Olson account coming along?" Leila asked Neil.

"It is going well, but we still have a lot of work ahead of us."

"Let me know if I can help," Leila offered, even though her workload was full at the moment. She was busy helping several other account executives.

"Thank you. We will need your help in the near future." Neil then glanced over to where Cameron was sitting and noticed he looked bored with the topic of their conversation. "I understand you're from Iran."

Cameron swallowed a piece of chicken cacciatore. "Yes, we moved here right after the revolution."

"You were smart. These days, you not only need a visa but also a security clearance before getting into the country."

"Yes after 9/11, the world changed."

"We have family in London," said Susan.

"I'm not surprised. England has a large Iranian population. In fact there's a delicious Persian dish I tried once. It was mashed eggplant with yogurt dressing.

"Kashkeh Bademjan."

"How do you say it? Kesh be-dee-men," he said and the Sultanis laughed.

"I make for you. You bring your fiancée."

Neil laughed on the inside. Sarah would never be willing to meet these people, let alone go over their house, he thought. "Thank you," he replied.

"Mom, will you play with me?" Sam asked Nicole. She was cute with her light brown pigtails, petite nose and mouth.

"Not now dear," Nicole said. "Why don't you go play in the living room and I'll come over later."

Sam did as her mother asked.

When dinner was finished, everyone helped clear the table. Leila loaded up the dishwasher and Anna Lisa washed the large platters that didn't fit into the washer. Nicole served hot Earl Grey tea and Anna her homemade apple pie with vanilla ice cream. Sam persuaded Neil and the Sultanis to play bingo with her. The rest of the evening passed in a pleasant manner, and everyone was having such a good time that no one wanted to leave until Nicole got up.

Neil was so engrossed in bingo that he was disappointed when Nicole said to her daughter, "C'mon honey, we have to go."

"Five more minutes," Sam bargained.

"No more minutes. It's way past your bedtime," Nicole responded while helping Anna Lisa clear the dessert dishes from the table.

Neil looked at his watch, surprised at how quickly time had passed by. It was 11. He helped Sam put away her game.

"You don't have any children," Anna said to Neil. "Why don't you stay a bit?"

"Thank you for a lovely evening," he answered sincerely, "but I have to get up early tomorrow."

Nicole and Anna Lisa came out of the kitchen into the dining room.

"Can't you convince Neil to stay a little longer?" Anna complained, looking at her granddaughter. "I hardly had a chance to talk to him."

"I would Grandma if I weren't about to pass out myself," Anna Lisa said. "We had a long day today."

"Oh, that's too bad," her grandmother said, extending her hand toward Neil, "it was nice meeting you. I hope to see you again."

"Likewise," he shook her hand.

Since everyone was leaving, The Sultanis got up as well and followed the rest of the guests outside as the gathering came to an end.

That night when Anna Lisa got home to her empty apartment, she lay in bed wishing it had been Paul at her grandma's house instead of Neil. How badly she wanted her boyfriend to be willing to spend time with her family and friends. She pictured her Grandma embracing him and him joking around with her friends. She was in love with him even if he did cheat on her. What if Kimberly was just a one-time fling? Anna Lisa would never know unless she spoke with Paul, but she was scared of the truth. What if he was in love with Kimberly? Then what? Would she fall apart and beg him to stay with her? Or would she say "Fine, get lost?" She didn't have an answer. Anna Lisa turned off the lamp next to her bed and forced herself to go to sleep.

TWELVE

"You go on trip. Let's see in, one, two, three...Yes, in three months...may be little sooner...But not with your boyfriend...No. You go with a man. A tall man, you don't know very well."

As the spring rain poured from the dark roaring sky, Anna Lisa packed her suitcase. Since she and Neil couldn't agree on the same marketing concept, Simon had agreed that they should go to London for five days so she could get a better perspective on the English market and get acquainted with the London office. This was Anna Lisa's first trip abroad and she looked forward to it. The Journey would not only give her the opportunity to get a glimpse at the taste of the English consumers but it also gave her a chance to unscramble her jumbled emotions toward Paul. She hadn't talked to him for a month since she had found him in bed with Kimberly.

Would she ever stop loving him, she thought as she added a dress and shawl to the four pants and blouses, and lace underwear already packed in her suitcase. Would she want to carry on with a dishonest man? Her answer was no but she missed him. His relationship with Kimberly could be just a passing phase. Lately, Anna Lisa hadn't seen Paul and Kimberly talking much to each other. Maybe Paul realized he had made a mistake and broke it off with Kimberly. Perhaps he deserved a second chance.

Anna Lisa closed her half-empty suitcase and checked her black leather purse to make sure she hadn't forgotten anything. Picking up her ebony wool sweater and jacket, she pulled her light suitcase down the stairs as the phone rang. It was the cab company informing her that her taxi was waiting outside. She told them she'd be right out and then rolled her suitcase outside of her condo and locked up. The taxi driver, a short hefty man got out of his car and helped her with her luggage.

Half-hour later, she arrived at LAX, paid the driver and rolled her suitcase into the British Airways terminal and stood in the short business-class line. She glanced at the coach class passengers and felt sorry for them. Their line wrapped around four lanes separated by long ropes. Once she checked in her luggage and received her ticket, Anna Lisa started looking for Neil. As she glanced around, she saw his tall figure approach her in black pants and dark gray turtle neck sweater, a matching scarf, a long coat thrown over one arm and a cup of tea in his hand. He looked so English, she thought.

"Hello Leeza."

"Hi, you look like you've been here for awhile."

"I got in 20 minutes ago." He glanced at the security check and noticed there was no line. "I think we should go in before people start to queue up."

Anna Lisa nodded in agreement and the two headed toward the security check.

After two meals, numerous snacks, a movie and visits to the restroom, their flight landed at Heathrow in the early afternoon and Neil's sister, Juliet, greeted her brother and asked Anna Lisa if her flight was comfortable.

"Yes, it was. Thank you for meeting us."

"A pleasure," said Juliet. When she noticed Anna Lisa had only one suitcase, she added, "Where is the rest of your luggage?"

"This is it." she glanced at her suitcase and then at Neil's sister, "I only brought one."

Puzzled, Juliet looked at her brother. "She isn't at all like Sarah. Is she?"

Anna Lisa was embarrassed. She thought she didn't measure up.

"What my sister means is Sarah usually travels with at least four suitcases."

"Should I have brought more things?" she asked with concern. "I only packed for five days."

Juliet smiled. "I have a feeling you and I will get along perfectly well. Would you like to come with us to my parents' for tea before you settle in at the hotel?"

Anna Lisa hesitated for a moment. "Thank you, but no. I'm sure you and Neil have a lot of catching up to do."

"I insist. My parents would love to meet you."

"Yes, you must come," Neil said.

Anna Lisa was tired. Weeks of throwing herself into her work in order to avoid thinking about Paul had taken its toll. All she wanted to do after the 10 hour flight was sleep but she didn't feel right to refuse them. "I'd be happy to meet your parents."

Neil's mother lived an hour away from the airport in the quiet neighborhood of Kingston Vale, southwest of London. Anna Lisa, who had taken the backseat of Juliet's silver Volkswagen Passat so that Neil could sit next to his sister, watched her drive from the left side. She wondered if she would be able to pull it off, had she the chance to drive. Her attention shifted to her surroundings as they neared the house. The pavement was wet from an earlier rain and the cool air coming in through her window smelled fresh and crisp. She saw well-groomed grass, large elms, oak and pine trees and postmodern homes with classically inspired styles. She thought of

Paul as Neil and Juliet talked to each other. How badly she had wanted to take a trip with him somewhere, anywhere, but he had always complained about wanting to save money for their trip to Greece. Now here she was in London and he at home.

"How do you like the scenery, Anna Lisa?" Juliet asked.

"I like it very much. Your neighborhood is beautiful."

"It is peaceful. isn't it? The city is always so crowded. Visitors have taken over and in certain areas it is impossible to walk on the street without bumping into people."

"I wouldn't know. This is my first time in London. Actually, this is my first time anywhere outside of the U.S."

"Really? Then we must show you a nice time so you'll come back."

"I'm afraid Sis, we'll be working the majority of time."

"That's a shame." Juliet looked at Anna Lisa. "You ought to at least take the London Sightseeing Tour. It only lasts an hour and a half and highlights the city's major attractions in London. You can hop in and out wherever you want and catch it again at the next stop."

"I'd love to do that. I hope I get to see a little of your city before I leave."

"I hope so as well," offered Juliet. "Neil, did you remember to ask Sarah to come over?"

"I asked her but I believe she and a friend had a spa appointment and then she was joining her parents for dinner at the Spencers, or was it the Taylors? Anyhow, I shall see her later tonight."

Juliet shrugged. "It's just as well. She never eats anyway."

Anna Lisa noticed the cool tone in Juliet's voice and wondered about the relationship between Sarah and Neil's family.

"Well, here we are," Juliet announced when her car pulled into the driveway of quaint white stucco house dressed with a dark-brown slanted roof and rust brick walls accenting the sides and the bottom half of the structure. It reminded Anna Lisa of the houses she drew in her art class when she was young. All it lacked was a white picket fence but instead there was a semi-circular brick wall and a gray stone pathway which led to the front door. Anna Lisa opened the car door, got out and looked around. All the houses in the neighborhood looked alike – they were what her grandmother would call cookie-cutter homes. But even so, Neil's parents' home was unique to Anna Lisa because unlike most tourists who stayed at a hotel and didn't get a chance to know the residents, she was about to have her first true English experience.

Juliet opened the frosted-glass-paned oak door. There was a stairway that led the way to the upstairs bedrooms. Near the stairway was the living room and a little further down, past a fireplace with a mantel was the dining room which had a doorway that opened into a large kitchen with a rectangular wooden table bordered by two long benches on either side. Charlotte Whittaker's face brightened as soon as she saw her son.

"Hello Mother," Neil gave her a peck on the cheek. "Where is father?"

Charlotte looked at her son with her small light brown eyes. "He'll be in shortly. He went for a stroll."

"I'd like to introduce you to my colleague Anna Lisa from the American office. Anna Lisa this is my mother, Charlotte," said Neil, aware that Anna Lisa did not like anyone to address her as Leeza.

"Very nice to meet you Charlotte," Anna Lisa said, extending her hand to shake hers.

Charlotte Whittaker was tall and slim with short sandy blond hair, coiffed like a football helmet.

"Glad you could make it," Charlotte said to Anna Lisa. "Juliet, tea is ready and I have cheesecake outside."

"Outside?" Juliet cried. "Really mother, you put an entire cheesecake alone with my husband and children?" She walked out into the yard with Anna Lisa following behind her. Luckily, the boys were too busy playing soccer with their father to notice the cake on the table.

The yard was carpeted with grass and bordered by golden form of black locust, Madronas, dove trees, day lilies, fuchsias, and petunias. On the north side, there laid a brick patio, a large round wooden table and eight chairs with taupe cushions.

"Mark, children, come here there's someone I'd like you to meet," Juliet yelled across the yard. Mark and three blond hair and blue-eyed boys ran over and Juliet introduced them: "This is Miss Gibson. She works with Neil at the U.S. office. Anna Lisa, this is my husband, Mark, my sons, Harry, Henry and Thomas."

Mark extended his hand and the children followed suit as each said, "Nice to make your acquaintance, Miss Gibson."

"Thomas is 11, he's my youngest. Henry is 12 and Harry 14," Juliet explained.

"Please call me Anna Lisa. It's nice to meet all of you."

"Will you join us in a game of football?" Thomas asked.

"Sweetheart, Anna Lisa just flew in and is very tired," Juliet said. "Go play with your brothers."

Anna Lisa didn't mind joining them except she had never played football before. She glanced at the ball they were using and noticed the ball resembled a soccer ball. Realizing their football is what the Americans call soccer, she said, "Actually I'd love to play football. Exercise helps get rid of jet lag."

Charlotte watched them play from her kitchen window and remarked to Neil, "She's quiet friendly, isn't she?"

Neil smiled at the irony of the word "friendly." It seemed as if it were only yesterday when the two of them were fighting over a jar of lemon curd. He never thought he'd be friends with Leeza, least of all inviting her to his mother's house. "Yes, she is," he responded, smiling.

"If I didn't know better, I'd say you fancy her."

"Before you allow your imagination run off with you, Mother, she has a longtime boyfriend, and need I remind you that I am to be married soon?"

"Yes, I know," charlotte sighed. "Where is that fiancée of yours anyway?"

"Don't worry Mother, she's not coming. She's off at a spa with her friend."

"Darling, I don't want you to think I don't like her. I do."

He looked at her skeptically.

"I just wish she were friendlier. I always feel like I have to be on my best behavior when I'm around her."

Neil did not wish to discuss Sarah. "C'mon Mum, let's go outside and have tea."

When they walked out and the boys saw Neil, they dragged him into the game. Soon enough Anna Lisa and Neil were competing against each other. After 30 minutes, Neil called a truce because he was tired and wanted to sit and have tea.

"Anna Lisa, you play well for an American," Juliet said.

"Did you say play well?" Harry said, "She massacred us." He looked over at the disappointed look on his uncle's face. "I'm sorry Uncle Neil, but she plays much better than you."

"That's because I get to practice at home," Anna Lisa admitted, "I have five young cousins."

"Ah," said charlotte, "that's how you have developed such great athletic skills."

"Yes, out of necessity," Anna Lisa replied and smiled. She then looked at the man sitting next to Juliet. He looked like an older version of Neil but still quite handsome and fit for his age. He was tall and lean and perhaps in his sixties. His round eyes were dark blue, his nose long and narrow and his salt-and-pepper hair was layered short in front and long in the back.

"Anna Lisa, this is my husband Oliver," said Charlotte.

"Nice meeting you, Oliver. There's a remarkable resemblance between you and your son."

"Yes, we look like brothers, don't we?" Oliver winked.

"You wish." Neil nudged his dad.

They all chuckled.

"So Anna Lisa, what brings you to London?" asked Oliver.

"Work."

"Oh, yes. You're Neil's partner. Neil never mentioned how pretty you are."

"Thank you," Anna Lisa blushed.

"Has my son been treating you well?"

Anna Lisa looked at Neil with an ironic smile. "Yes, very well."

"Good," said Oliver, "because if he gives you any trouble, all you have to do is call me."

"Did you hear that?" Anna Lisa said to Neil.

"Yes I did. I'm afraid my family seems to favor you over their own flesh and blood," Neil answered jokingly.

"C'mon everyone, try my cheesecake and tell me what you think." Charlotte started passing along the slices.

"Whatever you think, tell her you like it," Neil whispered to Anna Lisa. "For my mother doesn't take well to criticism."

"Like mother, like son," Anna Lisa whispered back.

After tea, Neil borrowed his sister's car and took Anna Lisa into London. He drove around Buckingham Palace and Green Park. He then invited her for fish and chips at his favorite pub in the Chelsea district. The pub was dim, had dark red leather chairs and booths and resembled an upscale diner. The menu offered everything from soups and salads to sandwiches to hot dinner entrées.

After their meals arrived, Neil blurted to Anna Lisa, "No, you don't put ketchup on that. You Americans want to put ketchup on everything."

"That's because there's no tartar sauce."

"Here, let me fix it for you." Neil poured vinegar over her fish and fries.

Anna Lisa, who didn't eat fish and chips often, usually had her fish with tartar sauce and her fries with ketchup. "Vinegar?" she cried. "Why would you put vinegar on my fries?"

"Here, try one." He handed her a piece.

She took a small bite skeptically. "Not bad."

"I told you so."

"You always like to be right, don't you?"

"Sorry, force of habit."

"That's okay, I'm the same way myself."

"Try these mint peas." Neil turned his plate so she could reach the peas easily.

Anna Lisa looked at the mashed green peas, tasted them and swallowed against her will. It tasted like mint and peas. What a disgusting combination, she thought.

"How do you like it?"

"It's an acquired taste. I think I'll stick with my whole green peas." She sipped the beer. It was warm but wasn't bad at all, she thought. "Now, this I like. It's tasty."

"So, how did you learn to speak French so well?"

"My grandmother sent me to Lycée; it's a French school not far from where we work. And when I was in college, I double majored in French and finance," she said. "And what about you? You speak so many different languages."

"Most Europeans speak at least two languages," he commented. "When I was a child, my parents told me I shouldn't expect everyone to speak English. So, I learned other languages."

"Exactly how many languages do you speak besides English?"

"Five," he said, "French, Italian, German, Spanish and Japanese." He took a forkful of fish.

"Japanese? You know how to speak Japanese?"

"Yes, I had to learn it. Our London office has many Japanese clients."

"I thought most Japanese speak English." She put a fry in her mouth.

"Many do, but not all," replied Neil, adding, "one is more likely to get an account when one speaks the client's mother tongue."

"But isn't it hard to learn so many?"

"Not really. Once you learn French, Spanish becomes easy and once you learn Spanish, Italian becomes even easier. But German, now that's a little more difficult. The verbs come at the end of sentences."

"How do you remember all these languages? Don't you sometimes mix them up?"

"I'm not as fluent as you are in French but I get by. And yes, sometimes I do mix them up."

"I still think it's incredible that you can speak so many languages." She took a sip of her beer.

"Not at all. I have always thought when you truly want something, all you need to do is go after it and keep trying until you get it."

"Even when it relates to a relationship between a man and a woman?"

"Yes, it applies to all situations. If you desire someone enough and you're certain the two of you belong together, you go after the object of your affection and never give up."

Anna Lisa disagreed with him in regard to relationships but didn't comment. Instead, she took another bite of her vinegar-laced fish. As odd as it seemed, it actually tasted good to her. She then looked at Neil's plate. He was almost done with his meal. She decided to let Neil talk while she enjoyed her dinner. As she listened, she also watched the people who came in with their friends and eavesdropped on their conversations. She loved the different expressions they used such as "They were having it off in the bedroom" or "I bought new bottoms" or "Rubbish!"

When Anna Lisa was finished with her meal, Neil drove her to her hotel. A nicely suited doorman opened the passenger door. Anna Lisa got out and Neil unlocked the trunk of his sister's car so that the bellhop could take her luggage.

"Till tomorrow then," Neil said to Anna Lisa.

"Thank you for dinner."

"My pleasure," he nodded before getting into his car and riding away.

Anna Lisa followed the bellhop into a taupe marble lobby furnished with elegant traditional furniture. She registered at the reception desk and took the elevator to the 10th floor. The bellhop who was already there unloading her suitcase on a luggage carriage greeted her once again. She tipped him and he wished her a pleasant stay before leaving her room.

Anna Lisa glanced around her. The sizable room overlooked a quiet street and was decorated with a blend of antique furniture – a gilt mirror, Queen Anne chair, vanity table and Victorian sofa. It had two comfortable-looking double beds, plenty of closet space and a spacious bathroom with luxury toiletries. She sat on one of the beds and realized how tired she was. Removing her shoes, Anna Lisa decided to lie down and close her eyes for a few minutes before washing up. But she never made it to the bathroom. She fell asleep and never once budged.

The next day and the two that followed, Neil and Anna Lisa had been to so many stores in London that their feet were burning. The two were barely able to move as they sat in the indoor food court of a department store and sipped on their cappuccinos. The large stand in the center of the court carried everything from roasted chicken to seafood to scones and pastries. More kiosks selling pizza on toasted bagels, bottled water, shakes and cappuccinos were scattered throughout the court.

"This is entirely your fault, you know," Neil said to Anna Lisa.

"My fault that your feet have blisters on them?"

"Yes, of course. If we had driven the company car as I had suggested, we wouldn't have been so tired. But no, you had to take the tube everywhere. I have never climbed so many stairs in my entire life."

"Well, I'm only here for five days and I thought I could get to know London a little better," she said, "and at the same time check out the packaging on different products."

"Please do tell how you are planning to carry these sample packages and the souvenirs you bought back to your hotel?"

"You will help me," she said. Seeing his frown, she added, "You're such a wimp. We'll take a taxi back."

"No, I wouldn't want to be a wimp. We'll take the tube back."

Actually Anna Lisa was tired and wished she had not called him a wimp, because now they had a long walk before getting to the underground and then there were all those stairs they had to take up and down when they changed cars. She simply didn't have the energy. "Fine, I admit it. I'm tired, too. In fact, I've surpassed tired. Sorry about your blisters but those are you own fault."

"My fault?"

"Well, yes. I asked if you wanted to buy a pair of sneakers but you refused."

"Gym shoes do not coordinate well with my Italian suit."

"Then you should've dressed more casually."

"This is how I always dress."

"Perhaps you should rethink your wardrobe."

"I'm too tired to argue with you," he said with a wave of his hand. "I want to enjoy my cappuccino in peace before I meet my in-laws for dinner."

The two sat back without speaking. They seemed like old buddies who were utterly at peace sitting next to each other without exchanging words. Their silence was interrupted as they both looked over. It was Sarah.

"Hello Neil, Anna Lisa, fancy meeting the two of you here," Sarah said holding a cup of tea with one hand and a garment bag with the other. She was looking for a seat when she ran into Neil and Anna Lisa by accident.

Neil didn't seem surprised as he got up and pulled out a chair for her. "Hello darling. Is that a new outfit I see in your hand?"

Sarah set her cup down on the table, draped her garment bag over an empty chair and took a seat next to Anna Lisa. "I needed an outfit for tonight. You are coming to my parents, aren't you?"

"If only my legs would move."

"Neil, you promised."

"Don't worry. I'll be there."

"And you too Anna Lisa, you must come." When Anna Lisa looked surprised, Sarah said to Neil, "You did ask her, didn't you? Darling really, I asked you days ago to bring Anna Lisa as well."

Neil smiled. He knew how tired Anna Lisa was and if he were to suffer, by God she should too. "I'm sure Anna Lisa would love to come."

Anna Lisa gave him a cross look. "Actually, I'm planning to go back to my hotel and soak my tired feet. But I thank you for the invitation."

"Neil, can't you persuade her to come? Mummy and Daddy will be so disappointed."

Anna Lisa interrupted Neil before he could answer. "I'm sure the two of you would like to have time alone and, as for me, I should try to call my boyfriend tonight," she lied.

"Then tomorrow, you shall have dinner with us and I will not let you back down."

Against her wishes, Anna Lisa agreed. It wasn't that she didn't like Sarah, but she was uncomfortable around her. Sarah was so full of ceremony and Anna Lisa had a casual personality. Besides, she didn't own a couture dress nor was she in the mood to go shopping just to please Sarah and her family. Yet, she owed it to Neil. After all, he and his family had been so kind to her. It was the least she could do.

When they left the department store, Sarah offered Anna Lisa a ride in her white Mercedes and dropped her in front of her hotel. Neil got out and moved from the back seat to the front.

"Thank you for the ride," Anna Lisa told Sarah.

"We'll see you tomorrow then." Sarah gave her a fake smile.

"Yes, tomorrow. Enjoy your dinner with Neil and your parents," Anna Lisa replied and walked away.

After Anna Lisa got back to her room, she threw herself on her bed and felt right at home. The traditional-looking furniture reminded Anna Lisa of her grandmother's house. And the large bathtub invited her over to relax for a good hour. She wanted to go downstairs and have dinner at the restaurant but felt uncomfortable eating dinner alone and ordered room service instead. As she waited for her dinner to arrive, she wrote a thank-you note to Neil's family for having her for tea and left a message for Neil at his apartment to let him know she was starting her day late the next day.

She relaxed on her bed and almost fell asleep when she heard a knock on the door.

"Yes?"

"Room service."

Dressed in a plush cream terrycloth robe with a towel wrapped around her head, she opened the door.

"Good evening," said the elegantly uniformed man as he set a tray down on a table.

"Thank you." She signed the bill and tipped him before he left. His dark eyes, his black hair tied back in a ponytail and the way he moved reminded Anna Lisa of Paul.

Wondering about what Paul was doing at the moment, she removed the lid on her club salad and started eating. Even though she missed him, she did not want to call him. If only she could see him without being seen or if she could hear his voice without being heard, she would be satisfied. He was a drug and she was the addict.

She turned on the television set and watched the news while eating. When finished, Anna Lisa prepared for bed, turned her lights out but couldn't fall asleep. At midnight, she called her grandmother. It was 4 in the afternoon in Los Angeles and her grandma was baby-sitting Joanne's daughter, Sam. Anna Lisa told her grandmother about how great London was and that they should take a trip together someday. She then tried to call Paul several times, but each time before the call could go through, she hung up. She decided that she would talk to him in person when she got back. Once again, Anna Lisa turned the lights out and after a long period of tossing and turning, she dozed off.

Wanting to make the most of her short time in London, Anna Lisa got up early the following day. She breakfasted at the hotel's restaurant which overlooked the beautiful Thames River. The polite waitress brought her fresh hot biscuits with lemon curd and tea with milk. The day was gray but she was not. Looking forward to being on her own, Anna Lisa took the London sightseeing tour aboard the red double-decker bus after her meal. The bus stopped at various locations and she got off at Westminster Abbey, the Houses of Parliament and Big Ben, but for the majority of the ride, she stayed on the bus as the commentator described the points of interest. Before she knew it, it was half past noon and she had to meet Neil at one. Running late, she took a taxi that dropped her off in front of a modern-looking glass-and-steel business building. She walked through a revolving door and found herself in front of a security officer. He asked for her I.D., where she was going and told her to sign in. He then checked his guest list to assure himself she was on it.

"Miss Gibson, this elevator will lead you to the 15th floor," said the security guard as he escorted her and used his pass card and a code to activate the elevator. In minutes, Anna Lisa found herself on the desired floor in front of a receptionist.

"May I help you?" said the well-groomed young woman behind a mint crescent-shaped marble table.

"My name is Anna Lisa Gibson, and I'm here to see Mr. Whittaker."

"I'll let him know you're here."

Anna Lisa sat on a comfortable black leather chair, opened her London guide and looked to see where to visit the next day. She highlighted Kensington Palace and the gardens.

"Hello Leeza, did you sleep well?" Neil interrupted her.

"Hi, yes I did, thank you."

"I take it you went sightseeing this morning."

"Yes, I did. How did you know?"

"I came by this morning to pick you up and they said you had already left."

"Didn't you get the message I left you last night?"

"Yes, I did. I thought I could show you around London for a few hours but I see you beat me to it," Neil said.

"I took the sightseeing tour your sister had suggested."

"You are quite the independent, aren't you? You seem not to need anyone."

"That's not true. Had I known you were coming, I would have waited."

"Well," he said in disappointment, "come, I'll show you around the office and introduce you to some of the people who work here."

To her surprise, the entire floor which was covered with silver-gray carpet had a contemporary and open-space atmosphere. She noticed the executive offices were made of clear glass and lacked privacy. The center of the room was furnished with black-laminated desks and leather chairs belonging to the subordinates and assistants. There were no cubicles. Vivid and modern geometrical paintings covered the white walls and added color.

Neil took her over to the offices of two of the partners who happened to be the company founders they worked for – Phil Howard and Shannon Brown. Both were pleased to meet her and said her reputation preceded her. She had a chance to meet the creative department and glanced through the impressive portfolio of the designs they had done for famous companies. She was told some of those companies were Neil's clients and Anna Lisa got to see the articles written about him in the British business magazines. His co-workers raved about him and said Neil was a celebrity. He had been interviewed on television numerous times and had won many advertising awards. By the end of her visit, Anna Lisa was too embarrassed to look Neil in the eyes.

"Something wrong?" Neil asked Anna Lisa when he noticed her staring blankly out of the window of his car.

At first Anna Lisa did not hear him but when she heard her name a second time, she said, "I'm sorry, did you say something?"

"I asked if you were alright."

"Yes, why?"

"You haven't said a word since we left the office."

"I was just thinking about how I've misjudged you," she confessed. "I thought I was so much better than you. But I realized today how little I know in comparison to you."

Neil looked at her for a while before he spoke. "On the contrary, I think you are quiet intelligent. You have your area of expertise, and I have mine."

"I'm a control freak. I need to have the last word even if I'm wrong."

"You don't think I'm that way? I was forced on you by the partners," he admitted. "I stepped in and expected you to hand me the reins to your client. I would've reacted the same had our situations been reversed."

"You would have?" Anna Lisa asked in surprise.

"Yes, of course. You and I are a lot alike," he said, "We're both sure of ourselves. I'll bet most people think us arrogant. Perhaps that's why we're always fighting."

"I am truly sorry for being mean to you."

"Don't worry about it, it's all in the past. We're friends now."

"In that case, my friend, please advise me as to what to wear to your fiancée's dinner. I've been nervous ever since she invited me."

"Wear what you like."

"But I really need your help. Sarah has impeccable taste and since your future in-laws are going to be there, I would like to make a favorable impression."

"Anna Lisa, you have nothing to worry about. Didn't you pack a dinner dress before you left?"

"Yes, the green dress I wore to the Simons'."

He remembered how beautiful she had looked that night. Her hair, now in a ponytail, had been loose and sexy. Her skin, hidden underneath a pink sweater had been smooth and glowing. "Wear that, then."

"You're sure you're not just saying that to make me feel better?"

"You have my word. Now, let me show you the British Museum before I take you back to your hotel."

"Drive on because now I'm in the mood to agree with whatever you have in mind."

What he had in mind was to frolic with her in bed for the rest of the afternoon. He was glad she wasn't able to read his thoughts as he smiled.

"What are you smiling about?"

"Nothing."

"C'mon, share."

I'm smiling about what it feels like to seduce you, he thought.

"I'm just in good spirits."

"Me too," she said, leaning back and enjoying the scenery.

"Two women...Very jealous of you. Be careful."

After visiting the museum and before meeting Neil's in-laws, Anna Lisa got ready at her hotel and took a cab over to a restaurant located inside a hotel in the Westside. The silver-haired doorman opened the taxi door. She got out, thanked him and walked toward the glass front entrance and into the art-deco lobby with dark purple and white marble floors, plush chairs and beautifully designed tables. She looked around, found the restaurant and went in.

The maitre d', a distinguished older gentleman, approached her. "Good evening, may I help you?"

"Hello, I'm supposed to meet my party here," Anna Lisa said and looked at her gold watch. It was 8:10. She was 10 minutes late.

"Which surname is the reservation under?"

"Weston," she replied as she looked around the dining room with chandeliers that dangled like inverted wedding cakes. "I think I see them over there," Anna Lisa said, pointing toward the table where Neil, Sarah and her parents were seated.

"Please follow me." The maitre d' told her and guided her through a series of large round tables covered with white linen and eggplant-hued chairs adorned by black-brown wood. When she reached the table, Neil got up and greeted her in his navy hand-stitched suit. The maitre d' pulled out a chair for her between Sarah's father and Neil. Anna Lisa sat down.

Sarah said, "Hello, Anna Lisa. Did you have any trouble finding us?"

"No, it was rather easy."

"I'd like you to meet my father, Barkley, and my mother, Camellia."

"Nice to meet you both," Anna Lisa said.

Barkley's eyes glinted as he looked over Anna Lisa. Camellia, a carbon copy of Sarah thanks to plastic surgery, didn't appreciate his excitement. She was slim with layered shoulder-length blond hair and bangs. Her green eyes widened as she said with a voice filled with superiority, "So, my daughter tells me you work with Neil at the American office."

"Yes I do." Anna Lisa responded.

A waiter came over, handed Anna Lisa a menu and asked her if she wanted something to drink.

"Try the merlot," Camellia offered. "It is exquisite."

Anna Lisa looked at the opened bottle of wine wrapped in white linen. "I think I will."

The waiter served her a glass and left.

"I suppose I should have a look at the menu," Anna Lisa said.

"There is no hurry," Neil replied. "Enjoy your wine."

Barkley glanced at Anna Lisa's breasts, looked up and uttered, "Actually I'm rather hungry and would like to order soon."

He was a short stocky man with a pink complexion. He reminded Anna Lisa of a pig except that she liked pigs but wasn't sure of her feelings toward Barkley. She opened her menu and noticed that the cuisine was European.

"Darling, you never told me how your day went," Sarah said to Neil.

"I met Anna Lisa at Howard Brown, introduced her to Phil and Shannon and gave her a tour of the office. Then we left and headed toward the British museum."

"Oh," Sarah said with a pinch in her voice. She didn't take well to Neil spending so much time with Anna Lisa. "Anna Lisa, did you enjoy the museum?"

Anna Lisa, who was still looking at the menu, looked up. "I did. Although, it was impossible to see everything in one visit, I particularly enjoyed the Parthenon sculptures on the first floor."

"May I make a suggestion?" Camellia asked when she noticed Anna Lisa looking back at her menu.

"Please," replied Anna Lisa.

"You should try the filet of monkfish on a bed of herb risotto. It is exquisite."

Anna Lisa decided to take Camellia's suggestion. After all, Camellia had probably eaten there before and was better acquainted with the dishes. "Why not?"

"Excellent," said Camellia and waived at the waiter. The waiter came over to take their orders.

"Two orders of baby sea bass with caviar sauce for me and my daughter, our guest will have the monkfish wrapped in Parma ham, stuffed leg of wild rabbit for my husband and Neil will have…"

"I believe I can order for myself, Camellia. Thank you," Neil interrupted her.

"Well," Camellia said touching the collar of her pale green Chanel suit, "I was simply trying to…"

"I shall have the Scottish baby lobster in lime butter," Neil told the waiter with authority. There was no way that he was going to let his mother-in-law make his decision for him.

"As you wish sir," the waiter said and left.

Anna Lisa looked at Neil's face. His lips were compressed, and she could tell he was mad.

Sarah said to Anna Lisa, "I hear you're going back to Los Angeles tomorrow."

"Unfortunately, yes. My time here went by so quickly. I hope to come back someday for a longer visit."

"And you shall," Sarah offered putting her delicate hand on her fiancé's arm as though she were marking her territory. "Neil and I will be married by then and you may visit us at our country home."

Neil passed Sarah a baffled look. "We don't have a house in the country."

"We don't have one now, but we shall once we get married."

He sighed in frustration.

"You may have anything you want, Pudding," Barkley told his daughter.

"Thank you, Daddy." She had on a simple red dress and as she got up to go powder her nose, she made heads turn. "Will you join me?" Sarah said to Anna Lisa.

Anna Lisa didn't need to but out of politeness got up and followed her.

"Are you still with what's his name?" Sarah asked once they were in the ladies lounge.

"You mean Paul? Yes, we're still together," Anna Lisa lied.

"I thought Neil and I saw him with what's-her-name at the movies."

"You mean Kimberly. Kimberly and Paul are friends," replied Anna Lisa, "I had plans that night, and I asked him to take her instead."

"You are brave, aren't you?" She took out a red lipstick out of her small black purse, uncapped it and rolled it out.

"What do you mean?"

She put on her lipstick, smacked her lips together and with her finger cleaned any leftover smudge around the edges of her mouth. "My mother once told me the reason men cheat is always a woman's fault. A woman needs to tighten the leash on her man."

"What makes you think Paul is cheating on me?"

"Perhaps he is and perhaps he is not, but Paul is not my concern. Neil is." Sarah started primping her hair and admiring herself in the mirror.

Perplexed about the topic of their conversation, Anna Lisa stared at Sarah. "I don't understand."

"I want you to stay away from my fiancé."

"What're you talking about?"

"You know precisely what I mean. He belongs to me and I will do anything, and I mean anything, to keep him."

"I think this conversation is over," Anna Lisa said walking out. "Crazy girl," she mumbled under her breath as she reached her table.

Neil did not miss the sudden change in Anna Lisa's composure when he asked if she was alright.

"I've got a small headache. Perhaps the jet lag is finally catching up with me."

Neil was about to ask her if she wanted him to take her home when Camellia interrupted him.

"So Anna Lisa, what do your parents do for a living?"

"My parents passed away soon after I was born."

"I'm sorry to hear that. What happened?"

"They died in a car accident. They were only 18."

At this point Sarah came back to the table and took her seat.

Barkley, who was sitting right next to Anna Lisa, slid his hand on her leg.

Anna Lisa's eyes widened and when she got over the shock, she pinched him hard. He let out a low screeching sound that only Anna Lisa heard or at least that's what she thought as he quickly removed his hand.

Camellia carried on with her inquisition: "What? Eighteen and they already had you?"

"Yes, well, they were young and in love."

"Who raised you, dear?"

"My grandmother and my two aunts."

"And what sort of work does you grandmother do?"

"She was a psychologist. She has now retired."

"I see," said Camellia, exchanging glances with Sarah. "It's a pity you have to work. I always tell my Sarah, work is a man's job."

Neil looked embarrassed and shifted in his seat.

Fortunately, the waiter came over and served their dinners.

But the silence only lasted a short period when Camellia said, "Anna Lisa, how do like your dinner?"

"I like it but I must say nothing beats the fish and chips and the warm beer I had the other night with Neil, isn't that so, Neil?" Anna Lisa said knowing that she was hitting two targets with one arrow.

Camellia choked on her expensive wine.

Sarah grinded her teeth when she heard Neil made time to have dinner with Anna Lisa.

Barkley, too afraid to look up, kept on stuffing his face with his stuffed leg of wild rabbit.

"Yes, that pub does make a great fish and chips," Neil said, knowing this would aggravate Camellia but figured she deserved it after treating Leeza with such bad manners.

The rest of the evening continued in the same pattern. Camellia asked Anna Lisa a question and then found a way to patronize her, Barkley ate incessantly, Sarah exchanged derisive glances with her mother and Neil tried to change the subject whenever possible to take the focus away from Anna Lisa. When dinner finally came to an end, Anna Lisa was never happier to leave such a dysfunctional family. It was obvious that the Westons thrived on putting others down and she wondered what Neil ever saw in Sarah besides her beauty.

"We'll give you a ride back," Neil said to Anna Lisa as he handed her her shawl.

"Thank you, but I think I'll take a taxi."

"Come, I insist," Neil said.

The Westons did not say anything.

Sarah kept quiet and hoped that Anna Lisa would take a taxi.

"No really, I'll be fine," Anna Lisa replied adamantly, got into a cab and left.

"You could've said something," Neil told Sarah when Anna Lisa was gone.

"You heard her, she preferred to take a taxi. What was I supposed to do about it?"

"Really Neil, you worry too much about that girl," Camellia remarked. "She's perfectly capable of taking care of herself."

"Yes, that's what I say," Barkley finally said to agree with his wife as he always did.

Neil didn't say anything but was truly disappointed about the way they had treated Anna Lisa.

"Come along darling," Sarah said to Neil when she noticed him hesitating to get into her father's dark blue Aston Martin. Neil reluctantly got in and Barkley drove away.

Anna Lisa felt sorry for Neil. What a family he was marrying into! But she had no right to interfere. She was surprised about his inability to see them for who they were. Then again, she was not one to talk. She was still in love with a man who cheated on her. As these thoughts occupied her mind, she packed her suitcase. It was her last day in London before going home that night. Neil was staying behind for a few more days. He wanted to spend time with Sarah and his family.

After packing, Anna Lisa checked out and left her bags with the concierge to pick up later before leaving for Heathrow. Once again, she breakfasted at her favorite restaurant at her hotel wishing she had more time to sit and look outside at the Thames while sipping her Darjeeling tea. The sky was clear, the sun was peeking out and the water looked tame. Her plan was to visit Kensington Palace and later walk around the breathtaking grounds she had heard so much about. She hadn't decided what she wanted to do in the afternoon. As she signed for her bill, a familiar voice said, "Hello Leeza."

She looked up and saw Neil. "What're you doing here?"

"I thought I'd catch you before you set out on your tour of the city," said Neil. "Dinner was a disaster last night. I'm truly sorry about the Westons. They can be such a – well, nevermind. What is your agenda for the day?"

"I'm visiting Kensington Palace and the gardens. I'm not sure what I'll be doing in the afternoon."

"Then would you like to join me for lunch and play at the Open-Air Theater in Regent's Park? We can eat at the theater bar before the performance."

Anna Lisa recognized the name. Earlier she was looking at her guide to see which subway exit she needed to take for Kensington Palace and she had noticed the Open-air Theater was only a few exits away.

"What sort of play?" Anna Lisa asked, surprised at his hospitality.

"To be or not to be, that is the question."

"One of my favorites – *Hamlet*. But, what about Sarah?"

"I'll be spending the next four days with her. I don't think she would mind sparing me for an afternoon."

In fact, Sarah would mind very much, Anna Lisa thought. "I'll catch the subway near Kensington Palace and meet you there. That way I can save a little time."

"How does one o'clock sound?"

"Perfect," she said and got up.

"Oh, I almost forgot. This is for you."

Anna Lisa looked at the square box in his hand. "What is it?"

"Why don't you open it?" He handed her the box.

She took it, removed the lid and found a jar of lemon curd. Her face brightened as she smiled. "This is very thoughtful. Thank you."

"My mother made it and wanted you to have it."

"I can't wait to try it. Will you thank your mom on my behalf?"

"I shall."

The two headed out of the restaurant. Anna Lisa gave the box to the concierge and asked him to take care of it for her. She then walked outside with Neil.

"I shall see you later." Neil started walking away.

"Oh, Neil?"

He turned. "Yes?"

"I overheard one of the assistants telling someone on the phone that you were in charge of fundraising for charitable organizations."

"Yes, I take different causes and raise funds for them. Last year, I was able to raise 30,000 pounds for a cancer foundation," he said proudly, "but this year I've done nothing because I was in America. Why do you ask?"

"I was wondering if you could help Brother O'Malley's youth foundation. I would do it myself except I don't even know where to start. I have no experience in that area."

"Well, it's too late in the year. I usually like to start planning at the beginning of the year," he replied. But when he saw the disappointed look on Anna Lisa's face, he added, "Perhaps I can do something on a smaller scale."

"Every little bit counts."

"Very well then, I'll get started on it right away."

"Thank you." She was so happy that she wanted to kiss him.

"Don't thank me yet. I haven't done anything. I'll see you this afternoon."

THIRTEEN

Resting in business class, Anna Lisa gazed out the window at the heavy smog that hovered over Los Angeles. After having a light lunch at the quaint outdoor café of the Open-air Theater in London followed by a great performance of hamlet, Neil had given her a ride to her hotel so she could pick up her luggage and then he had taken her to the airport. Anna Lisa reflected on all that had passed during her London stay. Meeting two British families, getting a glimpse of English life, carrying home plenty of information to help launch the Olson products, getting to know Neil better and receiving his help to raise money for the youth foundation. She had had a pleasant time in London but now was heading home to face Paul and Kimberly at work. She felt a profound sadness as she heard the final beep of the seat belt sign and the captain's announcement over the intercom.

"Ladies and gentlemen, this is your captain speaking. We'll be arriving shortly at Los Angeles International Airport. The temperature is about 25.6 degrees Celsius. That is 78 degrees Fahrenheit and …."

So typical of L.A. to have such a ridiculously warm temperature when the month of May hadn't even ended yet, Anna Lisa thought. She checked to make sure her belt was fastened and her seat was all the way up. She passed one last look out the window as her mind wandered off toward her relationship with Paul. What if he was over Kimberly and wanted to come back to her? Would she accept him after all that had happened? She missed him – of that she was certain but would she be able forgive him? She didn't know. As her plane landed on the runway of LAX, she was filled with a sense of dread and anxiety. Anna Lisa got off with the rest of the passengers, picked up her luggage and took a cab to her condo.

There were three messages on her phone when she got home. She played them. All three were from Leila to please call because she needed to speak with her. Anna Lisa got worried thinking something was wrong with Leila or her family. She picked up her receiver to phone her when the doorbell rang. It was Leila.

"Are you okay?" Anna Lisa asked when she opened the door. As worn-out as she was, she didn't fail to notice Leila's distressed countenance.

"Shouldn't I be the one asking you that question?" Leila responded pushing her way in. She knew Anna Lisa's flight was arriving today but wasn't sure about the time and since her friend hadn't responded to her messages, she had decided to stop by.

"What're you talking about?" She closed the door and stared at Leila.

"Then you haven't heard about Paul and Kimberly."

"If you mean they were seeing each other, I already know." She started walking into the kitchen to get a glass of water.

Her friend followed her. "Were seeing each other? They're still together."

She turned to face Leila. Her face was grim and she forgot all about her thirst.

"Why didn't you tell me about them?" Leila asked with concern.

Anna Lisa sighed. "Sit. Let me pour you a glass of port and I'll tell you all about it."

She took out a bottle from one of the cabinets and poured some into two small crystal glasses. She then went to the kitchen table, set the glasses down and explained all that had happened before she left for London.

Leila kept slapping her hand and repeating, "I don't believe it."

"Believe it, it's all true," Anna Lisa confirmed nodding her head.

"Why didn't you let me know sooner? I thought I was your best friend." Leila frowned.

"You are my best friend, but you also have a big mouth." She swigged her liquor to calm her nerves. "I didn't want the entire office finding out about my personal life."

"You don't trust me." Leila looked at Anna Lisa straight in the eyes.

"It's not that," she tilted her chair, reaching for the port sitting on the counter behind her and pouring more into their glasses, "You just can't keep a secret. You know that."

"You're right, you're right, me and big mouth," Leila admitted. "But everybody at the office knows."

"How?" She wondered if Kimberly had anything to do with it.

Leila lowered her eyes and circled the edge of her glass with her finger as she contemplated telling her friend. It tormented her to hurt Anna Lisa but she had to prepare her for tomorrow. "Paul and Kimberly drive to work together, lunch together and leave together. It's like they're inseparable."

Tears welled in Anna Lisa's eyes, and she tried not to blink. A sharp pain radiated through her chest and her head began to pound forcing her to close her eyes. Ever since her breakup with Paul five weeks ago, Anna Lisa had been living in denial and now reality was starting to hit home. She was about to have a breakdown she couldn't afford. Too many people at work were depending on her and Anna Lisa simply couldn't allow herself to fall apart.

"You are not well," Leila remarked when she noticed the agony on her friend's face.

Anna Lisa did not answer.

"I shouldn't have come."

"I'm fine," She finally replied, "I wish I could say the same for my head. Would you please get me a bottle of water from the fridge and two aspirins from my purse?"

"But you just had a drink. I don't think it's a good idea to combine pills with..."

"Please," Anna Lisa uttered forcefully.

Leila walked toward the fridge and took out a bottle of water and gave it to Anna Lisa. "Where's your purse?"

"In the living room."

She came back with the aspirins and Anna Lisa took them.

"I'm sorry," Leila said, gently holding her friend's hand. "I just thought you should know before you come in the office tomorrow."

"No, you did the right thing," she responded with a shaky voice. "Now, if you don't mind, I'd like to be alone."

Leila left feeling terrible about injuring her friend. But she had to tell her. She couldn't let Anna Lisa show up to work without knowing.

"I see changes. Many changes. I don't know. Maybe new job."

Once again Anna Lisa pushed her feelings away as she lay in the dark on the sofa of her living room for a long time, wondering what she should do. She called her Aunt Kate.

"Darling I told you that Paul wasn't good for you long ago."

"Is Steven still looking for an account supervisor?" The last time Anna Lisa had seen him was a year ago at her Grandmother's house. Steven Langley was Kate's brother-in-law and Anna Lisa's old boss. Anna Lisa got her first job because her uncle had recommended her to Steven. She had started in research and in a year worked her way to assistant account executive and later to account executive. Steven who was then an account supervisor was now the marketing director at Hamilton International Inc., an international marketing firm.

"I think so. He always asks about you when we talk on the phone and still wants you on his marketing team. I'll call him and see if I can set up an interview for tomorrow."

"Tomorrow? No, that's too soon."

Her aunt noticed Anna Lisa's frantic tone. "I tell you what; I haven't seen Steven in a long time. Let's all do an early lunch, say about 11 and then you won't be so nervous."

"You do understand I can't leave my current position until my assignment is over."

"Not a problem. Steven will wait for you. He really wants to steal you away from Howard Brown."

"I'll see you tomorrow at 11:00, then. Thanks Aunt Kate, you have no idea what this means to me," Anna Lisa answered with a voice full of appreciation and pain. "For the past five weeks my life has been hell. I kept thinking Paul and I could work it out. Now I know that's not possible...I...I don't know what I would do if you weren't here to help. You're my savior." She then stopped talking because she felt a lump forming in her throat and knew she was about to cry.

"Darling, you're not the first person to fall in love at work and you won't be the last. It happens. What's important is when a relationship goes wrong, you need to move on. You're doing the right thing."

"Aunt Kate," said Anna Lisa pausing a moment. "I don't want anyone to know about this until I have finalized my project. Even then, I want to be the one who speaks to Simon."

"I know how important Simon and the Olson project are to you. Don't worry, mum's the word," replied her aunt and meant it.

The following day, Anna Lisa called her office and left a message for Simon telling him she was jet-lagged and wouldn't arrive in the office until early afternoon. In her favorite peach suit, which minimized her wide hips and made her look five pounds thinner, she left home to meet her aunt and Steven Langley for lunch at a hotel in Beverly Hills. When Anna Lisa arrived, the valet parked her car and she walked up a red carpet before reaching the front entrance. Inside, she saw an inverted cone-shaped crystal chandelier, avocado green carpet and plush pink chairs. She noticed singer Rod Stewart coming out of the restaurant as she was going in. The maitre d', a bald older gentleman, greeted her with his Italian accent.

"May I help you, Miss?" he asked.

"I'm with the Langley party of three."

"You must be Anna Lisa," he stated but when he saw the look of surprise on her face he added, "They told me to keep an eye out for you. I'll show you to your table."

Anna Lisa followed him through the front bar and into the dining room brightened by spotlights and a large French window. Dark-green velvet booths encircled tables covered with pink tablecloths, each topped with a mixture of fresh white flowers. The Maitre d' stopped at the Langley table and pulled out a chair for Anna Lisa. Steven shook hands with her. Anna Lisa kissed her Aunt Kate on the cheek and sat down.

"I didn't pay attention before but you look a lot like your aunt," observed Steven as he looked from Kate to Anna Lisa. He was a tall 60-year-old with black hair, a square face, a large mouth and droopy cheeks. He looked more like cartoon character than a marketing director.

Anna Lisa eyed her aunt, thinking how affable and feminine she appeared in her pale-pink knit dress. A portion of her straight golden brown hair was pulled back with a simple hair clip. The eyelids of her hazel eyes were accented by mauve eye-shadow and smoky brown eyeliner. "Yes people often tell us we look like sisters," Anna Lisa admitted.

An attractive blond waiter came over, handed everyone a menu and asked Anna Lisa if she wanted something to drink.

"I'll have a sparkling water, please."

The waiter nodded and left.

"Let's have a look at our menus," Steven said, "and then we can get down to business.

They all looked through the menu which featured California cuisine. After a few minutes, Anna Lisa decided on the jumbo shrimp over stir-fried rice vermicelli, Kate wanted the grilled Alaskan halibut with grilled vegetables and Steven went for veal with mashed potatoes and roasted corn sauce.

Steven turned to Anna Lisa and said, "I was very excited when I heard you were thinking about working for us."

"Me too," Anna Lisa replied.

"Your Aunt tells me you're fluent in French."

"Yes, I am and in English as well," Anna Lisa said jokingly, and they all laughed.

"Most of our correspondence is international and we can definitely use you."

"I've put together a portfolio of the accounts I've been working on for the past five years and brought a résumé." She handed him her portfolio.

"It's really not necessary. I am familiar with your work," he said, "but since you have it with you, I'll have a look."

The waiter returned with Anna Lisa's drink. "Is everyone ready to order or would you like a few more minutes?"

"No, we're ready," Steven said.

The waiter wrote down their orders.

Steven opened Anna Lisa's portfolio to study her résumé and the advertisements she had worked on. Anna Lisa mouthed the words thank you to her aunt. Kate smiled and winked at her. Then the two glanced at Aaron Spelling who was sitting with a group of people at one of the booths. To his right, at another table were Gwyneth Paltrow and a guest.

After awhile, Steven closed the portfolio and looked up. "I like what I see. You seem to have a lot more experience than when you last worked for me," he remarked. "You were a good account executive then but you're probably a better one now."

"Thank you," Anna Lisa replied.

"I would like to hire you as an account supervisor."

She felt a pang of excitement and anxiety at the pit of her stomach. "Will I be the only account supervisor?"

"No. Besides you, there are two more managers."

"How many people would I be managing?" Anna Lisa asked.

"You'll be supervising three account executives. As you well know, you'll be less involved in day to day business of the client and more involved in campaign strategy. Do you think you can handle it?"

"I can handle it, but what kind of salary are we talking about?"

"I thought you might ask," Steven said. "That's why I brought a package with me." He gave Anna Lisa a black folder.

Anna Lisa opened it and glanced through. She would be earning 25 percent more than what she was making at Howard Brown. She would have a matching 401K plan, stock options and bonuses tied into the company's earnings. Her vacation time which was three weeks at Howard Brown would be doubled to six, but she knew with the kind of workload Steven was planning to give her, she wouldn't be able to use all of her vacation time. She closed the folder, looked up and smiled.

"I hope that smile means you're pleased with my company's offer."

"Yes, I am."

"Excellent. How soon can you start?" he asked, pressing her.

Suddenly, Anna Lisa felt too scared to trade her job, a great boss like Simon and the staff that she knew so well for a boss who had a temper and a company with which she was not familiar. Was she doing the right thing, giving up all that she loved because of a deceiving boyfriend? Yet if she stayed, she couldn't bear the idea of looking at Paul and Kimberly day in and day out. No, the only alternative was to get out while she could in order to save her own sanity. She glanced at her aunt. "As I told my aunt, I have to finish an important assignment before I leave."

"And when will that be?"

The waiter came over and served their meal.

"Everything looks so delicious," Kate commented.

"It sure does," replied Anna Lisa.

They started eating and after a couple of bites, Steven said, "You haven't answered my question, Anna Lisa. How soon can you start?"

Anna Lisa swallowed the shrimp in her mouth. "I'm hoping in September."

"That's only three months away," he noted. "We'll wait for you."

"You will?" she asked, surprised.

"Yes, I've been trying to get you on board for a long time. What's few more months?"

Her aunt raised her water glass. "To a happy union, then."

They all did the same and began to discuss Anna Lisa's future as the account supervisor at Hamilton International Inc.

When their lunch came to an end, Steven picked up the tab and the three walked outside to the valet parking. Anna Lisa shook hands with Steven and told him she was looking forward to working for him again. She hugged her aunt and said she'll call her. And when the valet brought over her car, she tipped him and headed for Howard Brown.

After reaching work, Anna Lisa strode toward her office, hoping to avoid Paul and Kimberly. Once inside, she set down her black briefcase and the sample packages she had brought back from London and was about to check her inbox when Leila walked in.

Anna Lisa was startled. "Don't you ever knock?" she cried. "You almost gave me a heart attack. I thought you were Paul."

"Is this how you treat a friend bearing good news?" Leila shut the door and made herself comfortable on a chair.

"I'm afraid the only good news you could give me is that I never have to see Paul and Kimberly again."

"No my news is not that great, but it'll have to do for now."

"Well? What is it?" her friend asked impatiently, sifting through her mail and phone messages.

"Both Paul and Kimberly are out with the flu," she reported with a big grin.

Anna Lisa's face lit up as though she had won the lottery. "Really?" she said with a tremendous relief, plopping down on her chair. "You just made my day. I hope they'll be out for a long time."

"You mean you hope that they'll be sick for a long time," Leila sniggered.

"No, I don't wish them ill. I just don't want to see them,"

"I can't say I blame you."

"You know, sometimes I wish I could get away from here and go somewhere where no one knows me."

"And what about me?" Leila complained. "You would leave and forget all about me?"

"Don't worry I couldn't run away even if I wanted to." At least not yet, she thought. She put her mail and messages back in her in box and decided to deal with them later. "I'm obligated to Simon and Jane. And as far as you're concerned, you'll always be part of my life."

"Just as you'll be part of mine."

"Thank you."

"You're welcome." Leila rose to her feet. "I suppose I should get back to work."

"And I should go see Simon." She picked up two folders, her briefcase and the samples and headed toward Simon's office.

"Do you think you'll have time to help me out later today with the Olson account?" Anna Lisa asked.

"Sure thing. Just give me a buzz."

"Will do." She tapped on Simon's door.

"Come in," he said.

She went in. Simon was standing next to a bookshelf about to pull out a reference book. "Anna Lisa, hi. How was your trip?" he greeted her warmly.

"Productive."

"Have a seat and tell me all about it." He moved to the sofa and set the book on the coffee table.

Anna Lisa joined him and placed her belongings on the table. "I met two of the partners, Phil Howard and Shannon Brown."

"And how did you like them?"

"I liked them very much. They're friendly and easy to talk to."

"Tell me, did you get a chance to talk to anyone else?"

"I spoke with couple of employees at the creative arts department," Anna Lisa said. "Neil and I have come to a decision."

"And what's that?"

"We believe the most effective technique to market Jane Olson's products is to use a separate packaging and media for our English consumers, if that's alright by you."

"Do you have any data to back up your strategy?"

"Here is the research on the English demographics and reports on marketing surveys for Jane's products done in our London office," Anna Lisa said as she handed Simon the data.

Simon briefly browsed through the information.

"Of course we already had this information before I left for London. But once I had a chance to feel out the English market by walking through their boutiques and department stores and eavesdropping on the customers, I realized that Neil was right. Our American package isn't going to work for the English market."

"Hmmm," Simon said as he pulled on his left earlobe.

Anna Lisa pulled out a binder and a DVD from her briefcase. "Here's a folder that exemplifies the English print media and a disk that illustrates the various television advertisements for cosmetics and beauty care products."

Simon glanced through the folder.

"I have also brought some sample packaging."

He examined them, "They do look different than what we had planned."

"If you take a look at the TV ads and the print media, I'm sure you'll agree we need a different packaging as well as television and magazine advertisement to promote Jane's products in England."

"I need time to go through all this," he scratched his head. "Give me couple of hours and I'll get back to you." But when he saw the unsatisfied look on her face, he added, "What's the matter?"

"Well, I'd like to get started on the changes as soon as possible. I think Jane is anxious to get the ball rolling."

"Why don't you work on it and see if you can get Leila to help you out," Simon said. "She just finished two of her projects, and I believe she has some free time on her hands."

Anna Lisa smiled on the inside at the concept of "free time" in the marketing and advertising world because it didn't exist. It was a fast-paced industry with a lot of long hours. "I'm already on it," said Anna Lisa.

"Good. Then go to it."

After leaving Simon's office, Anna Lisa went back to her desk and started to make changes in an outline form. When finished, she called Leila and asked her to come in.

"I'll be right over," Leila said.

A minute later, she showed up.

"Why don't you pull up a chair next to me."

Leila went behind Neil's desk and rolled his chair to Anna Lisa's desk because his was bigger and more comfortable than the other ones in the room.

Anna Lisa handed Leila the outline she had typed. "Have a look and let me know if you have any questions."

Leila rubbed her chin as she looked through it, nodded her head and said, "I think I can follow it." She was familiar with Jane Olson's products and had heard her friend talk often enough about it.

"I want you to write a preliminary proposal and have it ready by tomorrow."

"So, you're changing everything?!"

"No, just the ad campaign for the English market."

"I suppose I should write memos to keep the other departments aware of your new marketing plans."

"No, not yet. We have to wait for Simon's approval. Then Neil needs to see the proposal and we need to have a meeting with Jane. Once everything gets a heads up, then you can inform the creative arts department and do follow-ups to make sure our plans are executed according to schedule."

"It seems that you and Neil accomplished a lot in London."

"We did, but we have more work ahead of us. I want you really involved in this project."

Leila was thrilled to be working on such a large account. "Of course. This is a great opportunity for me."

Little did Leila know that Anna Lisa was planning to recommend her to Simon for an account executive position. Once Anna Lisa was gone, it would be up to Neil and Leila to make sure that the ad campaign was effective. They were the ones who had to follow up with Adam and find out if the Olson product line had reached its sales goal by the sixth month and if their market shares had grown according to plan. "Yes it is, and that means you'll have to put in even longer hours than what you're used to."

"That's not a problem."

"Well, you'd better get to work on that proposal."

"Yes ma'am," Leila saluted her jokingly when she stood up.

"Very funny."

Several hours later, Simon came in and stood in the middle of the room. "I want to let you know that I've looked through the information you and Neil provided and I agree with you. We need to have a different ad campaign for our English market."

Anna Lisa's face brightened. "I'm so glad you agree. I made an outline of the changes and Leila is writing up a proposal."

"Good," he said, rubbing his hands. "Now what you need is to get Jane Olson's approval."

"Maybe when Neil gets back, we can all get together and talk this over."

"Just make sure you have the figures to back up your strategy."

"I'm working on it."

"Excellent," he said and started for the door, "keep me posted."

After Simon Left, Anna Lisa wanted to call Neil but when she looked at her watch, she noted it was 6 which meant it was 2 in the morning in London. She could call him at midnight but didn't want to wait up that late. Her body and mind were exhausted and she needed to get to bed at a decent time. Anna Lisa decided to work for two more hours and call it a night. Planning to wrap things up before leaving Howard Brown but feeling guilty for hiding her intentions from Simon, she began working on two of her unfinished projects. Anna Lisa was certain that eventually she would get over Paul if she did not see him. How did that saying go? Out of sight, out of mind.

FOURTEEN

Four days after Anna Lisa's return from London, Paul and Kimberly were still out with Flu. Neil had returned from England but was coming in late. Anna Lisa was reviewing the list of potential U.S. publications where she wanted Jane's ads placed, comparing circulation and cost of a full page ad for a 12-month period and calculating to see if the expenditure was within their budget when her phone rang. It was Nicole wanting to know if Anna Lisa felt like going to the movies.

Since she'd been back from London, Anna Lisa had been in a depressed mood. No matter how many people were around her, she felt lonely and blue without Paul. "No, I don't really feel like going out."

"C'mon, it'll be fun. Once you get out of your office, you'll feel much better."

"Oh, I don't know."

"Please, do it for me. I miss hanging out with you."

May be Nicole was right. May be if she went out, she'd start to feel better. "Okay then," Anna Lisa replied reluctantly as Neil walked in. "Why don't you swing by my place at 7 and we can figure out what we want to see then."

"Sounds like a plan. I'll see you then, bye."

When Anna Lisa hung up the phone, Neil thought she was making plans with Paul and wanted to tell her they needed to work on the Olson account until late. Anna Lisa's eyes brightened at the sight of him and she said, "Hey, how was your trip?"

The office had felt so empty without Neil for the past few days. Funny, how six months ago Anna Lisa wanted her work space all to herself – now she was more than happy to share it with Neil. Perhaps he was a distraction she needed in order to get over Paul, she thought. Or perhaps she simply needed a male friend. Whatever the reason, she was happy he was there.

Neil, too, had missed Anna Lisa, their friendly bickering and the comfort he felt when he was with her. He hoped she would be his friend for years to come and that possibility made him crack a smile and reply, "Tiring. Too much turbulence. I'm glad to be on the ground."

"Sorry to hear that." She watched him walk over to his desk and take a seat. "Maybe you should go home early and rest up."

"About that," he said and then stopped because he didn't have the heart to break her plans with Paul, "Umm, never mind. Yes, I think I'll take your suggestion."

"By the way, did you want to go over the proposal before I give it to Leila for revision?"

"Absolutely. We need to be ready for tomorrow when we meet with Adam and Jane."

Neil began reading the proposal and Anna Lisa returned to reviewing the list of U.S. publication list, comparing circulation and cost of a full page ad and calculating to see if the expenditure was within their budget. She picked up her pen to jot down the name of a magazine but changed her mind. She couldn't concentrate. Her mind was preoccupied with what Neil thought about the proposal. She lifted her head up and looked at him, but he was too engrossed to notice her. She chewed on her pen cap.

He finally lifted his pen and made a few changes and handed it back to Anna Lisa.

She began reading through them, but was irritated by the proximity of his stance. He was looking over her shoulder, not giving her time to think.

"What do you think?" he asked impatiently.

She gazed at him and said, "You're hovering. I can't think when you're hovering."

He chuckled at her directness. "I apologize, I'm afraid it's force of habit." He went over to the coffee table, grabbed an *Ad Week* magazine and began paging through it.

After a few minutes Anna Lisa lifted her head. "I agree with your changes."

"Brilliant." He buzzed Kimberly so she could pick up the proposal and give it to Leila for adjustments, but Kimberly did not answer.

"Where the devil is that girl? She's never at her desk."

"She has the flu."

"Ah," he said. "I'll drop it off later."

The rest of the afternoon Neil and Anna Lisa worked out of the conference room because they needed space to spread their information and go through it. They analyzed five ad layouts for magazines, six logos consisting of Jane Olson's name and four storyboard layouts. In order to increase sales and market shares, Anna Lisa and Neil had to redefine Jane's products in contemporary terms. Once they were done, they had to decide on packaging, shapes and sizes, background color and cost.

They worked until 6 o'clock when Anna Lisa had to leave.

"I have to go," she said rising, "Can we meet tomorrow at 8 in the morning and finish up then?"

"Only if you bring me breakfast," Neil responded with a smile.

"I suppose you want toast, lemon curd and tea?" she asked.

He nodded his head smiling.

"You're so easy," she said as she walked out.

The next morning, after wrapping up their work from yesterday, Anna Lisa and Neil met with Simon, Jane and Adam in the conference room. They went over the increase in cost for advertising and explained their strategy behind their plan. Neil and Anna Lisa were able to persuade Jane and Adam to spend more money on packaging and magazine and TV ad in exchange for receiving a greater return for every dollar they spent.

After the meeting, Anna Lisa called Leila and told her to come by her office after 6 so that she could discuss the contents of this morning's meeting with Jane. She and Neil visited the media director's studio on the 17th floor to take part in selecting models for the television commercials, the billboards and magazine ads. And this was just the beginning. A lot more work needed to be done if they were going to launch the products before the September deadline.

At 5:30 that evening, Anna Lisa needed to talk to Paul – who finally was over the flu – so that he could prepare an expense report. She didn't want to see him and had Neil been around, she would have asked Neil to do it, but he was in a meeting with Simon regarding what he referred to as a subject of a "personal nature." She was curious as to what Simon and Neil were discussing behind closed doors.

Anna Lisa went over to Paul's office and found him behind his desk with papers strewn everywhere. Apparently, the few days he missed had backlogged him. He wrinkled his forehead as he added and subtracted on his calculator. She found herself still attracted to him. "Maybe, I should come back some other time."

"Anna Lisa!" he said in surprise when he looked up. "How are you?"

Her heart skipped a beat at the sound of his voice. His dark eyes mesmerized her and she wanted to run her hands through his hair the way she used to when they were in bed. "Shouldn't I be asking you that question?"

"Yes, well, I'm better now. How was your trip?" he asked as though nothing had ever happened between the two of them.

Anna Lisa stood there in disbelief. This man whom she loved so much behaved as though there was never anything between them. She became angry. "I'm not here to discuss my trip. Could you please write up an expense report for the Olson account? Here are the receipts," she said, tossing them on his desk.

He got up, approached her and seductively said, "We never did have that talk."

Her body shook because of the nearness of his presence and she hoped he wouldn't notice. "What's there to talk about? You cheated on me with Kimberly," she said, noticing her picture had been replaced with a framed photo of Kimberly, Paul and his mother on his desk with the Santa Monica Pier in the background. Suddenly all the strength in her legs disappeared. It was as though she became paralyzed. Then it dawned on her – that weekend. The weekend when she was in San Francisco for a conference and Paul's mother had visited him, he had been with Kimberly. She wondered how long his relationship with Kimberly had actually been going on. She stared at him and then at the photo. He turned red.

"But you never let me explain," Paul said, grasping her hand.

She pulled her hand away and replied, "A picture is worth a thousand words."

"Anna Lisa, I'm s–"

"Don't," she cried. "Don't say you're sorry when you don't mean it. Just give me the report by tomorrow." She stormed out. Feeling as though she were going to die, Anna Lisa turned a corner, when she bumped into Kimberly, who was heading toward Paul's office.

"Hi Anna Lisa, didn't know you were back," Kimberly said with confidence. She was wearing a white-and green-pin-striped shirt – the shirt Anna Lisa had bought Paul for his 29th birthday seven months ago.

Anna Lisa did not answer and kept on walking until she got to her office. Then the tears flowed. Worried that someone could walk in any minute, she sobbed in fear. She pulled out a small mirror from her purse and looked at her face. Her eyes were red and her nose looked like Rudolph's. She put two drops of Visine in each eye, drank the rest of the bottled water sitting on her desk, closed her eyes and let her head rest against the back of her chair for 5 minutes. Relax Anna Lisa, relax, she told herself. Just pull yourself together until you get home. She took in several deep breaths but couldn't calm down. She checked her eyes once more and noticed that most of the redness had faded away. Anna Lisa put the mirror away and decided to leave. She headed for the door as Neil walked in.

"I have good news," he blurted with a glowing face.

"What is it?" Anna Lisa asked attempting to hide her feelings.

"Simon asked me to stay here permanently."

"Good. I have to go."

"Is that all you have to say?" He wanted to tell her that Simon had offered him a raise and the possibility of a partnership in the near future if he stayed in Los Angeles, but she didn't seem interested in what he had to say.

"Sorry, I'm not myself right now," Anna Lisa said. "That is good news, but is that what you really want?"

"Well, I don't know. I haven't given it much thought."

"And what about Sarah? Will she be willing to move here?"

He stopped talking for a moment and then replied, "You know, I don't know. I suppose I should talk to her before making my decision."

"Will you excuse me? There's somewhere I have to be. Congratulations," she said and abruptly walked out.

Neil stood there for a while. He couldn't understand Anna Lisa at all. Why was she so hot and cold? She had behaved in the same manner the day he had come back from the dentist. She had a sense of humor but by late afternoon she had turned cold and out of sorts. Something was going on in her life that she wasn't telling him, but what? He went to his desk and as soon as he sat down, Leila came in.

"Hi Neil. Where's Anna Lisa?"

"I don't know," replied Neil with a puzzled look. "She said she had to be somewhere."

"Hmm. Strange. She asked me earlier to stop by so that she could update me on your meeting with Jane."

Neil handed her a file. "I have summarized the meeting in this contract report. You can read about the points that were agreed upon and the changes we made."

"Thank you," she said, starting to walk away when Neil's voice stopped her. "I was just wondering..."

"Yes?"

"Nevermind."

"What is it?"

"Well...umm...Have you seen a change in Leeza lately?"

"What do you mean?"

"Well, she was in good spirits when I left the office, but when I got back her mood had changed. I'm concerned."

"Oh," Leila said, "don't be. She's just having some personal problems."

"Perhaps I can help."

Leila contemplated if she should tell him. Everyone else at the office knew. "I don't think there's anything you can do to help her."

"I see. That's too bad."

"She broke up with Paul. She found out he was cheating on her with Kimberly."

"I am sorry to hear that," he replied calmly, but his body was tense and his face looked more grave than the words uttered.

"I'm not. I never liked him anyway," Leila commented, as she left to read the report.

The next day, Anna Lisa was alone in her office reading a report from the research department when Paul stopped by her desk to give her the expense report.

"Here's the report you asked for."

"Thanks," Anna Lisa managed to say.

He stood there for a while in silence until Anna Lisa became annoyed with him and blurted out angrily, "What? Do I have something stuck on my face? Is that why you're staring?"

Paul hesitated for a moment. "No, your face looks fine. It's just that…"

"That what?" she asked with raised eyebrows and wide eyes.

"It's just that I've missed you."

She clenched her teeth and wanted to scream at his stupidity. How dare he lie to her in that manner.

"You have no idea how important your friendship is to me." He looked at her with sad, puppy eyes.

Paul always gave her the same look when he did something to hurt her and she had always yielded to him, but not this time. "You have a funny way of showing it," she answered coldly.

From the blank look on her face, he could see she didn't believe a word he had said. He nervously walked back and forth, adding, "I just feel so comfortable around you. I feel like I can talk to you about anything. I've never felt that way about anyone before."

"Is that why you've been deceiving me for such a long time? Because you feel like you can talk to me about anything?" She wasn't going to hold back anymore. She was going to say whatever that came out of her mouth without giving it a second thought. After all, she had nothing to lose.

"Sorry, I didn't mean to fall in love with Kimberly," he uttered with a face filled with pain and regret. "It just happened."

She scrutinized him and wondered if he were faking his emotions. She knew how manipulative and deceitful he could be and nothing he said or did would make her trust him again. "What do you know about love?" she angrily cried. "You wouldn't know love if it hit you on the face." Anna Lisa got up to go open the door and leave. She could no longer stand being in the same room with him.

He grabbed her arm and turned her around so that they faced each other. "We're right for each other, Kimberly and I. She's the one."

She yanked her arm from his grip and stared at him with eyes that could kill. "Please, how many girls have you been with Paul, and how many times did you think each was the one?"

"This time it's for real, you'll see," he protested with conviction.

"And when were you going to tell me about you and Kimberly?" she shouted and started pretending to organize her desk by picking up files and tapping the bottoms hard on the desk. "When the two of you were married?"

"There never was a right time, and I didn't know how to break it to you," he answered raising his voice to match hers.

"Get out, will you?" she cried, pointing at the door.

"Can't we be friends?"

"You must be joking." she walked back to her seat. She wished he would just leave. This conversation was a waste of her time and it was starting to give her a migraine.

"No, I'm serious. I don't want to lose your friendship." Paul wanted to have it all. He enjoyed having women fight over him because it made him feel wanted except that Anna Lisa wasn't willing to fight for him. Maybe she didn't love him enough, he thought. Otherwise, why wouldn't she stick it out and try to win him back?

"You lost my friendship the day I discovered that trashy negligee in your car. How could you, Paul?" she yelled at him but the yelling was making her migraine worse. "How could you screw her knowing I was coming by any minute?"

"That wasn't my plan," he confessed. "She stopped by unexpectedly and then one thing led to another and before I knew it, we—"

"Stop," Anna Lisa interrupted. "Spare me the details. We're over." With shaky hands, she took a small bottle of aspirin from her purse, opened it, took three and forced them down with water.

"Does that mean you don't want to be friends?"

"Paul, I'm through teaching you right from wrong. Figure this one by yourself," she said pretending to be reading the research papers in front of her.

He stood there not knowing what to say next and then blurted, "Did you need anything else?"

"No, please go away," she replied quietly. Her head felt like bursting. The angrier she got, the more it hurt.

"Are you sure?" he asked, hoping to pull her back into the conversation. He didn't want her to hate him.

"I'll let you know if I need anything else," she said without lifting her head.

"It's just that–"

"That what?" she finally yelled looking up. Her head started throbbing again.

"I'm going on vacation–" he paused and cleared his throat, "That is, I'm going on vacation with Kimberly. I'll be gone for three weeks."

He was telling her this on purpose to hurt her, she thought. She would not fall apart in front him. She would not give him that satisfaction. Anna Lisa swallowed, "I see." She began tapping her pen on the paper in front of her in a rhythmic pulsating motion to calm herself.

"Jenna, the bookkeeper on the 18th floor, is covering for me while I'm gone, but if you need anything important, this is the week to ask."

"Fine."

"You aren't even going to ask where I'm going, are you?"

Her face looked cold and stern when she asked unwillingly, "Okay Paul, where are you going?"

"I'm going to Greece," he said with excitement. "I found this inexpensive deal and finally I get to see a piece of Europe." He wanted her to be happy for him. He wanted her to hug him and wish him well.

"Good for you. Now, may I get back to work?" Anna Lisa said lowering her gaze to the material lying on her desk so that Paul couldn't see the tears forming in her eyes.

Paul felt foolish. He stood there for a short time hoping that Anna Lisa would look up and say something. When she didn't, he left.

Anna Lisa put her head on the table to reflect on what had just happened. All those years he had promised to take her to Greece and now, he was going with Kimberly. She never thought she could hate anyone but she hated him. Why should he be so happy when she was so depressed, especially since he was the cause of her depression? She wished Paul and Kimberly would disappear and never come back, and for the first time in her life she understood why some people murdered their cheating partners. Temporary insanity, that's what it was. Paul was driving her insane and as much as she didn't want to admit it, she was falling apart slowly, day by day. It was as though Paul was poisoning her little by little, increasing the dosage each time and finally bringing about her demise. How insensitive and cruel he had been to her. Wasn't he the same guy who had looked out for her and been there when she needed him? At what point did he slip away? At what point did he stop caring for her? She hadn't the answers.

She started to feel nauseated and wanted to vomit. She picked up the round brown trash can next to her desk and put her head over it. Nothing came out. The throbbing in her head was getting worse. Anna Lisa went to lie down on the sofa. She closed her eyes and lay there like a dead person – cold and listless with a chalky complexion.

"I see changes. Many changes. I don't know. Maybe new house...or new job."

Half an hour later, Anna Lisa opened her eyes but didn't move. She lay there thinking – thinking of how tired she was of Paul, her life at Howard Brown and going home everyday to the same apartment. She needed a fresh start. She had to erase her past and start over and the only way to do that was to cut off herself completely from Paul. She had already decided to change jobs. Why not sell her place and move to a new one? After all, she had been thinking about relocating to a high-rise for some time. She went to her desk, pulled out the yellow pages and dialed a local real-estate agency to list her condominium.

FIFTEEN

Paul was already gone a week. In the past 10 days Anna Lisa lost weight and no amount of makeup could cover the dark circles under her eyes from lack of sleep. She looked sick and distracted at the office, but Neil did not say anything to her. They both sat behind their desks before lunch and worked quietly. Neil, poised upright on his chair, studied the reports form their television media buyer for the Olson account which determined the new and returning shows in fall, their content and appeal and the demographic of their audience. He was trying to decide on the TV stations where he wanted the ads to run.

Anna Lisa had her left elbow on her desk, her head tilted away from Neil and her hand supporting her head and hiding her face. She appeared to be working but she was not. Her mind, a thousand miles away, played the events that had occurred in the past couple of months – the day she found Kimberly's red negligee in Paul's car, the night she found Paul with Kimberly, the framed picture of Paul with his mother and Kimberly, the conversation about how much he loved Kimberly and when he told her about their upcoming trip to Greece. These awful memories ran through her head over and over as she stared at a promotional booklet and packaging layouts for Jane Olson's products.

"Leeza?" Neil said. She didn't respond. He tried again.

Anna Lisa turned and said, "I'm sorry, did you just call my name?"

"Yes, I was wondering if you wanted to go have lunch," he said, hoping that she would say yes. The fresh air and the sun would do her good.

She knew he was trying to cheer her up but she just wanted to be left alone. "No, thank you. You go ahead. I'm not very hungry."

He worried about her. She lacked energy, luster and a zest for life. "I can bring you something back and you can have it later."

"No, I don't have much of an appetite," she replied and passed him a half-smile, "But thanks anyway."

"Very well then." He got up and straightened his jacket. He looked at Anna Lisa's grim face and felt sorry for her. He walked across the room, opened the door and said, "I'll see you later."

The following day, it was almost noon and Anna Lisa still hadn't shown up at the office. It was not like her to come in so late and not let Neil know. Yesterday she looked so frail and unhappy and when he returned from lunch she wasn't there. At first he thought she was coming back because her work was scattered all over her desk and she always put her files away before leaving, but she never returned.

Concerned, Neil picked up the phone and called the art department to see if anyone had seen Anna Lisa but no one had. He checked with Diana and other employees on his floor and they said they hadn't seen her either. He called Simon. "Have you heard from Leeza?"

"Isn't she at her desk?"

"No, and no one seems to know where she is."

"Humph," Simon said, scratching his head, "She usually calls when she's going to come in late."

"Perhaps Leila would know."

"Let me know what's going on will you? I'm concerned about her as well." He knew Anna Lisa hadn't been herself lately because of her breakup with Paul.

When Neil hung up the phone, Leila was at the door.

"Hey, have you seen Anna Lisa?" she asked, "I tried calling her yesterday but her phone was busy all night, and today too, I couldn't get through. So, I tried making an emergency call but the operator said her phone was probably off the hook."

"No, I have not seen her," Neil replied with disappointment. "I went to lunch with Simon yesterday and when I came back she was gone."

"What do you mean gone?" said Leila furrowing her brows.

"I mean she never came back and I haven't seen her since." He let his fingertips touch and tapped his index fingers together, thinking about where she was.

"Strange," Leila commented. "Did she leave a note?"

"No, no note. And what puzzles me is she never cleaned her desk. She always straightens it up before she leaves."

"Maybe she wasn't feeling well." She knew how clean and organized Anna Lisa was. All sorts of thoughts ran through her mind. What if she had gotten into a car accident and was taken to a hospital? What if her friend was at home sick or injured? "I think I'll take my break now and go see if she's at home."

"Will you have her call me when you talk to her?"

"I will," Leila said and left the office.

A half hour later, Leila arrived at Anna Lisa's door step and rang the bell. She saw her car in the driveway and thought she might be home; but no one answered. She tried ringing the bell and knocking on the door at the same time. Still no response. "Anna Lisa? It's me, Leila, open up." Again nothing. She now pounded on the door much harder and the door finally opened.

"Please, stop pounding," a sleepy Anna Lisa answered and went back to lie on her living room sofa with her back facing the coffee table.

Leila followed her and noticed an empty bottle of vodka on the floor. She crouched next to the couch, put her hand on Anna

Lisa's shoulder and turned her toward her. "Please tell me you didn't drink an entire bottle of vodka."

"I didn't," she mumbled, turning her body away again. She drank quite a bit last night and spent half the night barfing in the toilet bowl.

All the pain, anger and hate she had repressed in order to avoid thinking about Kimberly's naked body straddled over Paul's were now emerging. She never allowed herself time to express her grief over Paul's betrayal. She kept pushing along – overworking when she shouldn't have, forcing a smile when all she wanted to do was cry, hiding her vulnerability, pretending that nothing got to her and that she was this strong well put together person. But she had finally cracked and she was going to hurt for a long time unless she was willing to accept reality – that Paul was a deceitful person who had only pretended to care for her.

"It looks to me you had a good portion of it or you wouldn't be laying there with a hangover."

"What's it to you anyway?" Anna Lisa muttered.

"We are feeling sorry for ourselves, are we?" said Leila putting her hand on Anna Lisa's shoulder once again and turning her limp body toward her. "You know, Neil and Simon have been wondering why you didn't show up to work today and frankly I can't wait to tell them that you have a hangover," Leila prodded, trying to get some kind of reaction out of Anna Lisa.

"Go away will you and let me sleep in peace," Anna Lisa said, rolling onto her stomach, burying her face into a yellow decorative pillow which was now covered with smudges of black mascara and salty tears. She was exhausted and couldn't care less about her work, the Olson account or Paul. The combination of alcohol and depression had worn her down and all she wanted to do was crash and forget about her problems.

Leila got up and opened blinds and the windows. She then went into the kitchen, and put the receiver that was dangling from its cord against the wall back into its cradle. She made a strong pot of coffee, poured orange juice into a juice glass, made toast spread with lemon curd and served it on a china plate. She poured the coffee into Anna Lisa's Yale cup, put everything on a cream-colored tray and brought it into the living room. She then turned on the television, making the volume as high as possible.

Anna Lisa jumped up holding her head with her hands. "Are you crazy? Turn that damn thing down and close the blinds."

Leila turned down the volume. "Good. Now that I have your attention, have some coffee," she said handing Anna Lisa her cup.

Anna Lisa passed her an angry look. She took a sip of the coffee and crinkled her nose. "Yuk. This is horrible. How much coffee did you put in there? The whole container?" She handed back the cup." I can't drink this."

"Then have some orange juice," Leila ordered, giving her the glass.

Her hair was in disarray, her eyes were swollen and her breath gave off the foul odor of vomit. "No, the thought of anything in my stomach makes me nauseous."

"What?" Leila shouted out loud on purpose.

Anna Lisa held her head. "I beg of you, don't shout."

"Then eat the breakfast I made you."

"Just so you know, you're Satan, not a saint," Anna Lisa said with a weak voice, taking a small bite of the toast.

"Yes, a Satan who is trying to get food into that empty stomach of yours."

The struggle to feed Anna Lisa continued for a good hour. Leila managed to get a slice of toast and six ounces of juice into Anna Lisa's stomach. Another hour passed before she was able to get Anna Lisa upstairs and into the shower. While Anna Lisa was in the bathroom, Leila called Neil.

"Neil speaking," he answered.

"Neil, it's me, Leila. I'm at Anna Lisa's."

"How is she? May I talk to her?"

"She has a..." Leila hesitated because she wasn't sure if she wanted to let Neil know Anna Lisa had been drinking. "She has a...bit of a hangover."

"I see," Neil responded gravely. It wasn't like Anna Lisa to drink and be irresponsible. She must be hurting over Paul, he thought. "Can I do anything to help?" he asked in a caring tone.

"You could let Simon know that she isn't feeling well. I'm going to take the rest of the day off and be with her."

"Certainly."

"I'll take her out so she can get some fresh air."

"Call me if you need anything."

"I will."

When Leila hung up the phone, she looked around her friend's bedroom. The organized Anna Lisa she once knew was now a slob. She saw an unmade bed, clothes, shoes, purses, accessories and makeup all over the floor and dresser. She started fixing Anna Lisa's bed and then picked up her clothes off the floor, hanging them up. After awhile, Anna Lisa came out of the bathroom with wet hair and in her usual white terrycloth robe. She noticed her bed was made and her things were put away.

"Thank you for fixing my room," she said. "Ursula is on vacation and I just haven't felt like doing anything."

"Don't worry about it," Leila offered. "Why don't you get ready and we'll go do something fun."

"I don't really feel like doing anything."

Leila ignored her. "Let's drive to Santa Monica and go for a walk."

"I'll get in the car if you want to drive around," Anna Lisa replied reluctantly, "but I don't feel like getting out."

"Okay then. While you get ready, I'll go make myself a sandwich." It was 2:30 and her stomach was growling.

Leila went downstairs and made a turkey sandwich. Anna Lisa dried her hair, pulled her hair up into a ponytail and changed into black sweats, matching her dark mood. She walked downstairs and saw Leila waiting for her.

"Did you eat?" Anna Lisa asked.

"Yes, I had a sandwich and you're right. My coffee was awful. I threw it out."

"It's the thought that counts," she said and forced a smile. She didn't feel much like smiling these days.

"Well," said Leila as she clapped her hands, "You're ready for that drive?"

Anna Lisa nodded. The two left her apartment, and drove west in Leila's white Mazda.

Leila took the San Vicente route because it was lush and green. She thought that pretty street, dotted with joggers on a wide stretch of grass would cheer Anna Lisa up.

During the drive, Anna Lisa was quiet. Leila put on the radio and kept her eye on the road. Every now and then she glanced over at Anna Lisa and saw her gazing outside into nowhere. After 15 minutes, Anna Lisa's mood seemed to have lifted a little when she finally said, "I like San Vicente. It's so beautiful and green."

Leila was pleased that her strategy had worked. "Good. You need to get outdoors more often. When the Olson project is over, you ought to take that long overdue vacation."

"I'll have no one to go with," she uttered, sadly.

"You have me." Leila loved Anna Lisa like she would her own sister. She wanted her friend to be up and about and energetic the way she used to be.

Anna Lisa glanced at her with a look of appreciation. "Yes, my loyal friend."

"Anna Lisa, there are lots of people who love you very much."

"Oh, please do not say that odious word love," she said, watching a red Ferrari zooming by and cutting Leila off.

"Damn crazy drivers. They think they own the road," her friend cussed. "Anna Lisa, love is not always painful. Besides, you don't need a man in your life to feel loved."

"You think?" she said without any emotion in her voice.

"Yes, I do." Leila was now on Ocean Blvd. overlooking the beach. She searched for a place to park and was lucky enough to find metered parking and pulled in. She turned her attention to Anna Lisa and said, "C'mon let's get out and go for a stroll."

"Fine," Anna Lisa sighed in frustration. Leila was persistent and arguing with her was futile.

They got out. Leila put her alarm on, inserted several quarters in the meter and walked toward the sidewalk, which was a shady path with an ocean view. Anna Lisa proceeded behind Leila. A woman was pushing a stroller with her toddler in it. A couple of joggers went by. A homeless man was taking a siesta underneath a large oak tree wearing torn and dirty rags with his life's belongings in a shopping cart.

"Look at him," whispered Anna Lisa to Leila as she pointed her chin in his direction, "I'll bet he doesn't have a care in the world."

"And neither do you," Leila said, cleaning her sunglasses with a tissue. "You're letting one person ruin your entire life and blind you to all the things you have." They started walking down toward the Santa Monica pier.

"What do I have? I have no children, no one to go home to. I work crazy hours and have nothing to show for it."

"I don't know how to knock some sense into you," Leila said in anger. "You have your whole life ahead of you and most people would give anything to be in your shoes."

"Money and position don't bring happiness as you can see," Anna Lisa said, turning her head away to look at the water. Her eyes were starting to sting and she didn't want to cry.

"Who's talking about money or position? You stand here feeling sorry for yourself. But if you stopped for a minute, you'd realize how rich your life is," Leila said. "My parents and I love you. And then there's your grandmother, your aunts, your nieces and nephews, Simon and his wife, Joanne and Neil."

Anna Lisa stared back at her friend and said, "Neil?"

"Yes, Neil. The man you dislike so much cares about you."

"Neil?"

"Yes. He told me to call him if you needed anything. You think he's cold and distant but underneath that cool exterior is a man who cares very much about you."

"I don't think he's cold. Well, maybe I used to think that, but he's alright."

"He's more than alright," Leila said and stopped walking. "He's perfect for you."

"I don't want him. I don't want anyone – ever." She sauntered toward a low wall bordering the sidewalk and overlooking a bluff, a highway and then the ocean.

Leila followed her but didn't argue with her. She knew no matter what she'd say at this point, Anna Lisa would not listen. They stood there for some time with a cool breeze against their faces, enjoying the roar of the ocean and the sound of the seagulls flapping their wings overhead. It was supposed to be another gloomy June day but instead the sun was out and the sky was clear.

By 5:30 they were ready to leave. Leila suggested that they stop by Anna Lisa's grandmother's house. She thought it would cheer up her friend to be around people who cared for her. Anna Lisa agreed, closed her eyes and took a nap while Leila drove. Lately, all she wanted to do was sleep. Leila flipped the channels on her radio until she found soft rock on one of the stations. The traffic was heavy but she didn't mind. She enjoyed driving; it relaxed her.

After a 30-minute ride, they arrived at her grandmother's house. Leila woke her friend up by lightly shaking her. They walked on the brick pathway to the front door and Leila rang the bell.

Anna looked through the peephole and was glad to see her granddaughter. She opened the door looking cheerful in a long yellow apron over a copper-color dress.

"Well, hello," she said and hugged Anna Lisa and then Leila. "Come in, come in." She was surprised to see Anna Lisa because her granddaughter never stopped by before calling.

They walked through the short hallway, went down a few steps and turned right into the kitchen.

"I've been cooking dinner, why don't the two of you join me?" her grandmother said, noting the dark circles under Anna Lisa's eyes and her somber aura. She knew her granddaughter was brooding over Paul. She went to one of the pine cabinets, pulled out three blue-patterned floral china plates and set them on the table.

"Thanks grandma but I'm not very hungry," she said, noticing there was a cold pitcher of lemonade and a basket of round sourdough bread and butter sitting on the table.

"Nonsense," her grandmother replied, "you can't leave here without having a good dinner."

Leila smiled. If there was anyone who could handle Anna Lisa, it would be her grandmother. "I'll help you set the table," Leila said with enthusiasm and went to a drawer to pull out the silverware but instead found clean kitchen towels.

"It's in the next one dear," said Anna when she saw Leila pulling out the wrong drawer.

"Ah," said Leila as she pulled out the right drawer and took out three knives and forks. She could smell the flavorful aroma of lamb stew wafting from the stove and rolling in her direction. Her stomach growled. She reached above her head, opened up a cabinet and looked for napkins. She saw stacks of china plates. "Napkins?"

"Try the third bottom cabinet," Anna Lisa said.

Leila opened the bottom cabinet and removed three dinner napkins.

Anna went to the stove and with two pot holders held the handles of a cast iron pot, picked it up and set it down on a trivet on the kitchen table.

Anna Lisa grabbed three glasses from one of the cabinets.

They all sat down to eat. No one spoke at first because they were too busy eating. Even Anna Lisa, who didn't have much of an appetite, savored the meal as she put a chunk of lamb and a morsel of bread in her mouth. She wondered whether it was the food that tasted so great to her or the fact that she hadn't been eating much lately and was starving. She swigged her lemonade to wash down the meal.

Leila watched her friend and was happy that she was eating. A good appetite is a sign of good health, her mother always told her. "I thought you weren't hungry," Leila said teasingly to Anna Lisa.

She smiled with her mouth full.

"Anna, this is a great stew," Leila said.

"Glad you like it," she replied, "I'll wrap some up for you to take home."

"No, I couldn't. It's rude enough for me to barge in on you when you were about to have dinner."

"Nonsense, you girls are always welcome here."

"Grandma, how's your tennis game going?" Anna Lisa asked just to make light conversation.

"Oh, fine. I played doubles yesterday with a friend of mine and we won."

"I didn't know you played tennis."

"Thirty years," Anna replied.

"You know, my mother used to play and..."

Anna Lisa listened to Leila and her grandmother as they conversed. She was glad to be there instead of being at the office where she was constantly reminded of Paul or at home where she felt so lonely. She made a pact to push herself and go out with friends instead of cocooning and getting depressed all the time. Perhaps Leila was right – she was concentrating too hard on what she didn't have instead of what she did.

When dinner was over, everyone helped clean up. Leila put things away and cleaned the maple table with a damp cloth, Anna Lisa loaded the dishwasher and her grandmother made tea, served pecan pie on china dessert plates, put everything on an antique silver tray and carried it into the living room.

"You mind if I turn on the TV Grandma?" Anna Lisa asked. She knew her grandmother didn't like the television on when they were eating.

"No I don't mind." She couldn't say no to her. Her granddaughter looked so unhappy when she had walked in and now she seemed to be in better spirits.

Anna Lisa flipped the channels and found a thriller about politicians and corruption. The movie had already started, but she had seen it before. She felt watching it would help keep her mind off her troubles. Anna rested her back against her recliner and extended her legs. Anna Lisa explained the beginning of the film and the three were pulled into the story until the end and then it was time to go.

Anna Lisa got up, realizing that her mood had improved after spending time with people who loved her. Leila went into the kitchen and grabbed the leftovers Anna had set aside.

"Thanks grandma for having us." Anna Lisa said, hugging her grandmother.

Leila came into the hallway with a white plastic bag and said, "Thank you for dinner and the leftovers."

"You're Welcome dear," Anna offered, watching Anna Lisa and Leila wave and drive away.

When they reached her condo, Anna Lisa said, "I appreciate you taking such a good care of me."

"You would've done the same if our roles were reversed."

"In a heartbeat," she said and embraced her friend. "I'll see you tomorrow."

Once inside, she was too tired to think of Paul. She climbed the stairs, set her alarm for 7 and went to bed determined to go to work the next day.

––––––––––––––––––

The next morning, Anna Lisa dreaded going into the office. She didn't want to be reminded of Paul, she thought as she pulled into her parking spot at Howard Brown. For the first time in her life, Anna Lisa wished she were rich like Sarah and could quit her work without notice, turn around and leave. Winters she would ski in Aspen and summers she would stay at a beach house in Newport Beach. She would never worry about money and would spend time buying high-fashion clothes, getting facials, fixing her hair and going to classy clubs. She would meet men, date them and dump them when she grew tired of them, she thought as she got into the elevator. But if she had that kind of money, would she be happy living such a life? She liked having a career and a reason to get out of bed every morning instead of running around aimlessly and worrying about a bad hair day. As far as men were concerned, she couldn't just move from boyfriend to boyfriend. She needed stability.

These thoughts ran through her mind until the elevator reached her floor. Anna Lisa got out, looked around the office and saw her fellow employees laboring in their cubicles. Everything seemed bleak and mundane – same carpet, same color walls, same offices, same co-workers, and same clients. She needed to get away, she thought as she walked over to her office and found Neil sitting behind his desk.

Glad to see her, he looked up and smiled. Neil never thought he would enjoy working with Anna Lisa but he really missed her when she wasn't around. They discussed and shared ideas, argued and compromised, fought and made up. And even when they didn't speak, he was content that she was there – her presence motivated him to work harder. Now he would have a hard time working alone. But Simon had promised him his own space if he decided to stay.

"Sorry about disappearing," she said, going over to her desk and setting her briefcase on it. "I don't know what has come over me. I think I need a vacation." She stared at her messy desk.

"Don't worry about it. We can all use a holiday after putting in such long hours," he said, noticing her prosaic countenance, sagging shoulders and drooping head, "But I must admit I was a bit concerned about you."

"I appreciate you looking out for me and being so understanding," she replied, removing her black jacket and draping it over the back of her chair, "but there is no need for concern. I'm doing well." She didn't want to alarm anyone at work about her troubles in her life. She had only confided in her grandmother, her aunts, Leila and Nicole. Her problems were her problems. Why should others worry about it?

Neil glanced over at her unkempt desk. "I suppose I should let you catch up. We can talk tomorrow about the Olson account."

"Thank you," Anna Lisa nodded and started organizing the mounds of work she left on her desk two days ago. She planned to go over them after she had a chance to look through her unread mail and unreturned messages. And so, she threw herself back into her work the way she did when she returned from London and was thrilled to be busy. By 8 in the evening, her desk was cleared and she had taken care of everything that was a priority on her list.

Anna Lisa swiveled her chair and looked behind her. The city lights were twinkling and she wondered what other people were doing at this very moment. Were they having dinner with their families or reading storybooks to their toddlers? Where they happy and content or were they troubled as she was? How much she desired to be married and to have children running about but in the course of a short time, all that had changed. All her dreams of the future were shattered by one love. She heard Neil calling her name and turned around.

"Hmmm?"

"Were you planning to take off?" Neil asked.

"Not if there's more work to do."

Neil looked at her for a moment from behind his desk and wasn't sure if he was doing the right thing, but he couldn't help himself when he said, "You know you can't hide in your work forever."

"What do you mean?" she asked with a puzzled look.

"It's not my business but –" and then he stopped as though afraid to finish his sentence.

Frustrated by his ambivalence, she raised her voice. "But what?"

He brushed his hand over his face and said, "Nevermind." He wasn't in the habit of prying in someone's business.

"Will you for once say what's on your mind instead of always being so proper?" she barked.

Neil could no longer hold his feelings back. "Fine, you asked for it. When was the last time you had a good cry?"

"Excuse me?" she uttered reprovingly and then glowered.

"You can't just push back your feelings, you know. At some point you have to deal with them."

How dare he tell her how to handle her pain? Had he any idea of the ache that tormented her every day? "And what makes you such an expert, Mr. Whittaker?"

"Ah, here we go. You're cross with me again."

Her body was tense and her face red with anger. "I just don't see what right you have to tell me how to deal with my feelings."

He lowered his voice. He could tell that she was getting upset and if he wanted to get through to her, he had to stay calm. "Because I once lost a friend. Different than what you're going through because my friend died in an airplane accident, but I pushed away my feelings for months until I almost had a breakdown," he explained with a caring voice. "I ended up in therapy, and I remember crying non-stop for a long time."

"I'm sorry about your friend but different people deal with their emotions in different manners," she stated, putting on her jacket and getting ready to leave. She wanted to end this unpleasant conversation as quickly as possible.

"Anna Lisa, you need to have a good cry or your feelings will eat you up alive," he said as he moved toward her.

She began to head for the door but he stopped her before she could get past the sofa by gripping her shoulders and holding her still. "Paul doesn't love you."

"Let me leave," she demanded.

"He's with Kimberly, together on a trip. What're you going to do about it?"

Her eyes filled up with tears and a lump formed in her throat. "You know I really hate you at this moment."

"Good," he said staring into her joyless eyes. "Hit me or something."

"Let me go," she cried and tried to jerk her body free but it was useless. His strong hands were firmly planted on her.

"He's with her, and there's nothing you can do."

This time Anna Lisa mustered all the strength she could find inside her and jerked herself free. She hit him in the chest with her fists a few times and then tears poured down her face. He slid one arm around her waist and the other around her shoulder, held her close and said, "That's it, just let it out. It's the only way for you to get better."

She didn't know how long she had buried her head in his chest before she lifted her head, moved away from him and collapsed on the couch. Losing Paul was not as painful as the humiliation she was suffering from at the moment. She felt as though she was worthless and that no matter how hard she tired, she would never be good enough for a man's love and affection. "You know the trip he's on, that's the trip we were supposed to be on." She shook her head as she gazed down at the carpet. "All those months of me trusting him and giving him time so that he could study, he was with that bimbo. I wish I were a bimbo. Men like bimbos."

Afraid of displaying his attraction to her, Neil joined her, but kept his distance. He tilted her chin up with his hand and said, "Maybe in the beginning, but it never lasts." He wanted to pull her into his arms, kiss her and make her pain go away, but couldn't. He was engaged to Sarah. Even if he didn't have a fiancée, he couldn't take advantage of someone so vulnerable. He couldn't give her the kind of love she expected and would only end up hurting her.

"He told me I was the most important person in his life. He told me when he saved enough money we would go to Greece together. It was all a big lie," she cried as more tears rolled down her face.

He handed her a tissue. "I know you don't believe me right now, but someday you will fall in love again."

"Never, I never want to go through this pain again." She wiped her face and blew her nose.

Neil wrinkled his forehead and said, "And what makes you think you will? Not all men are like Paul you know."

Her voice was now more relaxed and less emotional. "Maybe so, but somehow I seem to attract them."

"You're just going through a rough road," he said, giving her another tissue. "I promise you're going to pull through."

"I must've done something wrong in my life to deserve this," she said, blowing her nose once again, "I must be a terrible person, and now God is punishing me."

"On the contrary, you're a great person," he replied and moved closer because he couldn't help himself. She was like a magnet and he wasn't able to control his hand when it lifted and started caressing her hair, "Your only crime was to trust someone who betrayed you. But a life without trust, what kind of life that would be? You have to trust even if it means running into people like Paul."

"I just don't understand what's so special about her?" she sniffled. "Why does he love her and not me?"

"He doesn't love her. She's just the flavor of the month, you'll see." He gazed into her eyes with such a passion that had she not been so distraught over Paul, she would've noticed. "He's going to grow tired of her at some point and be unfaithful again."

"You don't know that," she said, hoping that he was right because if he wasn't, then there was something wrong with her. She was unworthy of a man's love. Men pursued her, but at the end, they fell in love with someone better and more deserving.

"You just wait and see. I know his type," he assured her as though reading her mind.

"How do you know?"

"His character is apparent in his work. He's dishonest; every time I ask him for something and he doesn't have it, he comes up with the most ridiculous excuses."

She nodded. "That does sound like him."

"And his work is quite sloppy. I doubt he will last here for much longer," he remarked nonchalantly with a wave of his hand.

Anna Lisa creased her forehead and replied in a serious tone, "I don't want him fired because of me."

"Don't worry," he said, patting her hand, "If he gets sacked, it'll be of his own doing."

"I'm sorry for hitting you," Anna Lisa said. "I hope I didn't hurt you."

"Well, my chest does hurt a little," he commented jokingly.

"I'm sorry for being mean to you."

"You weren't mean. Feisty, yes, but not mean."

She studied him. He was handsome with his short hair, seductive smile and sexy eyes, emitting kindness. Why hadn't she noticed before? "You know, some of the girls at the office think you're quite a looker," she uttered.

He was taken aback by her words and his ears turned completely crimson. He cracked a smile. "The girls at the office, hey? You girls gossip behind my back?"

"Not me, but there are women here who think you're attractive."

"You don't think I'm attractive?" he asked in disappointment.

"No... I mean yes... I mean no," she stammered.

"Well, which is it? Yes or no?" he pushed for an answer as he stared at her.

What has she gotten herself into? She should've just kept her mouth shut. Now she was cornered and didn't know what to say. She thought he was handsome but she didn't want to date him even if he wasn't engaged. They were friends and she wanted to keep it that way. "I think we should pack up and leave is what I think," Anna Lisa stated looking at her watch. It was 9. "It's getting very late." She started to stand and he yanked at her elbow.

"Not until you answer my question. Do you or do you not think I'm attractive?" Now, it was a matter of pride. He had to know what she thought of him.

"Oh gosh, I shouldn't have said anything." She desperately wracked her brain for a better way to explain herself without hurting his feelings but came up blank.

"Please," he insisted, "It is your turn to speak your mind."

Anna Lisa sighed and said, "Well, when we first met, I didn't like you much and so I didn't–"

His eyes widened and he interrupted her. "Thank you much."

"No, you didn't let me finish," she said in frustration, "You see, that's the trouble with you men, you never listen."

"Oh? And what have I been doing in the past hour? Not listening?"

"Man, oh man. You don't give a girl a break," she complained. "What I was trying to say was I didn't find you handsome because we weren't getting along."

"And now?" said he waiting impatiently for her reply.

"Now I realize I was wrong. I think you're very attractive," she said and gave out a breath of relief, "There, I've said it. Are you satisfied? Can we go home now?"

"I suppose," he replied, not sounding satisfied at all.

She seized his hand as she would a friend and lifted him off the sofa. "Let's go handsome. I'm tired and I want to get home."

"Fine, fine," he said, following her outside.

For the next few days, Anna Lisa's tears poured in the privacy of her home, the office bathroom and the office when no one was present. Eventually, she stopped crying and began living again. She called her friends, visited her family and began working out with Nicole. Her appetite returned and Anna Lisa started feeling like her old self. Neil became one of her dearest friends and she found herself thinking how lucky she was to have him and Leila in her life. The thought of Paul and Kimberly returning to the office no longer scared her. She began planning for things she wanted to do but never had the time for, like parasailing and taking her nieces and nephews on a roller coaster ride. She felt young and took pleasure in simple things life offered. After coming out of such a deep depression, Anna Lisa now felt an incredible sense of freedom.

PART TWO

SIXTEEN

The month of July was the start of a new chapter in Anna Lisa's life. At work she took her lunch breaks with Leila and Neil and ignored Paul and Kimberly as much as possible. If she needed something from Paul, she would have Leila call him, and if she wanted the help of an administrative assistant, she would ask Diana or another assistant but never Kimberly. Since she did not go into work as often on Saturdays, Anna Lisa had Ursula come in on Fridays instead so she could roam around her home without interruption. Now vibrant and energetic, she went back to hiking with Nicole, started parasailing twice a month on Saturday afternoons, spent more time with her nieces and nephews and developed a closer relationship with Adam. Adam, to her surprise, had been calling her often just to chat about nothing of importance and today, after her hike with Nicole, Anna Lisa was going to hang out with him.

She was lucky to have great male friends such as Adam and Neil, Anna Lisa thought as she parked her Saab in the parking lot of Paseo Miramar's hiking ground. She headed toward the large oak tree where she usually met Nicole.

"I beat you this morning," said Nicole in a coordinated gray T-shirt and shorts. Her wavy hair was tied back with a scrunchy.

"Yes, you did," Anna Lisa answered. She had a pink hair clip around her ponytail and wore a white tank top and khaki boxers. "How are you?"

"Tired, and you?

"I feel great," replied Anna Lisa with a big grin.

Nicole frowned. "How can you be so perky at his hour?" It was 9:35 in the morning and she hadn't slept well the night before.

"It's a beautiful day. The sun's out, birds are chirping and I'm well rested."

Nicole rolled her eyes. "C'mon perky, let's get started before I change my mind."

It was a scorching hot day and in a matter of minutes they broke into a sweat. They slowed down a few times to sip on their bottled water. The road was bumpy and at times they had to be careful where they stepped until they finally reached an apex and Nicole couldn't take it anymore. The 90-degree temperature combined with humidity was wearing her down.

Barely able to speak, Nicole huffed, "Let's stop here. I need a break."

Anna Lisa was only too happy to oblige. She opened the cap of her 1-liter bottle, which was half-empty and gulped her water.

Nicole did the same. Refreshed, she looked at Anna Lisa and said, "So tell me, are you still planning to leave Howard Brown?"

"I'm not sure anymore. I wanted to leave to get away from Paul but now that I'm over him, I may want to stay."

"I think you should considering staying. You love the people you work with."

"True, but I could use a change of environment. Besides, I would be making a lot more money and would have a better position," she said, pausing, "On the other hand, money and position isn't everything. I'd rather be surrounded by people who are kind. I suppose I have some serious thinking to do."

"And what about your condo? Are you still selling it?"

"Yes. I've made an offer on a new condo in Century City. I've been meaning to move for some time now and am excited about it."

"You should have a house-warming party then."

"Not right away because it takes time to settle in but I will eventually."

"I suppose we should get going."

This time, Anna Lisa and Nicole headed down until another steep hill came their way. They conversed a little and greeted a group of hikers who passed them by with their two German shepherds. But as the path became more difficult, Anna Lisa and Nicole quieted down until they reached their familiar lush and green break area where a thin body of water cascaded over a series of large and small rocks and landed into a creek. Feeling as though they were far away from smog and heat in the middle of a breathtaking forest, the two sat there and absorbed their surroundings – the cool breeze and the tall trees with elm and maple leaves that sheltered them from the relentless sun.

Anna Lisa broke the silence. "What're you doing the rest of the weekend?"

"Oh, the usual. I have to take Sam to a birthday party, Eddie's working till 6 and then the three of us are going out to dinner," said Nicole. "Tomorrow, Sam has karate in the morning and in the afternoon I'm taking her to see a cartoon. What about you?"

"I'm hanging out with Adam after here and tomorrow I'll be at my grandmother's."

Nicole passed her a mischievous look. "You've been talking a lot about Adam lately. Is there something going on between the two of you I should know?"

"No, nothing. We're just two friends who enjoy each other's company."

"Listen darling, he may be your friend but I'm sure he wants more than just a friendship. I bet at this very moment he's thinking about how to get you in bed."

Anna Lisa nudged Nicole and said, "You have a one-track mind, you know. Not every guy wants to have sex with me. First, you said Neil wants me and now you're pointing at Adam."

"I read somewhere that men think about sex 24 hours a day and if they're attracted to someone even if that someone is their friend, they want to fuck them."

"You're really crude sometimes. Can you tone down your vocabulary, please?" Anna Lisa rarely used profanity.

"Fuck, fuck, fuck."

"You're incorrigible," said Anna Lisa shaking her head.

"And that's why you love me," Nicole replied and blew her a kiss.

"Oh, please."

"So, what is going on between the two of you?"

"Nothing, I tell you," said Anna Lisa as she took out her cross-trainers and started shaking out a pebble that had snuck in. "Besides, I don't want to date him. I need time to sort out my life. Last thing on my mind is another relationship." She put her shoes back on.

"Maybe it's the last thing on your mind, but not on his," Nicole remarked making a crude gesture with her tongue.

"Stop that." Her friend blushed. "People are going to think we're gay."

"That's their problem. I like men, especially when they're well-endowed," she stated as she grinned and wiggled her eyebrows.

"That's it," Anna Lisa said and got up. "Let's finish our hike and maybe by the end you'll be too exhausted to think of sex."

"I doubt that," she replied getting up. They started walking downhill.

After the hike, Nicole left to pick up Sam from the babysitter and Anna Lisa went home to get ready before Adam dropped by. She took a hot bath, drank a cup of coffee with toast and lemon curd, blow-dried her hair straight, threw on a loose fitting cream and pink floral v-neck sleeveless dress because it was too hot to wear anything fitted and the dress made her feel pretty and feminine. She went downstairs to wait for Adam, but as soon as she sat down on the living room couch, the doorbell rang. Anna Lisa got up to answer it.

"Adam! Right on time." She was used to sitting around and waiting for Paul who was usually a half hour to an hour late.

"You look great," he commented. He was dressed in a casual pink Polo shirt and a pair of white slacks and was wearing a small silver earring in his left ear.

Anna Lisa was surprised to see him in a pink shirt and an earring. She was used to seeing him in more conservative clothes. "Thank you. You look nice yourself." In reality, Adam wasn't her type. He was too perfect looking and someone needed to mess him up. He looked as neat as a brand new book. Not a hair out of place, not a piece of lint on his shirt and not a speck on his white patent-leather shoes. He had a fantastic body – a tight behind, brawny arms, big shoulders, muscular chest and a small waist.

"You're ready or do you need a minute?"

"I'm ready. Just let me get my purse." She walked over to the couch and picked up her small pale pink purse that matched the daisy on each of her summery shoes. "Okay, let's go," she said, heading out the door. They got in Adam's black Aston Martin and started heading east toward Robertson Blvd., a chic street filled with trendy furniture shops, art galleries and restaurants.

Once parked, they strolled from one store to the other and Anna Lisa soon realized that Adam should've become a decorator instead of a CEO. He ooed and awed over different colors, fabrics and textures, explaining each piece with great zeal and pointing out his favorite paintings, vases, sculptures and furniture. Anna Lisa wasn't into furniture and decorating but didn't mind listening to him as long as they were inside a cool air-conditioned place.

"Remind me to ask you to be my decorator when I move into my new place," Anna Lisa joked as she admired a Tiffany table lamp.

"I know, I get carried away sometimes," he shrugged. "You want to go somewhere and have an early dinner or should I say linner?" It was 4:30 in the afternoon and all he had was two hardboiled eggs in the morning.

"What's linner?"

"It's a word I've made up. Just like brunch which is breakfast and lunch. I combine the word lunch and dinner and call it linner."

Anna Lisa sniggered and said, "Good one. I'll have to remember that."

"Well, how about it? Are you hungry?" Adam asked as he walked out of one of the furniture stores.

"Actually I'm starving. I've only had two slices of toast all day."

"I was thinking of a restaurant in Westwood called The Falcon. Their food is really tasty – it's a combination of European and American cuisine. Have you heard of it?"

Anna Lisa shook her head. "No, I haven't but I don't mind trying new places."

"Let's turn around then and walk toward the car," said Adam as they crossed the street and turned north toward Santa Monica Blvd – one of the city's busiest streets.

After leaving Robertson Blvd. and arriving at The Falcon, the valet met their car and the couple went inside.

"Table for two?" asked the hostess dressed in a black suit. She was pleasant and elegant just like the ambiance of the restaurant.

Anna Lisa looked around her. To her right was a large bar with two TV sets, rows of liquor and an espresso machine and to her left was an open kitchen where she could see the staff preparing meals. Tables clad in cream linen occupied the center and borders of the modern and stylish restaurant.

"May we sit over there?" said Adam pointing at a table by the window. The windows had a view of the street, but because of the radiating sun, the shades were rolled three-quarters down.

"Yes, of course," said the hostess, directing them to a comfortable table that could seat four people. She handed them the dinner and wine menus. "Your waiter will be with you shortly."

Anna Lisa noticed replicas of Picasso paintings covered the walls and circular-shaped chandeliers emanated rays that were soft and easy on the eyes.

A waiter came by. He had short, strawberry-blond hair and honey-colored eyes. He looked as though he had just turned 21.

Adam stared at him and ran his fingers through his hair.

"What would you folks like to drink?"

Anna Lisa looked at Adam and smiled.

"What would you like, Grandma?" Adam said jokingly to Anna Lisa. Since when did they become "folks"? They were not that old, he thought.

Anna Lisa bit her lip to stop herself from laughing. "I would like a bottle of flat water."

"I'll have the same," said her dinner date.

When the waiter left, Adam said, "Did you hear that? He called us folks."

She could no longer hold herself back and laughed. "Don't let it get to you. It's probably what he calls all the customers." She unfolded her napkin and laid it on her lap.

He frowned. "I wonder if all young men see me as old."

"Why should you care about how young men perceive you?" she asked, opening her menu.

He cleared his throat. "I don't. C'mon let's have a look at our menus."

When Adam's eyes were focusing on the menu, Anna Lisa studied him. His earring, his plucked eyebrows, his feminine pink shirt and the way he had touched his hair when the waiter came by – he had acted like a girl who was interested in a good-looking guy. She wondered if he were gay. "Adam?"

"Hmmm?"

"You mind if I ask you a personal question?"

"No, I don't mind," he said, looking up from the menu. "You may ask me anything. We're friends aren't we?"

She bit her top lip. "Yes, we are but I have a feeling that you haven't been totally honest with me."

"Why would you say that?"

Anna Lisa paused. She wasn't sure if she should ask him about his sexual preferences. Maybe he would tell her when he was ready, but she was curious. "Umm…are you…nevermind."

Adam knew his earlier comment regarding men's perceptions of him had cast suspicion in Anna Lisa's mind, because he had felt her stares while he was glancing at the menu. "If you're wondering if I'm gay, the answer is yes."

She smiled.

"Why are you smiling?"

"It's silly, really," she replied, shaking her head.

"What's silly?"

"The fact that all this time two of my friends thought you were interested in me."

He laughed. "If I were straight, I would be interested in you. You and I get along so well."

"Yes, we do get along well, don't we?" she said. "I wonder what all the people at my work would think if they knew. Most of the women think you're quiet a catch."

"Please, you cannot tell anyone," he nervously pleaded. "If word gets around and my aunt finds out, I wouldn't be able to face her."

"Don't worry, I'm not going to tell anyone. Although I don't see what the big deal is."

The young waiter came back with a large bottle and two wine glasses with a wedge of lemon on the rim of each glass. He poured the water into their glasses and left.

"Tell that to my aunt," he replied cocking an eyebrow. "She keeps encouraging me to ask you out."

Anna Lisa grinned. "I'm flattered. I like your aunt, and I think she's an open-minded person."

"Not when it comes to my sexual identity," he said, taking a sip of his water. "She would have an attack if she knew. And then there is my mom and dad, my two older brothers and their wives and children. I'm sure they wouldn't want a gay uncle hanging around their kids."

"If they love you, they'll accept you as you are."

Their waiter came back with a fresh basket of bread and set it on the table. "Are you ready to order or would like more time?"

Adam said to Anna Lisa, "The filet mignon is excellent and if you like seafood, you should get the almond-crusted scallops."

"I like scallops," she said. "I think I'll have that."

"And for you, sir?" the waiter asked.

"I would like the filet mignon," replied Adam as his finger roamed the menu. "I'd like it medium well, please." He closed the menu.

"A great choice as well," The waiter took their menus. "Would you like a salad to start?"

They both declined and the waiter left.

"I remember you mentioning you had broken up with someone you loved very much," Anna Lisa said, picking up the bread basket and offering Adam a piece of sourdough. He took one and then she took one for herself.

"What happened between the two of you?"

"He left because I wouldn't introduce him to my family as my lover," he said, lightly tapping his bread to olive oil and putting it into his mouth.

"I'm sorry to hear that."

"I'm over it," he answered with sad eyes that made Anna Lisa think otherwise, "You know, I'm glad I confided in you. With the exception of my gay friends, no one knows about my sexual preferences."

"I'm happy you told me," she responded, sipping on her water. "When people share a secret, it sometimes brings them closer."

"Yes, but my sexual inclination shouldn't really be a secret, should it?"

"No, it shouldn't. I have a feeling that someday you'll tell your family and they'll embrace you just as you are," she stated with conviction. But deep inside, she was unsure of how his family would react because she did not know them.

"I hope you're right," Adam answered looking at Anna Lisa with teary eyes.

Anna Lisa could tell he was getting upset and decided to change the subject. "You know, I was surprised by your knowledge of the arts and furniture."

"It's in the genes. Gay men excel in the creative. Haven't you seen that show – *Queer Eye for the Straight Guy?*"

"Yes I have. The gay men in it are very funny."

The waiter interrupted their conversation when he came over with their meals. "We have filet mignon with potato gratin." He laid the thoughtfully decorated plate in front of Adam. "And yours is the sea scallop with asparagus," he said putting Anna Lisa's dish in front of her. "Be careful, the plates are hot. Enjoy your dinner."

"Bon appétit," said Adam.

It was still early and the restaurant was half-empty. A large group of trendy dressed men and women were sitting at a round table several tables away. An Asian couple quietly conversed at the next table. To Anna Lisa's left, three tables over, was a family of four. No one was seated around the bar. Adam and Anna Lisa discussed their work, their families and their hobbies. Suddenly Anna Lisa spotted Neil coming in with a tall, older-looking gentleman. She was surprised to see Neil at first but then remembered that he lived in the area. The hostess directed them to a table that had a perfect view of Anna Lisa's table. Neil noticed Anna Lisa and smiled but when he saw she was with Adam, his smile faded away.

"Excuse me Richard," Neil said to his dinner partner, "I just saw one of my work colleagues. If you don't mind, I would like to go over and say hello. I shall be right back."

Richard nodded. "Go ahead. I'll have a look at the menu."

Neil, looking conventional in his pale yellow cotton shirt and black slacks, walked over to Adam and Anna Lisa's table and greeted them. "Hello, Anna Lisa, Adam. It's a small world."

"Yes it is," said Adam with surprise as he got up to shake Neil's hand. "I take it you like the food here as well."

"Yes I do. I'm here with my neighbor Richard," he replied pointing to his dinner partner. He then stared at Anna Lisa and Adam and couldn't think of anything else to say.

Anna Lisa said, "Adam and I were looking at furniture on Robertson Blvd. and then we both got hungry and decided to come here."

Furniture shopping? Why would they go furniture shopping together? He thought. "Yes the food here is great," he commented and then noticed that they were almost finished with their meals. "You should try the flourless chocolate cake with vanilla gelato for dessert."

"I couldn't eat another bite," answered Anna Lisa as she motioned toward her stomach. "I'm too full."

"We can share," said Adam. "I love dessert."

Neil wondered how they became so familiar with one another that they shared desserts. He didn't like their closeness. Adam had been calling the office asking for Anna Lisa too often and Neil was afraid that Adam was stealing her friendship away from him.

"Well, I should go back to my table," he stated.

"Enjoy your dinner," said Adam.

"Thank you," Neil coldly replied.

As he walked away, Anna Lisa watched him. Neil was a good person and a great friend. He had helped her through her darkest hours. Had it not been for him, she might still be dwelling on Paul. She wondered why his voice and manners were so cold and distant.

"Would you like some dessert?" the waiter asked.

"Yes, we like to try the flourless chocolate cake with vanilla gelato, a coffee for me and...," said Adam, looking at his date, "what would you like?"

"I'll have coffee as well."

"I'll be right back with your coffee and dessert," said the waiter.

"Neil is a handsome guy," offered Adam.

Anna Lisa grinned. "I take it you want to date him?"

"I wouldn't mind, but he seemed more interested in you than me. Why don't you date him?"

"He's engaged."

"Is he?" he asked with a puzzled look. "I would have never guessed by his behavior."

"What do you mean?"

"Correct me if I'm wrong, but I got the feeling that he was uncomfortable to see me with you. I think he likes you."

Nervous, she fiddled with the edge of a sugar packet. "I like him, too. He's my friend just like you are."

The waiter returned with two coffees, a silver creamer container and their dessert.

"Yes, but friends don't look at friends the way he looks at you," Adam commented pouring cream in his coffee.

She shook her head. "You're misreading him. He doesn't look at me like that at all."

"Think what you will, but someday I will prove you wrong."

"Funny, he told me that he thought you were interested in me. I think men make poor matchmakers," she said, digging her fork into the cake.

From where he was sitting, Neil could watch Adam and Anna Lisa. Richard, enjoying his salmon, was oblivious to what was going on in Neil's head.

Neil's head was clogged with emotionally pressing matters. He wanted to know if his friendship with Anna Lisa would disappear when he left for London to get married, if Anna Lisa was dating Adam and if so, was it turning into something serious? Had they had sex yet? Neil wondered what it felt like to kiss Anna Lisa and to enjoy one night with her free of attachment. Maybe he was getting cold feet. His wedding was right around the corner. Maybe he wished to be with other women before committing himself to one person. Yet he didn't want to be with other women, he only wanted to be with Anna Lisa. His thoughts were interrupted by Richard.

"This salmon is so moist and cooked to perfection," commented Richard. "Don't you think so Neil?"

"Hmmm?" Neil said, shifting his focus to Richard.

"I said," he replied and then noticed that Neil had hardly touched his fish. "Don't you like your salmon?"

"Oh yes, yes," he said taking a bite. "It's delicious."

Meanwhile, Adam and Anna Lisa were getting ready to leave. Neil glanced over, but when Anna Lisa caught his eyes he looked away.

Why is he acting so strange? Anna Lisa asked herself when she saw Neil looking her way and then away.

"You're ready to go?" Adam asked Anna Lisa.

"Yes, let's," she replied.

They both walked toward Neil's table to say goodbye.

Neil got up and shook Adam's hand. He turned to Anna Lisa. "See you Monday."

When Adam and Anna Lisa walked away, Neil watched them with envy, trying to figure out where they were going from there.

SEVENTEEN

Monday morning at work, Neil was studying the information provided by their research department for the advertising of Lady Caroline's perfume line. The data sitting in front of him included consumer surveys, mailed questionnaires, computer analyses, studies on consumer attitudes, trends and behavior, desires and interests. This information was helping Neil determine the kinds of packaging, pricing, distribution and promotion that would make his client's products more successful. But his brain didn't want to focus on statistics and figures. It wanted to find out what Anna Lisa did after she left The Falcon two nights ago. All morning he had tried to control himself and not pry but he could no longer contain himself. He was envious of Anna Lisa's relationship with Adam. He wondered if Sarah were living with him in L.A. would he still be worried about losing Anna Lisa to Adam. He dropped his pen on the research papers sitting on his desk and finally asked, "So, did you and Adam have a nice time on Saturday?"

"We had a great time," replied Anna Lisa from behind her desk. "I really enjoy his company and if it weren't for you I would still be sitting around moping and feeling sorry for myself."

Neil looked at Anna Lisa's black suede headband holding her hair away from her face and her black-and-white plaid dress. He realized there were changes in her – she kept her hair in a ponytail less often and wore dresses more often. Neil wondered if all this had something to do with Adam. "I'm glad I could help," he commented, cracking a smile. "Did you go anywhere else after you left?" he pried.

"No, we didn't go anywhere. Adam came over and we watched a movie – *As Good as It Gets*. Have you seen it?"

A romantic movie! He thought. Maybe they were dating. Maybe Adam did spend the night. "Yes I have," replied Neil. "It's actually quite good."

"We thought so," stated Anna Lisa as she watched Leila walk in.

"Would you guys be interested in seeing King Tut at Los Angeles County Museum of Art?" asked Leila who looked crisp in pleated lavender linen pants and white linen tank top.

"Yes I would," Anna Lisa blurted.

"Me too," replied Neil, thinking that he could go with Anna Lisa and spend an entire day with her free of Adam.

"Great, because I have four tickets that were meant for our clients but apparently our company bought too many and I was able to get these from Diana." Leila showed off the tickets.

"Why don't we all go together?" offered Anna Lisa.

Neil looked disappointed. "When is it?"

"The tickets are for Saturday at 2."

Well, at least it would be just the three of them, Neil thought. "I'm in."

"What're you going to do with the fourth ticket?" asked Anna Lisa.

Neil frowned.

"I asked my boyfriend but he has plans. You know anyone who'd be interested?"

"I can ask Adam," Anna Lisa offered enthusiastically.

Adam? Why does she have to include him, Neil thought.

"Let me see if I can find him," said Anna Lisa as she pressed on her speed dial and put Adam on the speakerphone.

"Hello?" replied Adam.

"Hey, it's Anna Lisa."

Neil looked at Leila and whispered, "She has his direct line? I always have to go through his secretary to reach him."

Leila chuckled.

"Listen, what're you doing this Saturday afternoon?" Anna Lisa asked.

"I have no plans."

"Want to go see King Tut with us at the museum?"

"Who are us?"

"My friend Leila, me, you and Neil."

"I know Leila. She's one of the assistants, isn't she?"

"Actually, she's an assistant account executive who is up for a promotion." That is as soon as I can convince Simon that she's fully capable of handling the workload, she thought. "Anyway, are you interested?"

"Sure. Why don't I pick you up?"

"I can pick her up," yelled Neil from across the room.

"Hi Neil," said Adam, "I live in Anna Lisa's neighborhood. It would be a lot easier if she and I carpooled."

Neil got up from his seat and moved toward Anna Lisa's desk. "I don't live that far from Anna Lisa. I'm in Westwood."

"Yes, but then you have to drive west and then east again; it would be out of your way."

"I don't mind at all," he persisted.

"I know you don't mind but it would be completely out of your way. It's much easier if I pick her up."

"Please, I insist."

Anna Lisa looked at Leila and rolled her eyes. Honestly, what was the matter with them? They were behaving like children.

"I have an idea that's going to make everyone happy," Leila interrupted. "Adam, you can pick up Anna Lisa and then Neil since they're both on your way. And because I live close to the museum, I'll get there early and save us a spot in line." This way the two of you can share Anna Lisa instead of fighting over her, she thought.

"I have no objections," said Adam who really didn't care whether or not he picked up Anna Lisa. By prodding Neil, Adam was trying to show Anna Lisa how much Neil liked her.

Leila looked at Neil. "What do you think?"

"Fine," he uttered reluctantly with his arms crossed in front of his chest.

"Okay then," said Leila. "Now that it's settled, let's meet in line around 1:15. Look for me at the head of the line."

"Sounds good," said Adam, "Listen, I'm hanging up now. There's a meeting of the board I have to attend."

"Excuse me," said Neil when Adam got off the phone, "I'll be right back." He left the room to use the bathroom and get a cup of coffee.

When Neil left, Leila plopped down on a chair across from Anna Lisa, looked at her and commented, "What's going on? Why's there such a rivalry between them?"

Anna Lisa shrugged. "I don't know. They sounded liked they were possessed."

"I think Neil's jealous of your friendship with Adam."

"He shouldn't be," Anna Lisa said, leaning back in her chair. "Although I do like Adam, I care more about Neil."

"You should tell him that."

"No, that's not such a good idea. He's going to be married soon, and I don't think Sarah would appreciate our closeness."

"Yeah, you're probably right," Leila agreed as she sat with one leg crossed over the other.

"Could you do me a favor?"

"Sure thing."

"Could you give these receipts to Paul?" her friend asked as she picked up a red folder from her desk and handed it to Leila. "And ask him to do an expense report?"

Leila took the folder. "Anything else?"

"Yes, then come back here. I want to familiarize you with my clients."

"I'll see you in a bit," she said, leaving the office as Neil walked back in holding a cup of coffee.

Neil glanced at Anna Lisa and settled in at his desk.

From the furrow between his eyebrows, Anna Lisa could tell he was in a bad mood. But why? Why was he so jealous of Adam?

It wasn't as though she had stopped being Neil's friend. "How's Sarah?" she asked, to make a light conversation.

He looked up. "She's doing well. We speak on the telephone every night. She is coming for a visit on July 28th."

Anna Lisa wondered how often Sarah would stop by the office and give her a hard time. "How long is she staying?"

"One week," he answered, imbibing his hot beverage.

Thank God her visit is short, she thought. "And your family, they're doing well?"

"Yes, they still ask about you, especially the boys," he smiled.

Anna Lisa's face brightened. "Really? They ask about me?"

"Oh, yes," he replied, putting his arms on his desk and interlacing his fingers, "They want to know when you're coming back to play soccer with them and I told them September – when you come for my wedding."

"I wish I could but I'll be visiting some old friends in Mexico," she lied. She was actually not going anywhere but was taking a week off before starting her new job.

"Can't you postpone it?" he asked staring at her in disappointment.

"I'm afraid I can't. My plans were made long ago," she replied looking back at him and regretting the fact that he was getting married. She knew her relationship with Neil would never be the same, once Sarah moved back here to stay.

"Well, I suppose I still have another month to convince you," Neil stated as Leila walked back in.

Anna Lisa smiled but knew nothing would alter her decision.

Neil went back to working on Lady Caroline's perfume line. Leila and Anna Lisa went over Anna Lisa's clients together. Leila was excited because she wanted to be more prepared when she moved up to an account executive position. Anna Lisa, who was over Paul but was still contemplating switching jobs, wanted Leila familiarized with her work in case Simon had questions if she were gone. Anna Lisa thought perhaps moving to a new environment and having new co-workers and new clients might do her good. She could be making more money and instead of putting most of it in her retirement account, she could save a portion for traveling and meeting interesting people. Perhaps she would even find that perfect guy.

On Saturday Anna Lisa got home from her hike, took a bath and got ready for her day at the museum. Since it was going to be another hot day, she only dried her hair halfway and then French-braided it. Not having done that in years, Anna Lisa was clumsy at first but after several tries, she succeeded. At the bottom of her braid, she added a hair ornament made of tiny white roses. She then threw on a loose, sleeveless peach summer dress, put on delicate white sandals and switched the contents of her black handbag into a white straw purse. She wanted to get away from her everyday career look and be more like a carefree girl who was on vacation with bunch of friends.

When Adam rang the bell, she descended the stairs and greeted him.

He was wearing a fitted T-shirt that showed off his muscular body and a pair of light blue jeans but no earrings. "Sorry, I'm a bit early. I hope I didn't rush you."

"No, you had perfect timing," she replied, walking outside. "I'll just lock up and we can go."

When they walked toward Adam's car, Anna Lisa said, "You know, if you like I can drive."

"No, let's just take my car. It's already parked on the street and ready to go," he said.

"Are you sure? You're always the one doing all the driving and I thought—"

"Please," Adam said, "Let's not argue the way Neil and I did the other day or else we'll be here all day."

"Why don't you go up to San Vicente, turn right, take it to the end and turn left on Wilshire. It's much faster that way," Anna Lisa commented as she turned around and yanked on her seatbelt.

Adam cocked an eyebrow. "Backseat driver."

"Sorry, I'm a control freak," she said, securing her belt. "You know, I never understood why the two of you were so persistent the other day over who should drive me."

"Oh, that," Adam smiled, "I was just giving Neil a hard time. He likes you, you know."

"He doesn't like me the way you think he does."

"And what way is that?" he asked glancing at her and then back to the road.

"You know what I mean," she answered crinkling her nose, "You goaded him the other day into an argument."

With an elbow resting on the window and his hand on the wheel, Adam said, "Don't you see, if he didn't like you, why should he have cared if I were the one driving you to the museum?"

"Did it ever occur to you that he might be jealous of our friendship? After all, I have been spending a lot of time with you."

"Friendship, *schmendship*. The bottom line is he wants you."

"Why would he feel that way about me and still be engaged to his fiancée? You're not making any sense."

"Maybe he doesn't love her but is afraid to get out of his commitment."

"What are you, a mind reader now?" she said with her arms crossed in front of her.

"No, just a romantic who likes to see you happy."

"I am happy. Besides, you're not exactly the queen of happiness. When was the last time you dated anyone?"

"I haven't met anyone that strikes my fantasy yet," he replied, pulling inside a fancy high-rise. A waterfall cascaded in the center of a round pond. Adam drove around the waterfall. A valet ran up to park his car. "We're waiting for a guest," said Adam as he saw Neil approach the car from his rearview mirror. He got out so that Neil could see him.

"Good afternoon," said Neil. "Did you have any trouble finding my place?"

"No, the directions were pretty straightforward."

Anna Lisa stuck her head out and was surprised to see Neil look so casual. He was in a periwinkle blue round-neck shirt and bluish gray sporty pants. "Hi Neil," she said admiring his clothes. "You look nice."

"Thank you," Neil smiled, glad that she had noticed him. He had bought his clothes the night before to impress Anna Lisa because she had always been on his case regarding how formal he dressed. He went around to the driver's side. The valet opened the door for him and he sat in the back. When Adam got in, Neil commented, "I like your car." He noticed that the interior was charcoal leather. "My in-laws have an Aston Martin except theirs is navy with tan interior. I prefer yours."

"Thank you," replied Adam as he finished his circle around the waterfall, waited for traffic to end and then made a right turn on Wilshire toward the museum.

Anna Lisa turned sideways, so she could talk to Neil. "What did you do today?"

"I ran on the treadmill and lifted weights this morning at the gym in our building."

Adam, who was into weightlifting remarked, "Oh yeah? How much can you bench press?"

Neil was embarrassed because he could barely lift 135 pounds. "One hundred thirty-five pounds including the weight of the bar."

"You must be a rookie," stated Adam, trying to show off.

Anna Lisa, who knew nothing about weight training, had a hard time getting involved in their discussion.

"How much can you lift?" Neil asked but regretted it as soon as he proposed the question because Adam was muscular with cuts in his arms.

"I can bench 230 on my slow days and on good days...oh, I can get to 300 and that's not including the bar," Adam gloated.

Neil's eyes widened. Three hundred pounds? He bet he could beat him in the leg press. He had strong legs. "I can leg press 350. How much can you press?"

"I don't know," Adam shrugged. "I just stack the 45 pound plates until there's no room left. I don't know how many plates that is," said Adam, "Let's see, I guess five on each side or is it six? Then multiply that by 45 pounds each–"

Anna Lisa interrupted them. "When the two of you are done comparing how much weight you can lift, please let me know because honestly, I'm really bored here."

"Sorry, we forgot there's a lady present. Perhaps we should talk about what happened on Lani Kay's talk show yesterday," Neil teased, winking at Adam in the rearview mirror.

Adam smiled and asked jokingly in a high-pitched voice, "What did Lani talk about yesterday because I was busy doing my hair and missed her show."

"Very funny," cried Anna Lisa, "I think I liked it better when the two of you were rivals."

Adam laughed. "Let's see, what's a safe subject to talk about?"

"Work," replied Neil. "That's always a safe subject to talk about."

"No, I don't want to talk about work," protested Anna Lisa, "Maybe we should save our thoughts and wait until we can share them with Leila."

"A good idea," said Adam.

So, the three of them sat there, looking outside at the cars, the old and modern buildings that surrounded Wilshire Blvd. and the pedestrians. Adam turned on his radio and found a station that played jazz, and it wasn't long before they reached their destination. They parked, crossed Wilshire and followed the crowd that was heading east toward the museum building where the treasures of King Tut were being displayed. When they arrived, they stood in a long line to give their tickets to a security personnel standing in front of a roped area. Once inside the roped area, they saw Leila and cut through the crowd as those waiting in line glared at them.

"It took you guys long enough," complained Leila looking sporty in her white t-shirt and taupe jumper. "I was afraid you were going to miss the exhibit." It was almost 2 o'clock.

"Sorry," offered Anna Lisa, "but there was a large crowd ahead of us."

Adam, who had a vast knowledge of Egyptian history, the pyramids, pharaohs and artifacts said, "Does anyone know the story behind King Tut?"

Neil wasn't about to let Adam show off. He may not have been an expert in the history of Egypt but he knew a thing or two about King Tut. "I do."

Anna Lisa gave Leila a look that said here we go again, the two of them trying to display their knowledge about this exhibit. Honestly, they were acting like five-year-olds. She decided to sit this one out and let the two of them fight it out.

"King Tut or rather King Tutankhamun's birth name was Tutankhaten, which meant 'living image of the Aten, the son of god.' He was a pharaoh who died at 18 or 19 years old and thus didn't accomplish much in his life," crowed Neil. "His fame is attributed to the discovery of his tomb by a British Egyptologist named Howard Carter in 1922 and the elaborate treasure that was buried in the tomb."

"How did he die?" Leila asked.

Adam jumped in. "His death was sudden and remains a mystery. I've heard that he may have been murdered by Vizier Aye – the high priest of Amun – who forced Ankhesenamun, King Tut's wife and half-sister, to marry him so he could stake his claim as pharaoh. Aye died four years after acquiring the throne."

Anna Lisa, who already knew this because she had borrowed a booklet from a co-worker who had visited the exhibit, remained silent.

"But where were his father, mother or siblings? Couldn't they have replaced King Tut?" asked Leila who had slept through most of her history classes.

"Don't forget he married his half-sister," said Neil nodding his head and raising an eyebrow. He spoke with an elevated voice filled with superiority, making sure that he caught Anna Lisa's attention, "and his father, who remains a mystery, died when King

Tut was young. Soon after, King Tut, who was about eight or nine, was given the throne."

As soon as Neil took a breath in between sentences, Adam interrupted him. "His father was believed to be Akhenaton, although some evidence points to Amenhotep III," Adam added wrinkling his forehead and looking serious like a college professor who was teaching his student. "His mother remains a mystery as well but she is believed to be Kiya."

The security started ushering the visitors into the museum. Adam held Anna Lisa's hand just to get a reaction out of Neil. Anna Lisa whispered in his ear to stop it or she was going to let everyone know he was gay.

Adam's eyes widened. "You wouldn't!"

"No, but you're really trying my patience," said Anna Lisa as she let go of his hand and started walking in front of him.

Neil, who had been observing them, was envious of their relationship and wondered what Anna Lisa was whispering to Adam.

Leila, oblivious of what was going on, was anxious to get into the room to look at the treasures of King Tut and the artifacts from other royal graves.

When they went in, they marveled at the amount of detail that went into each piece. The gold mask of Tut and a sculpture of him on leopard were among the many artifacts they saw. Leila and Anna Lisa read the descriptions on the bottom of each display as Adam explained the intricate detail. Neil was surprised by Adam's knowledge of Egyptian art. He always thought that L.A. residents were more interested in movies and the beach than cultural experiences.

After they exited the museum, it was already 4 o'clock. Outside, on a large patch of grass, round tables were covered with white plastic tablecloths embellished with orange sunflowers. Adam suggested they grab a table. Neil sat between Adam and Anna Lisa. Leila looked at Anna Lisa and smiled. Anna Lisa shook her head discreetly. They rested their feet for a few minutes, trying to decide if they wanted something to drink or eat.

"It's too hot to eat," Leila commented, "but I could go for bottled water."

"Me too," Anna Lisa uttered, "What about you guys?"

"I'd like a beer," Neil said getting up, "And I would like to treat everyone."

"Thanks," Adam replied, "I'll have a beer as well."

"Here, I'll help you," Leila offered as she got up, "You can get the beer and I'll get the water."

"That wouldn't exactly be treating you, would it?" Neil remarked.

"Don't worry about it. It's the thought that counts," she said, heading toward the bottled water vendor.

When they got back to the table, Neil noticed that Adam had moved next to Anna Lisa. He sure was possessive of her, he thought. She was his friend before Adam came along.

"Did everyone get the invitation to my aunt's party?" Adam asked. Jane was planning a party for everyone at Howard Brown who had worked on the Olson account including the assistants and the accountants. She had also invited the employees and the board of directors of Olson and Olson, Inc. Each person was allowed to bring a guest and the dress code was black tie.

"Yes," replied Leila, "It's Saturday, July 30th."

Anna Lisa opened the cap on her water bottle and took a gulp. She was going but had no one to go with. At one point she had even contemplated calling an escort service but later had decided against it.

"I hope you're all attending," said Adam.

"I am," Neil answered. "My fiancée, Sarah, is probably shopping this very minute for a new outfit," he commented jokingly.

"Wonderful. So, you're bringing her?" Adam reiterated.

"Yes, that is the plan," said Neil, but he didn't sound excited about it.

Leila said, "I'm bringing my boyfriend."

"What about you Anna Lisa? Do have a date?" asked Adam hoping that she didn't for three reasons. One, he didn't have anyone to go with and couldn't very well take another man with him. Two, Adam knew some of his co-workers had been speculating for some time about his sexual preferences because he wasn't married, didn't have a girlfriend and didn't show any interest in women. What better way to give the impression that he was straight by taking Anna Lisa. Third, he wanted to get a reaction out of Neil and prove to Anna Lisa that Neil desired her but didn't have the guts to tell her.

Anna Lisa embarrassed not to have anyone to go with, cleared her throat and sputtered, "I'll be attending by myself."

"We can't have that, can we Neil?" Adam asked, looking at Neil with a big obnoxious grin on his face. He then put his arm around Anna Lisa's shoulder.

Neil didn't respond but instead clenched his jaw. He didn't know why he was so jealous of Adam. He had a beautiful fiancée who loved him. Why should he care if Adam liked Anna Lisa? Yet, there was something about the whole situation that bothered him. Adam's arm around Anna Lisa irritated him. It was as though Adam was marking his territory. Neil looked at Anna Lisa and took a sip of his beer.

Adam said to Anna Lisa, "How would you like to be my date?"

Anna Lisa's face brightened. "Thank you. I accept."

"Perfect," said Adam. "Isn't this perfect, Neil?" He knew he was getting on the Brit's nerves and wondered at what point Neil would stake his claim on Anna Lisa. It was obvious to Adam that Neil liked her. Why didn't he dump that fiancée of his and go after the woman he really wanted? The man had no spine.

Neil passed Adam an unwilling smile and replied unenthusiastically, "Yes, that is just perfect."

EIGHTEEN

The Olson project was almost finished. People involved on the project were excited to see that after months of planning and working at odd hours, the fruit of their seed was finally paying off. And in celebration of everyone's hard work, Jane Olson had thrown together a party at The Wellington in Beverly Hills, minutes away from Century City where Howard Brown was located.

The Wellington was a luxurious hotel where many celebrities and politicians stayed when they were in town. Limousines dropped off and picked up their passengers in front of the spectacular all glass main entrance of the hotel. Beyond the cars and the attentive valets, large sliding glass doors showed off the sparkling cream-colored marble floors where the chic hotel guests socialized in their pricy suits and dresses.

The party was on the rooftop ballroom. Inside, 20 tables and 160 chairs were covered with white linen. A band played soft music behind a dance floor. Round tables were decorated with freshly cut pink-and-purple orchid bouquets mixed with white dendrobium. Beyond the tables and chairs was a bar manned by two male and a young female bartender. Waiters circulated hors d'oeuvres to the guests standing around and mingling.

"We should go to our table. I think they're about to take our orders," said Anna Lisa to Adam. Tonight she looked glamorous. Her hair was pulled back and set by a professional hairdresser. Her mauve eye shadow, dark eyeliner and soft pink lipstick were applied with perfection by a make-up artist. Her backless powdered rose dress complimenting her complexion loosely draped from the waist down, hiding her wide hips.

Adam, looking predictably perfect in his black tux and olive silk vest, was talking to a board member of Olson and Olson and her date. He excused himself and headed toward the front of the room with Anna Lisa who had chosen the guests at their table when she spoke with Jane Olson's secretary a month ago. The rest of the guests scattered around and went to their tables as well.

After everyone took their seats, the waiters took the orders. The choice was roast beef, roasted chicken or flounder. Adam, Anna Lisa, Neil, Sarah, Leila and her boyfriend and Diana and her date were seated at the table behind Simon's. Simon, Jillian, Jane and several members of the board of directors of Olson and Olson, Inc. were seated at the first table. Other tables consisted of employees of Howard Brown and Olson and Olson. Paul, Kimberly and some of the assistants sat toward the back of the room.

"It's nice to see everyone so relaxed," Adam remarked.

"I agree," replied Anna Lisa, who was seated in between Adam and Neil. "We're always under so much pressure at the office that we forget to smile."

"It must've cost a fortune to throw this party," commented Diana who was across the table from Anna Lisa.

Sarah, in a floor-length body-hugging black gown that was slit up to her right thigh, sneered at Diana's comment – how tacky it was that all Americans talked about was money. Ever since she had walked in, she had been envious of the way Anna Lisa was able to converse with ease with some of the movers and shakers of the marketing world. Sarah hadn't spoken much since she entered the ballroom – she felt out of place and uncomfortable. It bothered her that Neil sat next to Anna Lisa and that they were such good friends. Sarah found herself wondering once again if something was going on between her fiancé and his officemate. A few weeks ago, Sarah had agreed to move to Los Angeles, but tonight she was having second thoughts.

Anna Lisa noticed that no one was talking to Sarah and felt sorry for her. She decided to initiate a conversation with her even though Sarah had been rude to her in London. "That's a gorgeous dress you're wearing. Is it a Versace?" said Anna Lisa not having a clue about the styles of different designers. She usually bought what she liked and looked at the price not the labels.

Sarah's face brightened. "Thank you. I bought it in Paris at the House of Dior. It's haute couture."

"It's very sexy," Adam added. Adam may have been gay but he loved looking at women. To him, it was like looking at a beautiful piece of artwork.

"You really have great taste in clothes," commented Leila who wore a dark purple off-the-shoulder velvet dress. "I've seen you around the office when you visit Neil. I've been a great admirer of your wardrobe."

After that compliment, Sarah, who would never speak to someone like Leila, abandoned her arrogance for a miraculous moment. "We must go shopping together, and I can give you some pointers."

"I would like that," replied Leila.

Neil, looking suave and sexy in a classic black tuxedo, glanced at Anna Lisa with a look that said thank you for making my fiancée feel like part of the group.

Anna Lisa, who seemed to have read his mind, winked at him and smiled.

Sarah was too busy to notice. Everyone was asking her about wardrobe tips and Sarah was more than happy to answer. Then the subjects switched to London, the world summit in Scotland, the commitment to world hunger, the tragic terrorist bombing of the underground and the double-decker bus, and if it was safe to travel there.

"It was awful when it happened. I'm glad I don't need to take the tube," said Sarah to Diana.

"I was shocked when I saw it on the news," stated Diana. "I would have never thought something like that could happen over there but then look at what happened to us on 9/11. No place is safe anymore."

"I assure you that our government is doing everything possible to protect its citizens and the visitors," Sarah replied.

The meals arrived and the subject changed once again. This time they discussed the corrupt multimillion-dollar corporations, the thousands of employees who had lost their pensions, the stock market, and how unsteady it had been lately. Chuck, Diana's date said he had lost a "whole bunch of money" but Viktor, Leila's boyfriend said he had managed to make a few pennies here and there.

"You really can't depend on the company's prospectus or the analysts' point of view anymore. You don't know who to trust," said Chuck, a hefty man in his fifties who had eaten one too many pieces of fried chicken in his days.

"An insider's tip is what you need," replied Viktor, who sported a mustache and golden brown hair that parted in the middle.

"Yes, but you can get into trouble for that. Look at what happened to Martha Stewart." Chuck protested.

"I know, but if you look at it on the positive side, she made a lot of money because of what happened to her," Viktor commented.

"Yes, but you and I are no Martha Stewart," Chuck answered.

Everyone chuckled.

The conversation continued from investments to sports, movies and books until dinner came to an end and dessert was served. Sarah excused herself for the ladies' room. The band came back and encouraged the guests to dance. Leila and Viktor took their suggestion. Adam got up to stretch his legs. He went to his aunt at the next table to see if everything was to her liking. Neil turned toward Anna Lisa.

"Well, it's almost over. I bet you're glad to get rid of me," he said as he admired her perfect hairdo, her subtle make-up and seductive dress. Tonight, she looked like a movie star.

"You've been pretty tough to take," Anna Lisa said jokingly, "but I'll miss you." She wished they could be this close forever, yet she knew that was not possible.

"You talk as though we'll never see each other again," said Neil as he studied Anna Lisa's eyes. "I'm going to come back and stay here permanently."

She wished that Neil wasn't coming back because she was afraid of herself. Afraid of liking him too much. "Yes, but you'll be married and be very busy."

"I'm never too busy to make time for my friends," he said, touching her hand lightly.

"Men always say that," stated Anna Lisa, who had lost several of her friends after they had married. "But you see, wives don't like their husband's girlfriends."

Adam came back to the table, put his hands on Anna Lisa's shoulders and interrupted them. "Enough talking. Let's dance."

Anna Lisa let Adam lead her to the dance floor. Neil looked disappointed as he watched Adam put one hand around Anna Lisa's waist and whisk her away. Sarah came back from the ladies' room. Aware of her fiancé's attraction to Anna Lisa, she clung to him as though she were afraid to lose him. Neil switched his attention to his fiancée and asked her to dance. Paul was drinking at the bar and Kimberly was sitting with a group of people from work.

"Thank you for being my date," Adam said to Anna Lisa, giving her an appreciative smile. He was an able dancer, easy to follow.

"You're welcome. But are you ever going to let your family know you're gay?" she asked with one hand on his shoulder and the other in the hand of his extended arm.

"They'll never understand," he replied as he brought Anna Lisa closer to him. He placed his hand on her naked back because he noticed his aunt watching them.

"They're going to find out sooner or later," stated Anna Lisa as she wondered why in the world her gay friend was dancing so close to her.

"No, they won't," said Adam shaking his head. "I'll get married to some girl and that'll be that."

Anna Lisa tilted her head back slightly and objected with a voice full of disapproval, "What about the girl? Don't you care about hurting her feelings?"

Adam shrugged and said, "I'll tell her the truth right from the beginning."

"No one in their right mind would agree with your arrangement," she responded with a frown.

"There're many women out there who're only interested in money and position and I have both," he responded arrogantly.

Anna Lisa sighed in frustration. Adam was insane to come up with such a ridiculous solution. "You'll never be happy till you live the life you want regardless of what people around you think."

"And what about you?" he asked staring directly into her large, almond-shaped eyes. He admired her beauty, her honesty and her down-to-earth personality. Had he not been gay, he would've pursued her.

"What about me?" she asked giving him a puzzled look.

"It's time for you to start dating."

Oh God, he sounded just like her grandmother and her Aunt Kate. "I'm not ready to date yet."

"The sooner you get on top of a new horse, the sooner you'll forget the old one."

"I've already forgotten the old horse, but I have no plans of getting on top of a new one," she replied noticing that Simon and Jillian were now on the dance floor. She nodded when she saw Jillian looking her way.

"I think you're making a big mistake," said Adam as he checked out a handsome guy standing outside the dance floor talking to a short pudgy lady. He was tall with curly blond hair and baby blue eyes.

"I know what I'm doing," replied Anna Lisa who noticed Adam's eyes were focused on their receptionist, Bob.

Adam brought his attention back to her. "Funny how you can dish out advice when you have a hard time taking advice yourself."

"We make a lovely pair, don't we?"

"Not us, but perhaps you and Neil," said Adam taking a glance toward Neil dancing.

"Oh, are we back to that conversation again?" Anna Lisa remarked sarcastically. Honestly why did everyone think she and Neil made a great pair?

"I'm not blind, you know. I see how the two of you look at each other," said Adam, who started to move closer toward Neil and Sarah.

"He's my friend, and he'll be married soon," Anna Lisa dryly answered.

"Married to ice woman when he should be with you?"

Anna Lisa stopped dancing. "I have no feelings toward him other than friendship."

"Really? Then you don't mind if I cut in their dance and have you dance with your friend," said Adam gliding his date around the floor as though she were a feather.

"Please don't do that. I have no desire to dance with him," she pleaded pursing her lips.

But all the begging in the world did not stop Adam from heading toward Neil. "You mind if I cut in?" he asked Neil.

With a surprised look, Neil answered, "Not if Sarah doesn't mind."

Sarah found herself in an awkward moment. She didn't want Neil to dance with Anna Lisa but at the same time didn't want to be rude to Neil's client. "No, I don't mind," she responded unwillingly with a forced smile.

When Neil took Anna Lisa in his arms, she was nervous at first. Her heart was pounding loudly, her hands were clammy and she hoped he wouldn't notice. And had his heart not been pounding just as loud and his hands not been just as clammy, he might have noticed Anna Lisa's nervousness, but he did not. He held her close. Neither of them spoke. The energy they exchanged was stronger than words. The feel of his masculine hand against the skin of her back made her tremble. Why did he make her so nervous? He was just a friend. He was the same guy she went out to lunch with everyday at work. He was the same guy who sat next to her on the office sofa while she poured her heart out over Paul. So why did she suddenly feel like a schoolgirl on her first date?

The delightful smell of Anna Lisa's gardenia perfume, the feel of her breasts pressed against his chest and the smooth skin of her back drove Neil insane. He found himself wondering once again what it felt like to kiss her rosy lips and spend an entire night making love to her over and over. One night was all he wanted, but he knew he couldn't. He couldn't cheat on Sarah, and he couldn't risk his friendship with Anna Lisa for one night. He couldn't make love to her and leave her the next day but oh, how much he desired her. And as these thoughts occupied his mind, he was interrupted by Sarah who complained about how tired she was and that she wanted to go home.

Neil snapped back from his reverie and cleared his throat. "I'm sorry honey, you must be jet-lagged." He then walked off the dance floor with Anna Lisa and Sarah and started saying goodbye to a few people.

Anna Lisa walked back to her table and took a long drink of water. She turned to look at Neil's back as he walked away and wondered if she stayed at Howard Brown, would she be able to contain the mixed emotions she had felt when they had danced.

"Hello, Anna Lisa," said a voice from behind her. When she turned, she saw Paul.

He looked handsome in his tux and charcoal vest. His dark hair was tied back and his pitch black eyes were mesmerizing, but Anna Lisa felt nothing toward him. He was like a complete stranger to her. She responded coldly, "Hello Paul."

"You never asked me how my trip was," said Paul as he touched Anna Lisa's shoulder. He noticed her body stiffen. And when he saw the look of disapproval on her face, he removed his hand.

Impatiently, she asked, "And how was your trip?"

Kimberly approached them and stood next to Paul.

"We had a nice time and visited many places. My favorite place was–"

"Good for you," she interrupted. She no longer cared about what he had to say, what he did, where he went or who he saw and if he thought she was going to give a flying hoot about him, then he'd better think twice. As far as she was concerned he was a manipulative person who was trying hard to warm himself to her again. Fool me once, shame on you; fool me twice, shame on me, she told herself.

Kimberly, oblivious to how much Anna Lisa disliked her said, "I have pictures of our trip at the office. You should come by and see them."

She looked as slutty as ever with her silicone boobs practically hanging out of her white dress, Anna Lisa thought.

Leila, who had been watching them from afar, now came closer and said, "Would you mind if I steal Anna Lisa away?" She turned toward her friend. "Simon would like to have a word with you."

"Thank you for rescuing me," she replied to Leila when they had walked away. "What does Simon want?"

"Oh nothing. But let's go see him anyway so we won't look suspicious."

Jillian was hanging around with her husband near the bar. At 55, she had a fabulous body as she stood tall and sophisticated in her sleeveless, fitted, pear-colored sequined dress, when she said to Anna Lisa, "I saw you dancing with Neil."

Anna Lisa found it interesting that she would mention Neil but not Adam. "Yes, well. I seem to have lost my date."

"He's over there speaking to that good-looking blond fellow," Jillian responded as she pointed her almost empty martini glass in his direction. "Isn't Adam gay?"

Anna Lisa looked over and saw Adam talking to Bob. "Excuse me?"

"That's not our business," Simon said to his wife as he jiggled the ice in his scotch.

Anna Lisa frowned. His sexual inclination was none of anyone's business. "He's not gay."

"Think what you will," replied Jillian downing the remaining gin in her glass. "But I know a gay man when I see one."

"Jillian, can I get you another martini?" Leila interrupted to get her to change the subject. Jillian had no idea what she was talking about, Leila thought. There was no way that Adam was gay. He looked and acted like a straight man.

To this she responded, "No, I'd better not or else I'll wake up the next morning with a bad headache." She then faced Anna Lisa. "I hear you and Paul are no longer together."

She liked it better when Jillian was picking on Adam, Leila thought. Poor Anna Lisa, who was constantly reminded of Paul.

"I see news travels fast," Anna Lisa uttered, looking at Simon.

"I didn't tell her. I don't know how she knows these things," Simon replied, eyeing his empty glass. He could really use another drink, he told himself.

"I can't say that I'm sorry to hear about your breakup, as painful it might have been for you," Jillian commented with a caring voice that a mother would use to advise her daughter. "But he doesn't deserve you."

"So I've been told," Anna Lisa said. She knew Jillian meant well even if she was a busybody.

"Now Neil," Jillian said wagging her index finger, "he's a nice match for you."

Simon shook his head and left to get another drink. His wife was driving him crazy.

"He's engaged. Now, if you will excuse me, I think I'll go grab my date for a dance," Anna Lisa said politely, wiggling her way out of the conversation.

The rest of the evening went by more smoothly. Anna Lisa danced two more dances, one with Adam and the other with Simon. Paul and Kimberly left the party early. They did not look like a happy couple. Jillian dropped into people's conversations and at times, she just stood there, observing everyone.

"Sorry about my wife digging her nose where it doesn't belong but it's only because she likes you," Simon said to Anna Lisa when they were dancing.

"Don't worry about it. I like Jillian. And besides, my family is the same way. My grandmother is always trying to set me up with someone."

"I must say this evening has been more enjoyable than I had anticipated."

"I agree," Anna Lisa responded, eyeing Adam talking to Bob. They seemed to click well, she thought. She didn't know much about Bob except that he started working for Howard Brown nine months ago, and had always been friendly and polite to her. Anna Lisa wondered if Bob was gay.

When her dance with Simon was over, Anna Lisa went back to her table and found Leila and Viktor getting ready to leave. "You're taking off?" She asked Leila.

"Yes, aren't you? It is getting late. It's almost midnight."

"I am tired, but I have to wait for my date," Anna Lisa said, watching Adam approach her.

"How was your dance with Simon?" Adam asked.

"Great. I noticed you were talking to our receptionist, Bob," Anna Lisa commented.

"Yes, I was. As it turns out he's studying interior design."

"Your favorite subject. You two probably had a lot to talk about." Anna Lisa turned to Leila and said, "Adam loves decorating."

"How nice, I am terrible at it," Leila responded.

"I can teach you," Adam said, noticing most people had already left. He glanced at his watch. "I didn't realize it was so late. They're closing down the ballroom at midnight."

"That explains why everyone's taking off." Viktor replied and then they all followed the rest of the guests outside.

NINETEEN

One late evening, about a week after Jane Olson's party, Neil was clearing his desk. He was leaving for London in 18 days to prepare for his wedding. He looked up and saw Anna Lisa cleaning her drawers. "House cleaning?" he asked.

"Yes, the drawers tend to get so messy the longer you work here," she replied, thinking how handsome and cultured he looked in his navy suit, blue shirt and tie.

"Sometimes I like that. It gives it that home kind of a feeling."

"Yes, I suppose working the kind of hours we do, we might as well feel at home."

Neil smiled. "We've been so preoccupied with work that I forgot to ask how you've been doing."

"You mean after my nervous breakdown over Paul?" she said, tapping a group of folders on the table to line them up. She walked over to her file drawer to organize them. "I've been feeling much better, thanks to Leila and you. You both really helped me out," Anna Lisa said, lowering her head to put the folders in the proper file jackets, "I don't know how I could ever repay the both of you for being there when I needed you most."

Neil admired her sexy physique hidden underneath a conservative cream blouse and brown skirt. "We'll think of something," he replied teasingly. "Oh here, I think this belongs to you." He walked to Anna Lisa's desk to give her back a vintage pen he had once borrowed long ago.

"No, you keep it as something to remember me by," Anna Lisa offered as she got ready to leave. She picked up her briefcase.

"You're positive you don't want it back?"

"Uh-huh," she said nodding her head and heading toward the door.

Neil followed her, put the pen in his pocket and frowned. "Why do I get the feeling that I'm not going to see you again?"

She glanced back at him. "Don't be silly," she replied with an evasive smile, "We'll see each other when you get back."

"Are you certain you don't want to come to my wedding?" he asked, moving toward her and standing in between the door and Anna Lisa. "It would be a nice vacation for you."

"No, I'm going to be in Acapulco visiting old friends. I promised them long ago that I'd go see them," she lied.

"Well, if you change your mind…"

"Thanks, I'll think about it." She then tried to reach for the doorknob so she could leave, but he wasn't getting out of her way. She felt him standing too close to her and could smell the woody scent of his cologne. It reminded her of when they were dancing at Jane's party and she started to get nervous the way she had that night – wobbly legs, clammy hands and a heart that thumped incessantly. Why was he staring at her with eyes full of desire? It was as though he didn't want her to leave.

Neil stood inches away from Anna Lisa debating whether he should take her in his arms or let her go. Whatever you do, don't touch her, he told himself. Don't kiss her. You're engaged. Remember Sarah, your fiancée? But his heart wasn't about to listen to all the nonsense going on inside his head, and before he could stop himself, he was drawn like a magnet to Anna Lisa's soft inviting lips. And then it happened. He gently kissed her and when she responded back, he wrapped his arms around her and pulled her closer. Without reflecting, Anna Lisa brushed her hands against his chest and glided them up gently around his neck. He probed, lingered inside her and became more assertive. With a body that had a mind of its own and a brain which did not recognize right from wrong, Anna Lisa lost herself in his fantasy until she finally came to her senses and realized what she had done. She removed her hands from around his neck and pulled away. "We shouldn't be doing this," she said and bent down to pick up her briefcase.

"Leeza, I---"

"Don't. I don't want to be a Kimberly." She left him standing there.

The day that followed the unforgettable kiss was as awkward as hell. Anna Lisa tried to work out of the office of an account executive who was on vacation, but Neil would come by to ask her a question or to borrow something. She tried to avoid him when she went to get a cup of coffee or talk to a co-worker but wherever she went, she bumped into him. She had to get away from him. What she had done the prior night was unforgivable even if she did dislike Sarah. If women learned to control their attraction to unavailable men, then there wouldn't be so many cheating men.

For the longest time Anna Lisa had been contemplating staying at Howard Brown, but now, not even a raise or a partnership offer would entice her to stay. She was leaving Howard Brown a week after Neil's departure and with the exception of Simon, Leila and Adam, she had no intention of keeping in touch with anyone. A month ago she had thought she and Neil would be best friends for a long time, but now she knew better. She finally realized that women and men who are attracted to each other can never be friends and that there would always be sexual tension between them. That's why she could never keep in touch with him. When they had kissed, he had aroused feelings in her that she never knew existed. She was in love with him. She, who never thought she'd fall in love again. How crazy it was for her to fall in love so quickly with another man. It seemed like only yesterday that she was crying over Paul. No, she must be on the rebound.

Yes, that's what Neil was – rebound. Soon he would be married to Sarah and Anna Lisa would be starting a whole new life. She had put up her condo up for sale and was in escrow for a new one. A new job. A new home. A new Anna Lisa. No more office romances. She was finished with all that. Tired of always making the same mistakes with men, she was going to take her time before getting into another relationship. She had to sit back and analyze where she was going wrong and try to fix it. As these thoughts occupied her mind, she heard a knock on the door and invited the intruder in. It was her boss.

"I thought I'd stop by to tell you that we've had a great response to the ads you placed on the billboards for the Van Millen hair care products," Simon remarked. "I spoke with Van Millen this morning, and he was very pleased."

"I'm glad to hear it," said Anna Lisa, reaching behind her chair and putting on a sweater. The chilled air from the air-conditioner was giving her Goosebumps. She rubbed her arms in an effort to warm her body.

"Cold?" Simon asked.

"A little," she replied, taking a drink form her coffee mug.

Simon was about to turn and leave when he suddenly scratched his stubbly gray head and said, "Say, are you and Neil mad at each other?"

Good God, isn't anything sacred at this office? "No," she said frowning, "What makes you think I'm angry with him?"

"Well, you know that I don't like to snoop, but..." he paused.

"But what?"

"I was wondering why you moved in here?"

"Oh," Anna Lisa sighed. "You know me," she said, shrugging nonchalantly to evade suspicion. "I like to work alone and this office was empty. I thought I'd take advantage of it."

"Well, you needn't worry about not having solitude for long. Neil is getting his own office when he gets back from his honeymoon," Simon told her. "Then you can have all the space you need."

"About that…," Anna Lisa said. She had been thinking for a long time about how to tell Simon she was leaving the company.

"Yes?" Simon asked, raising an eyebrow.

Anna Lisa crinkled her nose. "Maybe it would be better if you sat down."

"You sound serious," he noted wrinkling his forehead, "I suppose I will." He wondered what Anna Lisa had in mind. He walked to her desk, pulled out a chair and sat down across from her.

"As you have seen in the past few months, I haven't been the most pleasant person to be around," she said, resting her elbows on her desk and interlacing her fingers.

"We all have our ups and downs," he replied, crossing his ankle over the top of his knee and relaxing back in his chair, "but we manage to get through them and I think you have."

"Maybe so, but I need to make some changes in my life."

Simon passed her a puzzled look. "I don't understand."

"I…I…I…" said Anna Lisa as she struggled with her words. Minutes ago she was cold and now a nervous sweat was forming above her top lip. She got rid of her sweater and draped it over her chair.

"What is it that you want to say?" he asked with a concerned look. He removed his ankle from the top of his knee and edged forward to give Anna Lisa his full attention.

"I have accepted a new job offer and my last day will be Friday September 2nd." She was leaving in about three weeks.

"What?" he said, raising his voice and staring at her incredulously.

"I've been hired by Hamilton International Inc.," blurted Anna Lisa as she scrunched her face.

"Are you joking?" he asked, exasperated.

Anna Lisa shook her head. "No, I'm perfectly serious."

"I'm sorry, but I can't let you leave," Simon replied adamantly as he collapsed back and crossed his arms in front of him.

"My mind's made up, and there is nothing you or anyone can do to change it."

"Are you unhappy here?" he asked.

"Of course not. You're the greatest boss an employee could wish for."

"Anna Lisa, you bring in a lot of business and you're up for a partnership position. Why would you jeopardize all that and go work somewhere else unless they offered you a better deal, a fatter paycheck or a higher position?"

"My decision has nothing to do with my paycheck," she said, still sitting with her arms on the table, afraid to move.

"Maybe if we made you a partner," he said desperately because he couldn't afford to lose her. He liked her. He was used to working with her. She was a productive employee.

Seven months ago her dream was to be a partner but now, after everything that had happened to her at that office, nothing could possibly lure her to stay. Anna Lisa shook her head in disagreement.

"Then why? Why are you leaving us?"

"Because I need a change of environment. A lot of things have happened since I started working here and I want a fresh start."

He tilted forward, looked directly into her eyes and asked, "I suppose there's nothing I can do to persuade you to stay?"

"Nope. It's time for me to go. But I have to ask you for two favors."

"Go ahead."

"First, is that I don't want anyone at the office to know when I'm leaving and where I'm going."

"Not even Neil?"

Especially not Neil, she thought. It wouldn't be right for her to keep in touch with him. She needed to move on and be with someone who wasn't involved. "No, not even Neil. Besides you, Leila and Adam, no one must know."

"But why?"

"I told you, it's important for me to have a new beginning. I don't want to keep in touch with my past."

"People are going to find out sooner or later."

"Let them. Right now I'm not in the mood to answer everyone's questions regarding why I'm leaving. Once I'm gone, they can speculate all they want. By then, I'm not going to care because I would've moved on with my new life."

Simon looked disappointed. "If you're ever unhappy at Hamilton, you know the door is always open for you here."

The look of appreciation that Anna Lisa gave Simon was beyond words. Her red eyes and expression of regret helped Simon understand how hard it must've been for Anna Lisa to tell him she was leaving. "What is your second favor?"

"It's actually not a favor but rather a win-win deal. I think you ought to let Leila replace me." She saw him shift nervously in his chair and added, "Just hear me out, and say no if you disagree."

"Go on," he said unsure of where she was heading.

"She's been working here for four years with three of them as an assistant account executive. She has only one class left before she finishes her master's and I've seen her work. She's detail-oriented and clients like her."

"I will consider promoting her, but she could never replace you. I couldn't possibly give her the kind of large accounts you've been handling."

"Here are some of the clients she has worked on," said Anna Lisa as she handed him a folder. "On many of them, she did most of the work but unfortunately it was the ad exec who got the credit."

"I'll study it and see what I can do."

"Thank you."

"You know, this isn't fair." He wrinkled his forehead. "I can't even give you a proper goodbye party."

She looked at him kindly. "I know, and I thank you for being so thoughtful."

Simon got up and extended his hand to shake hers. "I will miss you. We all will."

Anna Lisa stood up and shook his hand. "And I will miss you. But I will keep in touch. Just don't tell anyone where I am."

"Don't worry. I'm not even going to tell my wife. I wish you good luck," he said and headed out the door.

When Simon left her office, Anna Lisa felt very sad. She was leaving a comfortable environment for the unknown. True, she had worked with Steven Langley before, but he was the only person she knew at Hamilton International. Would her co-workers be nice? Would they treat her with respect? Would they be competitive and hate her guts? She didn't know, but what she did know was she was going to miss everyone at Howard Brown except for Paul and Kimberly. And what about Neil? She had spent almost eight months sharing her office with him and soon she would never see him again. She was so disappointed in him for kissing her last night. It was wrong of him to do so. Neil had lured her into accepting his kiss and Anna Lisa wondered about his character. Was he like Paul? Would he cheat on Sarah with other women once they were married? If so, Anna Lisa didn't want to have anything to do with him the way she didn't want to have anything to do with Paul. Why did these types of men enter her life? Why did she attract them? She never asked for their attention and yet, they seemed to find her somehow, pursue her, be with her and then dump her. Well, she's had enough of her share of dishonest men. This time she was going to truly study a man's character before committing herself to a relationship.

TWENTY

Neil sat with his legs extended on the black leather sofa of his living-room and thought about Anna Lisa. It was right around his bedtime but he wasn't tired. Three days had passed since he had kissed Anna Lisa but they hadn't talked much except to exchange a few words. He couldn't figure out why she was so angry with him. It wasn't as though he had coerced her to kiss him. All he had done was instigate it. Yes, it was wrong and he shouldn't have done it, but he couldn't help himself. It was as though he was pushed by the devil to do the wrong thing, except that what he had done didn't feel wrong. He had enjoyed it. Why did something so wrong feel so right? His emotions were completely entangled and Neil felt utterly confused. Did he want to marry Sarah? He had made a commitment long before he met Anna Lisa, and he was going to keep it. In a way, Neil was glad that Anna Lisa wasn't working out of her office because there was less temptation. He got up to get a glass of milk when his phone rang. He picked up the black cordless receiver sitting on the glass side table next to the sofa. "Hello?"

"Hi, it's me," said Sarah.

"Hello darling; you couldn't sleep either?" Neil sank on the chair to the left of the couch. He relaxed his arms on the high leather handles. It was 11 p.m. in Los Angeles, which meant it was

7 a.m. in London. Neil was surprised to hear from Sarah at that hour because she usually liked to sleep in.

"No, there's a lot on my mind," she said sounding upset. She was lying on her replica of a Louis XVI bed underneath a white plush comforter filled with goose feathers at her parent's house.

"What's the matter?" he replied frowning. "You're not sick are you?"

"If I tell you what is wrong, promise you're not going to get angry with me?"

"Of course not. You can tell me anything," he said resting his head on the back of the chair. "We're getting married soon and if we can't communicate now, we shall have an even harder time communicating later."

Sarah sighed. "Very well, then. Here it goes. I do not wish to live in Los Angeles."

Neil wasn't surprised. Lately when they talked on the telephone, she made hints about how she was going to miss her family and friends once they moved and how she wished he could work out of the London office. He had tried to calm her in the past and tell her that he could give her things she wanted if he worked in L.A. He was making more money than when he was in London. "Darling, I can provide a better life for you in L.A."

"We already have a good life in London. We can have anything we want right here."

"Your parents can. We cannot."

"What is the difference? They shall help us." She turned to lie on her side.

He sat up, stiff, angry and frustrated by her comment. "I don't need their help," he bellowed, and went to the bar to make himself a glass of neat whiskey. Forget about the milk, he required something much stronger than milk to calm his nerves.

Sarah started crying on the other end of the receiver and Neil felt awful for hollering at her. "I'm sorry I shouted at you. It's just that I thought you might at least give L.A. a try before you judge it so harshly."

She heaved. "I don't want to live there. Most of my friends are here."

"But you can make new friends," he said, pouring an ample drink and going back to the sofa.

"And what about my family? I need them."

Neil cussed underneath his breath. Her family was one of the reasons he wanted to get her away. He didn't like them meddling in their lives and controlling them with their money. He was about to say they could come to L.A. and visit her but decided against it. Instead he said, "You can go back and visit them whenever you want." He drank his whiskey.

"It won't be the same," she pouted.

"Darling, I cannot get up and leave at a whim. I have a boss to answer to. He is expecting me to continue working here."

"Why can't you tell him I don't want to move out there? Please Neil," she pleaded, "don't make me live there."

Neil swirled the whiskey in his glass and didn't reply for a long time. If he pushed Sarah to move, they would probably have all sorts of problems. Sarah would complain everyday about how unhappy she was in L.A. and he didn't need that. After a lengthy day at work, he wanted to come home to serene surroundings and a content wife. He preferred to enjoy his free time with her instead of squabbling all the time. Besides, part of him sympathized with her. Sarah didn't work. She would get lonely here by herself. It wasn't fair of him to pressure her do something against her will. Yet on the other hand, he didn't like being back home near his in-laws. They spoiled Sarah too much and prevented her from growing-up and learning to stand on her own feet.

Sarah heard silence on the other side of the phone. "Neil? Did you hear me?"

He nervously ran his fingers through his hair contemplating his dilemma, "Yes, I heard you. I was thinking." He took another sip of his whiskey.

"I'm sorry. I just had to tell you how I feel. Los Angeles is so big and spread out. It has no culture. There are no good operas or plays. The city's museum exhibits are limited and the restaurants are nothing compared to here."

He didn't know what to say. He had grown fond of L.A. and the locals' laidback and liberal attitudes. He enjoyed the beautiful sunny days, the warmth and the friendliness of the employees when he walked into a store and the mélange of residents who made up L.A. It was a flavorful city.

Sarah was getting more agitated and scared by the minute. She wished to talk to her fiancé face to face so she could read him better. Did L.A. mean so much to Neil that he was he going to part with her and stay? Because if that was his plan, then she would have to move out there. What choice did she have? She loved him and wasn't about to lose him.

Neil finally spoke. "Are you certain you will not change your mind?"

She was petrified to answer him. "I love you Neil," she replied with a shaky voice, "and I don't want anything to come in between us. But I would be lying if I said I desired to live in Los Angeles."

Disappointed and saddened by Sarah's decision, Neil wrinkled his forehead. "It's too bad you feel that way. I was hoping you would give it a go, but I can't force you to do something against your wishes."

"What are you saying?" asked Sarah. All the color drained from her face because for a moment she thought Neil was going to break off the engagement and stay in Los Angeles. She knew how much he had come to like L.A., especially now that he was friends with Anna Lisa. Anna Lisa – that was the real reason why Sarah wanted her fiancé to come back home. Neil and Anna Lisa were too close. Sarah had noticed it the night of the Olson party – the way they exchanged glances, how close they had danced and how he had admired her. That night, Sarah felt non-existent in Anna Lisa's presence, but she was not about to give up Neil. Sarah had interrupted their dance and had feigned exhaustion when she pulled her fiancé away from Anna Lisa's clutches.

Noting the apprehension in his fiancée's voice, Neil forced himself to say, "Relax darling, I'm going to tell Simon I can't stay." Neil had decided to give into her. If Sarah wanted to live anywhere else, he would've refused, but after all, London was where his family and friends were and he would get to see them more often. Plus, maybe it was better for their marriage to keep some distance between himself and Anna Lisa.

Sarah's face lit up, and color returned to her cheeks. She sat up in her bed and smiled. "Really? You would do that for me?"

"Yes. I hate to see you unhappy."

"You're the best. I love you," she said, throwing him kisses over the phone.

"I love you too," he said, but he was no longer sure if he still meant it. He downed the rest of the whiskey in his glass and slammed it on the table before going to bed.

That night, Neil lay in his bed, unable to move underneath his crisp and unwrinkled gray and maroon sheets. He had always believed that as time passed his love for Sarah would grow but instead they had grown apart. Neil had been spending too much time away from her. Perhaps after moving back home and spending more time together they could recapture the intimacy they shared before he left London. Yet, he was pulled between a life in L.A. and a life in London. London was and always would be his home, but in L.A. he had discovered new friends and a second home.

The day following his telephone conversation with Sarah, around 4 in the afternoon, Neil, who had procrastinated all morning, decided to finally stop by Simon's office to let him know he couldn't stay in L.A. He went in and noticed his boss holding the phone with his head tilted to one side and writing on a white note pad. Simon lifted his pen and waved at him to sit. Neil pulled up a chair across from Simon's desk.

"Two pounds of veal, a carton of eggs and what? Trader Joe's breadcrumbs? Uh huh...does it have to be from Trader Joe's? Why can't I go to Gelson's and buy it? Oh, I see...Trader Joe's tastes better," he said rolling his eyes at Neil. "Well why can't you send the help to get it?...They're busy? Doing what? Oh never mind, I have to hang up now. I'll see you at 6," Simon said and hung up. He looked at Neil who was waiting for him patiently. "Sorry, my wife's having another one of her small dinner parties for four. What can I do for you?"

"I have something to tell you and you're not going to like it," Neil said, sitting erect.

"You have picked the right week for it," Simon replied, resting his body against the back of his chair. Exasperated by a series of unwelcome events, he unbuttoned the first two buttons of his white collar, which was too tight for his thick neck and unraveled his navy-and-yellow-striped tie. "Bad news has been hitting me left and right. The infomercial we did for one of our clients got a lousy response and we have to re-shoot. The ad we placed in a magazine for another client came out at the wrong time. And to top all that, one of my employees is leaving for greener pastures. So believe me I'm getting immune to disagreeable news."

Neil wrinkled his nose. "Sorry, perhaps I should come back another day," he suggested as he started to get up.

"No, sit, sit," replied Simon with a gesture of his hand, "Don't let my crazy life scare you. I'm used to this. That's why I have no hair."

Neil forced a smile. He wasn't happy about what he had to say, "When I go back to London, I'm not planning to come back." He was leaving in about two weeks.

First Anna Lisa and now you, he frowned. "But why? I'm losing all my good employees."

Neil sat there holding his hands in his lap and with a voice full of disappointment said, "Had I not been attached, I'd stay, but as it is, I have a fiancée who is not fond of Los Angeles."

Simon edged forward, put his elbows on the desk and rubbed his face. "Women. As soon as you marry them they take over your life. Can I do anything to change your mind? I really need you here."

"You could try to convince my fiancée to stay, but I doubt you would have much luck."

Simon chewed on the corner of his mouth and shook his head. He was losing two of his best employees and there was nothing he could do to stop it. "I assume you'll be going back to our London office?"

"That is my plan, and I cannot tell you how sorry I am to spring this on you so late."

"I would like to take you out to lunch before you leave. Perhaps Anna Lisa and some of the employees could join us."

"Thank you but no." As much as Neil wanted to see Anna Lisa, he thought it best to stay away.

Simon huffed. "I don't understand you young people. No one wants a farewell party these days."

"I am forever grateful for your understanding of my sudden departure," Neil stated and shifted uncomfortably in his chair. "A goodbye luncheon is not necessary. It would only make me feel guiltier for leaving all of you."

"Well," he said sadly and sighed, "I hate to see you leave but I can certainly understand. I know I would do anything to keep my wife happy as much as I complain about her."

"How long have the two of you been married?" he asked, seizing the opportunity to ask Simon a few questions in order to get this wise man's perspective on love and marriage. Ever since Neil had moved to L.A., he had been confused and unsure about his engagement to Sarah.

"Twenty-six years and counting," Simon chuckled. "I'm joking, you know. I love Jillian. We were truly in love when we got married and we still are. I honestly think she's my soulmate."

"How did you know you were in love with her?" Neil asked like a student taking notes.

Simon got up, walked to the mini fridge located in the bar on the left side of the room and grabbed a bottle of Crystal Geyser. "Want one?"

"No thank you."

Simon twisted off the cap and went back to his chair. He quaffed his water. "Months before Jillian and I got married, we got into a big fight. I can't even remember what we fought about but I will tell you I was very angry and words were exchanged that shouldn't have. Anyhow, we didn't speak to each other for a whole month, and I was really depressed. I was drinking more than I should have and my life felt empty and pointless without her. I loved and needed her and couldn't imagine living without her. That's when I knew she was the one."

Neil listened to Simon's story with envy and wasn't sure if he felt the same way about Sarah. The truth was he wasn't excited about going back and getting married and he blamed it all on having cold feet. "Well, I've taken up enough of your time. I think I will go and work on Lady Caroline's perfume."

From Neil's serious face, the nature of his question about love and the way he hung on every word made Simon realize Neil's ambivalence. For the past four months, Simon had seen Neil's behavior around Anna Lisa and as much as he wanted to deny that his wife was a terrible matchmaker, he had to admit that in this one case, Jillian was right. Neil and Anna Lisa belonged together. He had noticed how Neil sometimes looked at Anna Lisa and how close he had held her the night of the dance. The guy was in love and didn't know it. Yet, Simon couldn't meddle. All he could do was point him in the right direction. "A word of fatherly advice, and then I'll let you go," said Simon when he saw Neil getting ready to leave.

Neil stood in front of Simon's desk silently and let him finish his thought.

"Marriage is hard work," he said shifting forward with both arms on his desk, "and it's even harder when you're not sure about your feelings toward your partner. So if you have any uncertainties about getting married, you'd better resolve them before making a lifetime commitment."

Neil nodded. "Thank you, Simon. I shall think about your advice."

After Neil closed the door behind him, Simon sat in his chair for a few minutes, thinking how content he was to be happily married. Sure they fought the way any normal couple did, but they also loved each other deeply. How lucky he was that he found his match, he thought as he got up, readjusted his necktie on and left work early to surprise his wife.

TWENTY-ONE

A memo was sent to all employees of Howard brown: Neil will be leaving permanently after Friday August 26 and to forward all client inquiries to Anna Lisa after that date and Anna Lisa will be going on vacation starting Monday September 5 and to forward all client inquiries to Leila after that date until further notice. Simon had abided by Anna Lisa's wishes and was planning to inform everyone of her departure after she was gone, but he wasn't letting anyone know where she was going.

Anna Lisa stepped in her office late in the morning and found the memo in her inbox. She read it over and over and couldn't believe her eyes. Neil was leaving. But why? She thought he liked L.A. Was he leaving because he was unhappy here or was he leaving because he wanted to get away from her? She was sad and relieved all at the same time. Sad, because she would never see him and relieved, because she would no longer be tempted to contact him. He was out of her life and everything that had happened between them was nothing more than a distant memory. Soon he would be married and living in London and she would start her new life. Yet, she sensed a deep void – a combination of solitariness, glumness and despair – but she wasn't going to show it. She had to be brave and keep her distance from the man she loved but couldn't have. As these thoughts ran through her mind, Diana walked in.

"Did you get the memo I put in your box earlier?"

"Yes I did," Anna Lisa said with her elbows on her desk, her arms extended in front of her and her fingers interlaced as she tapped her thumbs together anxiously.

"What do you think about Neil leaving so suddenly? It's all so odd."

Anna Lisa tried to hide her feelings. "I don't know. Maybe he likes it better in London." She looked at Diana, puzzled. "Is there something you needed?"

Diana cleared her throat. "I was wondering if you could do me a favor."

"That depends on the favor. What is it?"

"Everyone at the office has contributed money to buy Neil a farewell present and I was wondering...I mean since you know him better than everyone else, do you think you could pick out a present for him?"

"Oh," she uttered, surprised. "Why don't you buy him a business card holder or some nice set of stationary?"

"He's such a nice guy, we wanted to get him something more personal like a shirt."

The last thing in the world Anna Lisa wanted was to go shopping for Neil but unfortunately she was stuck. Obviously she could always say no but that wasn't her nature. She always liked helping out. "I'll do it," she replied reluctantly, "but I'm kind of busy for the next few days."

"As long as you get it done over the weekend."

"Fine. Anything else?"

Diana handed her a small envelope. "There's $60 in there. We also bought him a card. Some of the employees have signed it. Thought you might want to write something in there." She gave the card to Anna Lisa and waited for her to write in it.

"Could you leave it here and I'll look at it later? I'm right in the middle of working on Xian soap products," she lied because she had no idea what to write.

"Oh, okay." Diana said and left her office.

Anna Lisa opened the large envelope and removed the card. The outside had a picture of giraffe, kangaroo, chimpanzee and various other animals standing up and looking sad. Inside it read, 'Farewell to our co-worker. You will be missed.' It was a cute card, Anna Lisa thought, as she read the inscriptions from some of the employees. She picked up a pen to wish him well but wasn't sure how to say it. She closed the card, put it back into its envelope and took out a scratch pad to draft what she wanted to say. 'Dear Neil, Sorry to hear you're leaving. My best wishes for a happy future. Anna Lisa.' She scratched it out, crumpled up the paper and threw it in the wastebasket. 'Neil, I will always cherish our friendship, Love, Anna Lisa.' She scratched it out , crumpled up the paper and threw it in the waste basket. After 15 drafts she finally gave up and went back to work.

After lunch, Diana poked her head in, pointed at the large envelope and said, "Are you done with that yet?"

"No, not yet."

"I'll come back later."

Two hours later Diana came back for the card. "If you're finished with this I would like to take it," she said, picking up the card.

"I haven't had a chance to look at it," Anna Lisa complained.

"What's there to look at?" Diana responded with a frustrated voice, "You sign it and stick it back in the envelope. How difficult is that?"

"Come back in 10 minutes and I'll have it ready."

Diana put her hands on her waist. "You know, I want to at least get a couple more signatures before the day is over."

"Ten minutes, I promise."

"Fine." Diana left.

Anna Lisa thought and thought but her mind was blank. She finally scribbled some nonsense and signed it as Diana walked back in.

She shook her head and passed Anna Lisa a disappointed look. "Finished?"

"Yes."

"It's a miracle!" She took the card and left.

The weekend came by and left but Anna Lisa still hadn't bought Neil a present with the money Diana had given her. It was 6 in the evening on a Wednesday and Neil was leaving Howard Brown in two days. She dreaded shopping for him. Why was she the one who had to be constantly reminded that he was leaving? Diana had already bugged her about his gift several times, and Anna Lisa regretted the fact that she had agreed to shop for him. What could she possibly buy for a man who had everything?

Diana came into her office and found her standing near her desk, getting ready to leave. "So, what did you get him?" she asked anxiously.

"Nothing yet," Anna Lisa said as she threw on her red jacket.

"Anna Lisa you promised to buy him something yesterday," Diana frowned.

"I'll get to it when I get to it." She pulled out her ponytail that had gotten tucked underneath her jacket and straightened her collar.

Diana moved from the door to where Anna Lisa was standing and stared at her. "His last day is this Friday. Were you planning to wait and mail his present to London?"

She hated her overwhelming attitude. Who was she to push her around? "If you're so concerned, why don't you get it yourself?" She picked up her black leather purse.

Diana lightly pulled on Anna Lisa's sleeve to stop her from walking away. "C'mon Anna Lisa. You made a promise and you should keep it."

Anna Lisa wrinkled her forehead. "I don't know what to get him," she whined.

"Are you telling me that you worked with the guy for eight months and know nothing about him? I find that hard to believe," she replied with exasperation.

"Stop pushing me around or I'm not going to get it."

"I thought you out of all people would care more about him, but I guess I was wrong," Diana cried disapprovingly. She started to walk out of her office when Anna Lisa interrupted her.

"Wait, don't go." Her co-worker had every right to be angry and Anna Lisa knew it. She had been putting off shopping for Neil for days and now time was running out. The truth was she didn't want to think about him leaving. She just wanted to be left alone.

Diana turned to look at her.

"I'm sorry. You're right. There's no excuse for my procrastination," she replied, approaching her, "I'll have his present wrapped and ready by tomorrow."

Anna Lisa left work and went to an indoor mall where she had picked out Tennis shoes and casual clothes for Neil for the O'Malley basketball game. She went from store to store but nothing pleased her. One shirt was too plain, another too bright and a third not his style. Anna Lisa finally realized what the problem was. She preferred to buy him something casual and fun instead of some stuffy shirt and tie. That day at the game, Neil had been so delighted with his attire. She decided to go to the same store as before to buy his present. There she found what she was looking for right away – A khaki long-sleeve shirt with yellow stripes along the shoulders and sleeves and a pair of coordinating sweatpants. Anna Lisa also picked out a pair of brown sandals for him. When she took them up to the cashier, she had to add $40 of her own money to what Diana had given her but she didn't care. She knew Neil would enjoy his gift.

When she Left the mall and got home, she removed the prices off of each item, wrapped the sandals in a cream tissue, folded the clothes neatly and thoughtfully and placed them in a taupe box the store had given her. She took out a pretty maroon plaid paper, wrapped the present and made a beautiful bow with a matching ribbon.

The next day when Diana picked up the present from Anna Lisa's office, she was pleased. "I love the bow. It's so creative. Did you do it yourself?"

"Yes I did," she smiled, "Glad you like it."

"What did you get him?"

"I got him a khaki sporty shirt, matching sweatpants and brown sandals."

"Would he like that? He always dresses so properly. I thought for sure you'd get him a shirt and a tie."

"Trust me, he'll like it. He needs more casual clothes in his wardrobe."

"Okay then, would you like to give it to him yourself?" Diana offered.

"No, just tell him it's from everyone at the office," she answered, trying to remember something she had wanted to tell her and then it suddenly came to her. "Oh and there's a gift receipt attached on the inside of the box."

Diana nodded, took the present and left to go get the farewell card from her desk. A minute later, she knocked on his door and he asked her to come in.

Neil, working behind his desk on Lady Caroline's perfume, looked up and was surprised to see Diana give him a beautifully wrapped present and a large card. "What is this for?"

"It's a small gift from all of us at Howard Brown. We hope you like it."

"Thank you." He put the card and the present to the side and planned to have a look later.

Diana stared at him and said, "Aren't you going to at least open your card?"

Neil smiled. He was speechless at the kindness of the staff as he removed the card from its envelope, admired the front and then read the inside. There were many comments and signatures signed at different angles but the first one he looked for was Anna Lisa's. He read it and frowned. 'To Neil, best wishes, Anna Lisa.' How cold and distant her note was. At least the others had written "Dear Neil" or "Love so and so" or "We'll miss you."

Diana noticed his displeasure. "Don't you like it?"

"Yes. Yes. It's lovely," he answered and put the card away.

"You don't look very happy," said Diana, wringing her hands. She always liked to impress her superiors in case she ever needed their help to get promoted. She wondered what he thought of the present. Maybe she should've gone with Anna Lisa's idea and bought him something generic.

"I am touched and only too sad to leave all of you."

"In that case, you have to come back and visit us," she offered, her stance more relaxed now that he seemed pleased.

"I shall." He started to open his present very carefully. It was wrapped so beautifully that he didn't want to tear it up. And when at last he opened the box, he was moved by how perfect his gift was. He could wear it for his workouts or lounge in it at home and khaki was one of his favorite colors. "This is perfect. Words cannot express my gratitude."

"We thought you'd like it and if you need to exchange it for another size, there's a gift receipt in there."

"Thanks very much," Neil reiterated.

"You're very welcome." Diana left and closed the door behind her.

Neil opened his card once again and stared at Anna Lisa's writing. The scribbles of her thoughtless note hurt him deeply. It was as though she didn't care about him and they were nothing but strangers. But when he picked up his present and admired it, he wondered if Anna Lisa had anything to do with choosing his gift. It looked like her taste. And she was always on his case for not having enough casual wear. She must've picked it out. The others at the office didn't know his shoe size but she knew from the time they had gone shopping for the basketball game. He shook his head. Perhaps he was wishing desperately for some sign of her affection for him. He wasn't sure. Confused and upset about the negative turn of events in the past, he folded his gift and the wrapping paper in the box, put it away along with his card and went back to work.

Two weeks after giving notice, Neil had no reason to be at Howard Brown on his last day in Los Angeles. It was Monday. He had wrapped up business and said his goodbyes the Friday before, but he had to see Anna Lisa one last time before his flight took off. He approached her office, went in and closed the door behind him. "Will you please talk to me?" he said, walking toward her desk.

Back in her own office, Anna Lisa looked at his neat hair, freshly shaven face and perfect attire that always seemed to be right out of the dry cleaner's door. When and how did she fall for this Englishman who wasn't her type? She was drawn to grungy looking men who resembled Paul – loose long hair, a face with a four o'clock shadow and funky, relaxed clothes. Eight months ago Neil seemed stodgy to her and now he was everything she wanted but couldn't have. "I have nothing to say to you," she said, wishing he would go away. She was afraid of herself – afraid to show her feelings toward him. She figured that by being cold she could push him away.

He stared at her hair that she tied back into a bun like Mrs. Butterworth on the syrup bottle. Her eyes glared at him. How much he had missed her in the past few days. How did they end up being so close when they had such a bad start? When Neil had first met Anna Lisa, he didn't care much for career women – they were always so uptight. She wasn't like any woman he had dated. She was independent, feisty and opinionated and he cared for her deeply. He put his hands on her desk. "Are you angry with me because I kissed you?"

"Bingo," She replied, fidgeting nervously in her swivel chair.

"I would take it back if I could," he said with a frown. "I hate to see you cross with me."

She got up and paced the room not knowing what to say.

He waited for her to say something.

She turned and asked with an unyielding face, "Why did you do it?"

"I don't know. It felt as though it was the right thing to do at the time," he answered but didn't budge from where he was standing. He could feel the tension between them and didn't like it.

"Well, it was an inappropriate thing to do," she said, walking back to her chair and sitting down. "You're getting married, for God sakes."

"I know, and I apologize. It will never happen again." He wasn't sure if he could keep his promise. He was attracted to her but still wanted to marry Sarah. He and Sarah had a longer history together and came from the same culture. They understood each other.

"What you did, made me change my opinion of you," she said in a reprimanding tone. "I used to think you were different, but you're just like the rest of them."

"Nothing happened." He knew better. Something did happen. When they kissed, he forgot all about Sarah and had Anna Lisa not pulled away from him, he would've seduced her right there in the office.

"Nothing happened because I stopped you," she replied as though reading his mind. "What were you thinking?" She started pacing the room again.

"I made a mistake," he shouted. "Can't you forgive me?"

She turned to face him. "You don't get it do you? It's not about forgiving. I feel like I don't know you at all, the way I never knew Paul," she said. "Paul and I were friends once too, just like you and me."

"Are you comparing me to Paul?" he asked with an angry tone.

"Yes. He did the same thing with Kimberly behind my back as you did with me three weeks ago behind Sarah's back." Not that she gave a damn about Sarah, she told herself, but wrong was wrong.

"Everything is not as black and white as you think when feelings are involved."

"Go away, will you?" Anna Lisa plopped down in her chair, put her elbows on the desk and started rubbing her temples with her fingers. Three weeks ago they were friends and now she didn't know what they were.

Neil moved from the opposite side of her desk and got closer to her. "Are you ending our friendship because of a kiss?" he said, staring at her.

Anna Lisa didn't look at him nor did she answer. She had no answer.

Neil reached in his pocket, took out an envelope that he had been carrying in his pocket for some time but didn't have the guts to give to her. Ever since he decided to go back to London, he had promised himself to stay away from Anna Lisa. Except today he had broken his promise. He laid the envelope on her desk. "There's $10,000 worth of checks in there for Brother O'Malley's youth foundation," he said, his hand still on the envelope. "It was the best I could do in such a short time."

Without looking at him, Anna Lisa waited for Neil to remove his hand and when he did, she picked up the envelope, opened the flap and stared at the checks in disbelief. "I never expected you to raise that much. I don't know what to say. Brother O'Malley will be grateful, thank you."

"My pleasure," he answered. "But I didn't do it for Brother O'Malley, I did it for you."

The thought of him going out of his way to please her touched her heart. She looked directly at him but didn't speak.

"Can't we be friends?" he asked searching her face for a sign or a glance that said it's okay, we can get past this.

His stare was making her more agitated, and she was scared. What if he were able to read her face? What if he could see that she wanted him more than he wanted her? She reminded herself to be strong and do the right thing. "I don't think that's such a good idea after all that has happened."

He wondered why he was making such an effort to keep their friendship going when clearly she wanted nothing to do with him. "You don't forgive easily, do you?"

"It's not that, it's just that–" she paused for a moment, "I need time to think things through."

"You shall have all the time you need. I will not be coming back," he said and moved away from Anna Lisa. He went back to the opposite side of her desk.

Anna Lisa, already sensing the growing distance between them, looked over at his empty desk. He had no idea how much she was going to miss him. "Simon told me you were leaving. I was rather surprised. I thought you liked it here."

"You see, Sarah changed her mind," he said clasping his hands in front of him, "and doesn't want to live in Los Angeles. We'll be staying in London permanently."

He looked grave and stiff, she thought.

"I may need your help every now and then since I will not be here."

"I hope you'll have a nice wedding," she forced herself to say.

"I'll call you after our honeymoon," he replied and stood there waiting for Anna Lisa to say something.

She didn't want to promise to keep in touch. It wasn't right to keep in touch with a married man when she had strong feelings for him. "Goodbye, Neil. Have a safe trip."

"Until we see each other again," he said. He felt he had lost her forever and there was nothing he could do to change her mind.

TWENTY-TWO

It was two days before her departure from Howard Brown. Leila and Adam still had no idea she was leaving, but Anna Lisa was planning to tell them today at lunch at a casual indoor and outdoor restaurant inside a hotel near work. Trying hard to forget Neil, she had kept busy to avoid thinking about him. Anna Lisa had considered staying ever since she found out he was leaving but ultimately decided against it. Much had happened to her at her current job and she needed to get away. She opened up a file folder for Xian soap products and began writing a report when Leila entered the room.

"You're ready?"

"Almost," she said penciling in a few quick notes.

Leila looked at her watch. "We're going to be late."

Anna Lisa closed the file. "I'm done. Let's go."

They planned to meet Adam at 12:30 at the restaurant. A few minutes late, they found him waiting at a poolside table.

"Sorry we were a bit late," offered Anna Lisa.

"No problem," replied Adam.

The three sat in shade underneath an umbrella and glanced over the menus.

"This was a great idea." Adam removed his jacket and hung it over the back of the chair because it was warm outside. He glanced over at the hotel guests lying in the sun and children jumping in the pool. "It feels good to be outside."

"I agree," Leila replied, "It's nice to breathe fresh air instead of that dry air form the air-conditioner."

Their waiter came by. "Are you all ready to order?"

Everyone said yes. Anna Lisa decided on the roast beef sandwich, Leila had the club and Adam pasta primavera with shrimp.

"I asked the two of you to lunch because there's something important I needed to tell you." Anna Lisa said, removing the paper on her straw with shaky hands.

"You're getting married," Leila said jokingly.

"No, nothing as grand as that," she replied and paused. "I'm...I'm leaving...Howard Brown that is. Tomorrow is my last day."

"Very cute," Leila commented, "Now, tell us what's really on your mind."

"I just did."

"Why would you want to leave your job?" Adam asked in disappointment as he repositioned his body uncomfortably in his seat. He was worried about who was going to handle his company's account after Anna Lisa left. "I thought you enjoyed working for Simon."

"Believe me, this has been a very tough decision." She started playing with her straw nervously, moving it up and down in her glass. "For days I've been going over the advantages and disadvantages of staying but in the end, I realized the right thing to do was leave. I need to make some changes in my life."

Surprised and heartbroken, Leila replied, "I can't imagine not working with you."

"You're breaking up our team," Adam frowned.

"We'll still see each other outside of work. It's not like I'm leaving town," she replied, picking up the bread basket and offering it to everyone.

Adam and Leila each took a slice. Anna Lisa picked up a cracker stick.

"What did Neil say about you leaving?" Adam asked. He spread a small amount of butter on his sourdough and took a bite.

"I didn't tell him. You, Leila and Simon are the only ones who know and I would like to keep it that way."

"Why wouldn't you want others to know?" Leila asked.

"I'd like to leave quietly and don't want a fuss. I don't feel like answering everyone's questions as to why I'm leaving and where I'm going."

"Where are you going?" Adam asked.

"I'll be over at Hamilton International."

"Our competitor!" Leila cried with wide eyes as she knocked the butter knife off the table, "And Simon was okay with it?"

"He wasn't at first, but once I explained to him why I was leaving, he understood." She bit her cracker and chewed it agitatedly.

"You should at least tell Neil," Adam offered, "How's he going to get in touch with you?"

"I don't want him to be able to contact me. He'll be in London with his new wife, and I'll be here living my life."

The waiter came back and served their meals.

"You can't just drop him like that," Leila protested, "He's your friend." She removed a toothpick from one section of her club sandwich and took a bite.

Anna Lisa didn't want to tell them that she and Neil had kissed and that she had feelings for him she shouldn't have. Instead she said, "It's better for us to cut all ties. When I was in London, Sarah made it very clear she wanted me to get lost."

"She did what?" Adam exclaimed.

She regretted telling him about the London incident but didn't know how else to explain why she never again wanted to see the man she loved. "Sarah pulled me to the side and accused me of pushing myself on Neil and told me to back off."

"Did you tell Neil?" Leila asked as she listened in disbelief. Sarah was a foolish girl. Anna Lisa would never in a million years make a move on an engaged man.

"No and I don't want him to ever find out."

"But you can't let the ice woman break up your friendship. He loves you," he blurted, digging his fork into his pasta and chicken.

"First, he does not love me and second, I don't want to be in a relationship. All my life I've fallen into these impossible relationships and now it's time for me to take charge of my life. I need time to think about what I want in a man. I'm not going to fall for someone just because he happens to be conveniently present in my life."

Adam sighed. "You know, the two of you are so stubborn that neither one is willing to admit how you feel about the other."

"The first part of your statement is correct. We are both stubborn and as for the second part, I will let fate decide our paths."

"You mean you're not even going to try."

Leila didn't say anything. She knew Adam was wasting his time. Once Anna Lisa made up her mind, there was nothing he could do to change it.

"Right now, all I'm concerned about is spending time with my family and friends, working, traveling, enjoying life, and helping people in need. Anyway," she put her fork into her fruit salad and decided to change the subject, "enough about Neil and me. Tell me, how is your aunt these days?"

"She's doing well. She'll be very disappointed when she hears about you leaving the company. In fact, now I'm thinking about moving our account to Hamilton International."

Leila wrinkled her forehead. Olson and Olson was a big client and she was hoping for a chance to work with them.

"It would mean a lot to me if you didn't do that." Anna Lisa had no intention of stealing a client away from Simon.

"But I'm concerned. With you and Neil gone, who is going to handle our account?"

"The same person who has been handling it all along – Simon. Neil and I had to run everything through him before we finalized it. You have nothing to worry about."

"Are you sure my aunt and I will be well taken care of?"

"I guarantee it. Until Simon finds replacements for us, Leila is fully capable of handling all aspects of your account. She's quite familiar with it."

"Don't worry, I'll take good care of you," Leila assured him as she got up and brushed off a few breadcrumbs off of her dress. She excused herself to go use the ladies' room.

The waiter came back with a pitcher of ice-tea and poured it in Anna Lisa's glass.

Anna Lisa turned to Adam and confided, "I trained Leila myself and if you're ever unhappy with her work, talk to her. Although, I can't imagine you having any problems with her."

"I'm going to trust you on this," he said wagging his fork at her.

She raised her eyebrows and said, "Have I ever steered you wrong?"

"No and that's why it's so hard to lose you."

"You will never lose me. I'm right behind you when you need me."

"I appreciate that." He kissed her on the cheek.

When Leila came back to the table, the three talked about Anna Lisa's new condo in Century City and how excited they were for her. Adam asked all sorts of questions as to the type of facilities in the building, how big the structure was and if they had a well-equipped gym. Leila wanted to come over and use the pool. Then they changed topics to Hamilton International, the number of employees it had and Anna Lisa's new position. When their lunch came to an end, Adam and Leila insisted on treating Anna Lisa.

On her last day at Howard Brown, everyone thought Anna Lisa was going on vacation to Acapulco and so all day long people had been wishing her an enjoyable trip and telling her it was about time for her to go away. She felt guilty for not telling them the truth but content that she was going away quietly. She knew they were bound to find out sooner or later but hoped that it would be later because by then she wouldn't care. She would be too happy living her new life. No more Neil, Paul or Kimberly, Anna Lisa thought as she stood by the door of her office and looked around her. A calendar, desk mat, filing trays, pen holder and staples were arranged neatly on Neil's desk. She remembered their first workday together, fighting over a stupid parking ticket. Anna Lisa chuckled at how much they had disliked each other at first. Her eyes shifted near the sofa, recalling the time when she had cried over Paul and had buried her face in Neil's chest. Looking back, she realized how close they had been that night. She thought about the kiss they had shared weeks ago – right there by the very door she was standing near. It felt odd not to ever see him or hear his voice again. She glanced over at her own empty desk. For seven years she had worked with Simon and her co-workers and now she was leaving them all behind. Yesterday she was excited to leave but today, she felt a sense of loss and regret at how her life had turned out. She took one last look around her, turned off the lights and closed the door behind her.

TWENTY-THREE

With the exception of Neil getting married and Anna Lisa gone, not much had changed at Howard Brown. Paul had just started his fall term at California State University at Northridge and was hoping to finish school so he could get out of accounting and transition into the marketing department. Kimberly was still an entry-level assistant with no prospect of moving up the corporate ladder any time soon. Diana was promoted as the new office manager. Having been with Howard Brown for 10 years with plenty of experience handling client demands, she was hoping to soon become an account executive.

Unfortunately, Diana only had a bachelor's degree in liberal arts, which could get her only so far. In order for her to become an account exec, she would need a master's in business and would have to take a cut in salary and start on the bottom either in research or as an assistant account exec, and she wasn't willing to do that.

"Have you found someone to replace Anna Lisa?" Diana asked Simon when she brought him the newly typed contracts he had requested from their legal department.

"No, I haven't" he sighed, sitting behind his desk, with his reading glasses on. He was looking over the response to the ads they had placed for the Olson account and they looked good. "I'm swamped with work and with Anna Lisa and Neil gone, I'm not sure what I will do."

"You might want to consider hiring from within," Diana smiled as the edges of her mouth curled up. She was excited to seize the moment and make her dream come true.

"I already have," he said glancing at the contracts Diana had brought him and then back at Diana. "I promoted Leila to an account executive but I still need one more person."

"I know someone who would qualify to be an account exec."

"Who?" Simon asked looking puzzled.

Diana gathered up her courage to recommend herself. "I thought, may be I–"

The buzzer on Simon's intercom went off and he was told that Neil was on line one. "Excuse me," Simon said, picking up the receiver. "Neil! It's great to hear to from you. How are you?" he replied resting back against his chair, but when he heard the lack of energy in Neil's tone, he asked with concern, "What's wrong?"

Diana just stood there hoping her boss would get off the phone soon but he seemed to be interested in what his former employee had to say.

Simon finally said to Neil, "Hold on." Turning to Diana, he said, "Is there something you wanted?"

Diana felt foolish. "No, I was just leaving," she answered and slowly walked out of his office in a rotten mood. On her way to her desk, she ran into Kimberly seated in her small cubicle, chatting away on the phone. She had her platinum blond hair braided around her head and her large implants were hidden underneath a dull blue shirt that matched her skirt. Diana leaned over and put her hands on Kimberly's desk. "Don't you have work to do? Because if you don't there are plenty of things I can give you," she barked, taking out her anger on Kimberly.

Startled by Diana's comment, Kimberly told the person on the other end of the receiver she had to go. She looked at Diana. "I was talking to the printers, making sure the coupons for BLG's multigrain cereal were going to come out on time."

"That's not your job," said Diana, still angry.

"But Leila asked me to," protested Kimberly as she stared at Diana with her big blue eyes.

Diana's face tightened and the veins on her high forehead appeared as though they were going to pop at any minute. "Yes, but you needn't spend an hour socializing with the printing department every time you get on the phone with them."

"Sorry," Kimberly said, picking up the letters from her desk that needed to be faxed and walking away. She began mumbling to herself, "Who put the burr up her butt? Who does she think she is talking to me like that, all because she got promoted? She's not the boss of me and next time I'm going to tell her exactly what I think."

Unfortunately for Kimberly, Diana was right behind her and her large and attentive ears heard Kimberly's comments. "The next time you're going to tell me what?"

"Shit," Kimberly whispered to herself. She turned around and said, "Nothing."

Diana crossed her arms in front of her chest. "I thought I heard you say you were going to tell me exactly what you think of me."

Kimberly stared at Diana with narrowed eyes. "I wasn't talking about you. Besides, you shouldn't be listening in on other people's conversations."

"Oh, is that what you were doing? You were having a conversation with an imaginary friend. I think you need to take time off," to go the loony bin that is, she thought.

"As a matter of fact, I've been thinking about taking off a couple of days and going somewhere with my boyfriend Paul."

"Dream on," cried Diana putting hands on her hips. "You already took your vacation, and you won't get another one for a long time."

"It's not up to you. It's up to Simon," replied Kimberly arrogantly.

Diana raised an eyebrow. "I have to approve it and without my signature Simon would never allow it. So, the next time you mumble, you should consider saying nicer things about me," she said, storming away.

The day after Kimberly's spat with Diana, Paul walked into his office tired and bored. He was tired because he had been out drinking with Kimberly and his friends the night before. He was bored because he believed he was going nowhere with his life. He was wearied of doing accounting all day, but needed the money. He wished he could have Anna Lisa's job. She was so lucky to do what she liked. And now she was working for another company, probably making more money than before, he thought as he sat on his chair. He opened his ponytail, shook his hair loose and wished he could go against the company's dress code and not have to pull his hair back. Paul turned on the computer in his office and stared at the screen. The intercom buzzed.

"Yes?"

"Paul, could you come into my office? We need to talk," Simon demanded.

"Yeah, sure," he replied, wondering what Simon needed this time. He tied his hair back again and headed for Simon's office.

"Oh, hi Dorothy," Paul said to his boss's new secretary, "Simon asked to see me."

Dorothy, a middle-aged frail-looking lady buzzed her employer, "Excuse me sir, Paul is here to see you."

"Send him in," Simon replied, "And Dorothy?"

"Yes sir?"

"Please don't call me sir, this isn't the army. Simon will suffice."

"Yes sir."

"You did it again."

"Sorry sir...I mean Sorry, Mr. Simon."

Simon shook his head. Calling him Mr. Simon was worse than sir but he didn't feel like correcting her.

"You may go in," Dorothy said to Paul.

Paul entered Simon's office and said, "You wanted to see me?"

Simon removed his reading glasses. "Yes, I did. We have a problem. Would you shut the door behind you so we can talk in private?"

"What is it?" Paul asked with a curious look on his face. He closed the door.

Simon frowned. "You seem to have misplaced a half a million dollars."

"What?" He approached Simon's desk. Impossible; he would never make such a large mistake, Paul thought.

"Here, have a look," Simon said handing him a copy of the general ledger from across his desk. Paul had debited and credited the wrong accounts. "You made a mistake in your journal entry."

Paul stared at the ledger in disbelief. He sat down slowly on a chair across from Simon and paged through the paperwork wondering how he had underreported the company's earnings by $500,000. He kept going from page to page to see where he had gone wrong.

"Don't bother; it'll probably take you too long to figure out your mistake," Simon said. "You see, you did a poor job of keeping our books. Do you have any idea what the IRS is going to do to us for underreporting our income by such a large amount?"

Paul's heart dropped. The IRS? He didn't like the idea of dealing with the IRS. "I don't know what to say," Paul said sheepishly.

Simon's facial muscles tightened as he loosened one of the buttons on the collar of his now perspiration-stained mint shirt. "Lucky for you, one of the partners is friends with a supervisor at the local IRS office."

"Am I going to get fired?" Paul asked nervously. He spent a chunk of his savings on the trip with Kimberly and couldn't afford to lose his income.

Simon drummed his fingers on the table. "No, but I am forced to demote you."

"Demote me?" blurted Paul, "Why that's almost worse than being fired."

"I've hired a CPA who will take over the firm's accounting and all the bookkeepers will report to him."

"But I've always been this floor's bookkeeper."

"Look Paul, consider yourself very fortunate. Were you working for another firm, they'd drop you on the spot," Simon said. "In fact, the partners asked me to get rid of you but I told them you've been with us for a long time and this was your first mistake."

His employee wrinkled his forehead. "I suppose you're right. I should consider myself lucky. Am I going to have to take a cut in pay?" he asked, handing back the ledger to his boss. There was no use trying to find his mistake now. Simon and the partners had already made their decision.

"No, you'll get the same salary," said Simon, scratching his stubbly gray head. "I should've never made you the person in charge. You weren't ready for it and this is partially my fault."

"I guess there goes my transition into marketing," he replied hopelessly.

His boss chuckled, "That should be the least of your problems. Besides, you're not even finished with your bachelor's. From now on, you need to prove to me that you can handle the work."

"But I don't like being in accounting," he complained.

Simon sighed. "Sometimes in life we do things we don't like in order to get to where we'd like," he said, unscrewing the cap of a bottled water sitting on his desk and taking a swig. "Let me give you fatherly advice…Instead of spending most of your time chasing women, stay focused on your work and school. I promise if you work hard, you'll achieve what you want."

Paul's looked extremely discontent. "When is this CPA coming in, anyway?"

"His name is Herman, and he's starting tomorrow. I suggest you go tidy up your files and show up to work on time because he's a stickler for organization and punctuality."

Paul nodded and walked out of Simon's office toward his own with his head drooping. Worried and uncomfortable, he sat down behind his desk and wished he hadn't made such a large mistake. How could he have made an error like that? He thought. Now, he had to report to some fat, bald thick-glassed middle-aged prick with a bow tie. What kind of name was Herman anyway? The thought of having a boss breathing down his neck made him uneasy. Maybe he should just quit, but he needed the money. Well, he could probably do without a salary for a few months, but then what? Where would he find a cushy job with a decent paycheck? No, he had to stick it out. Herman would have to force him out before he would leave on his own. He'd show Herman what a great bookkeeper he was. He'd be the one forcing Herman out of a job. As these thoughts ran through his head, a stranger walked in carrying a large box of files, folders and office supplies.

"Hello Paul, my name is Herman. I understand we're to work together," he said with a deep voice.

He was startled. "You weren't supposed to be here till tomorrow."

"True, but I never like to leave for tomorrow what I can accomplish today," said Herman, dropping the supplies on Paul's desk.

Paul swallowed. He didn't like Herman's philosophy already. He took a closer look. He didn't look at all like what he had imagined. Herman was young; maybe in his early thirties. He had light brown hair and plenty of it, too. He had on a pair of square, frameless glasses but they weren't thick. He didn't wear a bow tie and was incredibly skinny. He wore a black tie, a gray shirt that matched his pants and a knitted vest. Maybe he was going to be a nice man after all.

Two weeks with Herman and Paul was ready to quit. Forced to change his entire filing system, he had to reorganize and turn things around to Herman's liking. Not only did he lack a moment of peace but when he took his lunch breaks, he had to return exactly on time or he would get a long, tedious lecture from Herman. Every second of his day was accounted for on a timesheet, which Herman reviewed. He told Paul he wasn't using his time efficiently as he took over Paul's schedule and squeezed all that he could out of him.

He couldn't take it anymore. Once home, he collapsed into a worn La-Z-Boy chair. He popped the top open on a beer can and gulped its contents as he turned on the tube. Soon after, he felt a pair of arms around him. It was Kimberly.

"Did you miss me?" she asked. Her layered hair was smooth and straight and her nails had a fresh coat of fuchsia polish.

"How can I? We see each other every second," Paul said sarcastically without turning to look at her. He was in a bad mood and wished he could just be by himself without having to cater to anyone.

"You didn't complain when we started dating," she remarked, kissing him on the cheek. Not much bothered Kimberly when it came to Paul. He could put her down and cuss her out and she would still be there like a doormat begging for more.

"Yes well, that was then and this is now," he replied, gulping his beer.

"What're you saying? That you're tired of me?" she asked, still hanging onto him, not realizing that her neediness was driving Paul crazy.

Paul set down his beer can on a rickety wooden side table. "I need my space," he said, removing Kimberly's arms from his shoulders.

Kimberly moved from the back of the chair and stood in front of him. "Don't you love me anymore?"

His jawbone protruded as he gritted his teeth. "It's been a long day and I just want to sit here, drink beer and watch television. Is that too much to ask?" he snapped, pushing her away with one hand so that he could see the screen and began flipping the channels with his remote.

"Don't talk to me like that." She snatched the remote out of his hand to get his attention and set it down on the coffee table.

"Like what? I've been nice to you for weeks. We go to work together, we go to clubs together and we spend time with my friends together, what more do you want from me?" Paul yelled.

"Don't yell at me," Kimberly said, perching on his lap and putting her arms around him one more time. She needed him. She had always had a man in her life and didn't know how to live on her own.

Paul felt as though her arms were a heavy chain around his neck. "Will you please get off of me? How much you weigh anyway?"

She had put on an extra 18 pounds since she had moved in with Paul. "I'm not fat," she said.

"You could've fooled me. Why don't you go run around the block. You sure could use the exercise."

"Why are you being so mean to me?" she replied tearfully. Even Kimberly couldn't take that much abuse, especially when he made fun of her figure.

"You don't give me much choice," he said, belching.

"Maybe I should go back to my husband then," she screamed. Billy Ray, who was soon to be her ex-husband, was from North Carolina. He moved to L.A. with Kimberly a year ago, but when he found out she was cheating on him, he filed for divorce.

"Maybe you should," Paul yelled back. He was sick and tired of spending every moment with her and wished he hadn't asked her to move in with him.

"Fine, I'll go pack," she uttered thinking she could scare Paul by threatening him.

"I don't care what you do as long as you leave me alone," he said, finishing off his beer, squashing the can with one hand and throwing it into a corner. He got up, walked over the cheap brown shag carpet of his living room and onto the chipped yellow linoleum in his kitchen. He opened his fridge and took out a six-pack.

Kimberly followed him. "So, this is what I get after all that I do for you. I cook you dinner, do your laundry, clean the house, keep up with my appearance and never complain," she cried.

"So?" He went back to his chair.

"So? So, you're lucky to have me," she said with her hands on her hips.

"Kimberly, will you please go away and give me a moment of peace?" With a clank, he dropped the beer cans on the coffee table. He took out a can, popped the top open and started guzzling.

Kimberly stormed into the bedroom and slammed the door.

Kimberly sat on Paul's La-Z-Boy, waiting for him to come home. She told him they needed to talk because she couldn't handle his comings and goings any longer. Ever since their fight a week ago, Paul was drinking heavily and coming home late every night. She even found lipstick marks on his shirt a couple of times. At work he ignored her, claiming he was too busy to talk to her. Alone and friendless, Kimberly was also unhappy with her boss Diana, who was always on her case, treating her with disrespect and complaining about everything she did wrong. She didn't know what to do. Kimberly hardly made enough to live by herself, didn't know anyone she could room with and didn't want to move back home to Tucson, because she didn't get along with her stepfather. Her only choice was to move back with her husband. He was a boring but attractive man from North Carolina, worked in construction and made good money but wasn't exciting like Paul. Billy Ray didn't have Paul's charm and wasn't a big city boy. Kimberly needed nightclubs and parties; she wanted to try new things and live an exciting life. Yet, there was no one who was willing to help support her lifestyle. Maybe she could live with Billy Ray temporarily until a better opportunity came by, she thought as she waited for Paul to arrive. After waiting for him late into the night, Kimberly got frustrated, packed all her belongings and set them by the door.

At 2 in the morning she heard the door open and her boyfriend walked in reeking of alcohol and perfume. He didn't even notice Kimberly's luggage by the door.

"What're you doing up so late?" he slurred.

She did not respond. She went into the bedroom and slammed the door but he didn't care. He was used to sleeping on the sofa and, in fact, he was happier there, because he didn't have to listen to Kimberly bitch. He turned off the floor lamp, curled up on the sofa and went to sleep.

When morning came and Paul finally woke up, he saw Kimberly sitting on the coffee table, staring at him.

"Good. You're finally awake," she said.

Paul rubbed his eyes and dragged his tired body into a sitting position. His mouth felt dry and he wished he had a glass of water on the table instead of Kimberly.

"Yesterday, I was going to break it off with you in a note," she said with a calm and controlled voice, "but I changed my mind. I wanted to see the expression on your face when I told you I was leaving."

"Huh?" he said still half-sleep and still thinking about how thirsty he was.

"You heard me. I'm leaving you," she repeated with a satisfied look on her face.

Paul staggered toward the kitchen, pulled out a yellow plastic cup from one of the cabinets and filled it with tap water. He drank the whole thing and filled it again.

"Paul, did you hear me?" Kimberly cried, following him into the kitchen, "You and I are through. Finished. Kaput."

"You and I were through weeks ago. Now go on, get out of here," he demanded bitterly.

"Don't you at least want to know why I'm leaving?" she asked, wishing that he wanted her back.

"Does it matter? The point is when the going got tough, you gave up on us." Paul had always been looking for someone who wouldn't give up on him no matter what. He had never forgiven his mother for giving up on his father. He thought she should've stuck it out and stayed with him.

"What us Paul?" she shouted, "It has always been all about you." She moved out of the kitchen into the living room with Paul trailing right behind her.

"You know," he said, pointing a finger at her, "Anna Lisa would've never treated me this way."

She turned and glared at him. She was so sick of how perfect everyone thought Anna Lisa was. "And what way is that?"

"She would've never abandoned me in my slump."

"What're you talking about? She didn't even put up a fight for you."

"She has class, which is something you would never understand."

Kimberly went to the phone, picked up the receiver and snapped, "Why don't you call her if you're so crazy about her. Go ahead, I dare you."

"Don't think I haven't tried but she changed her number."

"Poor pathetic Paul," she slammed the receiver down. "You have no work. You stink of alcohol. Anna Lisa has disappeared and now you're about to lose me."

"Losing you is the best thing that could happen to me. Go on, get of here," he hollered and threw the water glass in her direction but missed on purpose. He just wanted to scare her.

She was shocked by his behavior. She turned on her heels, dragged her luggage out and said, "I hope I never have to see you again." She shut the door behind her and never looked back.

When Kimberly left, Paul reached in his pocket, taking out some girl's phone number he met at a bar the prior night. He called her and made plans to meet her that evening.

Kimberly took a cab to Billy Ray's apartment. Once there, she dropped her luggage in front of her husband's door and rang the bell.

Billy Ray lived on the first floor of a beige and brown apartment building in a modest, family oriented neighborhood of Burbank. He was a 29-year-old blond and blue-eyed hunk with an athlete's body. Billy Ray was not surprised to see Kimberly when he opened the door. She always came back when she fell on her butt. "What happened? Boyfriend kick you out?" he said, staring at her tight pink shirt and white mini-skirt. Her eyes were red and her face looked grim, but he didn't feel sorry for her. Not after the way she had treated him.

"Please, can I come in? I have no one to turn to," she asked in desperation.

Billy Ray, who looked simple in a T-shirt and a pair of dark blue jeans, moved away from the door but did not help her with her luggage. If she can dump him at a drop of a hat and move out, she damn well can move herself back in, he thought. "So, what's your story this time?"

She bent over and hauled in her two large brown suitcases, one at a time. "I want a second chance," she said as she straightened up. "Do you think you can give me a second chance?"

He had his back against the wall and a hand in his pocket. "And why should I believe you this time?"

"Because I've changed; you have no idea what I've been through," she said through teary eyes and runny mascara.

"You look like you've filled up pretty well. Your life couldn't possibly be that bad," he said looking her up and down. She looked sexier and more voluptuous than when she left him, he thought.

"Please Billy Ray, don't you be cold," Kimberly said and went to hug him. "I sure could use a hug."

Billy Ray didn't hug her at first but when her tears began to wet his shirt, he couldn't take it anymore and put his arms around her.

Kimberly held onto him for a while before pulling away and wiping her face. She noticed his apartment was empty and his bags were packed. "You have no furniture!"

"I'm going back home to North Carolina."

Kimberly's eyes widened. If he went home, she wouldn't be able to live there. "Why?"

"It's too expensive here. And I don't like the people."

Kimberly stood there speechless. She looked around the empty apartment and wondered had she not left him would they still have a chance to make it in L.A. But the damage was done and there was nothing she could do. Trapped in a rotten situation, without an alternative, she asked, "Can I go with you?"

"I don't know, Sugar. You really broke my heart."

"I won't run away again, I promise. I really want us to make it," she said, hoping that she sounded credible.

Billy Ray shook his head and didn't respond for a long time.

After a lengthy silence, Kimberly said, "Please, Billy Ray. I'll be good."

He still loved her. Damn, that soft heart of his, he thought. "You can come back but if you screw it up this time, that's it; no more chances."

Kimberly nodded her head and promised to be the perfect wife he wanted her to be even if she didn't have a clue what that was. At least Billy Ray appreciated and loved her. Besides, if things didn't work between them, she could always take off again. For now, she was glad to find someone who was willing to take care of her.

TWENTY-FOUR

In the same month Paul and Kimberly were having problems with their jobs and relationship, Anna Lisa and Neil were dealing with difficulties of their own. At 3 in the morning, a week after Neil left Los Angeles, Anna Lisa couldn't sleep in her new condo. She tossed and turned, pulled the covers over her head, pushed them away, forced herself to shut her eyes but nothing worked. She sat shivering in only her white tank top and bikini underwear and cursed herself for falling in love with an engaged man. She promised herself never to fall in love with anyone until she was certain of his character and here she was sleepless over someone who would be married soon. How dare he have kissed her? She was perfectly content before he made a move on her. Why did he do it? He was probably expecting to have a one-night fling before getting married and then he was planning to toss her aside. It was obvious he didn't love her or else he wouldn't be getting married. Angry and furious, Anna Lisa put on a robe, went into the kitchen and turned on a yellow spotlight underneath the whiskey-colored kitchen cabinets, walked toward the freezer and pulled out a container of rocky road ice cream. She grabbed a spoon from a drawer near her sink and went to sit down behind her rectangular kitchen table which coordinated with the cabinets and the leather cushions on her chairs. She removed the lid of the untouched container, spooned out a hefty chunk of ice cream and placed it in her mouth to comfort herself. She played the night of the kiss over and over in her head. Why did it happen? What possessed him to do it? Then the answer came to her. He wasn't the only person at fault. They were both at fault. At some point during their friendship, she had fallen in love with an engaged man. He must've known or felt it. She stuck her spoon back into the ice cream, scooped another chunk and gnawed it. Is this what Paul felt for Kimberly? And if so, why had he lied to her? Why had Paul confirmed his affection for her if he had been in love with someone else? He should've told her long ago that he didn't care for her, but instead he had manipulated her and led her on. Was Neil just like Paul? Had she been fooled by Neil's gentlemanly behavior? Anna Lisa didn't know and it didn't matter because she had no intention of ever seeing him again. With her old condo up for sale, her telephone numbers changed and most of her ties cut off from Howard Brown, she wished to trade her past for a new beginning. This time with a lot of experience behind her, Anna Lisa was planning to make all the right moves to secure her happy future. Feeling more serene, she stuck her ice cream back into the freezer, dropped off the spoon into the sink, turned the spotlight off and went back to bed.

While Anna Lisa was struggling with her feelings for an engaged man, Neil was having second thoughts about marrying his fiancée. A week had already past since he left Los Angeles, Neil reflected as he stretched his legs on the dark brown sofa in the living room of his London apartment near Hyde Park, in an upper middle-class neighborhood. He was wearing the outfit Anna Lisa had picked out for him before the O'Malley basketball game – a pair of jeans and a charcoal T-shirt. The same brown sandals she had bought him as a going away present lay neatly on the hardwood floor near the sofa. He couldn't get the kiss out of his mind. Neil couldn't comprehend why he had felt such a profound desire for Leeza and why he had not come remotely close to feeling that way toward Sarah. Neil had many girlfriends in his lifetime but not one had been able to trigger the torrid passion he felt for Leeza. Had she not pushed him away and refused him, he would have seduced her on the floor of their office. He wished he had. Yet, that would have meant he would have cheated on Sarah – the woman he was marrying in five days. He knew her longer than Anna Lisa and had more in common with her. They came from the same culture and understood each other better. He should want to be with an English woman and not an American. Sarah was younger, more flexible and not opinionated like Anna Lisa. Well, except that Sarah had refused to move to Los Angeles but he couldn't blame her. She didn't care to leave her family and friends and go to a strange country.

Neil thought about Anna Lisa again. He remembered holding her and not wanting to let her go. He longed to see her. Did he want what he couldn't have? What if he could be with her and grew tired of her afterward? Was Anna Lisa right? Was he just like Paul? Was it just lust between them? It wasn't just about lust. Neil wanted to make love to her but there was more to it than that. Working with her side by side, having lunch with her everyday and becoming familiar with her moods established a closeness between them. She was part of his life. Their differences didn't bother or scare him; he respected them. Neil liked the fact that she made him see things in a different light. As his mind was occupied with these thoughts, Sarah opened his apartment door with a set of spare keys he had given her two years ago. Knowing that Neil liked her in rose hues, she had decided to wear a pink Dolce and Gabbana dress, her silky dark blonde hair pushed back with a matching headband.

"Darling, you're alright?" she said when she saw his unhappy composure.

He found it odd that he hadn't heard her come in. "Yes, I'm perfectly fine," he said and tried to hide behind a forced smile.

"You look troubled." She had been standing there for some time but he hadn't noticed her at all.

"And is this how you greet your fiancé? Don't I at least get a hello kiss?" Neil said teasingly, trying to divert her attention from his concerns.

Sarah sat next to him, put her arms around his shoulders and kissed him. He felt nothing. "Will you try again and this time do it as though it's the first time you've ever kissed me."

She looked at him, puzzled. "What's the matter? Something is wrong; isn't there?"

"Nothing's wrong. I just want us to kiss the way newlyweds do." He sat up with an ambivalent expression on his face. "You know that eternal ardent kiss full of want, love and passion? The kind that makes your heart race and your body ache for more."

Sarah shook her head. "You know that's just a fantasy, darling. Such love doesn't exist and if it does, it wears off quickly."

"Do you love me?" he asked, looking serious.

Her eyes widened and she said, "Have you gone mad? What kind of question is that? Of course I love you."

"I mean, are you in love with me?"

Confused and lost she replied, "What's the difference?"

Neil stared at her. She did not know what he meant and he wouldn't have known the difference either had he not met Leeza – the woman who had managed to turn his world upside down. "Let me rephrase my question. Why do you want to marry me?"

"What? I cannot apprehend what has come over you," she tearily replied. "You're making me very upset."

"I'm sorry. I just...I just..." He slid his hands over his face and shut his eyes for a moment, trying to collect his thoughts.

Sarah's body shook nervously, waiting for him to speak.

"I've been thinking about us for a long time now, and I'm no longer sure if we're right for each other."

"Of course we're right for each other," she confirmed.

"We don't have similar goals. You want a house in the country with cooks, nannies, chauffeurs and all the luxury items that come with it, and that's not for me."

She raised her voice. "You knew my background before we went out. You knew about my family and the way I was raised. I'm used to a certain lifestyle and do not wish to give it up."

"I'm not asking you to give it up. I'm saying that kind of lifestyle does not excite me. What I want is a simple life with children running around a comfortable home. Perhaps a babysitter to help us out when we need it. But what I don't want is some stranger raising our children. I want to spend time with them the way my parents did with me and Juliet."

Sarah's lip quivered and she looked as if she were about to cry. She didn't want to lose him but she was having a difficult time picturing the boring life he had described. "Up until the time you left for America, you and I thought alike. What happened to you?" she looked at him with narrowed eyes.

He didn't know what happened to him. All he knew was that when Leeza had visited him at his parents' house in London and played soccer with him and his nephews, he had truly enjoyed himself. "I've changed. I'm not the same person you agreed to marry a year ago."

"But I love you," she pouted.

"No you don't. You love the old me. I'm not that person anymore."

Sarah started crying hard and Neil hugged her. He hated causing her so much pain but couldn't go on lying to himself and had to face the truth. Feeling nothing toward her except compassion, he couldn't force himself to marry someone he didn't love. He reached for a tissue on the end table and handed it to her.

She wiped her face and excused herself to use the bathroom. Inside, Sarah was appalled by her disheveled appearance as she cleaned her runny mascara, powdered her face, put on blush and lipstick. Neil belonged to her and no one else was going to have him. She decided that instead of crying, she had to change her strategy. Sarah had to stay calm, cool and collected, leaving her fiancé's apartment with grace. Then she would collaborate with her mom as to what steps she should take to get him back. She had to convince Neil to marry her.

Worried and anxious, Neil waited for her to come out of the bathroom.

When she finally emerged, she said, "I'm better but I think we should talk about us tomorrow. I would like to go home now."

His face was stern and his body tense. He couldn't hold out any longer. "No, we're going to finish our talk today. Right here, right now."

"Please Neil. I'm pleading with you not to make a rash decision. Let's discuss this later when you're more sensible."

"I am sensible," he yelled. "I've never been more sensible in my life."

"You see…there…you are shouting at me."

Neil took in a deep breath and let it out. There was no easy way to say this than just to say it. "I'm not in love with you."

She went over to him and clung to his face tightly with her delicate hands. In a panicky tone, she said, "Darling, you're just having cold feet. It's natural. We'll be married soon, and you'll forget all about this nonsense."

He looked down and then back at her. "No. That is not it."

Removing her hands from his face, she asked, "Are you angry because I don't want to move to Los Angeles? Because if that's what this is all about, I'll go back with you," she offered. But when she saw him look away, she took her hand, put it on his cheek and made him look at her. "I'll do whatever it takes to make our marriage work."

God help him because he was about to break her heart. Damn it, she should save herself and let him go. "Sarah if I was in love with you, it wouldn't matter where we lived."

"Darling, you're scaring me. Our wedding is coming up in five days," she said looking directly into his eyes.

Neil was frustrated by her persistence. He was only trying to convey five simple words – I do not love you. Which part of the phrase did she not understand? He controlled his boiling temper as he removed her hand from his face, pulled it gently by her side and held it in his. "I can't marry you Sarah because I'm not in love with you."

She let go of his hand and looked at him with her desperate eyes. "But what will I tell my parents and our friends?"

He was irritated by her response. Is that all she worried about? What her parents and friends thought? "Tell them you have changed your mind. Tell them whatever pleases you. It doesn't matter to me."

She shook her head. "It's her, isn't it? It's that bloody American."

He stood up, turned his back on her and proceeded to the middle of the room but did not say anything.

Her voice became angry and her hands turned into fists. "I knew it the first time I met her. I knew she would do everything possible to have you to herself."

"She does not want me," Neil said disappointedly and looked outside at the dark murky sky. It seemed as though it were about to rain.

In order to get his attention, Sarah went to Neil and stood between him and the window – the direction where his gaze was focused. "Then why? Why are you doing this?"

He frowned. "Because we are not right for each other, and it is better to realize it now than after we have been married. I am sorry."

Devastated that none of her ploys had worked, she felt defeated for the first time. She had tried everything possible – making him move back to London, crying, begging him to wait and talk at a later time and even agreeing to relocate to Los Angeles, yet nothing had helped to alter his adamant mind. "Fine," she finally conceded and stormed toward the front door. She grabbed her car keys and purse from the hall table and hurled his apartment keys at him. "I hope you're happy. You have ruined my life," she said, opening the door and slamming it behind her.

When she left, he collapsed on a chair, feeling as if a tremendous burden had been lifted off his shoulders. He was finally liberated from his commitment to her and from having to deal with her appalling parents and accepting their charity every single time Sarah wanted to buy something beyond their means.

He was finished with that life. It was all behind him and for the first time in months he felt as unrestrained as a shuttle floating in space. And the sky was not the limit.

The wedding was off and Neil felt a long-awaited relief. His friends and family were supportive of his decision and he wished he could say the same about Sarah's family, but they had cut him off completely. In fact, they made sure he got booted out of a prestigious private club that he belonged to but he did not care. The social status that had impressed him long ago no longer mattered. He felt free to be himself again. He could come and go as he pleased without abiding by the social rules. He spent his time playing soccer and tennis with his friends, visiting his parents and working at the London office. But he wasn't happy. He missed Leeza. He missed her scolding him. He missed bickering with her. He wanted her.

He called Simon.

"Hello?" said Simon sitting at his desk at 4 in the afternoon. Diana was in his office as well. She had just brought him the newly typed contracts he had requested from their legal department.

Dressed in his pajamas with a brandy in one hand, Neil sat up on the sofa of his apartment at midnight while talking to Simon. "Hello Simon. This is Neil," he said nervously.

"Neil! It's great to hear to from you. How are you?" replied Simon resting his back against his chair.

"I've been better," Neil said sadly.

Simon heard the lack of energy in his voice and asked with concern, "What's wrong?"

"Sarah and I broke off our engagement and I was wondering…" he swallowed, "if the offer you made me before I left Los Angeles still holds." Simon had offered Neil a higher salary, rent and car lease reimbursement for one more year and the possibility of a partnership offer in the near future if he stayed in Los Angeles.

Simon noticed that Diana was lingering around and so he said to Neil, "Hold on." Turning to Diana, he said, "Is there something you wanted?"

"No, I was just leaving," she answered and walked out of his office.

Simon returned to his conversation. "I'm sorry it didn't work out between the two of you, but I'm sure glad you want to come back."

"You are?" said Neil, who wasn't expecting such a warm welcome. He had been worried that his position had been filled already.

"Oh yes. We need you. With Anna Lisa gone, we've been short on help." Simon frowned. He still couldn't get over losing her to Hamilton International.

"I beg your pardon?" he asked. "I'm sorry, I thought for a moment you said Leeza was gone."

Poor boy, Simon thought. He knew how much Neil liked her and how close they were. "No, you heard right. She is gone," Simon confirmed.

His chest tightened and he froze for a few seconds before uttering, "Gone where?"

"I don't know where." Simon lied because Anna Lisa had asked him to keep her whereabouts a secret. "She said something about wanting to start over again."

Bloody hell. How could she do this? How could she leave without telling him? Why would she hide her whereabouts? He shall never understand what goes on inside that head of hers. "There must be someone who would know where she is."

Simon who had been sworn to secrecy, said, "I'm afraid no one knows."

He sighed in frustration and his former boss heard it.

For a second Simon worried that Neil would change his mind now that Anna Lisa was gone. "So, do we have a deal? Are you coming to L.A. to work for us then?"

Angry about Anna Lisa's disappearance and faulting himself for not trying hard enough to keep in touch with her, he uttered, "Yes. I shall be in the office a week from today."

"Fantastic," Simon answered joyfully. "I'm looking forward to it."

"Me too," Neil replied. He decided to get ready right away. He had to find Anna Lisa and tell her he was in love with her before it was too late, "I'd better go now. There are some things I have to take care of." He had to pack, figure out where to stay once in L.A. and say farewell to his family again. He was worried that his family would think he had gone absolutely insane.

"We'll talk later then."

"Yes, thank you Simon. Thank you very much. Goodbye."

Right after Neil hung up with his boss, he called Anna Lisa at her apartment and heard a loud warning tone, "iee iee ooo" followed by, "We're sorry, the number you have dialed is no longer in service and there's no new number. Please check your number and try again." He couldn't believe his ears. He tried several more times and got the same message. Neil tried her cell phone and heard, "Code 568, the mobile phone you're trying to reach is no longer in service." He slammed down the cordless receiver hard and was lucky it didn't break. Where could she be? Why in the world would she disconnect all her numbers? She was making him crazy. His phone rang and he thought by some miracle it was Anna Lisa calling. He fumbled for the receiver, dropped it and picked it up hastily. "Hello? Hello?"

"Hello," replied a lady with a nasal voice. She sounded like she was calling from outside the country. "May I speak to Gertrude please?"

Disappointed that it wasn't Anna Lisa, he yelled "There's no Gertrude here and you shouldn't be calling her at this time of night anyway. It's after midnight."

"I'm sorry," the voice said and disconnected.

Neil felt bad for taking that kind of tone with the woman. He was going mad. Now he was yelling at people he didn't know. Settle down, will you, he told himself. He finished his brandy in one gulp and felt it burn his guts. When he finds Anna Lisa, the first thing he is going do is to scream at her and shake her hard so she would never do this to him again. Damn that girl and damn himself for falling in love with her.

The following day, Neil was at Hyde Park, sitting on a scraped wooden bench where he sometimes met his sister. After a long sleepless night, he had called Juliet from work and arranged to meet her for lunch. She told him she'd bring a picnic lunch for them to share. He was brushing off the scattered dried leaves from the seat when he noticed his sister approaching.

Juliet looked so much like their mother, he thought. Her downward slanted eyes, her tall and slinky figure and the way she swayed her hips when she walked.

She smiled and her lips faded into a thin line. "How is my brother, these days?" she asked him teasingly. She had two brown bags in her hand and gave one to Neil.

"Must you ask?" He looked at her with tired eyes. He took the bag, opened it and removed a sandwich wrapped in plastic. He was starving since he hadn't had breakfast that morning.

"That's a leftover from Mum. I went over last night with Mark and the children and she gave me a lot of food."

"Which reminds me, I need to talk to her and father sometime this week."

"About?"

"Let's eat and I shall tell you."

Juliet opened her bag. She made sandwiches out of the gigot her mother had given her and brought two cans of tomato juice and her mother's pecan tart for dessert.

Neil bit into his. "Mmmm, this is good. What kind of spread did you use?"

"Horseradish."

"It's delicious," he said, devouring every morsel.

"Guess who I bumped into yesterday?" Juliet said as she removed the lid from the can of tomato juice and drank some.

Neil passed her a puzzled look. "Who?"

"Your former fiancée, who was on a shopping spree at Burberrys."

He didn't like discussing her but was curious. "What did she have to say?"

"A few unkind words that I'm not sure you would not want to hear."

"This I like to hear." Ever since Neil had called off the engagement, he had refused to utter any adverse comments behind Sarah's back. He had blamed himself for everything.

"She accused our family for meddling in your affairs."

"What?" he blurted, astonished by Juliet's revelation.

"She said had we been more accepting of her, you and Sarah would still be together."

"That's a fine thing to say. First she accuses Leeza for coming between us and now she's blaming my family."

"Anna Lisa?" Juliet asked, flabbergasted. "What could she possibly have to do with your breakup?"

"Absolutely nothing." He prevaricated because he wasn't ready to disclose his feelings about the woman he loved.

Unfortunately, his sister knew him too well and was able to read right through him. "Hmmm," she replied looking at him skeptically. "You know, you needn't be afraid of talking about Anna Lisa. I like her and so do Mum and Dad."

"You have talked about us?"

"Ah-ha! There is an us," And when he didn't reply, she poked him further by blurting, "You're in love with her, aren't you? That's why you broke it off with Sarah."

"Eat your sandwich, will you?" he answered irritably. "You have no idea what you're talking about."

"Very well then, look me in the eye and tell me I'm wrong. Tell me that you feel otherwise."

He grunted at her astute observation. Why were women always so intuitive? He wondered. "Fine. You win. I am in love with her. You're happy now?"

She stared at him in surprise. It was one thing when she speculated about his feelings toward Anna Lisa but another to hear him say it. "And is she in love with you?"

"I don't know." He hoped she loved him because he was risking everything for her.

"Have you talked to her?" Juliet asked with a concerned look on her face.

The emotions churning inside him were new to him and he was uncomfortable discussing them. "Stop asking me so many questions." He took a bite out of his pecan pie.

She put her hand gently on his shoulder. "You have to tell her how you feel. You owe yourself that much."

He furrowed his eyebrows and said, "I cannot find her."

"What do you mean you can't find her?"

"I mean she has left her old job. No one seems to know where she is. I tried calling her last night but all her numbers have been changed."

"Do you mean to tell me that my intelligent brother cannot find the simple whereabouts of a work colleague?" she asked condescendingly.

"Believe me, when I get to L.A. I'm going to hunt her down and then I'm going to strangle her for giving me the runaround," he replied, making a circling gesture with his hands as though he was choking Anna Lisa right there.

Juliet laughed hard. "That girl has been riling you up from day one. I remember you wanting to terminate her after your first day of working with her."

"And I still do."

"I cannot wait until I tell Mum and Dad. They'd be very pleased. They're finally going to get a daughter-in-law they like."

"Juliet," he said sternly, "Anna Lisa and I are not getting married. I'd be lucky if she speaks to me."

"Why wouldn't she talk to you?"

"Because I kissed her."

"You kissed her while you were engaged to Sarah?" she said, her eyes popping out of their sockets.

"Yes and she got very cross with me. Said it was better if we didn't keep in touch." His face was grim. He wished he hadn't kissed her and waited until he had broken it off with Sarah.

"Well, can't say I blame her." She rested her back against the bench, crossed her legs and bit into her dessert. "After all, you were engaged. But I must confess that after hearing this, I like her even more."

"Do you?" He threw his wrappers in the nearby trashcan.

"Yes. She's the type of girl who would always do right by you. I like that about her." She gave him her empty tomato juice can and he discarded it.

Neil was smiling for the first time in days. He was glad his family liked Anna Lisa. But when he saw the grimace on Juliet's face he said, "Why are you frowning?"

"Did you say you were going to Los Angeles to find her?"

"Yes." He sat next to her.

"Are you planning to come back?"

Feeling guilty for taking off again, he put his hands in his lap and looked down. He knew it was hard for his family to see him come and go. "No. I called my boss in L.A. and asked him for my job back."

Juliet wanted him to stay in London, yet she knew it would be selfish of her to try to keep him there. "I suppose this is why you wanted to meet."

He noticed the disappointed look on his sister's face and said, "It's not as though I'm leaving forever. I will come and visit on holidays."

"I shall miss you but I am happy for you."

"Thank you for understanding."

"Tell me, how did you fall in love with Anna Lisa? Didn't you dislike her at one point?" she said, studying his face.

"Yes, but that's all in the past. As I got to know her better, I realized how much she and I are alike."

"I'm not sure if that's such a great thing. There are times the two of you are like bulls locking horns, neither side willing to back down."

Neil chuckled and said, "We do squabble now and then, but it doesn't bother me. How should I put it...It adds a certain oomph to our relationship."

"I know what you mean," Juliet nodded. "It reminds me of my relationship with Mark. Sometimes he drives me crazy but I do love him."

"What do you think mother and father will say about all this?" he asked with concern.

"I believe they shall be thrilled. Anna Lisa is a better mate for you than Sarah and I'm sure if they were here right now, they would agree."

"Thanks Sis," he said and kissed her on the cheek.

Then the two basked in the sun for a few more minutes and enjoyed the fresh air until it was time to go. Juliet returned to work and Neil to the office to tie up loose ends before his departure.

TWENTY-FIVE

Third week of September, Anna Lisa left work and drove home dispirited and jaded. Her new supervisory job overseeing the work of other account executives at Hamilton International was depleting all her energy. Her office, situated on the 14th floor of an ultra-modern building, overlooked downtown Los Angeles, was larger than her former work space and had pricy contemporary furniture. Anna Lisa even had her own personal secretary outside her door, ready to fetch whatever she needed. However, she didn't care about any of that and often thought about her previous employer. She kept telling herself that it took time to adapt to a new environment. Yet how was she to adjust when she traveled so much? She had already been to Chicago, Washington and Houston and was weary of sleeping in hotels and waking up in a different city each time. She had to stick it out. What choice was there?

When she got home, she changed into brown sweatpants and taupe tank top and pulled back her hair with a red hair band. In the kitchen, She filled a pitcher with chilled sugar-free cranberry juice, put cheddar-cheese rice cakes in a yellow ceramic bowl and set them on a clear glass tray along with two tall glasses and carried them outside to the balcony of her new condo. She was expecting Leila any minute. Anna Lisa poured juice in her glass and tried to relax as she gazed out.

Her old condo was in escrow and her new one was in a security building with valet parking, a swimming pool, tennis court, basketball court and fitness center. Her balcony overlooked the city and on a clear day she was able to see the Pacific Ocean. Anna Lisa was comfortable but not happy. She missed Neil. She missed him when she took time off for herself; she missed him when she sat in her new office at Hamilton International, and she missed him now. Except, it was wrong to long for a married man. It was wrong to be friends with a married man when she had feelings for him. She was better off staying away.

Even if he wasn't married, Anna Lisa didn't want him. She wasn't ready to have a boyfriend and needed time to sort things out. She was tired of making the same mistakes in her relationships and no longer trusted her own judgment. Maybe she should let her grandmother and her aunts pick out her next boyfriend. As these thoughts occupied her mind, her intercom rang and the security announced Leila.

A few minutes later, Leila came up to the 20th floor. Anna Lisa opened the cream door of her condo but before she could greet her friend, Leila started: "Have I got news for you. Paul quit his job and broke it off with Kimberly, Kimberly went back to her husband and–"

"Stop. I told you I don't want to know anything about what's going on in that office," said Anna Lisa walking back to her balcony.

Leila followed. She had come straight from the office in her work clothes – wearing an orange skirt and a white round-neck blouse. She looked pretty with her incredibly short black hair. She had a haircut two days ago – bluntly trimmed bangs angled to the side and curt sideburns showing off her delicate small ears.

Anna Lisa relaxed her back against her chair. "Did you say Paul quit?!"

Leila stared at her friend with eyes that portrayed defiance. "I thought you weren't interested."

"I am not. I don't care about Paul or Kimberly, but I am surprised he quit."

"He misplaced a half million dollars," Leila said, taking a seat on a large comfortable chair with white handles and a green cushion. A square glass table divided her from Anna Lisa.

"What?" said Anna Lisa, shifting to the edge of her seat and sitting up erect with a look of disbelief in her eyes.

"When he reported the gross profit, he underreported it by a half million dollars and Simon found out later when the firm was audited. Of course Simon was furious and hired this guy Herman who has a master's in taxation and is a CPA, and demoted Paul. The accountant in charge was so strict that he was driving Paul crazy and so Paul quit," Leila said, pouring the juice in her glass and hers, drinking most of it.

Astonished and perplexed, Anna Lisa stared at Leila as her jaw dropped open. Leila was talking at 100 miles per hour and Anna Lisa had a difficult time grasping all that had happen since she had left Howard Brown.

Leila set her glass down and went on as though she was racing to get to the end of her story. "Then Kimberly left. Apparently she was from Tucson but lived in North Carolina and she came out here with her husband but when her husband found out she was cheating on him, he kicked her out of the house and she moved in with Paul. But because she attached herself to Paul like a leech, she drove him crazy and so he broke it off with her. And when they were no longer together, Kimberly couldn't afford her own place and she moved back in with her husband who wanted to move back to North Carolina and now she's in North Carolina; I guess trying to work things out with her husband." Leila paused to catch her breath and then continued, "And now Neil is back and he's not married. He's been looking everywhere for you but I–"

"Slow down, will you? Kimberly was married?"

"Yes, like I said–"

"Neil is not married?" Anna Lisa knew Neil was back because he had left several messages for her at work and she hadn't returned any of his calls but she had no idea that he wasn't married.

"No, he's not," said Leila as she slapped the back of her right hand against the palm of her left. "Try to keep up, will you? I'm trying to bring you up to date with–"

"Why isn't he married?"

"I don't know. All I know is when he came back there was no ring on his finger. I asked him where his ring was, and he said there's no ring because he didn't get married."

Anna Lisa fell back into her chair, her face drained of color and her body limp. He was not married.

"What should I tell him?" said Leila as she poured some more juice in her glass and noticed that Anna Lisa's glass was still full.

Anna Lisa had been so engrossed in Leila's story that she had forgotten all about her drink. "About what?"

"About you," said Leila setting down the pitcher. "He's been driving me crazy asking all sorts of questions."

Anna Lisa stuck her hand in the bowl of rice cakes, grabbed a bunch and started putting one in her mouth after another, chewing on the pieces nervously. "Nothing. Tell him nothing about me. You promised to keep my whereabouts a secret," she said, pointing a rice cake at Leila.

Leila frowned. "But that was when he was getting married. Wouldn't you like to be with him?"

She shook her head. "No."

"Why not? I thought you wanted him," cried Leila.

She didn't trust him anymore. He was not the man she thought he was. "I did. I mean I do but I just don't want to see him," said Anna Lisa, getting up and pacing her balcony and wringing her hands. Oh, God. She wished he were married already and done with it. Why was everything in her life always so complicated?

"Do sit down for two seconds, will you," said Leila. "Seeing you pace back and forth is giving me motion sickness."

"Sorry," said Anna Lisa and did as her friend asked.

Leila peered at Anna Lisa. "I'm confused. How could you have feelings for this man and not wish to see him?"

Because I've been hiding the truth from you, she thought. "I might as well tell you what happened. I don't want to be with him because he kissed me."

Leila's black eyes widened as though someone had just slapped her awake. "He what?"

"He kissed me before he left for London to get married," said Anna Lisa and scrunched her face.

"He kissed you?" Leila said in astonishment. "He kissed you and that's why you don't want to see him?"

"Don't you get it? He was about to get married when he kissed me. If I were to get involved with him, how could I be sure he wouldn't go after other women behind my back?"

Leila grabbed Anna Lisa's shoulders. "Because you aren't just another woman; he is in love with you."

"That's what I used to think about Paul. I thought he loved me," said Anna Lisa, moving to the edge of her balcony and holding onto the copper railing that had weathered to aqua green and rust. She gazed at the city that was slowly starting to glitter.

Leila looked at Anna Lisa's back and said, "Anna Lisa, you're comparing filet mignon with meatloaf. Neil isn't anything like Paul. He's a good man."

With teary eyes, Anna Lisa turned and shook her head, "I can't. I can't do this anymore. I don't want him to find me." She had been hurt too many times. First, her parents abandoned her when they died and second, she had gone from one bad relationship into another. She had always searched for the fairy-tale romance her parents shared. But each time she had tried, it hadn't worked. Her parents were lucky to have found each other, she thought.

"But what should I tell him? He knows you and I are best friends."

"Tell him–" said Anna Lisa biting her lip, "tell him, I'm too busy with Adam and it looks like our relationship has taken a serious turn."

"You're kidding, right?" said Leila. She didn't know Adam was gay or she would've been even more displeased by Anna Lisa's ridiculous excuse.

"No, I'm perfectly serious. If this is the only way to get rid of Neil, so be it."

Leila sighed. "I think you're making a big mistake."

"Then it's my mistake and not yours. You just make sure you pass along my message."

"Fine," said Leila with a wave of her hand and a sarcasm in her voice. "Your wish is my command your majesty." How foolish her friend was to give up such a great man, she thought.

———————

"I cannot comprehend why she refuses to see me," Neil told Leila the day after Leila had paid Anna Lisa a visit.

Leila was in her new office about to file a few folders. Her work area, which was half the size of Anna Lisa's old office, had an oak desk, a few cream filing cabinets, an oak bookshelf and a partial view of a running track, a field and a congested street. Leila turned with folders in her hand, looked at Neil and felt sorry for him. How long could she stall him and not tell him that Anna Lisa didn't want to have anything to do with him? Anna Lisa was stupid not to grab him. Leila knew he would have no trouble finding another girlfriend, but she had to make sure that didn't happen. He and Anna Lisa belonged together, and she knew it in her gut. *Forgive me, Anna Lisa for not passing along your message to Neil,* she thought. "It's not you. She needs time alone and you need to be patient." *I will continue working on her until I get through that thick head of hers,* she told herself.

He rubbed his face. "Then why doesn't she at least return my calls?"

Leila was astonished that he had called her. Why hadn't Anna Lisa told her? But then again, her friend had been secretive about many things lately.

He noticed the surprised look on her face and said with a raised his voice, "Did you think I wouldn't find out that she works for Hamilton International? Of all the stupid ideas that girl has. Why would she get a job at our competitors?" He had found out about Anna Lisa's whereabouts from Diana who had a friend who worked for Hamilton International.

She gasped and said, "She never mentioned you had tried to contact her."

"I must have left her a dozen messages with her secretary."

"Sorry," she replied sympathetically, "but like I said, you have to give her time."

He felt that Leila was holding out on him. He could tell from the tone of Leila's voice and the way she was looking at him that she was somehow deceiving him. But what option did he have other than to wait? "Very well then," he said jotting down his new address and phone number on a white pad sitting on Leila's desk. He tore off the top sheet and handed it to Leila. "Will you give this to her and tell her to call me?"

Leila took the information from him, folded it in half and put it in her black leather purse. "Sure thing," she said, studying his face, "But you still haven't told me why you didn't marry Sarah."

"You shall find out soon enough, that is if Anna Lisa will ever allow me to see her," he said, walking out of Leila's office dissatisfied. Neil didn't want to stay away from the woman he loved but didn't have an alternative. He could probably find her if he tried. All he had to do was wait somewhere outside her office building and follow her home, but Neil didn't want to succumb to that. She needed space and Neil was giving it to her. He had faith and if they were meant to be, all the space in the world would not keep them apart.

TWENTY-SIX

On a chilly October night, Anna Lisa lay on her bed, keeping warm underneath a black afghan, feeling sorry for herself. She was on her cycle and her hormones were wacky, making her cry at a drop of a hat. She felt lonely and tired. Originally Anna Lisa had planned to work less, but her boss kept her incredibly busy. The combination of frequent traveling, working at clients' job sites, not getting enough sleep and not having time for herself, family and friends was wearing her down. She wished she could go back to working for Simon. A year ago, Anna Lisa had it all – a career she enjoyed, a boyfriend she loved and time for herself and family. Now all she did was work, come home, sleep and repeat the same monotonous day. The worst part of it all was that she didn't need to work that hard because Anna Lisa didn't have a family to support. She could get a less stressful job that didn't pay as much, lease her condo and live at her grandmother's house and be a lot happier. She reached for a box of tissue sitting on her nightstand and pulled out one tissue after another as she cried and blew her nose for a good 30 minutes, thinking about her misfortunes and the turn of events in her life.

Enough, she told herself. Get a grip. Anna Lisa got off her bed, went into the kitchen, and like any good girl on her cycle, searched her cupboards for something rich and sugary. She settled for a jar of lemon curd. It was almost her bedtime and before turning in she had gotten into the habit of watching BBC World

News, which she taped earlier on her VCR. She flipped on her TV, lay back in her bed and after 20 minutes dozed off.

"I see love and commitment...I don't know," Susan replied, *the edges of her mouth tilting downward. "May be from this man you go on trip with."*

The following day, on a Friday afternoon, right before Halloween, Anna Lisa walked hesitantly into her favorite British shop – Little Brit, with her shoulders hunched and an anxious expression plastered on her face, afraid to run into Neil. He had already been in town for a month but she had not seen him. Attired in a fitted rust-colored skirt suit after work, she stood near the entrance eyeing each aisle but found no trace of him. She picked up a metal shopping basket, went to the second row and unlike the time when she had first met Neil, she noticed there were at least 10 jars of lemon curd on the third shelf. She reached for two along with a few more items such as an English breakfast tea, a package of small scones and a narrow cylindrical box of English candy by the cashier's counter, which looked liked M&Ms but the pieces were flatter and larger, the colors were different and the morsels tasted better to Anna Lisa. She handed her purchases to a tall old clerk with a humped back. As he rang up the items, she opened her brown leather purse and looked for her wallet when she heard a man's voice from behind her.

"Pardon me, but I think you have my lemon curd."

"What're you talking about?" said she and turned to look behind her. "There's plenty left on–" she said and suddenly stopped talking when her eyes fell upon the man she had been struggling so hard to forget.

Neil Scott Whittaker in his signature black Armani suit, white shirt and burgundy tie stared at Anna Lisa and said, "Hello Leeza."

She felt butterflies in her stomach as her heart pounded hard against her chest. "Hi," she managed to say without meeting his eyes.

"That'll be $15.19," said the cashier.

Anna Lisa turned back to face the cashier, paid him, picked up her white plastic bag and moved away. She then looked at Neil, "How've you been?"

"I've been better," he said looking glum and solemn.

"How is your family?" she asked trying to keep their conversation light and uncomplicated.

"My family is keeping well. Thank you for asking." He stared at her wondering why she did not look happy to see him. All this time he had been searching for her, thinking about her, missing her and yet here she was cold and distant as though they were never friends. He didn't comprehend the girl at all.

Feeling guilty for avoiding him all this time, she felt awkward and uncomfortable around him. "Well, it was nice seeing you. I have to go now," she uttered and walked out.

Neil followed her to her car. Her legs felt weak, blood rushed to her face and she felt warm, extremely warm. She unlocked the trunk of her car and put her groceries in.

"Will you at least look at me?" Neil said from behind her.

She closed her trunk, turned around slowly and saw his eyes fixed upon her. "Sorry, I'm in bit of a hurry. I'm meeting Adam," she lied to push him away.

Adam? So they were officially a couple now? Well, he didn't care. He and Leeza belonged together. He didn't come all the way out here to lose the woman he loved to Adam. "Adam can wait, this can't," he said, putting one hand under her shoulder blades and the other behind her head, pulled her toward him and kissed her.

Anna Lisa welcomed the intrusion in reflex, putting one arm about his shoulder and the other around his back. She found herself lost and witless for a long time until she was completely out of breath. She pulled away and looked at him panting, her palms sweaty, her knees week and her head hazy. She couldn't do this.

She was afraid to get hurt again and this time around she knew she would not be able to recover. "I have to go."

He knew in his heart that she loved him. The way she had responded to his kiss, the way their bodies had melted into each other and the way she looked at him with a great passion. Why was she denying them both a happiness that was so rare to find between two people whose souls connected and intertwined? He took her hands into his and said, "Leeza, what are you running away from? Love?"

With a serious look on her face, she said, "I must go," but he wouldn't let her go. He had trapped her between him and the trunk of her car.

He fixed his eyes upon her until she was forced to look at him. "You're in love with me. Admit it."

She was angry at his arrogance. So sure was he that she loved him. What an assumption to make when she hadn't admitted to anything. "I'm with Adam now and you, you were supposed to be getting married."

The sound of Adam's name gnawed on his nerves but it didn't stop him from saying, "I didn't marry Sarah because I was and still am in love with you."

Confused and surprised at all that was happening in such a short time, she said, "Please, let me go." She released her hands from his grip, pushed him away, got into her car and drove away.

Neil stood there for a long time looking at the empty space where Anna Lisa's car was situated before she took off in a hurry. There was no doubt in his mind that she loved him but she wasn't ready to commit herself to a serious relationship. Leila was right. Anna Lisa needed time and space before she would come back to him. He would have to learn to be patient and wait.

Back in her kitchen, Anna Lisa put away her groceries and reflected on what had just happened. She cussed herself for not doing her shopping on Saturday instead. The guy was impossible and didn't give up easily. She sensed a mixture of emotions from anger to love to confusion. She was angry that he had kissed her because while driving home, all she could think about was how much she had been enraptured by his touch and entranced by the tender expression in his eyes. He had imposed himself on her but rather than objecting, she had welcomed him. He loved her. He had said it, finally, at last. The words she needed to hear. But were they just words or did he mean them? Oh, how much she needed to talk to someone. Anyone. But how could anyone help make up her mind about him? No, she had to do it herself. She opened her fridge, searching for something salty, sweet, heavy or gooey that could help calm the turbulence brewing inside her but instead settled for a bag of mixed vegetables. She chomped on a carrot followed by a cauliflower and broccoli but they weren't gratifying her. Anna Lisa pushed the bag away and thought the hell with it. She needed the good stuff – chocolate candy. Grabbing them from a distant cabinet, she popped the lid, took out several pieces and let each piece melt gently into her mouth. She played with the cylindrical box as she rolled it back and forth in her hand, contemplating if she should eat its entire contents but decided against it. Shutting the lid, she put it back where it was, went to her bedroom, changed into a T-shirt and a pair of sweats and started cycling her turmoil away.

The night of her encounter with Neil at Little Brit, Anna Lisa had dinner at her grandmother's house. They had finished eating pot roast and were about to have hot chocolate for dessert. Anna Lisa got up from the kitchen chair, put the salt shaker in the fridge, took out the whipped cream and set it in the spice cabinet. She then walked over to the dishwasher, removing the clean plates and utensils from the prior day and placing them on shelves where they didn't belong.

"What's wrong, honey?" Her grandmother asked. She had just finished fixing her hot chocolate tray.

"Nothing, Grandma," said Anna Lisa as she inserted the dirty dishes in the dishwasher.

Her grandmother went to the fridge, took out the salt shaker that Anna Lisa had accidentally put in there and stuck it in the cupboard where the whipped cream was, picked up the cream and set it on the tray. She turned and gave her granddaughter a puzzled look.

"Really, I'm fine. What makes you think I'm not?" Anna Lisa said, shutting the dishwasher door without putting soap in and turning it on.

Her grandmother shook her head, walked over to the dishwasher, turned it off and opened the door.

"What did you do that for?" Anna Lisa glared at her grandmother.

"You forgot to put soap in there," she said, taking out a box of detergent from underneath her sink, pouring it in the dishwasher's soap container and closing the lid. She shut the door of the dishwasher, turned it on and put the soap back. "Now, would you like to tell me what's bothering you?"

Anna Lisa shrugged defiantly. "Nothing's bothering me."

"Honey, you've been putting the salt in the refrigerator, the cream in the cupboard and I can't find any of my dishes where they belong. Now, you either tell me what's going on or soon I will not be able to find anything in my own house."

She crinkled her nose. "Sorry Grandma, my mind has been elsewhere lately."

Her grandmother lifted an antique silver tray bearing a pink floral china pot, two matching cups and saucers and fresh whipped cream. "Come child, let's go to the living room and sit down," she said.

Anna Lisa followed and sat next to her on the sofa.

"Now, tell me what's bothering you," her grandmother said as she poured hot chocolate into their cups. She put a dollop of cream into each cup just the way her granddaughter liked it.

Anna Lisa chewed on the inside corner of her lip and sat in silence for a few moments before she spoke. "You remember Neil?"

Her grandma picked up the two cups with saucers and tiny teaspoons. She handed Anna Lisa one. "The nice Englishman you brought over a couple of times. Is he married yet?"

Anna Lisa took the hot chocolate from her grandma and replied, "No, and that's just the problem. He didn't get married because he says he's in love with me."

Her grandmother stirred her hot beverage and took a sip. "And are you in love with him?"

Anna Lisa frowned. "That's not the point. The point is – oh, I don't know what the point is anymore," she sighed.

She looked at her granddaughter and remarked, "You should be happy he's in love with you, unless you don't feel the same."

"Paul really hurt me," she said, drinking her hot chocolate. "I'm not ready to be in love again. I'm not sure if I'll ever be." Anna Lisa never had an ideal male figure to look up to while growing up. She was raised by women all her life and her uncles were always busy and hardly came by.

"My dear, love isn't going to wait for you and come into your life at a perfect time. Look at your parents. They had no money, no job and not even a place of their own but they fell in love and then they had you," replied her grandmother with a grim face. How she wished that they were still alive.

Anna Lisa noted her grandmother's sadness. "Did you like my father?"

"Not at first. I just thought your mother was too young to get married. But afterwards, when she got pregnant and you were born, I thought I was the luckiest person in the world to have the three of you and then the accident–" Anna stopped talking because a lump formed in her throat and tears filled her eyes.

Anna Lisa set her cup down on a walnut side table next to the sofa, grabbed a tissue from a silver container and gave it to her grandma. "I wish I had known them." As much as she loved her grandma and aunts, as a child, she had felt a certain void in her life. On Parents' day, while other parents showed up with their kids, Anna Lisa was accompanied by a female family member.

And on Father's Day, she had always envied the children who showed up to school with their dads.

Her grandmother wiped her tears and said, "I wish you had too." She held Anna Lisa's hands and gently squeezed them. "Don't be afraid to fall in love. Love is a wonderful thing when it's right. It gives you direction and a sense of purpose."

"But how can I be sure when it's right?" she said looking very serious.

"Just trust your instincts," replied her grandmother, passing Anna Lisa a kind smile.

She shook her head in disagreement. "My instincts have always led me to be wrong." Her voice was sullen, her forehead wrinkled and her neck and shoulders tense. How come other people had it so much easier? She thought.

"No my dear, ignoring them is what led you to be wrong," said her grandma. She let go of Anna Lisa's hands, hunched over and refilled her cup. "Take Paul for example. You knew his character before you went out with him. Your gut feeling warned you to stay away from him."

"True but he pursued me till I fell for him," said Anna Lisa and turned to pick up her cup. She spooned out the whipped cream and put it in her mouth.

"Now, you know better. And this English fellow, I remember you saying you felt good about him, so he can't be all that bad."

What her grandma said was true. Anna Lisa had thought Neil was an honorable man up to the point when he had kissed her. After that she had been confused about his intentions. Now that he wasn't married, she didn't know what to make of him. Was she comparing Neil to Paul on purpose just to push him away? Because if that was the case, then she had no reason not to love him except her own fear of commitment. "Oh, I don't know, Grandma," she replied, her voice filled with apprehension.

"You don't have to make a decision right now. Just think about what I have told you."

She nodded and kissed her grandmother on the cheek. "Thanks for listening to my troubles."

"Anytime," said Anna, patting her granddaughter's hand with her freckled bony one. I'm always here for you."

"And I for you," replied Anna Lisa thinking how fortunate she was to have such a loving grandmother in her life.

Anna Lisa did not brush off her grandmother's words. She thought about everything she had said and then observed it when she had dinner at Nicole's house, a week later. Nicole's boyfriend, Eddie, who looked domestic wearing a green apron over his white T-shirt and brown velour pants, was barbecuing chicken in the backyard. Nicole's daughter, Sam was busy playing with a new puzzle Anna Lisa had brought her.

It was the first free Saturday afternoon Anna Lisa had since she started working for Hamilton International. The sun played hide-and-seek beneath the clouds and a soft breeze meandered through the air. Nicole came out of the back door of her kitchen looking comfortable in a loosely fitted white rayon dress with red flowers; her hair hanging loosely around her shoulders. She held a bottle of beer in each hand, one regular and the other non-alcoholic. She gave the regular one to Anna Lisa, who was relaxing in her jeans and sweater, admiring the small pond Nicole had recently purchased and installed. A statue of Venus stood in the middle of it while water circulated from the top of the statue's head emptying into the pond.

As Anna Lisa took the beer from Nicole, she noticed that her formerly thin friend had put on a little weight. "Nicole?"

"Hmmm?"

"You're glowing."

"Am I?" said she with an ambiguous smile.

"If I didn't know better, I'd say you're pregnant."

Nicole beamed.

"Oh my God! You are pregnant!" replied Anna Lisa with wide eyes. "Eddie, my sneaky friend," Anna Lisa yelled across the small yard, "Why didn't you say something?"

Eddie, who was turning ears of corn on the barbecue heard her and smiled. He was tall and overweight with honey-colored hair and eyes. His stomach hung over his pants, his butt was wide and his manners mild and friendly.

Anna Lisa said to Nicole, "But didn't you say you weren't planning to have any more children?"

"Yes, that's what I said but this one wasn't planned. It was an accident really, but we're thrilled about it."

"Come here, give me a hug," said Anna Lisa, opening her arms and embracing her friend. "Congratulations. How far along are you?" she asked touching her friend's belly.

"Four months."

"You hardly look it. I mean you're glowing but you're not showing as much as most people do during their second trimester."

"My clothes are getting tighter. I had to go up a size," commented Nicole. "C'mon, let's go sit."

Anna Lisa followed her and took a seat next to Sam. There was a pretty etched-glass candleholder supporting three tall pink candles in the center of the table. "If it were me, I would have had to go up five sizes," Anna Lisa said and they both laughed.

"Will you help me?" Sam asked as she looked at her puzzle and then at Anna Lisa.

"Honey," said her mom, "we're talking. Do what you can and then we'll help you after dinner."

Sam pouted and continued playing.

Nicole looked at her friend. "So, how've you been?"

"I'm better," said Anna Lisa but she didn't look happy. She missed Neil.

"I have another surprise for you," offered Nicole, who was too excited with her good fortune to notice the sadness on Anna Lisa's face.

"You do?"

"Eddie and I are getting married next month and both you and your grandmother are invited. It's a small ceremony, but we prefer it that way."

"I thought you vowed to never get married again."

Nicole smiled. "That was the old me. I used to think all men are like my ex, but Eddie is great," she said, looking over to Eddie who was flipping chickens. "He works hard. We make decisions and handle all money matters together. He's wonderful with Sam. I can't ask for any more than that."

"In that case, once again congratulations are in order. I'm happy for the both of you."

"Now tell me, is there someone special in your life?" she asked, quaffing her non-alcoholic beer.

Anna Lisa shook her head. "No. I'm just trying to enjoy my new freedom."

"I understand," Nicole said, resting her back against her chair. "When Sam's father left, I was really hurt. I didn't want to be with anyone, but look at me now. I'm getting married again. That's a big step for me, you know."

"I know. I remember how difficult it was for you," said Anna Lisa, drinking her beer. She envied the way her friend had been able to overcome her doubts and bitterness toward the opposite sex.

"Someday, you'll be ready too. But don't wait too long," Nicole said, rising to go into the kitchen to grab utensils.

Anna Lisa followed her.

Nicole picked up a small stack of red plastic dishes and paper napkins from her white-tiled counter and handed them to Anna Lisa. "I wasted a lot of time crying over a bad man. Learn from mistakes and move on quickly," she said, picking up forks and knives and a wooden bowl filled with salad.

Anna Lisa helped Nicole set the table. The sun had disappeared and it was starting to get dark. Nicole lit the candles on the table with a long blue lighter. Eddie brought the barbecued chicken and corn on a large white plastic platter and set it down. He removed his apron and told Sam to put her puzzle away. He went into the house with Sam so that they could wash their hands. When the two of them came back, they joined Anna Lisa and Nicole for dinner.

That evening while everyone enjoyed their meal and conversed, Anna Lisa couldn't help longing for Nicole's lifestyle. Her friend had a nice job, giving her plenty of time to spend with her family, a kind-hearted boyfriend, a well-mannered and loving daughter and a baby on the way. Would she someday have all these if she allowed Neil in her life? As scared as she was, she had to admit that she loved him and he her. Why else would he have flown all the way out here and given up his life in London just to be with her? He had made the mistake of kissing her while he was engaged but for how long was she going to punish him for his past action? She decided to get in touch with him. She wanted to give them the chance they deserved.

TWENTY-SEVEN

Ten days to Thanksgiving, most of Neil's belongings still sat in boxes at his newly leased apartment in Santa Monica near the beach. With Anna Lisa gone from the office, he was bombarded by a heavy work load, and although some of Anna Lisa's clients were transferred to Leila, Neil still had to help Simon out by overlooking the work of other account executives and handle some of Anna Lisa's large clients until Leila was ready to take over. Simon had told him to interview new people for Anna Lisa's position but he hadn't had the time. She was irreplaceable, he thought, as he went into the kitchen to turn off the stove because the kettle had been whistling for some time. He decided to make his tea later and went back to sit in front of his tube in the going-away-present Anna Lisa had picked out for him three months ago – a khaki long-sleeve shirt with yellow stripes along the shoulders and sleeves and a pair of coordinating sweat pants. He was watching the late night news, using chopsticks to eat his Chinese food out of cartons and wondering if she ever thought of him. His doorbell rang.

He looked through the peephole and was surprised as he opened the door and said, "What are you doing here?"

"I've missed you," Sarah said, standing in front of him in her taupe Donna Karen dress, a matching Burberry cashmere scarf and a brown leather headband holding her beautiful silky hair back. She had her luggage with her.

She was lovely, he thought, like a flawless model on the cover of a magazine yet he felt nothing toward her. Neil wasn't happy to see her, but let her in anyway, and helped her with her luggage. "Did you just get in?"

"I got in two hours ago," she said, closing the door. "I could use a cup of tea."

"Have a seat," Neil suggested, removing the newspapers from his black leather sofa, and putting them on the two-tiered glass table.

With a wrinkled forehead and a puzzled look on his face, he asked, "How did you find me?"

"I got your address from your father," she replied, untying her scarf and plopping into the sofa. She removed her pointy shoes and rubbed her feet.

"Oh," he uttered and went into his white kitchen. He reached in one of the cabinets, took out two green mugs and Earl Grey tea bags, which he dropped into a small tea pot. He poured hot water over them and let them simmer for a few minutes but before he could turn around, he felt Sarah's body against his and her hands caressing his back. He cursed underneath his breath.

"All I do is think about you," she murmured, "I will do anything to make it work and promise not to get in your way."

Neil turned around anxiously, stared at her and shook his head. "Sarah, you and I don't belong together. We have different values. You want an ostentatious lifestyle and I don't." She was much too close to him and he knew it. Except that Neil didn't want to hurt her by pushing her away. After all, they were engaged once.

"But I love you," she said, brushing her hands against his chest.

"No you don't," he replied adamantly, grabbing her hands and holding them. "What you're feeling is not love. It's dependency."

"That is not true," she stated, her lips quivering and her voice disturbed.

He joggled her hands and said with reproach, "Sarah, you ought to get out there and experience life. You cannot depend on me or your parents for the rest of your life."

She kissed him softly on his lips and his body stiffened. He thought a bit of cold decorum was in order. He had no intention of having his way with her and regretting it in the morning. He let go of her hands and moved away from her to create distance between them.

She pursued him.

"Please, stop," he told her. "Why don't you take that chair," he said, pointing to a black laminated chair behind a matching oval table, "and I shall serve us tea."

She did as he asked and blurted, "Don't you see? I'm willing to come out here to improve."

"Coming out here isn't going to change anything," he answered, pouring tea into the cups and setting them on coasters on the table. He grabbed the sugar bowl. He knew Sarah didn't take sugar but he did. "You don't even know who you are. You need to go get a job, meet new people, people outside your social circle."

"Don't you love me?"

"Not enough to want to marry you." He put two teaspoons of sugar in his tea, stirred it and tossed the spoon in the sink. Feeling guilty that she was having such a hard time letting him go, he pulled out a chair next to her.

"Maybe we can live together," she said tugging on his shirt.

"No," he said, removing her hands. He remembered how hurt Anna Lisa had been when she and Paul had broken up. Neil didn't want Sarah to go through a similar pain and preferred to soften the blow of their separation, but not at the risk of compromising his integrity.

"Why not?" she pouted. "We almost did when we were in London."

"And it's a good thing we didn't," he said clearing his throat. "You're young and you have a lot to learn."

"But all my friends my age are married."

"Your youth has nothing to do with your age," Neil said. "How should I put it? You're immature. You have a lot to learn about who you are before you commit to anyone."

"I'm so tired," Sarah said. The combination of the long flight and the hopelessness of not being able to reconcile her relationship with Neil were wearing her down by the minute. She needed him. She was lost without him. She was supposed to be Mrs. Neil Whittaker with at least two children and a house in the country and had it not been for that American seductress, she would've been married by now. It was all Anna Lisa's fault, she thought.

"Here, have some tea," Neil handed her a mug. "We need to find you a place to stay."

"Please Neil, can't I at least stay the night?" she implored, staring at him with her desperate eyes, "I'll sleep on the couch. I don't want to be alone tonight."

Neil put his hands over his face in his dilemma. He didn't want her in his apartment but felt guilty kicking her out. He let out a frustrated sigh. "One night and that's it. You have to go to a hotel tomorrow."

"Thank you," she said, drinking her tea and trying to think of a plan so that she could stay there longer.

"You can sleep in my bed, and I'll take the couch."

"Are you certain because–"

"Yes, I'm certain. I just need to go upstairs to grab a blanket and a pillow," he said and headed toward a closet where he kept extra towels, blankets and pillows.

"Two women...Very jealous of you. Be careful."

Anna Lisa was up and ready early in the morning because she couldn't sleep. Dressed for the nippy temperature of New York – a white round-neck cashmere sweater and black pleated wool pants – she was going for an overnight trip to meet with a client but before leaving, there was something important she needed to do that couldn't wait any longer. She threw her red carry-on suitcase and travel bag in her car trunk, got in and looked over the directions to Neil's new apartment. As she drove to his place, she remembered what he had told her in London: "If you desire someone badly enough and you're certain the two of you belong together, go after the object of your affection and never give up." Today, more than ever, there was no doubt in her mind that Neil was the object of her affection and that they belonged together. Anna Lisa had thought about him the rest of the weekend after the barbecue at Nicole's and even picked up the phone several times to contact Neil, but had hung up, frightened to make the initiative of going after the man she cared so deeply about. And yesterday her schedule had been so crazy that she hadn't had time to talk to him. If she didn't speak to him today, she was afraid to lose her courage and never regain it.

When she got to Neil's place, she climbed up a set of stairs and found herself inside a modern but stylish brand-new pale peach apartment building. She looked for apartment 6 and after finding it, she stood in front of it, too scared to ring the bell. Her heart was pounding hard, her breath was barely coming out and her hands were shaky. She finally rang the doorbell.

Inside, Neil was in the shower upstairs and didn't hear the bell at first but Sarah did. She went down, looked through the peephole and was horrified to see Anna Lisa in front of it. Biting on her nonexistent cuticle, she tried to figure out how to get rid of her and then an idea came to her. She ran back upstairs, discarded her black lace negligee, went to Neil's closet, grabbed a blue shirt, put it on and left the top three buttons open. She messed up her hair to make it look like she had just left Neil's bed and had been interrupted by the bell. She then rushed downstairs as the doorbell rang again. But this time Neil, who had just turned off the water, heard it.

Outside, Anna Lisa was anxious and about to leave when the door opened. Startled, she saw Sarah in front of her with tousled hair and wearing Neil's shirt with no pants. Anna Lisa was speechless.

"Who is it?" Neil said as he climbed down the stairs with wet hair and a towel wrapped around him.

Anna Lisa took one look at him and one at Sarah and ran out.

"Leeza, wait," he said, chasing after her in bare feet. The morning air chilled his body and the ground underneath his feet was cold and rough, but he didn't care. He finally caught up with her near her car, clutched Anna Lisa's wrist with one hand and held on to his towel with the other and said, "This is not what it looks like."

"I don't care," she said glaring at him defiantly. "Let me go."

He frowned. "Please stop for one moment and listen." She was trying to wiggle her way out of his grip.

"No. I'm glad I saw you this way because now I don't have to go through all the heartache I went through with Paul."

"Damn you," he shouted, "I'm not Paul."

"No you're not, you're worse. Let me go." She managed to free herself and drove away.

Neil was furious at Sarah's deviousness. He ran back to his apartment, took Sarah by the forearm, dragged her up the stairs and yelled, "Put your clothes on. You're leaving this instant."

Sarah did not argue. She was frightened by his behavior because she had never seen him with such a violent temper. She picked up her clothes and went into the bathroom to change. Neil threw on his tan robe, stuffed Sarah's negligee into one of her four suitcases and took them all downstairs and left them outside his door. He called a cab.

By the time Sarah was ready, her luggage was in the trunk of a taxi waiting outside. Neil opened the taxi door for her but did not speak to her. He directed the driver to a hotel in Beverly Hills.

After Sarah left, Neil got ready quickly and headed toward Hamilton International. When he got there, the security wouldn't let him in because he was not on the guest list. Furious, Neil left and drove to his office. He had no other way of contacting Anna Lisa except to harass Leila and this time he wasn't going to take no for an answer. He was going to get Anna Lisa's address and that was that.

Neil barged in Leila's office, and blurted, "Where is she?"

Bewildered, Leila, who was sitting behind her desk, going over the ad layouts for Xian body soap, said, "Where's who?"

"You're going to give me Leeza's address or so help me God..." Neil said angrily. He was behaving like a lunatic and knew it but couldn't stop himself. His rage had taken over and he could no longer control himself.

She looked at his frantic face and ordered, "Calm down. Tell me what happened."

He put his hands on Leila's desk. "There's no time. I must speak with her."

"I can't give you her number. I swore I wouldn't give out any information about her. Besides, she's probably on her way to New York."

"New York! You can't be serious," he screamed, wrinkling his forehead.

"She told me she was going there on business. Now, sit down and tell me what happened."

Neil sat down, took in a deep breath and let it out to relieve the frustration he had felt ever since his doorbell rang that morning. He then explained to Leila all that happened the night before and the following day.

Leila kept repeating, "Oh, my God!"

"Will you stop saying that? Think. Where's she staying?"

Leila shrugged her shoulders. "I don't know."

"You're lying to me; I can feel it."

"No, Neil, I honestly don't know." Anna Lisa hadn't told her where she was staying. However, Leila did have Anna Lisa's cell phone number, but she wasn't about to give it to Neil. Leila knew her friend too well and how angry she must be feeling at that very moment. Neil should give her time to cool down. She looked at Neil and said, "Why did you let Sarah spend the night, last night?"

Neil grinded his teeth. "Because I was being nice. Apparently doing the right thing doesn't count anymore."

Leila studied his tense facial muscles and his nervous manner and felt sorry for him. What luck did he have. Had Anna Lisa showed up the day before or the day after, they would be together now. "I'm sorry. It's just that Anna Lisa's very vulnerable right now. Had you seen her the day I found her after she had disappeared from the office, you would understand. You have to wait and let her come to you."

"I did wait and look what happened. No, some things cannot be left to fate. I must find her," he said, but had no idea what course of action he was going to take to find the woman he loved.

TWENTY-EIGHT

The day Anna Lisa arrived back in Los Angeles from New York, there was a message on her cell. It was from Leila asking her to call her as soon as she got the message. But Anna Lisa had been in such a hurry to leave her apartment the morning of her trip that she had forgotten to remove her phone from the charger and take it with her. In New York, she hadn't called in for her messages. She figured her work and family knew her number at the hotel in case they needed to get in touch with her. Wondering what was so important, Anna Lisa called Leila at work and spoke with one of the secretaries whose voice she did not recognize. The girl told her Leila was in a meeting.

"Would you like her voicemail?"

"No, I'll try back later. Thanks," Anna Lisa replied and hung up.

She turned on the TV in her bedroom and watched the news as she undressed and got ready to take a bath. It was 6 and she had to get ready to meet Adam later for dinner. Anna Lisa soaked in her bath and tried to relax.

After her bath, she got ready. Tired of always rushing and not looking her best, she put on a simple but sexy black dress to make her feel pretty. Anna Lisa called Leila again but couldn't get ahold of her. This time she left a message on her voicemail.

"Hi, it's me. Sorry to get back to you so late but I forgot my cell phone at home before I left. I'll be with Adam tonight. I'll try calling you tomorrow from work," she said and hung up. She picked up her small satin black purse and ruby shawl, checked her red lipstick and her wavy chestnut brown hair in the hallway mirror and left.

When she arrived at the restaurant, Anna Lisa looked for Adam and found him sitting at the bar. Biscotti, a trendy Italian restaurant located northeast of Century City where Anna Lisa lived, was situated in a hip neighborhood, owned by a couple of famous actors and frequented by youthful clientele who enjoyed celebrity hunting. Inside, there were two rooms, a patio and a dim dining room enclosed by darkened windows. Ebony curved booths and inky chairs surrounded the tables with black leather tablecloths. Anna Lisa walked over to the bar and greeted Adam who was squished between large groups of young drinkers.

"Hi," said Adam when he saw Anna Lisa. Attired in a fitted olive shirt and black slacks, he pushed himself through the crowd. With a glass of half-empty sangria in one hand, he embraced Anna Lisa with the other and said, "I've missed you." He hadn't seen her for a month.

"And I you," said Anna Lisa, kissing him lightly on the cheek.

"Would you like something to drink?" he asked looking as handsome as ever with his newly layered haircut.

Anna Lisa admired his good looks and thought it was too bad for the female population that he was gay. He was like a perfect portrait one hung on the wall and stared at every day. "Yes but I'll get it myself, and don't forget it is my turn to treat you," she insisted.

Adam chuckled, "Fine. You can treat."

"Thank you," said Anna Lisa who was always frustrated by Adam's persistence to pay when they went out. She went up to the bar and waited for the busy bartender to notice her but was interrupted by Adam. "Our table is ready."

"Oh, okay," she said and followed a petit brunette hostess to their table with Adam trailing behind her.

The tables were small and the chairs were crammed into a tiny space with hardly any elbow room but Anna Lisa didn't mind. She was just happy to see her friend.

"Finally, we are able to get together. Between your schedule and mine, it's almost impossible for us to hook up," said Adam.

Anna Lisa nodded in agreement. "Hamilton International makes sure they get their money's worth out of me. There are days I wish I had stayed at Howard Brown."

"You know, my aunt is still mad at you for leaving."

"How is your aunt?"

"Feisty as ever. She wanted me to thank you again for putting our products on the right track."

Anna Lisa smiled. "You have a good product. I just gave it a small facelift."

"You're too modest," Adam commented. "We weren't doing that well and you know it."

Their tall waiter with short dark-blond hair parted to one side came by and interrupted them. He recited the specials and asked them what they wanted to drink.

"I'll have a kir royale," said Anna Lisa.

"And I will have another sangria," replied Adam.

"I'll be right back with your drinks," stated the waiter.

Adam and Anna Lisa opened their menus and looked through them. Anna Lisa decided on the saffron risotto with braised veal and Adam the pan-roasted swordfish steak.

"So," said Adam, "Tell me what you've been up to?"

"Mostly work. I just got back from New York visiting a client."

"How do you like your new job?" he said, finishing off his sangria.

"It's not Howard Brown," she said looking a little sad. "But the people are nice. No one gives me a hard time except I don't like the traveling. Next week I have to be in Chicago again."

"At least you get to travel," said Adam trying to point out the positive.

"Yes, but I rarely have time to see anything. By the time I get to my hotel, I just want to sleep."

Their waiter came back with their drinks, took their orders and left.

"To friendship," said Anna Lisa and clinked his glass.

Adam set his glass down and asked, "Why did you leave Howard Brown?"

"It's a long story," Anna Lisa answered as she glanced at her drink, gently swirled it and thought about how her life had taken so many turns and twists in the past 10 months.

He clapped his hands lightly and commented, "We're not going anywhere. C'mon spill."

Adam was like a girlfriend with whom one talked all night. He was warm, soft-hearted and a good listener, thought Anna Lisa as she accounted for her relationship problems she had encountered in the past year. While Anna Lisa told her story, their waiter brought their meals. And when Anna Lisa got to the part where she walked in on Neil and Sarah, Adam asked "Why did you take off like that?"

"It's called self-preservation. I didn't want to get hurt," said Anna Lisa, putting a piece of veal in her mouth while she talked. "It was obvious to me that he didn't love me or he wouldn't have slept with her."

"How do you know he slept with her?" asked Adam, frowning. "You didn't give the guy a chance to explain."

"There was nothing to explain," Anna Lisa shrugged. "It was crystal clear as to what happened. Don't you think?"

"Sometimes your eyes can deceive you," said Adam, enjoying his swordfish. "You can't run away every time things don't go your way. You need to communicate."

"He betrayed me," replied Anna Lisa. She ate a forkful of her saffron risotto.

"You don't know that and besides, didn't you tell him you don't want him?"

"Yes I did."

"Then what do you expect? He's a man with needs, if you get my drift," said Adam as he wiggled his eyebrows.

Anna Lisa wrinkled her forehead and said with a raised voice, "Yes, but I didn't think he's going to hop into bed with his ex right after he finished telling me he didn't marry her because he was in love with me."

Adam had to strain his voice as well because the rock music coming in over the speakers above their head was getting louder and louder and he could barely hear himself speak. He was beginning to regret taking his coworker's recommendation and choosing this restaurant. "It could have been just pure sex and nothing more to it. I mean she is gorgeous, and after all he's a man."

"Now, I want to strangle her," said Anna Lisa as she squeezed her water glass tightly.

"You don't have it in you," Adam chuckled. "Why don't you call him and see what he has to say?"

"No, I will not humiliate myself," she said adamantly.

"Alright, don't call him, but let me give you a second scenario of what you saw and you can judge for yourself," he said, crisscrossing his arms on the table. "She drops in unannounced and pushes him to let her spend the night. He's a gentleman and can't throw the girl out in the cold as tempting as that might be. So, he agrees. They sleep in separate beds, he gets up in the morning to take a shower and get ready for work, she hears the bell and borrows his shirt to go answer the door," Adam says. "How am I doing so far?"

Anna Lisa picked up her fork and played with her food. She was no longer hungry. "Why would she borrow his shirt? Doesn't she own a nightgown?"

"Who knows? Maybe she likes to sleep naked or maybe she forgot to pack a nightgown. The point is until you speak with him, you won't know what the truth is," said Adam, looking directly at her with concern, "Give him a chance to explain."

"I sure have made a mess of things," she said, dropping her fork. "Haven't I?"

"It's not too late to fix it."

The busboy came over and asked them if they were finished. They both nodded and he cleared the table.

Anna Lisa started making imaginary doodles on the tablecloth with her finger. "It is too late," she said to Adam with discontentment written all over her face, "I blew him off and now he's probably with Sarah as we speak."

Adam took her hands into his. "You don't know that."

"But if he is with her, my heart can't bear it. I love him more than I have ever loved anyone."

"Then trust your instincts and go after him," he ordered as he shook her hands.

Her eyes started to moisten. "I don't have the courage anymore."

"At least promise me you'll think about it."

"I will," said Anna Lisa and decided to change the subject. She didn't want to cry and ruin their dinner. "I feel like I've been talking about myself the entire night. Please tell me, what's new with you?"

"Well...I have a new boyfriend." He had a big grin on his face.

Anna Lisa's eyes widened. "Who?"

Adam ran one hand through his hair. "Remember the receptionist, Bob?"

"Yes, the curly blond with baby blue eyes," she replied, remembering Adam admiring him the night of the dance.

The waiter came over and asked them if they wanted coffee. They both said yes.

Adam said, "Can we get low-fat milk with it instead of cream?"

The waiter nodded and went away.

"So, tell me about Bob," Anna Lisa said.

"We started dating two weeks after the dance," he explained as his eyes twinkled with joy.

"And your aunt and the rest of your family?" she asked giving him a puzzled look, "Do they know?"

"Yes, they do," he answered, sipping his water. "I thought about what you said the night of the dance and decided to tell them the truth about me."

Anna Lisa smiled. "Good for you. Don't you feel better now that everything's out in the open?"

The waiter returned with their coffee.

"Yes except no one's speaking to me but my aunt," he replied, pouring milk in his coffee. "Want some?"

"Yes, please," Anna Lisa said, watching Adam pour milk into her coffee.

"I suppose I'm the black sheep of the family."

"No, you're not," she said, kicking him lightly under the table, "You're a great person." She put a packet of diet sugar in her coffee and stirred it. "They'll come around and if they don't, who cares? You need to be true to yourself."

"Thanks," he said and touched Anna Lisa's hand. "Your support means a lot to me."

"And your friendship means a lot to me."

When their dinner came to an end, Anna Lisa and Adam both walked outside to get their cars from the valet. After their cars arrived, they hugged and kissed and each got into their cars and drove away. Adam went to his house where his boyfriend was waiting for him and Anna Lisa went back to her empty condominium, thinking how lucky Adam was to have someone special in his life.

———————————

Back at Howard Brown, Leila and Neil were burning the midnight oil. Leila, engrossed in her work, finally noticed her flashing message light. She pressed the play button. Neil sat on a chair across from her desk.

"Hi, it's me. Sorry to get back to you so late but I forgot my cell phone at home before I left. I'll be with Adam tonight. I'll try calling you tomorrow from work."

Neil's hands, which were resting comfortably on his lap, became tense. "So, she's spending the night with Adam."

"No, she's not," Leila replied, erasing the message. She looked at Neil with compassion and said, "Believe me, there's nothing going on between them." At least she hoped not for his sake.

"That's not what I heard in her message," he snapped and abruptly got up, "She said she'll be with Adam for the rest of the night." He started walking back and forth in Leila's small space and the walls seemed to be closing in on him.

Good God, she wished he would stop that. He was making her nervous. "You're jumping to the wrong conclusion. I know Anna Lisa. She doesn't get into bed with just any guy."

Neil stopped moving and put his hands on Leila's desk. "Adam is not just any guy. They know each other very well."

She raised her voice. "Yes, but that doesn't mean she's sleeping with him."

Neil straightened his body and frowned. "You mind if we call it a night? I'm suddenly tired and want to go home."

What a good idea, she thought. In his state of mind, they wouldn't get anything done anyway. "Sure thing. We can go over the meeting tomorrow."

Neil started for the door.

"Neil?"

"Yes?" he said and turned to look at her.

"Have faith."

"Right." Neil appeared sad and hopeless. He walked out of Leila's office and headed toward his own. When he got there, Neil went through the client roster and found Adam's address but no home telephone number. There was only a work number. He went online and looked up the directions to Adam's house on MapQuest, printed a copy, folded the paper and stuck it in his coat pocket. He then left his office and headed out to his apartment.

Once home, Neil paced his living room, trying to decide if he should pay Adam a visit. It was almost 10 p.m. and Adam was probably having his way with Anna Lisa by now. He hoped he was wrong. Damn Sarah, who had destroyed any chance he might have had with Anna Lisa had she not been there that day. What did it didn't matter? The deed was done and there was nothing he could do. He went upstairs and took a shower. When he got out, his nerves were frazzled. He decided that sleep might calm him so he crawled into bed and passed out.

Around midnight, Neil awoke and sat up in his bed with his heart beating hard against his chest and his head throbbing. In a nightmare, he had seen a faceless man come after him with an ax. He moved from the bed into the bathroom and splashed cold water on his face to get rid of his fearfulness. He opened his mirrored medicine cabinet above the sink, took out two aspirins and washed them down with a glass of water. Neil walked back into his bedroom and sat on his bed. He found himself agitated and uncomfortable. Anna Lisa was with Adam tonight and he had to stop them or else his relationship with Anna Lisa would be completely over. He could never forgive her for spending a night with Adam, he thought as he changed into a pair of dark blue jeans, a black turtleneck and a jacket and left his apartment. He took out his directions to Adam's house and drove there at breakneck speed.

In 20 minutes, he found himself in front of Adam's Victorian style house. Neil looked for Anna Lisa's car but it wasn't around. Perhaps it was parked in Adam's garage or perhaps Adam had picked her up from her apartment, he thought. After another 10 minutes passed by, Neil found the courage to get out of his car and walk toward a large and intricately cut reddish-brown door brightened by two torchieres on either side. It was late, very late, past midnight late, but if she were there, he would go in, get her out and leave. He rang Adam's doorbell. No answer. Maybe he was at her apartment. He rang the bell again and this time he didn't remove his finger.

"For God's sake, stop ringing; I'm coming," Neil heard Adam shout from the inside. Adam opened the door in an elegant brown and beige silk robe. "Where's the fire?" he asked.

Neil pushed him aside with his hand and walked in. "Where is she?" he yelled, frenetically.

Startled and confused, Adam said, "Where's who?"

"You know who, Leeza.'"

"Anna Lisa!" Adam said with wide eyes, "You think she's here?"

"Stop playing games with me," Neil demanded as he started searching from room to room with Adam following him.

"Are you insane? What are you doing?" Adam shouted. "Quit this madness and let's talk."

Neil did not listen. First he went into a library, then a room with a pool table, then a family room, but there wasn't a trace of Anna Lisa. He climbed up a set of oak stairs as Adam ran after him.

"No, don't go in there, please," Adam yelled as Neil turned right and approached another door.

Neil ignored his plea and opened the door to find Adam's naked boyfriend, Bob, chained to the bedpost with a pair of handcuffs. "Excuse me," Neil said, shut the door quickly and stared at Adam. "Who was that? Was that our reception...Are you...?"

"Yes, I am," Adam said, angrily.

"But...I thought," he said and turned to look back at the door and looked at Adam. He shook his head, "No, it can't be."

"Yes. Yes, I am gay, get over it," Adam replied in frustration.

Neil frowned and said, "No, it's just that...I thought you and Leeza...that Leeza and you..."

"Oh, for heaven's sake," Adam yelled. "The two of you need to get together, fuck all night long and get whatever it is out of your systems," Adam said, going downstairs and walking to the front door. He opened it to get rid of Neil.

Neil followed him. "Where's she? Please, I must speak with her."

"She's back at her apartment sleeping like any normal person," said Adam and pointed toward the door to get Neil out of his house.

"But I don't have her address. I'm not leaving until you give it to me."

Adam rolled his eyes and ordered, "Stay there. I'll be back. If I don't give him the damn address he'll never leave."

Neil did as he was told.

Adam went into his library and pulled out a thin drawer, took out a silver pen and a beige piece of paper with his initials monogrammed on it and jotted down Anna Lisa's address and telephone number. He walked back to Neil, gave it to him and said, "I wouldn't go there tonight if I were you. You need to cool down."

Neil took the paper and kissed Adam on his cheek. "Thank you for being gay."

Adam smiled and was glad his boyfriend didn't see the kiss or else there would be hell to pay. "Go on. Get out of here."

"Thank you," Neil said once again and left.

Adam shook his head at the craziness of the whole situation and went back to his boyfriend.

TWENTY-NINE

"Everything is going to change for you... In six months or less, but it's all good. At first, not so good, but then you will be happy. You'll see."

Exhausted from an incredibly long day, Anna Lisa could think of nothing else but plunging into a relaxing hot bath. It was the day following her dinner with Adam. She had been at work since 7 in the morning and it was now 7 in the evening. Anna Lisa opened her apartment door, turned on a light and immediately knew Ursula had been there. There was a fresh clean scent in the air and the dust on her hardwood floor had disappeared. She set her purse down on the hall table, dropped her keys into a round clay dish, took her dark green jacket off and hung it in a nearby closet. Anna Lisa went straight to her bathroom, turned on a pair of gold faucets above her bath and poured lavender scented granules in her tub. She started unbuttoning her white silk shirt as she walked into her bedroom to remove her clothes and was startled when she saw Neil sitting against her headboard, eating her lemon curd out of a jar with his body stretched out on her peach and cream bedspread.

"Oh my God...Oh my God!" she cried and stamped her feet, "You scared the wits out of me."

"Hello, Leeza. May I join you for a nice hot bath?" he said with confidence and arrogance. His glance shifted from Anna

Lisa's eyes to the lace bra underneath her shirt. He undressed her with his eyes. The connotation behind his words and the seductive look he gave her made Anna Lisa blush. Surprised by his sudden presence, she found it difficult to articulate her words. "How long have you been here? Who let you in?" she demanded, trying to still recover from the shock of finding him in her apartment.

He, on the other hand, was calm and collected. "Let me see," he said, putting his index finger on the corner of his mouth, "Shall I answer the first question or the second one?"

Anna Lisa wrinkled her forehead. "Who let you in here?"

"My good friend Ursula, of course," he said as he stared at her shiny hair, which was pulled back in a ponytail, and the natural rosy glow of her lips. He wanted to pull her in his arms and kiss her.

"Ursula let you in!" replied Anna Lisa with wide eyes.

"Yes, she was quite friendly actually," he smiled and got off her bed, "You must give me her number. I have been in need of a good housekeeper."

Anger and joy battling within her, Anna Lisa cursed underneath her breath. She was angry because Ursula had allowed him in her private space and joyful because of his mere presence. "Look, I've had a tough day and I'm tired. All I want to do is take a bath," she said, walking into the bathroom and turning the water off. She then walked to the front door.

Neil followed her.

She opened the front door and said, "Will you leave if I promise to call you tomorrow?" She wasn't ready to face him yet.

"I'm not leaving until we have a talk – a talk that we should have had long ago."

Stubborn man, no wonder he always got what he wanted. Well, she was not ready to talk. Besides, from the way he was looking at her, he seemed to have a lot more in mind than talking.

He moved closer to her so that there was hardly any distance between them.

Talk? She couldn't possibly talk when he stood so near her. The fresh masculine scent of his body was intoxicating to her. Her heart started beating fast and Anna Lisa felt nervous and worried that he was going to kiss her. She let the door go and moved away from him into her living room. Neil started to come after her but she made a halting gesture with her hand and cried, "Please stop. Don't come any closer."

He stared at her from only a few feet away with eyes that could melt a girl's heart and said, "Why are you afraid of me?"

"I'm not afraid of you," her voice cracked and her body trembled with agitation, "I just want you to keep your distance."

"Then I'll talk from here," he said, still keeping direct eye contact with her, "The other day when you came by–"

"Yes, I know. I spoke with Leila this morning and she told me what happened."

His face lit up and he said, "Then, you're not mad?"

"No, I am not."

He eyed her with a puzzled look and said, "Why do you run away from me, then?"

"Because..."

"Because why?" he asked, moving a little closer.

"Because when I'm around you, I can't think straight," she said, feeling butterflies in her stomach like a schoolgirl with her first crush.

Neil closed up the distance between them and this time Anna Lisa didn't run. She couldn't even if she wanted to. Her feet were glued to the floor and her knees had no power left in them.

He looked at her tenderly and said, "I'm in with love you." He watched her with steady gaze and could tell from the thoughtful expression on her face that he was finally getting through to her.

She let his earnest confession linger in her mind for a long moment before she spoke. "And I with you," she conceded, her words choked up with emotion, her spirit trembling with bliss, her eyes moistening with tears, "But it scares me to love you. I'm afraid to get hurt and never recover."

He brushed a strand of her hair away from her face. "I'm not going to hurt you, not intentionally, anyway. But it is you who can hurt me."

"Me? How could I possibly hurt you?"

"Yes, you. I can't concentrate at work. I can't sleep at night. I'm desolate without you," he replied, putting his hand behind her head, removing her hair clip and letting it drop down to the floor. He put his hand through her soft chestnut brown hair and brought her lips near his but did not kiss her. He peered at her with his midnight-blue eyes for what seemed to be an eternity to Anna Lisa and said, "I'm going to kiss you now."

She could feel his breath against hers, and it was driving her insane.

"Please tell me if I kiss you, you're not going to be cross with me and you're not going to flee because—"

"Neil?"

"Yes?"

"Kiss me already, will you?"

With that invitation, he parted her lips with his, penetrated her slowly and explored her, and when Anna Lisa glided her hands around his waist and responded willingly, he became more demanding. Never had a woman so much control over his senses. So, this is what it felt like to be in love.

Her head was fuzzy and her heart thumped hard against her chest as she caved in and accepted his probing. He could make love to her right there and she would not be able to resist. She let go of her independence, surrendered to him and tasted him as she would a warm lemon curd on a breezy summer afternoon when he pulled her closer one final time so she could feel him. For how long he was going to torture her in this manner, she wondered. Then to her disappointment, he pulled out and released his grip.

"I'm going to take Adam's advice," he said as he interlaced his fingers through hers.

She looked at him perplexed. "I don't understand."

"You will in a minute," he replied and led her to the bedroom.

You may contact the author at the address below.

Homa Pourasgari
C/o Linbrook Press
PO BOX 2325
Beverly Hills, CA 90213

Or at: www.HomaPourasgari.com

Printed in the United States
62305LVS00004B/67-72